What You Don't Know About Charlie Outlaw

Also by Leah Stewart

What You Don't Know About Charlie Outlaw

Leah Stewart

G. P. PUTNAM'S SONS
Publishers Since 1838
An imprint of Penguin Random House LLC
375 Hudson Street
New York, New York 10014

LIBRARY OF CONGRESS CATALOGING-IN-PUBLICATION DATA
Names: Stewart, Leah, date.
Title: What you don't know about Charlie Outlaw : a novel / by Leah Stewart.
Description: New York : G. P. Putnam's Sons, 2018.
Identifiers: LCCN 2017006220 (print) | LCCN 2017011339 (ebook) |
ISBN 9780735214347 (hardcover) | ISBN 9780735214354 (epub)
Classification: LCC PS3569.T465258 W48 2018 (print) |
LCC PS3569.T465258
(ebook) | DDC 813/.54—dc23
LC record available at https://lccn.loc.gov/2017006220
p.   cm.
International edition ISBN: 9780525536284

Printed in the United States of America
1   3   5   7   9   10   8   6   4   2

Book design by Gretchen Achilles

This is a work of fiction. Names, characters, places, and incidents either are the product
of the author's imagination or are used fictitiously, and any resemblance to actual persons,
living or dead, businesses, companies, events, or locales is entirely coincidental.

For Jeremy O'Keefe & Elwood Reid,
who made this book possible

For you have but mistook me all this while.
I live with bread like you, feel want,
Taste grief, need friends. Subjected thus,
How can you say to me I am a king?

—SHAKESPEARE, *Richard II*

I.

The actor's instrument . . . is himself; he works with the same emotional areas which he actually uses in real life. The self that the actor presents to the imaginary Juliet is the same as the self he uses in his most private and intimate experiences. The actor is both the artist and the instrument—in other words, the violinist and the violin.

—LEE STRASBERG, *A Dream of Passion*

One.

Something terrible is about to happen to Charlie Outlaw. This terrible thing will slam into his life with such shocking force as to seem impossible, implausible, even as it's happening. If we could reach into his story and warn him, he'd struggle to believe us. For the last three weeks, Charlie has been so miserable that it's hard for him to imagine his life could get worse. Also, he is famous, and people tell him all manner of untrue things.

Charlie Outlaw is an actor, currently the male lead of a hit television drama. In his roles he's had to grieve and rage and die, and yet his own life—or shall we say his life as Charlie, because even when he's someone else it's all his own—has been blessed with an absence of horror. He has, like all of us, known fear and anxiety and guilt and heartbreak, known them more intensely, perhaps, than many of us, because he was born with the heightened sensitivity of an actor and because he became one, and so subjected himself to the highs and lows of that existence, the intensity only inconstancy can bring.

Heartbreak is what chased him here, to this island nation off the coast of a foreign continent, to this clearing in a rain forest where he sits and eases off his backpack, pretending not to notice the surreptitious glances of the woman beside him. Heartbreak, and also fear and guilt and shame, and a desire to escape the gaze—the many, many gazes—of those who know too much about him and imagine even more. Later he will relive again and again the sequence of events that brought him to this place and time, starting with the interview he gave *Vanity Fair*. Without the interview, none of the rest of it would have happened, not the backlash from fans and coworkers, not the stricken look on Josie's face, not the insomnia-driven impulse to book a flight. He wouldn't have spent last night alone in a rental cottage, struggling to resist calling Josie again, would never have hiked into the jungle today without his phone. A person to whom something terrible has happened is as obsessed with causality as any plotter of stories. I did A, and B followed. Is that what it means to deserve something?

Right now Charlie's mind is on the right strap of his backpack, which he's struggling to loosen. His pack is very full, because he's planned an overnight hike—eleven miles of walking today, and then a night, maybe two, spent under the stars on an otherwise inaccessible beach, and then eleven miles back again. There are a handful of other hikers in the clearing—napping, eating, adjusting the laces on their boots—and though he intends no conversation, he's glad to see them. He dislikes solitude, but he has chosen it, as penance, as quest. He has to remember he's a person, not a compendium of other people's opinions. He has to remember who he is when he's alone.

The woman beside him turns out, when he glances at her, to be quite beautiful. She goes on watching as he fiddles with his strap. There are only three reasons to observe him performing this extremely uninteresting task: One, she knows who he is; two, she thinks he's attractive; or three, she's bored. *All of the above* is also a possible answer. He tries to resist meeting her gaze, but even now, when he should know better than to make eye contact with strangers, it seems rude, or cowardly, to ignore someone who's looking at him. She smiles and doesn't look away. Not just bored then. He smiles back automatically, then returns to his backpack. *Please don't talk to me*, he thinks. But he can tell she's going to.

For quite some time now—possibly his whole life—a good deal of Charlie's processing power has been devoted to reading other people's reactions. He's highly attuned to the feelings of others, an instinct that can have the eerie accuracy of telepathy. He can usually tell what someone wants from him, and most of the time he tries to provide it. He strives never to offend, because he hates to hurt others and because he himself is easily hurt, though jokes and charm and good looks assist him in concealing that. Of course, in trying to please one person (a reporter, for instance), you might offend everyone else. Since the interview, he's been stuck reliving every one of his stupid, thoughtlessly hurtful words: the memory of saying them, the memory of reading them, the memory of everyone else quoting them back. Even if Josie had forgiven him, even if she hadn't broken up with him, he'd be struggling to forgive himself. Why hasn't he learned by now to deflect, to produce an enigmatic smile? Why does he still answer every single question he's asked?

He presses his thumb and forefinger hard against his eyelids, takes a breath, shifts his mind back to the strap.

"American?" the woman asks.

Because he doesn't want to talk to anyone, he doesn't want to talk to her, lovely though she is, but he can't tamp down his reflexive politeness, his hardwired desire to please. "Yes," he says. "You?" Though from her accent he'd guess no.

She puts her hand on her chest and says, "Brazil."

So she won't sense his reluctance to talk, he asks another question. "Are you going all the way to the beach?"

She purses her lips and tilts her head from side to side. "Maybe," she offers finally. She waves a hand at her feet. "These boots . . ." She makes a face.

"Ah," he says. "Boots are important."

She smiles as if this were a clever thing to say. The show doesn't air in Brazil; at least he doesn't think it does. But still she might know who he is. With the internet, all things are possible. If she does know, he wonders if she's seen all the nasty comments about him. The homicidal vitriol. Some people probably even hate him in Portuguese.

From his pack he extracts a bag of lychees he bought from a kid with a cooler on the side of the road. He offers some to the woman and they both eat. He makes a joke and she laughs, meeting his eyes with obvious interest. He wishes he could reciprocate. He wishes he wanted to. That would be an approved way for this story to unfold, the story of how he tried to get over Josie. But to sleep with another woman would feel like a betrayal. Like another one.

"You are alone?" the woman asks. "You hike alone?"

"Yes. You?"

The woman shakes her head, gesturing at two women stretched out on the ground with their hats over their faces, their booted feet crossed at the ankles. "My friends." She rolls her eyes. "They are tired already."

"Me, too," Charlie says. "I don't really like hiking."

"No?" She raises her eyebrows. "Why, then?"

"Why don't I like it? Or why am I doing it?"

She laughs, though what was funny? "Both."

"I actually do like hiking. Just not by myself."

"So why?"

He shrugs, then presents her with a sheepish smile. "I'm on a spiritual journey." He can say "spiritual journey" only if he puts it in quotes. Not because he doesn't mean it. Because he means it so much. People mistake irony for disdain, but how, without irony's blessed distance, could you avoid succumbing to every one of your raw and tearful yearnings, every ridiculous thing you feel?

Save it for the close-up, Charlie. That's what he says to himself, in life, when he can tell he's about to cry. He said it to himself last night, alone in a rental cottage intended for two, and then cried anyway. When did the habit start? Before he was an actor, if there ever was such a time.

"I understand now," she says. "For a spiritual journey, you must be alone."

"Is that true? I guess that's true."

"So now I ask another why."

"Why what? Why did I need one?"

She nods.

Yes, why? Why Charlie?

The reporter had read deeply about acting, interviewed a multitude of actors. She was dangerously insightful. She asked questions about his process, about his ambitions and aesthetics, about the experience of newfound fame, like she already knew the answers, and so it seemed mere confirmation to give them to her. It felt like they had a mutual understanding. "Her loyalty is to the magazine, not to you," his publicist said, with a weary patience, after the article appeared. Charlie knows that, of course he knows that. His task was to project the publicist-approved version of Charlie Outlaw, hers to see through that to his messier, more complicated, genuine self. She succeeded by making him fail. Can he blame her when it's his job, too, to generate trust? "You can make a truth out of anything," he said to the reporter, during the part of the interview that was an earnest discussion of craft. "You just have to make people feel."

Still, he hates that these days he gets punished every time he drops his guard. His show's success was nearly instantaneous, and he's had months and months of interviews and events and people who melt into puddles or turn spiky and awful at the sight of him. He wants to stop feeling like every interaction is a chess game, each side anticipating moves. It's exhausting being careful all the time. It makes him sad how frequently now "Charlie Outlaw" feels like another part he plays.

When we think of actors as changeable, manipulative, performative, we forget the willingness to be vulnerable, the crucial impulse toward honesty. Fame insists that vulnerability be armored in wariness, but Charlie has not been famous very long. He resists the lesson. He still wants to be himself. The interview began to go awry when the reporter asked him whether he'd watch his own show if he weren't on it. He answered the question honestly. He gave it serious thought. He said no.

What can he tell the Brazilian woman, who may already know all this and many other things about him? That it turns out to be possible to know he said what he said, about the show being a little boring in its tidy resolutions, a little limited in its will-they-won't-they concerns, and yet feel taken aback to see it all in print. The "boring" quote was the one that really pissed people off. That, and the part about liking "more challenging" shows.

To be a fan is to bear a love that by its very nature separates you from the loved one, a wind pushing away what it wants to hold. All the people who'd been so ready to offer up their love, so insistent he receive it—he could never love them back like they loved him, and they knew it, and so they were just waiting for him to give them a reason to hate him. He released them from their purposeless longing, and frantic with relief, they took to their keyboards to call him names.

So he thinks his fans are stupid, people wrote. *He thinks he's better than us. But we made him. Ungrateful s***head. He'd be nothing without us. He'd be nothing without that show.*

He could tell the woman he is afraid that this is true.

Plenty of people wrote, *I still love him,* but—alas for human nature—those words floated away, while *I hate him I hate him I hate him* settled like shrapnel in his mind.

The woman nudges him with her shoulder. "I am in suspense."

"My girlfriend broke up with me," he says. "That's why I'm alone." To say this aloud is a self-inflicted wound.

The woman looks at him with such sympathy, which maybe she wouldn't if she'd read the article. "I know this feeling," she says. "Terrible. She does not love you now?"

"I don't know." He wants to protest that of course she still loves him. She must! It's only been nineteen days. He believes in love at first sight, having felt it both on and off the stage. He fell in love with Josie the night they met. But surely the end of love takes more than an instant, more than nineteen days. Can an emotion stop so abruptly, like a road cut off by a wall? Not in his experience. Not even when the emotion belongs to a character, and you walk off the stage as yourself.

"There is another man?"

Charlie shakes his head.

She points at him in playful accusation. "Another woman?"

"No!"

"So . . ."

He finds an answer that is neither a full confession nor a lie. "I said something about her to someone else, and she found out."

That makes her wince. "What did you say?"

Why does everyone want to know his secrets, even the ones that are secret no longer? And how, *how*, did the reporter get him to tell Josie's? He remembers discussing the effects of fame—sure, that was the theme they kept revisiting—and then the reporter brought up Josie's career, how Josie no longer got anything like the level of attention Charlie was getting now. What did he think that might be doing to her self-worth? Charlie should have said something cheerful and evasive. Instead, he answered haltingly, feeling his way toward the truth. A small, uneasy part of him knew he should shut up, and as if she sensed that, the reporter changed tack. She complimented his relationship with Josie, saying how happy they seemed in photographs, so beautifully real that she wondered if it was all just another act.

Once, he'd been waiting in the car for Josie while she auditioned and she emerged buzzing—with anger or elation, he couldn't quite tell—and instead of going to lunch like they'd planned, they drove to a deserted part of the garage, where she climbed on top of him despite, or perhaps because of, the dangers of security cameras, of some producer's assistant pulling up next to them as she parked her car. It wasn't like Josie to be reckless, to let passion win, and that's why he remembers the scene with such painful vividness, the sound of her breathing and the determined way she moved. He loves that fierce, unconquerable part of her, loves it still more, perhaps, because she so rarely lets it out.

Their relationship was the realest thing in Charlie's world, and he told the reporter so. He remembers that part clearly. He said it with confidence. Then the reporter asked, "Is she the love of your life?"

And he hesitated. She was, she *is*, but in the beat after the question, he stopped to wonder what Josie would say if someone asked her that about him. Would she say yes? Lately she'd been a little distant. Would it make her uncomfortable if he said yes? Would he seem annoyingly sappy? They'd had a very uncomfortable conversation after his suggestion that they buy a house together, a conversation he'd done his best to forget. In the reporter's expression he saw that his hesitation had gone on long enough to seem like a negative answer, and so he said, "Yes!" hastily, loudly. Then, uncomfortable with his vehemence, he added, in a worried way, "So far."

Everything in this description is accurate—the way he said *so far* suggested insecurity, not womanizing arrogance—but he should have used a different phrase, like *I hope* or something, anything else. Because in print it didn't look the way he'd meant it. *Asked if Josie Lamar is the love of his life, he said, "So far."*

Two words. Five letters. Josie shouted them back at him more than once. Her fury left him stricken and fumbling. His apologies couldn't unsay it. None of his explanations explained. In all that terrible scene, these were the two worst things: The despair in her voice when she said he'd made her look pathetic. And the flat finality with which she asked him to leave.

The Brazilian woman nudges him again. "You don't want to tell me what you said. This means it is very bad."

"Yes. It is very bad."

"You said she is ugly? You said . . . you hate her mother?"

"No." Charlie laughs. "Nothing like that."

The woman waves a hand. "I won't make you tell me. You said sorry to her?"

"Many times. It didn't seem to matter."

"But it is good for you. For *you*." She touches his chest with her index finger. "To say what you feel."

"I don't know about that," he says. "That's what got me into trouble."

"Really? I say what I want to say." She laughs. "Maybe this is bad."

Charlie gives her a rueful smile. "It's bad when I do it, I guess."

"Say something you want to say. What do you want to say right now?"

"To who?"

"To anyone. To your girlfriend. To me."

Josie. You said I cared too much what other people thought, and then you broke up with me because of what other people think. Josie, you said to leave you alone, so I did. I came all the way here, I let my phone die and stashed it in a drawer; I hiked miles into the jungle. Was all this a terrible mistake? Is there something I could have said or done if I'd stayed, if I'd tried again? Can I fix it, even now? Do you still want me, Josie? Should I run back up the trail and come home to you?

"You are thinking something," the woman says.

"Yes."

"But you don't say it."

He shakes his head.

"Ah!" She laughs, leaning back on her hands. "We are always ourselves."

He appraises her. She cocks her head, gives him a challenging smile. It's easy to guess what she wants from him. The test is whether he'll offer it. He feels a rush of anger at Josie for lecturing him about success in ways that suggested he was wrong to enjoy it, for falling silent when he recounted praise from a famous fan, for disappearing from a party so that he hunted for her for half an hour, calling her phone, until one of his costars told him she'd left. For refusing to buy a house with him once he started making money, citing her attachment to her own house, the skittishness left over from her long-ago divorce. That was the first time he'd felt doubt—and only because it seemed like she did.

During the last year, the world has become a hall of mirrors, everywhere he looks a different version of himself until even he doesn't know which one is real. But Josie does. Josie knows him. How can she believe the person he is in that article over the one he is with her?

"I have an idea," the woman says. "You can go with us instead of alone."

"That's nice of you," Charlie says. "But . . ." The word hangs in the air. Any second now she'll ask, "But what?" What should he say? He can hike to the beach with this woman, maybe spend the night with her there, insist to himself that it really is over with Josie. He can put her off with a joke or maybe sincerity, proceed up the trail alone, continue his penance in solitude. He can grab his backpack without another word and run back the other way, plug in his phone, call Josie, propose. There are other choices, too, so many possibilities, and he doesn't know which is right, and he doesn't know where any of them will lead, and so he wishes he didn't have them. The woman shifts her body toward him, about to speak again, but a sudden commotion intrudes. For an instant—before he separates the noise into the rumble of wheels on dirt, voices raised in confusion and alarm, before he turns to see the car and the van—he's grateful for the interruption.

Before someone shouts, a strangled, fearful sound.

Before the doors of both car and van open and eight people thrust themselves out.

Before he sees that they have guns.

Before they point those guns at him and the other people in the clearing.

Before they force him into the trunk of the car.

Later the memory of that grateful instant will make him feel bitterness, regret, longing—longing most of all—for Josie, for the time when he still got to choose.

Two.

Josie Lamar used to be a hero, and now she isn't. Or—because she remains a hero to the many fans of the cult show on which she starred—it's more precise to say that she no longer feels like one. What she feels like is a half-awake, intermittently employed actress in line at a Coffee Bean & Tea Leaf wearing yoga pants and a hoodie, her long red hair pulled up in a messy ponytail. How often do you have to act to still call yourself an actress? More and more she's been thinking about quitting so that not working will be her choice, so that she will no longer have to ask herself such questions.

Once upon a time, Josie was Bronwyn Kyle, beloved of fangirls and fanboys, a fighter, a Chosen One. She punched and she kicked; she suffered and she triumphed. Bronwyn Kyle didn't have it easy— to be a leader takes a toll, and so does the inevitability of the new fight that follows each victory—but still, still. Bronwyn knew her worth. She knew her power. And so, because Josie was she and she was Josie, Josie knew her worth and power, too. Josie knew how it felt to stare down an evildoer—to tell him with her expression *I will destroy you*—and have him turn and run. Josie knew how it felt to matter. Josie tries not to miss being Bronwyn Kyle, but she does miss it, and if she knew what had happened to Charlie, she'd miss it even more. Bronwyn Kyle could rescue Charlie from the people who've taken him. What can Josie do?

The man in line in front of Josie wears a concert T-shirt and jeans, like a crew member or an off-duty actor, but he's got the serious, clean-shaven face and close-cropped salt-and-pepper hair of a businessman, so maybe he's visiting from out of town. Maybe he's on vacation. Maybe he slept with someone at a nearby apartment and now he's stopping here before he goes home. Maybe he goes out really early for his coffee and then goes home and puts on his suit. That last scenario seems the least plausible. He glanced at her a moment ago, and she saw in his face the subtle performance of suppressed recognition. If he did recognize her, in a moment he'll glance at her again. People have a hard time repressing that urge. Josie understands that. Sometimes she, too, has to force herself to look away from a famous person—the director of her favorite movie from childhood, the roguish movie star whose poster used to hang on her wall.

It's 5:45 a.m. Josie has a 6:30 call time at a studio in the Valley. It's on a lot so small she'll have to park a mile away and catch the production shuttle. She should make it in plenty of time, as it's early enough that the 405 shouldn't be a problem. She's not a morning person, and two decades of early call times have failed to make her one, so what's on her mind right now is how tired she is, and how slowly this line is moving, and how she hopes this guy doesn't talk to her because she's not sure she's awake enough to summon the necessary politeness. Especially if he doesn't know where he recognizes her from and wants help figuring it out. She's not worried about the fact that she's pregnant because she has no idea that she is. She's only five weeks along. She's forty-one years old. Though theoretically she wanted to have children, in the last few years the panicky indecision induced by her uncertain career and her waning fertility has given way to acceptance, so while children are still biologically possible, they no longer seem so to her. It hasn't yet dawned on her that she missed a period. She's never been regular, even less so since she hit forty.

In a remarkable coincidence neither she nor Charlie is yet in a position to appreciate, Josie is playing a kidnap victim this week. Later, when she looks back from the end of this story, connections like this—each link on the chain back to Charlie—will seem to Josie both inevitable and amazing. This is how we come to believe in fate. For now, all she knows is that she's guest starring on a cable procedural, a show that cuts back and forth between victims and the FBI agents out to rescue them. It's called, appropriately, *Kidnapped*. Josie is not the first recognizable actor to play one of the victims, though some viewers will be sad to see her in the part, shaking their heads at what becomes of us all, and others will feel the weird nasty triumph we can feel at the sight of a once-successful, now-diminished stranger, and others will get a thrill out of seeing her and imagine she took the part for fun, not out of need, and still others won't think about her at all, except as her character, whose name they probably won't recall. They won't recognize her, won't realize she was ever even close to famous. The character's name is Karen. Karen Woodward. Josie auditioned for the part and was glad to get it. She needs the money, sure, that's never not the case, but also her friend Cecelia is a regular on the show, and also, most of all, she just wants to work. She always wants to work. You can't be an actor unless someone will let you act. That's why she so often dreams of writing or painting—anything, really, that would give her a creative outlet over which she had some control.

The man glances at her again. He says nothing but turns away with a secretive smile, so she knows he recognizes her. He must have been a fan of *Alter Ego*. No one who knows her from her other work ever looks quite so delighted. Now he's got his phone out. She can't see the screen, but she imagines he's texting someone, and she's right. He's texting his wife and teenage daughter, both of whom will be thrilled to hear that he saw Josie Lamar and will want to know every detail of the sighting when he gets back to their hotel room. He'll report that she's taller than he might've guessed, and really, really skinny, and that she ordered an Americano with an extra shot and room for cream. He'll say she looks great, and they'll look up her age on IMDb, and his wife will admire her for resisting plastic surgery and his daughter will wonder why she never married again or had children, and they'll remind each other of the famous men she's dated. In response to their jealousy over the encounter, the man will tease them that this is what they get for lazing around in bed while he goes to fetch their coffee. It'll be a moment they reference for years to come—the time Dad saw Josie Lamar and they missed it, and it was so unfair because, though Dad loved her show, they were the ones who were the real fans, Mom watching it when it aired and then years later rewatching it with her daughter, Josie's character a role model for them both, a girl so smart and brave that sometimes Mom teared up at the sheer joy of Bronwyn Kyle's existence, at her ability to show this character to her daughter and say, look, there's something out there for you besides hookers and girlfriends, I promise. I promise there is.

For Josie, it's not that kind of moment. She won't remember it later, faded into the mass of such encounters. She remembers only the dramatic ones: the linebacker of a man who couldn't stop saying her name as if it were a proclamation while he stood between her and the exit from Bed Bath & Beyond; the woman in a crisp suit who burst into hysterical tears when she saw Josie at the next table in a restaurant eating scrambled eggs; her cousin's girlfriend, who slid in beside her in the pew during her grandmother's funeral, so close their thighs touched, and asked in a very audible whisper for her autograph. The girlfriend held out a hymnal with the funeral program atop it, proffered a pen. When Josie made no move to take it, the woman pointed to a blank space on the program underneath a Bible verse, as if the problem were that Josie didn't know where to sign.

Now, in the coffee shop, Josie's braced and alert, trying to prep for a scene in which she can't predict the lines. Both cash registers open at the same time, and Josie and the man step to them side by side and place their orders. She's aware of him while pretending not to be, just as he is of her, though she's better at the pretending, having had years of practice. It was hard for her, during the time when she was truly famous, not being able to observe people without being observed herself. To be a good actor one has to *notice*—the particular way the man hiding his anger turns away from his wife, the self-conscious carriage of the teenage girl, newly curvy, who wants to be looked at but can hardly stand it when she is. It's the problem of an anthropologist in the field—you can't observe natural human behavior when your very presence alters it.

An anthropologist who wanted to examine how people react to celebrity would find Josie a good interview subject. She's sympathetic to the starstruck—the ones who are nice, at any rate—and she's honored and often moved to hear that she impacted someone's life, and yet it's by necessity a distancing sympathy, tinged with caution, the way you might feel about a little-noticed acquaintance who abruptly presented you with a love poem. What people want is eye contact, recognition, to register in the consciousness of the person so deeply embedded in theirs. They are eager to touch you, and often they do, your sleeve, your hair, your hand. They ask to take your picture, or they don't ask and take it anyway. They say: "Oh my God, I just really want to hug you," lost in a desire so compelling they're helpless not to express it, as if they're children, or drunk, or on the rapturous verge of speaking in tongues. They've approached transcendence. They're near the source. Their hearts thunder. Their legs shake. They feel the heat coming off your body. You're real! You're real! They were right to believe in everything you've ever made them feel.

It was so much worse twenty years ago when she was on TV every week, in people's living rooms, and they lacked any sense of separation between their lives and hers. Then when people approached her, they'd attract other people until a crowd had gathered around her, and in those crowds, Josie felt vulnerable, overly exposed, unsafe. Now she doesn't mind, in no small part because these days one fan doesn't usually lead to more. Most of the time she even likes the interaction, exhausting as it is trying not to end up the butt of a joke on someone's blog, the villain of someone's Twitter feed— trying to be what people want. But today she fears a fan encounter, because people have been theorizing in the virtual world about her reaction to Charlie's interview, and therefore someone might have the temerity to ask her about it in the physical one. After a night lost to Twitter and the comments sections of celebrity gossip sites, she forbade herself to look again. *He just said the truth* was one opinion. *She's washed up.* Another: *What I don't get is how she ever got hot in the first place.* Another: *She was great on* Alter Ego, *but as she ages, she comes off shrill and unlikable.* Another: *She's too old for him. He's so cute and she's a hag.*

How is she supposed to forgive him? Charlie did not, of course, say that she was washed up. Charlie didn't say anything like that. But what he said could be interpreted that way. It was fine for him to tell the reporter that he was afraid of coming to rely on fame, that he was afraid of the world becoming his mirror, of growing so used to attention that when it vanished he'd be bereft. But he shouldn't have said that this was what had happened to Josie. He shouldn't have talked about her struggle, which was not his to expose; he shouldn't have said he thought it was hard for her now to watch fame happening to him; and above all, he shouldn't have said *so far.*

At the thought of that phrase, she feels again the rush of shame and grief that has not, in the last three weeks, lost any part of its power. Her years as an actress have taught her to be vulnerable at work, guarded otherwise, but for Charlie she lowered the wall, so when he hurt her she had no defenses. If she hadn't trusted him so thoroughly, it'd be easier to forgive him now. That article was a repudiation of everything she'd believed their relationship to be. Was he the love of her life? Yes, yes, he absolutely was. Her certainty is unbearable in the face of his qualified answer. She misses him with a horrible intensity. She can't allow herself to call.

Please talk to me, his last text said. Every day for the last two weeks she's picked up the phone to respond, then stopped herself. And in all that time, fourteen days, he hasn't tried again. So it really is over. It's over. How can it be over? But it is.

She knows that as he grew more famous she occasionally subjected him to abrupt withdrawals, to glimpses of an anger she refused to acknowledge. Yes, she admits it. And she knows how sorry, how wounded, he is. She would have known that even without his saying so because she knows him so well. She's sure he feels as if the whole world has taken up arms against him, with her at the head of the charge. But how could he say such things? How could he fail to predict the consequences? She knows what it is to ride high on adoration, and yet she can't forgive him for succumbing to it so completely he believed it was his to keep. He made a public example of her and at the same time proved that he himself had learned nothing.

She resolves—again, again—not to think about Charlie, which takes an effort so monumental it feels physical and is, she knows, a resolution made particularly ridiculous by the fact that this morning she put on the necklace he gave her. She's wearing it right now tucked under her shirt. Her longings are contradictory and manifold.

The barista calls out, "Chris!" and the man in the concert T-shirt retrieves a cardboard tray with three cups of the largest size coffee they offer. As he passes Josie on his way to the creamer station, he says in a low voice, "You're terrific," and though she says, "Thank you," relieved, her voice full of genuine pleasure, she's not sure he hears her as he walks away. Some people treat these encounters as though they're spies at a meet, barely looking at her, whispering a compliment as though it were a secret. These are the fans who feel grateful for what she's already given them and want only to give something back, and she feels her own responsive gratitude to them for demanding nothing. The teenage barista calls out, "Josie!" and hands over her drink with a disinterest approaching disdain. Josie smiles at her anyway, carrying the warm glow of her secret, believing again for a moment that she is terrific, which is, after all, what we all want to believe. Terrific is the opposite of how she's felt since she lost Charlie.

Three.

It's not enough, of course, to perform a convincing emotional response to a situation: A good actor must adapt that response to the overall tone of the piece. On a comedy, even heartbreak is occasion for a joke; on a procedural, even murder cleans up tidily, and if you're playing a relative of the victim, you probably shouldn't cry. Some stories have no room for raw desperation. Charlie has played being trapped in the trunk of a car three times—twice on comedies, once on a procedural—and on none of those occasions was he asked to scream or sob or have a full-blown panic attack. On one comedy, the scene was a reference to the famous one in *Out of Sight*, his character trying to play the charming take-it-all-in-stride rogue to an eye-rolling girl. On the other, he performed a series of contortions in concert with another actor, struggling to retrieve a phone from that actor's back pocket with his teeth. On the procedural, he shook his head wildly as the bad guy duct-taped his mouth, and then after the trunk closed and the car started, he looked around in grim and purposeful resolution, and began kicking out the tail-light.

Alone in this trunk, this real live trunk, in this real live moment, there is no romantic banter, no comic acrobatics, no heroic display of any kind. It does not occur to him to try to kick out the taillight. It does not occur to him to do anything. He's completely overtaken by panic. He's hyperventilating and sweating, and while he's aware of the movement of the car, it's a dim awareness, afflicted as he is by the tightening vise around his chest against which his heart desperately flings itself. Being forced into a trunk by gun-wielding strangers was terrifying enough to cause these effects, but his claustrophobia intensifies them, his mind telling him over and over that he will die instantly if he spends one more second in this tiny enclosed space. He's been claustrophobic since childhood for no reason he can recall, though his second-oldest sister guiltily thinks it might be because of the time she shut him in the closet for nearly an hour when he was two. Whatever the cause, he'll bound up ten flights of stairs to avoid an elevator. He worried, when he had to play those trunk scenes, that he'd ruin a day's shooting with a panic attack, but his claustrophobia never kicked in. Perhaps because he wasn't being himself.

Right now, he has no one else to be. He's all he's got. Charlie Outlaw, thirty-four years old and six-feet-two-inches tall, quite tall for any man but especially an actor, too tall to be fetal-positioned in the oven-hot trunk of a midsize sedan, making himself even hotter with his frantic breathing until at last he loses consciousness. Let's leave him there a moment, poor Charlie, because nothing more will happen to him until the car stops.

Charlie has always wanted to be an actor. Three months ago, when his parents moved from their big suburban house to an apartment in downtown Cincinnati, his mother sent him a box labeled CHARLIE'S CHILDHOOD in her almost illegible handwriting. In it he found a book report on the autobiography of Marlon Brando, written when he was nine, that offered a random assortment of facts about Brando before segueing into a disquisition on his own ambitions. *When I grow up, I want to be an actor. I will be a Method actor in the style of Marlon Brando, who learned from Stella Adler how to make his emotions seem real.*

He'd forgotten all about this, and he's not sure now if it was lack of confidence or masculine embarrassment that made him wait so long to audition for a school play, which he did finally as a sophomore in high school, and only then because his girlfriend persuaded him to try out with her. The play was *Grease*, and he got the part of Kenickie. His girlfriend was cast as an extra and quit the play in anger—she was the star of the school's drama program, but *Grease* is a musical and she couldn't sing. Charlie didn't ever say that to her, of course. He listened to her rant about the drama teacher's betrayal with patience and understanding. Partly because of that, she stayed his girlfriend a while longer, swallowing her own hurt feelings to come see him every night he was in the play. Also, she couldn't resist his performance. Even then he'd been that good. Sitting in the audience, she could feel the way he magnetized the air. When his castmates spoke, she heard them say their lines. When Charlie spoke, she believed him. The other girls at school looked at him now with drugged and helpless yearning, but he was only hers. Every night in the auditorium she felt the power of having what everyone else wanted.

Why on earth, at nine, had he been allowed to read the autobiography of Marlon Brando? His father was the exhibitions director at the Contemporary Arts Center, site of the famous Robert Mapplethorpe controversy, and his mother was a First Amendment lawyer. They forbade him violent television, but beyond that, they resisted censorship. If they saw him with a copy of Judy Blume's *Forever* from his oldest sister's bookshelf, they'd say, "That's not appropriate for you, honey," but they wouldn't actually take it from him. They'd trust him to put it back, as if he could be counted on to understand the need to protect his own childish innocence. He usually did put it back, whatever the book was, because he liked being trustworthy. He was number three of four children, the others all girls, and every one of them a handful except for him. He wasn't just the only boy; he was the only good one. Until the play, he'd shown no evidence of special skill—his sister Caroline was a math whiz, Beth a talented artist, Alexa a three-sport athlete—but he was the good boy, and oh how his parents loved him for it. Though his sisters taunted him for those good-boy ways, they loved them, and him, too.

Everybody loves Charlie Outlaw. Or at least they used to. He's counted on that, always, without quite understanding how much. He's had an unconscious belief that he arrived first, whole and complete in himself, and the love pursued him. Only since the article has it seemed to him that everybody's love is the foundation on which the rest of him is built. He has big eyes and mobile, expressive features, an easy smile, good manners. Because he is a tall and broad-shouldered man, his inherent sweetness seems a charming discovery rather than a weakness. *You're so nice!* people say to him, as though his niceness were a miracle, and when your niceness wins you so much approbation, why wouldn't you continue to display it? In the last year, as his share of the world's attention expanded exponentially, he has been so, so nice. And he's gotten so much love—so much! The naked adoration in their faces. The outsize gratitude for any minor kindness, so that to have been nothing but polite makes him feel like a god. He's been mainlining love, a dose so strong that the high teeters on the edge of pain. It's terrifying to be worshipped, more terrifying still to imagine being worshipped no longer. For months now, even before the troublemaking article, he's been waking at four in the morning in the desperate sweaty grip of his own inadequacy.

The headline on the article was "Charlie Outlaw Takes the Stage," which didn't quite make sense, as he's in a TV show, not a play, but the copy editor couldn't resist doing *something* punny with his name. Few can. Outlaw Wears a White Hat, Outlaw Rides Again, etc. A quick internet search and almost every article about him confirms that the name is real, not invented, but people on the street still ask him, sometimes in a tone of sweet wonderment, sometimes in a way that tells him they already know and just want to confide they're in on the joke. Then he says yes, and they say *really?*, with varying inflections. And he says yes. They look skeptical or amused or oddly impressed. The skepticism perplexes Charlie. Why would a man who wanted to be taken seriously name himself Outlaw, given the choice of any name in the world? When an actor changes his name, he's not looking to sound like a self-deluded character on a sketch-comedy show. He's looking to distinguish himself from some other guy in the Screen Actors Guild. He's looking to sound like a star.

Who is he now, if people no longer love him? If Josie doesn't?

The car is slowing now in the face of some substantial bumps in the road. The jostling rouses Charlie, who would just as soon have not been roused, as at this moment there's no benefit to consciousness. When he slipped into his mind, he found Josie there. Outside it, she's gone. Nothing good about being him. He opens his eyes, then closes them. If only this feeling of unreality signified that none of it was real. They bound his hands in front of him with rope. He tries to loosen it and succeeds only in further chafing his skin. He tries to think, but in his brain there is only a humming silence harmonizing with the vibrations of the car. One clear thought finally surfaces, and it is this: *I must be in shock.* He is correct in this self-diagnosis, for all the good it does him. His pulse is rapid, his pupils dilated, his skin clammy. He feels like he might throw up. As the car continues to slow and then finally stops, he concentrates on vanquishing his nausea. All will be well as long as he does not vomit. For comfort, distraction, resolution, he pictures Josie's face.

Charlie and Josie first met as Benedick and Beatrice at the home of an actor who liked to gather groups for readings of Shakespeare plays. Charlie tagged along with a friend who'd been invited because he knew that Josie would be there. When he was a kid, he watched her show with his sisters, and he had a crush on her character, which, of course, he understood at the time as having a crush on Josie. By the time they met, he was sophisticated enough to know that he shouldn't conflate her and her character, but that didn't mean he wasn't curious to see how much she'd resemble Bronwyn, that he wasn't watching for signs of that. His friend had told him that she was surprisingly good at Shakespeare, given her lack of formal training or experience on the stage. "You don't even know if she knows what she's saying, but she makes you feel it," he said.

Then Charlie walked into a room and saw her, and despite himself, he was disappointed. She seemed too diffident, too quiet. As soon as they started to read the play, though, he knew that his friend had been wrong. She knew exactly what she was saying. He had a sense that her intelligence was always being underestimated, that she underestimated it herself. But what power she had in her! When she wasn't acting, she dimmed it. Or the world did.

Their relationship progressed very quickly in that way that makes you feel like your love is inevitable, irresistible, while everyone around you suggests that you might be moving too fast. For two years they never fought, which was in retrospect a mistake, because when they finally arrived at conflict, they had no practice in recovering from it. Even so, for two years they were a fantasy, a miracle. They drove everybody else crazy.

Please, Josie, he thinks, in the trunk. *Please, Josie. Please.* What is he asking her for? To come for him and transport him back to that time.

On the other side of the world, in Charlie's home state of Ohio, a teenage girl in the grip of boredom and longing enters Charlie Outlaw into Google. He comes up smiling, smoldering, angry, sad, determined. So many faces, image after image, as she clicks through looking for the version that most swells her heart. And there it is, the one that will shortly grace the home screen of her laptop, a shot a magazine chose from dozens, his gaze frank, his smile inviting. She sighs. "I still love you, Charlie," she says.

The trunk opens. The air and light rush in. Charlie Outlaw opens his eyes.

Four.

Every episode of *Kidnapped* is a variation within a strict form, like a sonnet. In the teaser, we see the victim proceeding through her day in the unknowing bliss of normalcy. Then comes the sudden intrusion of horror—the grab, the van, the gun. Cut to the title sequence. After the commercial, the agents get the case. The last scene is always the agents together over a cheerful meal or drink, advancing to an infinitesimal degree their repressed romance. Once the victim's rescued, she vanishes from the story. Like most procedurals, the show makes Josie dwell on everything it leaves out: the terror of the victim, the strain on the agents, everyone's accumulating post-traumatic stress. What happens to someone who's been on the receiving end of that much malice, that much indifferent cruelty? What happens to the agents exposed again and again to the worst that people can do? Rescue cannot possibly be the end. But five minutes later it's scenes from next week.

The first scene that Josie has to shoot today is her most taxing one, emotionally speaking. Tomorrow there's an exterior shoot involving running and falling and being dragged. For today's scene, she'll come to in a small dark room, chained to a chair, and she'll struggle and scream until her kidnapper comes in, and then she'll demand to know who he is and what he wants until he answers with some creepy quotations from the Bible. Then she'll struggle some more as he clamps a chloroformed cloth across her mouth. Or rather, as Josie would say, these are the things that a lawyer named Karen Woodward will do. Some actors use "I" in reference to their characters, some "he" or "she." Josie is in the latter group, very deliberately so. The "I" is inescapable in any performance whether you say it or not. An actor's body is her art: Josie herself will be chained to a chair, Josie herself will be screaming. Josie will do her best to believe when she is chained and screaming that what is happening is happening to her, and then later she will do her best to believe that it happened to someone else. Everything that has ever happened to one of her characters has happened to her. But imagine the trauma, the grief, the confused romantic yearnings, if she allowed that to be true.

She doesn't know the actor playing the kidnapper, which is probably for the best. They've exchanged a few pleasantries. Right now she's watching him chat up one of the makeup artists. She and her friend Cecelia Wright—who plays the female half of the FBI pair—are standing near, but not in, a line of people at an ice cream truck hired by the director as a thank-you to the cast and crew. Later today she and Cecelia are scheduled for their one scene together—Cecelia rescues Josie, Agent Corbett rescues Karen Woodward—but production is running three hours behind, so when a PA knocked on the door to tell them about the ice cream, they were hanging out in Cecelia's trailer playing each other in a word game on their phones. Josie took this job in part to hang out with Cecelia. They haven't gotten together much lately, with the long hours Cecelia works: here until eleven last night, back at six this morning. It's hard being number one on the call sheet. Josie remembers how hard and would nevertheless like those days to return.

"There's a lot of food on this set," she says to Cecelia.

"Really?" Cecelia's reading something on her phone, only half listening.

"That taco truck yesterday, ice cream today, plus craft services."

"I don't pay attention," Cecelia says. "I mostly don't eat it." She puts her phone in the pocket of her FBI agent blazer and frowns. "How do we feel about the *Alter Ego* reunion?"

"Is something up?" Josie looks at the outline of the phone in Cecelia's pocket.

"No, that was a text from my mother. Her cat's sick. I just wondered how we feel about it. Are we glad? Are we nostalgic? Are we wishing it wasn't happening?"

"We have mixed feelings."

"Right?"

"Right." Josie looks at the menu posted beside the window on the white ice cream truck. No one has asked if she and Cecelia are in line; everyone assumes the actresses won't be eating the ice cream. Normally this would be a reasonable assumption, but right now Josie would very much like some ice cream. It would be fair to say she has an intense and urgent desire for it. "I'm debating whether to hire a publicist," she says. "I mean, I know we're all doing interviews at the convention, but for individual stuff."

"Why bother? The studio will send them."

"Yeah, but they'll be all about the show," Josie says. "I mean someone for me. I could really use some good individual press."

"Oh," Cecelia says. "Right."

Josie registers that she's just made Cecelia uncomfortable. Contained within that exchange was the difference in their relative positions: Cecelia has for some time now had studio publicists serving her cause and so doesn't need to shell out thousands of dollars to get her picture in a magazine. So Josie doesn't go on with what she's thinking, which is that a well-placed interview might lead to a long-term job. She says, "I know they're covering hair and makeup."

"They want to sell those anniversary DVDs."

"Not stylists, though."

"Oh really?" Cecelia frowns. "I'm glad you're paying attention. I didn't realize that was on us."

At other times Josie would freely say to Cecelia that she's reluctant to spend the $1,000 that one day of a stylist's services would cost, not to mention the $5,000 or more she'd spend on a month with a publicist. But relationships between actors shift, in ways subtle and not, depending on whether they're working. The one without the job must be careful not to express jealousy, which means, as good actors have high sensitivity to the subtexts of interaction, that she should perhaps not bring up that she's feeling a little strapped in case she inadvertently expresses jealousy or at least alerts the other one to the possibility that she feels it. The one with the job might feel uncomfortable about her good fortune, conversationally constrained by the need to neither rub it in nor complain. Or she might perceive resentment from the other one and feel resentful in return at her friend's inability to take pleasure in her success or at her friend's blind notion that now all her problems are gone. There are some who like their friends better when they're not doing well, enjoying the position of superiority, of sympathy expressed from a loftier perch. These people disappear when you get a job even if your job is not as good as theirs. Cecelia isn't like that; no one Josie has stayed friends with is. Still, it's better not to talk about money with Cecelia right now. Josie wishes she hadn't brought up the publicist at all. "I might succumb to the ice cream," she says.

"I try to be social on set," Cecelia says in a low voice. "But it's always about standing around the food, and then I end up eating crap, and then I feel like crap."

"That Oreo milkshake sounds pretty damn good to me. When's the last time I had an Oreo milkshake?"

"I give up."

"High school, I think."

When Josie was a kid, her favorite treat was an Oreo shake from a regional chain called the Taco Box. This was in Clovis, New Mexico, where Josie grew up with a single mother who worked on the nearby airbase. Once, in an interview with the *Albuquerque Journal*, she reminisced about the Taco Box, and when she went home to visit her mother, she heard they'd framed the article and hung it on the wall. At the time, her show had still been on. If it had been five years later, after two unaired pilots followed by a completely barren pilot season, she might not have done what she did, which was to go over there thinking she'd offer to sign the article and give them a thrill. The kid behind the counter had looked at her with blank suspicion, and said, "We don't usually let people deface the artwork."

"It's not artwork," Josie said, taken aback. "It's an article. About me." Behind her, a man in a cowboy hat shifted impatiently, anxious for his burrito.

"I'll have to get my manager," the kid said. He disappeared into the back, abandoning the cash register. The man behind Josie groaned audibly. She turned, flashed him an apologetic smile, and then fled before the manager could emerge. Later, this became a useful self-deprecating anecdote. She even told it on a talk show, complete with hyperbolic imitations of the kid's suspicion and the man's annoyance. She multiplied the man into a long impatient line. She got big laughs. That was at the height of her fame, when ego-pricking humiliation could become a hilarious incongruity. Now a moment like that would seem considerably less funny.

"I mean, Josie," Cecelia says, "it's been twenty years since *Alter Ego*."

"I know."

"And it's still the main thing people care about."

"I know." Josie sighs. "But wait, really? Even now with this show?"

"Yes, absolutely. When people come up to me, *Alter Ego* is almost always what they want to talk about."

"But this show is a huge hit."

"Different demographic," Cecelia says. "Not the culty types. People who like this show like me on it, but they don't *adore* me. There's no reason to adore me. I'm not angsty and magical. I'm dedicated and professional."

"I think about myself back then and I feel a little hostile," Josie says. "Look at you, all plump and dewy and no inkling how lucky you are. And you're right, twenty years later everybody still loves that version of me the most. She's my main competition. Unappreciative little brat."

Cecelia laughs. "You weren't unappreciative."

"I wasn't?"

Cecelia shakes her head. "You were pretty good."

"I complained."

"We all complained. The night shoots! Jesus. All the *crying*."

"We did a lot of crying."

"You and Max especially."

"Max didn't cry so much as look like he was trying really hard not to cry," Josie says.

"He produced an occasional manly tear."

"Yes, the solitary tear. Very effective." Despite her tone, Josie's not being sarcastic. She's warding off a riot of confused feelings about Max. He played her tortured on-and-off love, whose name was the rather dramatic Malachi. Josie hasn't seen him in a while. A couple of years ago, she ran into him at a restaurant in Silver Lake, where he was having brunch with his wife. He was wearing a baseball cap pulled low and a set expression of unhappiness, which dropped from his face the moment he saw Josie. He and his wife have since divorced. When Josie goes to the convention, there he'll be. And suddenly she, too, is single. Josie tugs on Cecelia's sleeve. "Let's get in the line," she says.

"Oreo shake?"

"I'm pretty sure that's the way I'm going, yes." She moves to the back of the line, and Cecelia follows with reluctant steps.

"I'm standing here for moral support," Cecelia says. "Don't think you can peer pressure me."

"I wouldn't dream of it."

"Sometimes dedicated and professional feels a little boring."

"Shhh," Josie says. Cecelia's phone chimes, and while she tends to it, moving away, Josie tries not to feel irritated by her friend's complaint. Cecelia has every right to be bored. She plays one interrogation scene after another. She tells bad guy after bad guy to put his hands in the air. Three seasons into this show, Josie would probably be bored, too, but right now that's hard for her to believe. Right now Josie's fervent wish for steady employment means she'd be more than happy to point a gun, week after week after week, wearing a suit with implausible cleavage and a pair of uncomfortable, unrealistic heels.

It's Josie's turn to order. "Feel free to add extra Oreos," she says. The ice cream guy winks at her. He's young and cute, and she feels grateful for the wink. When he hands her the shake, he says, "I added extra everything."

"I believe you," she says. "It feels like it weighs twenty pounds."

"Enjoy."

"Thanks." They smile at each other for a lingering moment, and the pleasure she takes in this most minor of minor flirtations gives her a premonition of terrifying loneliness.

Josie rejoins Cecelia, who looks at Josie's shake with an exaggerated expression of longing. "Sometimes it's good not to have a job," Josie says.

"I have a half-naked scene next episode," Cecelia says.

"Love scene?"

"Shower. There's a bad guy in the house and I don't know it. Water's running, I'm stripping, the audience says, 'Look out!' One of those." Cecelia makes a rueful face. "A real acting challenge."

"Ah," Josie says. She should commiserate as a good and loyal friend. She's failing. She'd welcome the stupid scene, acting challenge or not. But later she has her own scene and for the moment she has this shake. She pulls the straw out and licks ice cream off the sides in a greedy way that makes her look sheepishly at Cecelia. Cecelia is gazing past her at the view: the flat paved lot; the ice cream truck; the clusters of crew members with their cones and shakes; the guy who plays the kidnapper now demonstrating a retro dance move to the makeup artist, who watches intently and then imitates him; and, farther off, the rows of trailers and the enormous nondescript building that is a wonder palace of make-believe—Agent Corbett's living room with its tasteful couch cushions; an FBI office with blinds and desks and recycling bins—but looks from the outside like a place where you might store auto parts.

Cecelia is still thinking about the *Alter Ego* reunion. It'll be at a convention, a panel discussion in honor of the show's twenty-fifth anniversary, and they'll film a separate group conversation for a one-hour special on Syfy. Cecelia played Josie's best friend, Genevieve, aka Vivi. In a later season, Cecelia's favorite, Vivi suffered tragedy, went bad, and became Josie's nemesis. There were passionate speeches and stage punches. Cecelia had such fun being evil that after her character reawakened to her inner goodness, she found herself feeling restless and confined.

Before she was cast as Vivi, Cecelia auditioned for the role of Bronwyn Kyle, which was the lead, the part Josie got. Once, at a bar, a drunken former casting assistant told Cecelia she should've gotten the part, but the decision-makers lacked the bravery to give a black girl the lead. At the time, this seemed a dangerous invitation to bitterness: It was the first year after the show ended, and Josie was a hot property while Cecelia had gone several months without even an audition. Now, when she thinks of that claim, which she mostly doesn't, life having recently been good, she wonders how the show would have done with a black actress as the superhero, the world being what it was—and is. Who knows? A thousand things happen, or don't. When will it ever come to pass that no one has to ask such questions?

"This is our life," Cecelia says.

"We're lucky," Josie says.

"Of course we are."

Before Josie's done with her milkshake, the PA comes to say they're ready for her. She hands the milkshake to Cecelia, who shakes her head and says, "I'm not going to finish it, but I will throw it away for you."

"Not in front of me," Josie says. "It's too sad." Then she follows the PA inside to a folding chair in the hall. She's not quite comfortable in the wardrobe they've given her. The waistband on her pants felt a bit too tight even before the encounter with the milkshake. The discomfort might work to her advantage in the performance, but while she waits in the chair for them to set up the lights, it just adds to her anxious impatience. She puts her earbuds in, dark, dramatic music cued up. She's asked the PA not to speak to her, just to tap her on the knee when it's time to go on. This has long been Josie's method for emotional scenes. In general, she withdraws on set, and in this she is very unlike Charlie, who treats a set like a cocktail party, making sure he knows everybody's names. He's frank about the fact that this isn't entirely the result of kindness; to do his best work he needs to feel the support of the room. So he makes sure he gets it. To do her best work Josie needs a kind of privacy.

One of the things she doesn't like about doing guest spots is explaining her ways to a production assistant she doesn't know, a new solicitous young person who will do whatever she asks but God knows what she's thinking or what she'll tell her boyfriend later, rolling her eyes. There's an unspoken rule on set that you don't act like a fan, you don't run up to an actor to rave about her previous roles, you make chitchat only if she seems amenable, you don't ask her to be her public self, you do your job and let her do hers. This is how it works. And yet it's a reflex for Josie to wonder if the production assistant has any idea who she is. She'd like to know, but she can't, because anything the girl said, good or bad, would mess with her head. In fact, the girl does know. In fact, the girl is thrilled, and happy for this glimpse of Josie's approach, and all she'll say to her boyfriend later is that Josie was very nice and that her hair color appears to be natural. She waits near Josie now, alert for the moment when she'll need to tap her knee.

The director of the episode is a former actor, a tall and handsome black man ten or twelve years older than Josie, and recognizable from the ensemble casts of two very popular shows that aired about fifteen years apart. In both cases, his character was kinetic and moody but capable of intense, almost frightening concentration. Josie knows better than to assume that this is who he is in real life, and yet their conversations today have ratified the impression that that's exactly who he is. She wants to be good for him. She doesn't like to imagine him watching her in the video village, muttering in angry disappointment at the monitor, turning to the script supervisor to complain that she flubbed a line. She turns her music up and closes her eyes.

The tap comes. She takes her earbuds out and hands the iPod to the PA. Then she walks onto the set, trying to keep her mind blank. She sits and is chained to a chair, trying not to register the jocular fellow in a Simpsons T-shirt who does the chaining. The buzzer sounds. Silence falls. The director shouts, "Action!"

Every artist is chasing those moments when their skill feels equal to their vision. They are beautiful and rare. This is one of those moments for Josie. God knows why, as the odds are against it—it's the first take, this character is new and underdeveloped and fleeting, and as the scene starts, Josie's still conscious that her pants are a little too tight. But she plays the scene and makes it true. When it's over, she can feel the spell she's cast, everyone's attention riveted to her. Every one of these people had a hand in creating the scene she just performed, and yet for its duration, she convinced them it was real. She smiles. For a brief exhilarating moment she doesn't remember that she'll have to do it again.

The director comes in. He crouches beside her so he can look her in the eye. She tenses even as she registers and appreciates his empathetic eye contact, his voice pitched low so only she can hear. "I have to tell you, that was good work," he says.

"Thank you," she says, full of wary gratitude.

He sighs his reluctance to say what he's about to say. "The thing is, it's not right for this show."

She nods, waiting.

"You played it real," he says, "but this show doesn't play it real. Can you do it less raw?"

"But she's been kidnapped," she says, though an exasperated part of her asks why she's bothering to argue.

"I know, I know. You're absolutely right. But for this show you can't play it like, Anne Hathaway as Fantine."

"Oh."

"Okay?" he asks, kindly, but with the kindness one shows the powerless, an animal or a child.

Guest spots, she thinks. "Okay," she says.

"Thank you," he says, touching her lightly on the arm. Then loudly, "Let's go again," rising to his feet.

She tones it down. And then she tones it down some more. By the end, her exhilaration is utterly gone and it seems to her that she's playing the scene as if being kidnapped were an annoyance on the order of bad customer service. She says the lines. They do close-ups. She says the lines. They change the camera setup and shoot again. She says the lines. The script supervisor notices that her hair, which was behind her shoulder at the start, has now fallen forward, and someone comes in to fix that. She says the lines. In the show, the scene will last less than two minutes. It's been more than two hours since she started saying the lines. Sometimes she sees acting as a noble profession fulfilling a crucial role in the culture. Right now she thinks it's self-flagellation for masochists.

The director comes in again, this time for words with the kidnapper. Josie stares in blank weariness down at her chained wrists and longs for Charlie. Maybe this is a long-distance psychic connection, as when Mr. Rochester calls out for his Jane Eyre. Reach out for him, Josie! Don't you hear him calling you? You'd never believe it now, but you can be the one to save him.

The necklace Charlie gave her is on the desk in her trailer near the pile of her actual clothes, and she pictures it there as though the image alone could summon it to her. She associates it with Charlie to a degree she'd find embarrassing were anyone else to know, so when she wears it in public, she usually tucks the pendant inside her collar so she'll never have to answer even the question of where she got it, about which she would lie. It *is* Charlie, this necklace. Or more precisely, it's his love for her. Objects are magical even in our real-life world, containing as they do the magic of our creating thoughts, the conjurations wrought by our insistent feelings. When Josie settles the small cool dome of the pendant inside the palm of her hand, she feels what it is to be loved.

After they started dating, Charlie ordered the pendant, a glass bubble containing a fragment of the play they acted the first time they met: the word *Beatrice* clearly visible on one side, *Benedick* on the other. Until recently, she wore it every day. She had developed a habit of lifting the pendant off her chest between her thumb and finger, stroking its smooth surface, wearing an inward smile. Sometimes she'd even press it to her lips. Since the article, she can hardly stand to own it. She hides it from herself, then finds it, then hides it again. This morning, half-awake in the quiet dimness of her house, she rescued it from the giveaway box by the front door and put it on.

For a moment, chained to that chair with the cameras pointed at her, she is not the kidnapped lawyer Karen Woodward nor is she the actress Josie Lamar. She is Beatrice. She is Beatrice, and she kisses Benedick. The chemistry she and Charlie had from word one—well, actors tell the truth when they say that might not translate to affection in what we call real life. But when Benedick and Beatrice kissed, so did Charlie and Josie, and there was for them and for everyone watching that alchemy that erases the distance between the make-believe and the real. *Peace! I will stop your mouth.* A cartoonist might have drawn a little sparkle of light at their lips. You can never be sure, of course, that such a thing, real or not, will linger. But when the play was done and the cocktails were in hand, she looked at him and he looked at her and it was still there. The light.

II.

Further, endeavor to penetrate the psychology of persons around you toward whom you feel unsympathetic. Try to find in them some good, positive qualities which you perhaps failed to notice before. Make an attempt to experience what they experience; ask yourself *why* they feel or act the way they do.

—MICHAEL CHEKHOV, *To the Actor*

One.

The house where they take him is blue and white, alone against thickening vegetation, one story, in need of paint. He sees the house with a spotlit clarity, stumbling toward it, though he's having a hard time registering details about the people hustling him inside. They are shorter than he is. They speak their own language in hushed and urgent voices. What does any of that matter? The point is that they have guns. They are brute force personified. They are the monsters in a dream.

The door to the house—a white door—swings open, and a young woman in a housekeeper's uniform steps aside to allow them entry. Charlie swings his head to gape at her even as the gun in his back and the hands on his arms urge him forward. She waits for them to pass with a deferential air and then steps to close and latch the door. This has to be a dream. The walls of the hallway look as if they'd be rough to the touch. In some places the paint is peeling. To Charlie, the hallway is interminable, though in actual fact the house is a small one, the hallway a standard length. There's nothing remarkable about the house at all, though to Charlie it's the strangest place on earth, the hole beneath the world. They shove him past two open doors. He's not able to glance inside, and if he could, he'd see nothing. It's an empty house. Ahead of him is another doorway, and as in a dream, he knows he mustn't go in there but can do nothing to stop himself. Even if he tried to scream, he wouldn't make a sound.

The room at the end of the hallway is very small, eight by ten, and like the other rooms, it's empty. The floor is concrete, the walls painted the dark, dark blue of a sky on the verge of night, the one window covered with boards. Into the floor someone has hammered metal stakes. At the threshold, the scrum around Charlie separates so that nothing touches him but the gun in his back. The gun in his back, which nudges him gently forward, as a dog might nudge your leg. Does Charlie know that this is his prison? Deep, deep down he knows it. But sometimes the things we know take quite some time to understand.

"Lie down," says the person behind him. A male voice.

"Where?" Charlie says.

"Floor," the man says.

Charlie's legs tremble so violently that lying down sounds like a decent idea. But his head shouldn't be by the door, so he wants to turn around before he complies. Will that be allowed? He doesn't yet understand the rules. He doesn't want to make a mistake. "Can I turn around first?"

The man hesitates. He is a very young man, only twenty-one, and though he's doing a good job of concealing it, he's quite nervous about all this. He's intensely aware of the others watching from behind him in the hall. His English isn't great either, and he's not completely sure he understood Charlie's question. "Slow," he says, finally, with a persuasive threat in his tone.

Charlie turns as slowly as he can. For good measure, he lifts his hands in the air as much as possible, bound as they are. He doesn't stop to look at the people with the guns but turns his gaze toward the floor, trying to determine how to sit without his hands to catch him. Finally he drops rather painfully to one knee. From there, he falls to sitting, and then he lowers his back down and stretches his long legs out along the floor. Against the cold comfort of the concrete he can feel that his whole body is shaking. There's a fuzziness at the edges of his vision that suggests he might black out again. He can't see anything now but the ceiling. It's an ordinary ceiling, with a light fixture that looks incongruously like the one in his childhood bedroom. Someone flips it on as he's looking at it, so that he shuts his eyes and sees bright spots behind them.

There's movement near him, and then a hand on his arm, and then a tugging at the ropes. He opens his eyes to see a man crouching beside him, cutting his bonds. He risks a glance at the man's face, but the man—an older one, who came in from the hall with his large sharp knife—keeps his own gaze fixed on the task before him. When the ropes separate, the man pulls them free, and Charlie instinctively rubs first one wrist and then the other. "Why are you doing this?" he asks, but the man doesn't respond, indifferent to Charlie's desperate need to know. There must be something Charlie could say to compel an answer. What's the right line?

The more kidnap victims believe it matters what they think or want or feel, the more they struggle to comprehend their loss of agency. If, in their normal lives, their actions, their decisions, and their words have power, they can't help but persist in the idea that they can change what's happening. They insist there's a misunderstanding, an overestimation of their value or threat, and they try to explain that they're not rich, that they're not spies. *I'm not the one you want.* Like others in his situation, Charlie wants to say this. But in his case he knows it isn't true.

The man speaks over his shoulder to the young one with the gun, and that one brings over chains. Limb by limb, they attach Charlie to the four stakes in the floor. "You don't need to do this," Charlie says. "You have guns. Listen to me. You don't need these chains. I'm claustrophobic. Please listen to me." Do they speak English? They don't answer. They don't meet his eye. As they chain his second wrist, he begins an active attempt to get the older man to look at him. If there's anything in the world he knows how to do it's make someone look at him. He watches the man—the top of his thick curly head, the tip of his prominent nose—and puts all his energy into compelling his gaze. Finally the man meets his eye. He does it reluctantly and immediately looks away, but Charlie feels a surge of triumph that he made him look at him at all. That triumph is the only thing he's felt except terror in what seems like hours, months, days, and he clings to it. He won't be less than human if he can make them look.

Their task completed, the men step away from him. Though they move at different times and in different ways, to Charlie's confused mind they are as synchronized as dancers. What is actually a slap-dash, on-the-fly operation—five novice kidnappers at this house, counting the woman who opened the door, and six with the other hostages—seems to Charlie confidently choreographed. The powerless ascribe to the powerful even more mastery than they actually have. That is one way power grows.

The chains are painfully tight. Charlie strains against the ones on his wrists, a pointless use of energy leading to additional pain, but he obeys the instinct anyway. Though it's nothing he can articulate yet, he'll come to understand that effort, even pointless effort, is what staves off despair. "Who are you?" he asks. "What do you want? When will you let me go?"

The men talk over him and he understands none of it. In his peripheral vision he sees their feet. They're wearing running shoes.

How did they know, how did they know who he was, where to find him? Someone must have recognized him on the street, at the bar. And then followed him, because he told no one about the hike. But why did they pick him up in the woods? Wouldn't it have been easier to snatch him outside the bar or at his rental cottage? *Woods* is the wrong word. Not woods, not woods—tropical rain forest. He read his guidebook cover to cover. It said nothing about kidnapping. It said the people were friendly. On the plane he memorized the list of helpful phrases, phonetically spelled, and on land he successfully ventured *Hello* and *How are you?* But for the things he wants to say to these people he doesn't have the words. What comes to mind is *Where is the bus stop?* He'd like to find the bus stop. He'd like to catch a bus now, please. He doesn't want to be a person this has happened to. He doesn't want to be someone people recognize.

Before he was famous, Josie tried to tell him what it was like. She said that when *Alter Ego* was on, going out in public felt like walking past a pack of police dogs with a pocketful of drugs. As though people were not individuals but one enormous inquisitive animal, quivering and insistent. "You make it sound terrifying," he said, and she looked at him with a mixture of sympathy and irritation, and said, "Because it is." But for him, back then, those moments of recognition were rare, so it was still a novelty, a rush, when a stranger's face morphed into surprised delight. He'd had a few uncomfortable encounters—the girl who kept insisting she knew him from a show he'd never been on, raising her voice, following him when he tried to walk away. But most people were sweet, encouraging, like the flight attendant who leaned in low when she handed him his water and stage-whispered her compliment. They were beneficent. Like they knew he needed them.

Now he puts on a baseball cap like everybody else, walks with his head down. He's been accosted for an autograph while peeing in a urinal. He's been asked to pose for a photo while fumbling drunkenly with a hotel key, while hustling his sister's tantruming toddler out of a mall. Shivering on a hospital bed with food poisoning, fetal-positioned around a basin filled with his own vomit, he looked up to see a nurse beaming at him with childlike delight. "They told me you were here but I didn't believe it!" she said. I'm here, yes, but don't you see the vomit? The screaming two-year-old? The fact that my fly is down? He isn't a real person anymore; he knows that. He's the surprise cameo in someone else's story.

Josie used to say to him, before he was famous, *Let's quit. Let's quit and be flight attendants. Let's quit and open a bookstore. Let's quit and open a bed-and-breakfast in Taos.* Josie is from New Mexico and they'd intended to go there together sometime, but they never got around to it and now they won't. Why didn't he ever go with Josie to New Mexico? He'll turn back time, take that trip instead of this one, and never do that interview at all.

He tried to quit acting, or at least the show, after the article. He called his agent and asked how he could get out of his contract, and his agent said that would never happen no matter how mad the showrunner was. And she was mad. He was going to have to endure the sharp tone and caustic asides for as long as it took to achieve forgive and forget, and God only knew what embarrassing stuff she was planning for his character in season two. Whatever it was, he'd have to do it. He was going to have to buckle down and be the good boy he always, always had been.

I tried to quit, Josie, he thinks now, chained on the floor, as if persuading her of this truth might release him. *I tried. I tried.*

Though he doesn't know it, he passes out again briefly and has a dream that he is asleep in a bed in a crowded room, Josie beside him. He returns to consciousness to find a woman bending over him. She is not the woman in the housekeeper's uniform, but the one who appeared in the clearing with a gun. She stands with her hands braced on her knees, a considering expression on her face. She was debating whether to prod and wake him, but before she could nudge her foot into his side, his eyes opened. Her hair is in two long blond braids that swing down toward him, but he is not fooled into believing that she is sweet or girlish. She's meeting his eyes without hesitation, without compunction, as if there were nothing at all strange about what's happening here.

"Hello," she says.

He tries to say hello back but his voice catches on relief. She speaks English. She's speaking it to him. He swallows. "What's happening? What do you want with me?"

"We are glad to have you," she says. Her tone is conversational, as if she were the innkeeper, he the guest. "How do you like our country?"

He feels a flare of incredulous anger. "I liked it better yesterday."

She smiles a satisfied smile and nods, as if to say he's pleased her. "We hoped for you," she says. "And you are here."

Two.

The island nation where Charlie Outlaw has met such terrible luck is very small, so small you've never heard of it. Site of many arrivals and skirmishes, it has perilous and confusing politics and a racially diverse population. If you ever did hear of it, it would be the same way Charlie did, from an article in a high-end travel magazine with a headline like "Hidden Paradise" or "The Last Eden." Keep your gaze only on what nature has to offer, and the island is indeed a paradise: sparkling ocean, verdant land, bright singing birds. The human part of things is less ideal. Jobs are insufficient and poverty widespread while politicians, the small moneyed class, and foreign investors gain wealth from the one big resort and the smattering of rental cottages and boutique hotels. In one of those cottages are Charlie's forlorn belongings: clothes, the shampoo he likes, his currency and passport.

A second resort is in the planning, to be built by an American company, and crucial to the realization of those plans is the displacement of two small villages, one of which contains the house where Charlie is chained on the floor. The kidnappers are from these two villages, their plot hatched out of bitter complaining about the hotel corporation and America and their own government's obsequious kowtowing to those two entities. There are eleven kidnappers in total, nine men and two women. They range in age from seventeen to forty-eight and come from a variety of ethnic backgrounds. There's confusion of purpose among them—some believe they should make political demands for the release of the hostages, some financial ones—but the man named Darius, the oldest of the group, had sufficient charisma to persuade them to enact this plan before they'd agreed on all the particulars. His own conviction—that they can and will use their prisoners to scuttle the resort—is so persuasively total that he believes the others must share it no matter their indications to the contrary.

It would be misguided to assume that the kidnappers are less dangerous to Charlie because they're amateurs with a half-baked scheme. Their rookie uncertainties are no guarantee that they won't kill or otherwise harm him. They are nervous people with guns in their hands, and if they didn't possess the all-too-human capacity to view another person as somewhat less than real, they wouldn't be in this story. On day one of Charlie's captivity, they leave him chained up alone for more than an hour without considering that he might need food or drink or the bathroom, or that a gap in the boards on the window is sending a beam of sunlight directly into his eyes. Every time he opens them, he winces into a blinding vision, but keeping them closed does nothing about the heat on his face, so that in addition to his numb terror he has to cope with the physical discomfort of feeling as if someone has stuck the top of his head in a microwave. These two feelings merge into one, so the heat seems to amplify his terror, his terror the heat, and then an itch develops on his ankle where a mosquito bit him. He wants to scratch the inflamed bump so badly that he keeps moving his hands toward it though they're nowhere close to reaching. He tries to roll his ankle to scratch it on the floor, which does nothing for the itch and, in fact, seems to tighten the chain, and tears of helpless despair push their way from behind his eyelids, leaving a stiffening line of salt down his temples into his hair.

From the swamp of fear and panic, a thought surfaces: He's experiencing all aspects of this situation as if they were equivalent, the unreachable mosquito bite no less troubling than being chained to a floor. Then he notices the rapidity of his breathing, then the way he's clenching his muscles as if to levitate off the floor. All this noticing is a trail of bread crumbs back to himself: Charlie is well practiced in simultaneously being and observing himself be. This skill, an essential one in his profession, can be a detriment in certain real-life situations, and he's sometimes felt ashamed of the voice in his head registering the usable material in the midst of some wrenching disagreement, but right now the ability to step aside and watch is going to save him. He's trained for this.

He tries an observation exercise. Counting to one hundred, he looks around the room as best he can, then shuts his eyes to test what he can recall. Observation. Imagination. Memory. These are an actor's tools, and as one of Charlie's professors used to say, all tools must be sharpened. That professor was given to aphorisms that didn't, on further reflection, apply as broadly as she seemed to think, but still she was a good teacher. One of Charlie's classmates used to do an imitation of her, announcing, "All tools must be sharpened," during lulls in the conversation or at moments when he might otherwise have been expected to offer sympathy or advice. There's a memory for you, one Charlie can use to evoke amusement, nostalgia, and, yes, a hint of scorn, because that classmate always had to make a joke, never was quite brave enough to proceed with the necessary sincerity, so was never as good as he might have been and failed to understand why. To defeat criticism, you have to be amazing. To be amazing, you have to be vulnerable. That's the real paradox of the actor, in Charlie's opinion: Vulnerability is your best protection. Because the worst thing you can be is bad.

The floor is a pockmarked gray. Not far from his face is a faded red streak about (he thinks) a foot in length, four inches wide. As if someone started to paint the floor and then thought better of it. His imagination says: blood. Imagination is no good to him now. Observation is what he needs; observation tells him the red streak is not blood, not the right color, too even in shape. Whoever painted the walls that midnight blue did a sloppy job: blue spots on the white ceiling, blue spots on the gray floor. It's quite a dark color for such a small room. Where the ray of sun hits the wall—a thick diagonal stripe made irregular by the shadow of a shelf hanging above it—the paint is unevenly distributed. Hard to get those dark colors just right. Who painted the walls? Maybe one of the gun-wielding boys, to cover up the blood.

There is no blood.

The walls are made of cinder blocks. He didn't have time within his self-imposed limit to count how many across, how many down. He'll have plenty of time for that later, time enough to count them again and again. Don't imagine that. The ceiling is white and has the snowflake look created by a spray gun except for a long smooth strip right above him that looks as though someone went over it with a roller. Why? To cover up the blood?

He opens his eyes, squints against the sunlight. Yes, he got it all right—cinder blocks, paint, shelf, shadow. If there's something on the shelf, he can't see it from this angle. The room is longer than it is wide. He's lying lengthwise, which is good because he'd feel even more claustrophobic on the short side, his head and feet just inches from the walls. As far as he can tell, both the door past his feet and the window behind his head are centered on the walls. The window is tall, or looks tall from this vantage point. It has a thick sill, also painted dark blue. The boards nailed across it look fairly new.

What else can he observe? He resists counting the cinder blocks, because that seems like the thing he'll do when he starts to go crazy. Will he be here long enough to go crazy? How long will that take? How would he play that if it were a scene—kidnapped man, losing his mind? He could count the blocks. He could thrash and scream.

Don't imagine.

He should observe his way to an escape route. He should make a plan.

Like what?

Like what?

He pictures the blond woman's face above him, her swinging braids. There's an exercise where you look at a stranger, assign her a name, then an occupation, a family history—but he can't even give the blond woman a name. Her face induces terror. He used to struggle to conjure terror when a scene demanded it, and now here it is uninvited, all the terror he could possibly want. But it's not useful terror, because how can he ever use it in performance? He can't imagine a future in which he gains an objective distance on any of this. To picture this woman's face will be to shut himself in a tiny room. He will not be able to act. He will be using all his resources trying not to scream.

Is it ransom they want? He hopes so. He hopes he's a commodity to be traded rather than a symbol of American cultural imperialism, a propaganda star. It is too easy for Charlie to imagine what notions his celebrity might give a terrorist, the power of diminishing by torture or death the object of your enemy's worshipful attention. He hopes the studio will pay the ransom, not his family. Everyone in his family is upper middle class, but still they have mortgages and car payments and student loan debt and college savings plans. After his oldest sister and her husband bought their house, she had fifty-six dollars in her checking account. The kidnappers may have unreasonable expectations about what his family can afford. He knows about K & R insurance, but he can't imagine the production company has a policy on him. They don't travel to Third World countries for the show. They hardly ever leave the lot. What if the kidnappers approach Josie? She'd have to sell her house to raise money, and she loves that house. Despite everything that's happened in the last nineteen days, and though it would leave her without assets, he knows she would sell her house for him. There's comfort in that thought because it brings with it a return of the certainty that Josie loves him, that if she could see him chained on the floor right now she would do anything to set him free. He feels a stab of guilt, as if the house were already sold, Josie already broke and without a place to live. Maybe he can pay the ransom himself, go online and transfer funds. But he has $38,000 in his bank account, and he knows people expect him to have millions. He hadn't had a steady job in five years before he landed the show, which meant substantial credit-card debt and no savings. Will they believe him when he says that's all the money he has?

It has to be ransom they want. It has to be.

This room has blue cinder-block walls and one shelf and one window and blue paint mistakes on the ceiling and floor. What is going to happen to him here?

Three.

The contents of Charlie Outlaw's backpack are strewn across the enormous table in the kitchen. A long-ago owner built the table inside the room, and it's far too big to fit through the door. So it will stay in here until someone takes an ax to it. It's the only furniture in the house, which is small, with one bathroom. The kitchen, too, is small, but all the kidnappers are gathered here now. Everyone leans against a wall or a counter, eating bowls of noodles, except for Darius, who stands at the table sifting through Charlie's possessions again, studying each one as though it might eventually become a thing the kidnappers wanted: Charlie's passport, his money, his phone. They'd all expected a little windfall, a first payment of some kind. Instead: a bedroll, a dish, extra socks. Charlie packed from the list they gave him at the outdoor store, checking off each item as he went.

Darius drops Charlie's flashlight on the table with a sigh of disgust. He catches Denise watching him over her noodles and instantly smooths his face, gives her an authoritative nod. "Stay here," he orders the room, as though anyone were planning to follow him. He retrieves the key to Charlie's cell from the nail by the kitchen door.

It's on a key chain imprinted with the resort's logo, a native tree endangered by deforestation. The resort's marketing campaign emphasizes their environmental efforts, the concern for the community, the replanting of trees. Normally any reminder of the company infuriates Darius, but right now he's so distracted that the logo brings no stab of murderous irritation. He didn't even notice it. He thinks they should call the prisoner's room *the guestroom* in case of anyone overhearing.

He doesn't really want to go in the guestroom. But what can he do? He set these events in motion but no longer feels in control of them. He makes himself stride down the hall as though he hasn't a single doubt. The hinges creak when he pushes the door open, and the man on the floor opens his eyes. "Hello?" he says, or rather tries to say, the word as hesitant and creaky as the hinges, and then he lifts his head to look at Darius, but the way he's bound he can't lift it very far. Maybe they need to loosen his chains.

Darius, to be courteous, moves to where the man can see him just by turning his head. But he won't crouch. After one glance down, he puts his gaze on the wall and keeps it there. The empty shelf looks odd. Shelves shouldn't be empty. Then what is the point of them? He doesn't want to look at the man.

"Who are you?" asks the man on the floor.

"I am Darius."

"No, I mean, what is this group?"

Darius glances down again, frowning, and waves an impatient hand. "No money in your backpack," he says.

"I didn't bring any on the hike."

"No passport in your backpack."

"I didn't bring that either."

Darius makes a frustrated sound. "Why?"

"I didn't think I'd need it in the woods."

Darius wants to pace, but the room isn't big enough. He walks to the back wall and for no particular reason reaches out to touch it, looks up at the ceiling. The man on the floor takes up a lot of space. Darius does not want to step over his long splayed limbs, which limits where he can go in the room.

"The *forest*," the man says.

"What?"

"It's not woods. It's tropical rain forest."

Darius looks at the man—he can't help it—and sees he's closed his eyes again. Not with a sleeping face, a peaceful face, but with forehead and eyelids scrunched, like someone bracing against pain.

Tropical rain forest, tropical rain forest, Charlie thinks, as if these were magic words.

From above him, he hears the question: "Where is your money?"

He keeps his eyes closed. "At the rental," he says. Last night he was sorry to be staying alone in a cottage instead of at a hotel among people. He'd paced from the canopied bed to the table bearing a bottle of champagne and two flutes, suffering a fervent wish to be in a blank hotel room instead of this honeymooned hell.

Now he's glad. No key card in his bag printed with the name of the hotel, therefore no easy way for these people to raid his room. On this first day in captivity, his perspective has not yet caught up with his reality; he still cares whether they steal his passport, get his phone with its famous contacts, see his photos, read the texts and e-mails between him and Josie. Maybe that was even their plan: to sell that stuff to tabloids and gossip sites. Maybe they're hoping he's got naked photos of his costar.

On some level, he knows that motive is nonsense, yet the idea has the weight of reality. All things seem possible now.

"What is in your pockets?" Darius asks.

"My pockets? Nothing."

Darius makes a skeptical sound. Charlie's wearing hiking pants, which have a lot of pockets, but everything was in his backpack. He hates having things in his pockets. At home he carries a messenger bag. No, *wait*. He does have things in his pockets, put there just before the morning's catastrophic collapse: in one, a half-eaten protein bar, in another a pocketknife. He'd taken the knife from his backpack to peel a lychee, then tucked it in his pants after the Brazilian woman laughed at him, plucked the lychee from his fingers, peeled it with her own, and popped it in her mouth. She'd spit the glossy black seed impressively far. Before putting the knife away, he did a little comedy routine. "What, I don't have to attack it?" Pulling out another lychee, pretending he was going to impale the thing.

"Wait?" Darius asks, and Charlie realizes he said that word aloud. Oh shit. What should he do? He has a knife! Surely he should try to keep it.

He opens his eyes. He is very good at sincerity. He tries to meet Darius's gaze, but the man won't look at him. "I have half a protein bar."

"Protein bar?"

"Food," Charlie says. "Hiking food."

"Where?"

"Top pocket. On your left." Charlie points with his chin.

Darius squats and reaches in for the bar, a tricky proposition involving wiggling his fingers into a space near Charlie's groin. He frowns and looks away, as if to pretend he doesn't know what his hand is doing. He fishes out the bar and his frown adds a quality of disgust. The bar has started to melt. He has chocolate on his fingers. He goes hastily from the room without checking the other pockets, taking the bar with the obvious intent of throwing it away.

Charlie is nauseous with relief. He still has the knife. The man didn't find the knife. Now how does he keep it? He looks around again, but there's no good hiding place in here even if he could get the knife out of his pocket to hide it. Which he can't. His adrenalized sense of purpose begins to ebb back into despondency. The knife will stay where it is, which means eventually he'll be caught with it. Someone will think to search him, someone less squeamish than that man. He sees again the blond woman leaning over him, braids swaying. Her appraising eyes. His instinct tells him she'll feel no compunction. Not about putting her hands in his pockets. Not about anything she does. What will the consequence be for failing to disclose a knife in his pocket? Maybe he should call the man back and confess. What could he do with it, anyway? A tiny little blade that won't cut through chains and will dramatically fail to intimidate anyone holding a gun.

Now Charlie realizes he's hungry. The protein bar was the only thing he'd eaten in two hours of hiking and he hadn't even finished it. Because it wasn't that good. Many times in the days to come he'll think with envy and scorn of the person he was when he put that half-eaten protein bar back in his pocket *because it wasn't that good*. He should've tried to keep it instead of the knife.

The hero thinks of a plan, Charlie. The hero doesn't opt for a half-eaten protein bar over a knife. The hero takes risks, because he knows that if he doesn't the world will end. Charlie knows he'd be less frightened if there was someone else to save instead of just himself. That's the function of babies and sweet grandmothers and wide-eyed girls—to keep the hero from admitting he's scared. He thinks of something Josie once said to him after glumly accepting what she called a "screaming-girl part": "Once you've been the badass, it's hard to go back to damsel." She made her eyes big, her voice breathy and high-pitched. "You saved me," she said to him. "Oh, Charlie." She pressed her hand to her heart. "You saved me *so well*." Discomfited, he tickled her until she shrieked with laughter then rolled over on him and pinned his wrists. She kissed him aggressively. She liked to be on top. Why discomfited? Because he hadn't really minded her looking at him like that.

He'll ask to go to the bathroom. They must be prepared for that eventuality. They'll have to unchain him. When they do, he'll have another chance to scope out the room, and he'll pay attention this time when they take him down the hall: Where are the open windows? Where are the doors? In the bathroom, he'll find a hiding place, and then once the knife is hidden, he'll have some time to figure out what to do with it. That is his plan: bathroom, knife, hiding place, quickly, quickly, before they open the door. What if they don't let him go alone, don't let him close the door? He'll have to move with confidence so it doesn't occur to them to object. Maybe he'll have to shame them, look them in the eye, say, "Why do you want to watch me urinate?" His heartbeat quickens at the thought of the performance he'll have to give. What if they search him before they leave him alone? Well, then, he forgot. He has to believe he forgot. *I forgot, I forgot*, he says to himself. *I didn't know it was there.* He closes his eyes, fixes these beliefs in his mind: that he forgot he had the knife, that he has the right to use the bathroom unobserved. He breathes in through his nose, out through his mouth, in through his nose, out through his mouth, in, out, in. He opens his eyes. "Hey!" he shouts. He waits a beat, hears nothing, shouts again. He thumps the floor with his heels, rattles his chains. There's a weird exhilaration in making all this noise.

Finally someone comes in. It's the young one who, a million years ago, ordered him onto the floor. He's slight and sweet faced, so Charlie imagines he's even younger than he is, which is twenty-one. "How are you?" asks the boy.

"How am I?" Charlie repeats. "What kind of question is that?" He feels anger urging him to say more, but the boy still has his rifle. "I need the bathroom," he says.

The boy—his name is Adan—frowns. He looks over his shoulder as if hoping someone will appear to give him an order. In obeying

Darius's command to go check on the prisoner, Adan hadn't thought that anything further would be required. Is he allowed to take the prisoner to the bathroom? "One minute," he says.

He leaves, then returns. With him come two other men, one to unchain Charlie and one to join Adan in training rifles at him. When Charlie tries to stand, his legs give way, and Adan lets the gun barrel drop so he can grab Charlie's arm. Charlie utters an involuntary cry, as if the catch had been a blow. "I help you," Adan says irritably. Charlie could swear the look on the boy's face is reproachful.

They march him back down the hall, one man in front, two behind. One of them checks the bathroom, as though to make sure Charlie doesn't have an accomplice in there, and then nods him inside. This is Charlie's cue. He steps confidently forward, turns to shut the door. He sees the hesitation on Adan's face and gives him the reassuring, resolute look his TV character gives his patients' families. Adan lets him close the door. Heat in his face, blood throbbing in his skull—he notes the physical symptoms of nerves but his mind is lucid and calm. It's like being onstage. The bathroom is very small— toilet, sink, no tub or shower, not even a cabinet. He can hear the men just on the other side of the door, the three of them, talking, shuffling, thumping against the walls like little boys who can't stand still. There's really only one option, so he lifts the lid off the tank, slowly, slowly, wincing against the sound he's afraid he'll make but manages not to, then he sets the lid on the closed toilet seat, drops the knife in the tank, replaces the lid. His shoulders are clenched, his heart rioting. He almost forgets to use the toilet before he opens the door.

On the way back down the hall, Charlie begins to shake. He doesn't want to go back in the chains. He slows his steps. They pass the woman with blond braids watching from the doorway of an empty room. Her eyes stay on his face the whole time, and Charlie, reflexively, tries to smile.

Back in the room, they instruct him to lie down. "Please," Charlie says. "I need some water." He looks at Adan, whom he's begun, unreasonably, to think of as the nice one. "What is your name?"

Adan looks at Darius, who nods. "I am Adan," he says.

"Adan, I need some water," Charlie says. "It's very hot in here. Please."

"Lie down first," Darius says. "First the chains."

"How can I drink if I'm chained on the floor? Please." Charlie brings his hands into a prayer position, looking first at Darius, whom he now assumes is the leader, then the other two. "Please. You could just do one ankle. Then I could sit."

Darius narrows his eyes. He takes a deep loud breath through his nose. "For now," he agrees. He nods at his subordinates.

Having won a small victory, Charlie knows to be submissive. He sinks immediately to the floor, proffering his left ankle for the chaining.

Darius tells Adan to watch Charlie, and the other man—Thomas—to get water. Darius himself goes outside to the spot that gets the best cell reception—next to a wild hibiscus, not the white one but the red. He's been googling—*kidnap* and *U.S. embassy, hostage* and *demands*—because only now that stage one of the plan has been executed has he realized he has little idea how to accomplish stage two. How exactly does a kidnapper issue his political demands? Is there someone he should e-mail? He can find the main number for the embassies of the various citizens he's detained, but if he just calls, they'll be able to trace it. Won't they? It's a conundrum he needs to resolve quickly. It's important that no one working for him realize that he doesn't quite know what he's doing.

So it's inevitable that the person who should come outside as he's standing in consternation by the hibiscus bush, staring at his tiny screen, is Denise. Denise seems to suspect him of being unqualified for this mission—has, in fact, seemed to suspect him from the moment he asked her to take part. He couldn't rescind the invitation, though, because to do so he'd have had to acknowledge to himself her evident doubt, and then that her doubt bothered him, and then perhaps he would've arrived at the conclusion that her doubt bothered him precisely because he knew it was justified. That was a conclusion Darius couldn't—can't—afford. So here comes Denise, that walking accusation.

"He will be trouble," she says, in their shared language.

"No, he won't," Darius says irritably.

She shrugs. She taps on the gun in her waistband with one judgmental fingernail, a new habit of hers that irritates Darius so violently that it's beginning to cause him physical pain. "Go back inside," he says. "Check on him."

Tap, tap, tap. Then she shrugs again and retreats. For the moment, she still obeys his orders. There may come a time when she doesn't, but this, too, Darius cannot afford to acknowledge. Adan is her younger brother, the other young man, Thomas, Adan's best friend. She is at the center of a web of loyalty and cannot be gotten rid of.

It is too bad for Darius that this is true. Too bad for Charlie, too.

Four.

Charlie's first steady job was a small part on Alan Reed's show—*one* of Alan's shows. He was twenty-eight when he got the part. Alan Reed was a TV star, a man in his late fifties, veteran of two long-running and high-rated comedies. So this show was a star vehicle, a workplace sitcom set in a restaurant, with Alan as the brilliant, hot-tempered chef, and Charlie as his sweet bumbling nephew, the world's worst waiter, fired and rehired repeatedly throughout the show's two seasons. It was his job to say the adorably literal thing that set Alan's character off on a hilarious rant.

"Ah, for a need." That was something Alan would mutter sometimes between takes. Other times, he'd look at Charlie and say, "Bored yet?"

At this, Charlie would smile and shake his head, and usually Alan would smile back and say, "That's good, that's good. I envy you."

But once, that first season, in a grim mood, Alan told him instead, "You will be. I promise. I know how happy you were to get this part. Hell, I was happy to get this part. And I know when this show ends we'll both be desperate for another one. You know what I worry about more than anything, anything in the world? My next job. But there's no actor on a TV show who by season two isn't desperate to get off it."

They were only two months into filming, and Charlie was still awash in gratitude. That Alan, of all people, was worried about his next job, that Alan was anticipating desperation of any kind: This made no sense to him. "Why?" he asked.

"Ah, for a need" was Alan's reply.

"Is that a quote or something?" Saying this, Charlie felt as dumb as his character. In Alan's presence, he helplessly played the ingénue whether or not the cameras rolled.

Alan shrugged. "It might be Shakespeare. One of the Henrys. Or maybe I made it up. The point is, kings get bored. That's why we have wars."

At the time, Charlie didn't believe a word of it. It was easy to say from the top of the mountain that the view got boring after a while. At the upfronts that first season, advertisers came up to take pictures with the cast, everyone crowded onto a small platform for the purpose. Charlie was never their favorite character; Charlie was never the one they were excited to meet. The advertisers invariably stood right in front of Charlie, already at the back because he was tall and on the edge because he was unimportant. One time he fell off the back of the platform just as the flash went off. People noticed, of course, and asked if he was all right. But for a moment after he stumbled backward, it seemed to him that he could fall off the world and nobody would bat an eye. He looked at Alan accepting some fan's gratitude for his arm around her shoulder, for his polite smile, and felt a baffled resentment. Bored? How dare he use that word to describe the condition of having it made? In Alan's position, Charlie would never be anything less than grateful. Charlie would never be bored.

And yet he has been bored.

Ah, for a need.

Now Charlie has experienced a sudden and vertiginous reduction in his sense of what he needs. The water that Adan brought him is warm and has a chemical sharpness, but so what, so what, it is water. He starts out gulping, then makes himself slow down, tilting the glass only a little so the inflow diminishes to a trickle, letting it pool on his tongue before he swallows. Concentrating on the relief of liquid on a hot, dry throat. He's closed his eyes to aid that concentration so he doesn't know that Adan has looked away, unable to bear the sight of Charlie's desperate pleasure, while Thomas watches with open fascination, as if Charlie were an anthropological experiment.

Charlie hears someone come in—footsteps, a tap, tap, tap that's a fingernail on a gun. He opens his eyes. He sees the blond woman and gulps the rest of the water before she can take it away. She regards him with disdain, then looks at Adan, who snatches the glass from Charlie. Charlie wipes his mouth with the back of his hand. He's still so thirsty. He decides to risk it. "Can I have some more?"

The woman considers this request, all impassivity. Then she nods at Adan, who hustles out of the room. If Charlie couldn't tell from her bearing that this woman was someone to be feared, he'd know it from her effect on Adan. She walks very close to Charlie, stepping over his legs without appearing to look down to avoid them, and he flinches out of her way. At the far wall, she turns to regard him. She manages to give the impression of having just noticed he's there— no, of having just *decided* to notice. She stands with her legs apart, her chest open, making clear his status as a nonthreat. It's as if she's practiced, as if the director told her before the take, "You're confident, you're intimidating." Charlie would rather think her a good actor than imagine this is just who she is.

"Who are you?" he asks.

"My name is Denise."

"But I mean who are all of you? What is this group?"

Denise shrugs. Does that mean she doesn't understand? Or just that she won't answer?

He tries again. "What do you want with me?"

"We want you."

"But what for?"

She shrugs again. "Another time," she says, so casual. So irritably dismissive. As if he were a fan on the street asking for a selfie, not himself on the floor asking for his life.

The boy still in the room stands with his gun pointed at Charlie, lazily swinging the muzzle from side to side. Charlie gives him a nervous glance. "What's his name?"

"That is Thomas."

"Is his gun loaded?"

She scoffs. "Of course."

"Could you ask him not to point it at me? It's making me nervous." He looks back at Thomas. "Thomas, would you mind pointing that gun away from me?"

Thomas looks at Denise, who responds with a slight nod. Thomas lowers the gun toward the ground.

Emboldened, Charlie sits up tall and deepens his voice. "I need to know what's happening."

"Why?" Denise asks.

Why? His mind stutters. He feels as if there's a correct answer, one that will unlock the information he wants. But what is it? Because I deserve to know? But this woman doesn't care what he deserves, or, even worse, she thinks that's what they're already giving him.

"It will not help you to know," she says.

Just like that, all courage is gone. Courage was an illusion! The world is a vortex of fear. "Because you're going to kill me?" he manages.

Denise laughs.

"Why is that funny?" He hears his voice swerving louder. "Are you going to kill me? Tell me!"

She sighs extravagantly. "You are crazy," she says. "You will be fine."

He searches her face. He believes her. Queasy, he makes a *ha* sound under his breath, smiles in the angry way you smile at someone who just terrified you for fun. "I'm crazy," he says. "I'm the crazy one."

She moves her hand to her gun with slow deliberation. Tap, tap, tap. *Be careful*, Charlie instructs himself. *Watch your mouth.* "I do not tell you things," she says. "You tell me things."

"Like what?"

"You tell me who you are."

Who he is? Is this a metaphysical question? Does she want him to describe his personality? *I'm a Gemini*, he thinks, with stunned hilarity. "What do you mean?"

"Who are you?"

"Who am I?"

"What is your name?"

He stares at her. "What is my name?"

The look on her face tells him he's an idiot. "Yes," she enunciates. "Now you say your name."

His mind flickers with the possibility that he's gotten this situation all wrong. "You don't *know* my name?"

She clicks her tongue in irritation. "No. That is why I ask."

"But you said you hoped for me."

"We hoped for an American." She shakes her head. "Not for *you*. You are nothing."

"I am nothing," he says.

"Yes, yes." She's dropped her don't-care stance to lean over him, frustration twitching through her. "You are nothing. What is your name?"

Adan returns with the water, providing a convenient interruption. Charlie takes a sip. How should he answer this question? He doesn't know. He's distracted by a giddy urge to laugh. He's nothing! That's why he came to this place, to be nothing. Anonymous American, mid-thirties white male. Good for you, Charlie, you did it. No one wants your autograph here. He'd had himself convinced that anonymity would have spared him. He thought they'd taken him because he was *something*. Well, aren't you full of yourself.

Denise looks at Thomas, who knocks the water out of Charlie's hand with astonishing speed. Charlie stares at the inexorable spread of the puddle from the cup. Deliberately, Denise puts her foot in the puddle. She crouches to retrieve the cup, hands it back to him. "Go ahead," she says, and he drinks the two sips remaining, survivors of the waste. "Good," she says, when he's finished. "Be good." She grips his chin and turns his face back and forth, as if deciding how to photograph it, how to make it up. His best side is the right. When he's posing for a photograph, he has pretty good control over how he looks. What expression is on his face right now, as she puts her hand on him, as she controls him, he has no idea. He can tell his jaw is clenched because his lips are going numb.

The woman—Denise—releases him. She rises and takes two steps back. "What is your name," she says again, her voice gone dead, her voice flatlined.

How can he possibly know whether it's best to tell them who he is? When he thought they knew, it seemed like a bad thing—maybe they wanted to execute him on the internet or bankrupt his family, or Josie. But if they don't know, does that make him more disposable? What if they turn out, by some miracle, to be fans of his show? Maybe if he says his name they'll let him go. "We didn't recognize you!" they'll say. "We thought you'd be taller!" They'll ask him for his autograph. Who can blame him for this sorrowful little fantasy? He's been ushered to the front of so many lines, feeling self-conscious, even unsavory, no less because part of him enjoyed the special treatment. Maybe there's some sort of celebrity upgrade for kidnap victims, a bigger room, cushy padding on his chains. Being recognized makes things better except when it makes them much, much worse.

He needs more background! He doesn't know enough. He risks a last attempt. "Is this about money?"

"Money," she repeats, as though it's the first time she's considered the notion. He wonders if he's made a terrible mistake. "It's about"— she spreads her hands and smooths them across an imaginary table—"everything."

"But what is everything?"

She ignores the question. "Your name," she says.

But he can't decide, he can't decide. "You're Charlie Outlaw!" people say on planes, in restaurants, passing on the street. "Oh my God, you're Charlie Outlaw!" Sometimes they get confused and call him by another actor's name. Even when he says they're wrong, they'll continue to insist. They think they know better than he does who he is. Sometimes they call him by his character's name. One woman ran into the street when she saw him on the other side, narrowly missing death by vehicle, shouting *Charlie Outlaw! Charlie Outlaw!* At least once a day a stranger tells him his name.

He senses movement behind him, glances back, and so turns into the blow. It's Thomas who has hit him in the face with the butt of his gun, but in the moment Charlie doesn't register the particulars, only the pain. The pain is bad. Charlie has been in a number of fights in his life, but not one of them has been real. Being hit very hard in the face knocks you back more than choreographed fisticuffs typically suggest. There is blood, there is throbbing, throbbing, there is the stunned confusion that results from the sudden infliction of pain on someone wholly unused to receiving it. Poor Charlie. He suffers pain and fear but also an unreasonable sense of inadequacy. Because he's been taught, you see, how to grab a gun, throw a punch, vault down a fire escape: and there is a part of him that believed his training applied to real-life danger as well. Now that part of him is exposed as a self-deluded sham. He's only ever had to fight back against people who were paid to let him do it.

His face throbs and bleeds against his hand. His eyes are filled with tears—of course they are, but on TV a blow has never made him cry. He looks at Denise through the blur and says, "Ben Phillips."

Eight years ago, back when Charlie still had roommates, he was living with a friend when the friend got his first part in a movie. The part was a small one—an American prisoner in a foreign jail who shares a cell for one night with the movie's hero—but the friend was very nervous and excited, and began commandeering the television to watch episode after episode of a reality show about people imprisoned or held hostage in foreign countries. Interviews with the formerly imprisoned, actor reenactments of their imprisonment. Charlie and the friend watched as a man captured by guerrillas in Colombia gave a fake name to protect his adult daughter, his only child, from fear and impossible ransom demands. It was a striking act of heroism. "Someone should make a movie about this guy," said Charlie's friend.

Does Charlie remember that show, that man, how much he admired his selflessness? Not at this moment. Art determines life determines art. Sometimes that's buried deep.

Denise is satisfied by the name he's given. She nods. "What is your job?"

"I'm a waiter," Charlie says.

She frowns. She was hoping for something better than a waiter. A lawyer, a doctor, a businessman. These are the jobs she assumes Americans have, and yet Darius snags a waiter. If Charlie were a fish, she would throw him back. If Darius were a fish, she would throw him back, too. For a moment she considers giving this whole thing up in disgust, but Denise believes in perseverance. She believes in surviving. She believes there will yet be something she can get out of this.

"Ben Phillips," she repeats.

"With two *Ls*." As far as Charlie can tell, she believes him. He is surprised and not surprised; he trusts his powers of persuasion, but that doesn't mean they won't fail him after someone hits him very hard in the face. Ben Phillips was his character on Alan Reed's show. Honest, innocent Ben Phillips. It was a challenge to portray him so he seemed a pure soul, not just an idiot. Charlie loved that character, felt an intense protectiveness toward him, and yet by the second season, he felt increasingly constricted when he put him on, like a growing child still confined by last year's clothes.

"You don't have to hurt me," he says, with the wounded sweetness that would have been in Ben Phillips's voice had anyone ever hit him in the face with a gun. "I'll tell you what you want to know."

"You did not say your name until I hurt you," says Denise. As if she's scored a match point, she strides in triumph from the room. "I," she said, though it was Thomas who did the hurting.

Charlie has always wanted to play a spy, a multitude of parts contained within the one. A good performance for a spy is not money or praise or another juicy role; it's survival. This is something Charlie can understand. He said something like that to Josie once, about performance being survival for him. If that notion came to his mind now—which it doesn't, his mind being entirely with his throbbing, bleeding face, his fear—he'd have to shiver at the irony. How he's always loved the high-wire act of acting! The risk. The reach. The audition akin to stripping naked so that someone can throw knives at you. And then surviving, and surviving, and surviving, to the resounding echo of applause. But danger, emotional or physical, is only fun when it's voluntary.

With Denise gone, Adan comes around in front of Charlie and crouches down to examine his face. "Hurts?" he asks, with sympathy or a good imitation of it.

Charlie nods. He takes his hand from his face to look at the blood. Adan looks at it, too. Then he moves his gaze over Charlie's head and says something in their own language to Thomas, who answers in kind. Charlie was already braced against his awareness of Thomas standing behind him, but at the sound of the boy's voice, he has to work not to flinch. He feels a flicker of rage at the fact that this boy can make him flinch. Skirting Charlie's chains, Thomas exits the room. These two are clearly lowest on the totem pole. They must follow orders. And yet they're allowed to leave the room without permission. Adan points at the gash on Charlie's cheek and says, "We will clean it." He looks at Charlie expectantly, and Charlie, raised to be polite, says, "Thank you." Adan smiles as if enormously pleased.

Thomas returns with a bowl and a rag, and Adan stands to allow him access. It is Thomas who crouches in front of Charlie now. Charlie has become a child; faces appear in close-up before him, then rise into the air. Thomas doesn't make eye contact so Charlie stares right at him. He's a slight person, really. Charlie probably outweighs him by fifty pounds and could most certainly overpower him if not for the gun. Maybe he could do it anyway. Maybe if he revisited all his training, rehearsed the moves in his mind. Summoned that muscle memory. Waited until he got Thomas alone. And then wrestled the gun away and hit the boy with it as hard as he could. While Charlie imagines this scene, Thomas is cleaning the wound he inflicted with a weird, unsettling tenderness. He finishes by drying Charlie's face with delicate care before administering two Band-Aids in a cross. Is he penitent? Maybe it's all the same to him, hit Charlie or doctor him. Maybe he just does what he's told.

"Sorry, Ben," Adan says, after Thomas leaves with the bowl. "It is because of your country."

"What about my country?" Charlie asks.

Adan waves his hand toward the window. "What they do."

"I don't know what you mean. It wasn't me."

"But you are here. You are here." Adan points at the floor. "Lie down."

"Can't I stay like this? I can't go anywhere." Charlie tugs his ankle chain to prove its strength.

Adan hesitates. "Lie down."

"I'm claustrophobic," Charlie says. "I have asthma. I might have a panic attack."

Adan looks puzzled, shakes his head.

"It makes me sick to chain me up," Charlie says. "Sometimes I can't breathe. This room is too small. It might give me asthma." Adan looks no less confused so Charlie breathes shallow and rapid. "Asthma," he says. "Like that."

Now Adan looks worried, but this time when he shakes his head it means no. "Not the boss, Ben."

Charlie says, "But . . . ," and sees frustration flex in Adan's jaw. He doesn't like the position Charlie's putting him in. Charlie makes a quick calculation to retain his goodwill. "I understand, Adan," he says. "You're doing your best." He lies down and lets himself be chained, wrist, wrist, ankle.

Adan pats him on the leg when it's done. "Be good," he says. "Maybe they will change."

"I will be good," says sweet, compliant Ben Phillips, while Charlie Outlaw pictures the knife sunk to the bottom of the toilet tank like a clue in the aquarium in all kinds of movies. Charlie Outlaw wonders if he can really use it to escape. Charlie Outlaw wonders if there's any chance on earth he can get back to Josie before they catch him, before they find the knife, before they figure out he lied.

III.

The need to be loved and protected is at a peak when we feel abandoned and are particularly vulnerable to difficult circumstances. Most people will have experienced something comparable more than once before they have finished their teens, so it should be relatively simple to find a transference for this reality.

—UTA HAGEN, *A Challenge for the Actor*

One.

The PA smokes a cigarette while he waits by the parking lot for Josie Lamar. He's twenty-three and only recently took up smoking. It was part of fashioning his LA identity, shaking off the guy from Mayfield, Kentucky, who graduated from Murray State. And, yes, he sees the irony of avoiding tobacco in tobacco land only to succumb in the kingdom of self-conscious health, but his parents are religious, middle-class, small-town, hetero-normal conservatives, and his whole life until he came here was about pretending he was, too. Later, the habit will come to seem a grim enslavement, but that's many years and personal ups and downs in the future. For now, he's still young enough that smoking gives him that chin-lifted so-what feel of insouciant rebellion.

A car approaches, hesitates, and then turns into a spot a few spaces from where he stands. The PA—his name is Mason—sees the red hair of the woman at the wheel and knows this must be the actress he's awaiting. He didn't even know who Josie Lamar was until someone told him. He looked her up so he'd recognize her, and now he has seen photos of her at every age since she became famous and some from before (as one middle school and a couple of high school shots popped up in "Before They Were Famous" posts). He's formed opinions about her various hairstyles and her fashion choices and the effects of aging on her face. Despite never having been even remotely famous himself, he feels superior to her because she's not as famous as she once was. Don't judge him too harshly, though, for the smug pleasure he takes in his own indifference. We're so often helpless in the face of celebrity: helpless not to behave like malfunctioning robots in a famous person's presence; helpless not to click on headlines as the stars romance, rehab, and reproduce. Perhaps it's no wonder that we feel a small triumph about the ones we manage not to care about.

Mason doesn't put out his cigarette or approach the car just yet. It's his job to guide her to the stage, offer her coffee, take her into the conference room, be polite and welcoming, etc., and he'll do all that, but he doesn't have to hop to. He doesn't have to stand there looking eager while she checks her face in the mirror. He wants to be a writer, and in modeling himself on this show's writers, he's imbibed their disdain for the actors—"those black holes of need," the showrunner calls them. He's filed away some of her other comments, too. "An actor and a writer are two people with guns at each other's heads," she said once. And another time: "An actor's dream is a script with twenty-two characters, and you tell her she's playing every one."

Now the car door opens, and Josie Lamar gets out and spots him. "Are you here for me?" she asks, and though she says it with a smile and a pleasant tone, Mason feels a shiver of irritation. "I'm with *You & Me*," he says. "I'll take you to the stage."

"Okay, great," she says.

One thing does impress him about Josie Lamar, and that's the fact that she got to make out with Max Hammons. She got to make out with him so many times! "I'm totally going to ask her about it," he told his friend Alex—with whom he's been intensely, and apparently unnoticeably, flirting—and Alex said, with crushing dismissiveness, "No, you're not."

Yes, he is. He's determined to report back that he did, and his hilarious, titillating, victorious retelling will be the moment when the music changes and Alex Patroski sees him anew. He just has to find a segue.

Josie asks his name, and then repeats it aloud, and then repeats it a couple more times in her head. "Nice to meet you," she says. Once upon a time, she was unerring with names, but as she crossed the border into forty, she seemed to leave that skill behind. And, my God, the last couple weeks—or longer?—she can't remember anything for more than thirty seconds. She thinks, *I should write that down before I forget*, and by the time she's grabbed her phone and clicked on Reminders, she's already forgotten. It's important to remember names. She knows how people interpret it when she can't remember their names.

The PA—shit, she's already forgotten—sets off at a brisk pace, and she follows him, not quite keeping up, which is fine because it removes the obligation to chat. Martin? Something with an *M*. This job is a guest spot on a sitcom—a multicamera comedy, staged like a play and filmed in front of an audience the way they've done it since Lucille Ball. It's Josie's first time on a comedy, let alone a multicam. She never would've *auditioned* for a multicam, knowing she'd either have to dazzle them out of their preconceptions or wait for the I-knew-it looks to appear, smug or polite or politely smug, when she proved to be just okay or even awful. It's possible she'll be awful on this show. They might be worried about that. God knows she is. But they wanted her anyway: They wrote the role for her, or at least that's what the passion letter from the showrunner said.

She's nervous about the table read, which is the only thing on the schedule for today, and though it's not a particularly long walk from the parking lot to the stage, it feels like one as she picks up her pace, now, to catch up with this speedy PA. She's beginning to feel tweaked by his pointed lack of interest in her. She stops walking. "Hey," she calls, and then her brain helpfully supplies his name. "Mason."

It takes him a second to turn, his mind obviously completely elsewhere, and when he does, he seems flustered to find her standing ten feet behind him. She puts her hands on her hips in a pose that Mason—had he ever seen an episode of *Alter Ego*—would recognize as her badass stance from the last shot of the credits. That's right, Josie. That was you who struck that pose. "Are we late?"

He shakes his head as he walks back toward her. "Sorry," he mumbles, and now he looks so abashed and young that she feels a modicum of shame for calling him out on being a dick even though the kid was definitely being a dick. Maybe it's his first day and he's nervous. Maybe someone just chewed him out. Maybe his cat died.

"My mom always says I walk too fast," he says. Granted, he didn't exactly say it in a snarky way—more a weird combination of wistfulness and triumph—but that can't have been an accident, that clichéd attempt at a jab. She dislikes him again. She's nervous, and he's making it worse. His *mom*. She probably could be his mom, too. Which is depressing. She's nervous and depressed and angry at herself for letting a crack about her age sting. Exactly how you should feel before your first time ever on a comedy.

Now they're walking again, more slowly than necessary, and whether Mason's being considerate or pointed is difficult for Josie to determine. She gives up on trying, stares at her feet. Who cares. Who gives a shit. Life is fraught with pointless prickly encounters, hard little pings against your soft matter. A good actor is an instrument of exquisite sensitivity. It's a difficult way to go through the world, registering every slight. Exposing yourself over and over, and then having people come at you eager for more exposure. Wanting to excavate.

Mason stops abruptly, and Josie looks up to see they haven't yet reached the *You & Me* stage, the side of which features a giant billboard advertising the show. No, they're standing outside the building next to it, which features a giant billboard advertising Max. She looks at Mason in bewilderment, then follows his gaze to see they've stopped at Max's very parking spot, right by the stage and labeled with his name. Mason has brought her to Max's parking spot. Why? Did Max ask him to? She has a giddy image of Max muttering, "Hey, kid," from under a detective's hat, pressing a folded twenty into Mason's hand.

Of course she knew Max's show shot on this lot, but she's been trying not to wonder if she'll run into him. She didn't realize she'd be shooting right next door. He's here—his car is in the spot. Well, she assumed he'd be here. He's number one on the call sheet; he's probably here from seven in the morning until nine at night. He's probably here all the time. That doesn't mean she'll see him. Does she want to see him? Not exactly, and yet she knows she'll be disappointed if she doesn't.

Max's car is a Mercedes SUV. No surprise there. That first year on *Alter Ego*, Max spent an outrageous portion of his income on a Range Rover so he had to go on crashing for months with his girlfriend and her three roommates or with whichever friend had thrown that night's party. *Alter Ego* was Max's first job. Before that, he'd been manning the front desk at a gym.

"What are we doing?" Josie asks.

"Um," Mason says. Whatever attitude powered his various walking speeds seems to have abandoned him now. He looks stricken. Josie's sympathy for him returns. Sometimes it exasperates her how easily her sympathies are stirred.

"Did you want to show me Max Hammons's parking spot?" she asks patiently.

"I didn't know if you knew he shot here," Mason mumbles.

"Yeah, I knew," Josie says. She gives him another beat to recover, out of baffled curiosity as much as kindness. Then she points at their destination and says, "Don't we need to go *there*?"

He nods without looking at her and sets off again, fast as a race walker, before catching himself and slowing to a normal pace. Josie fights an urge to laugh and then another to glance back at Max's car. She sighs inwardly, remembering what it was like to have her own parking spot right by the *Alter Ego* stage, her name on a sign. At first it was a thrill, and then it was routine, and then it was gone. It's not the thrill she misses—it's the routine. She feels a pang of longing at the thought of taking something for granted.

Mason continues twitchy and embarrassed all the way to the conference room, where tables are set up in a U-shape, place cards and small bottles of water at each chair. In the presence of his utter weirdness, Josie triumphs over her nerves, and there's something that settles her, too, at the sight of her name on her place card. By the time Mason escorts her up to the showrunner, mumbling about what she'd like in her coffee and then scurrying away, she feels a queenly calm, which in turn makes her feel a tender gratitude toward him. When he hands her the coffee, she meets his eye and says, "Thank you, Mason."

"You're welcome," he says, surprised by her sincerity into matching it.

Poor Mason. He won't have any further alone time with Josie—when she arrives tomorrow and the rest of the week, she'll need no escort from the parking lot—and he knows it and knows Alex was right that he wouldn't have the balls to ask about Max. He retreats dejected to the back of the room, like a person who should just go on home to Kentucky.

The table read goes well for Josie, meaning that her lines get laughs. Predictably, appreciative surprise is a component of that laughter: No one really expects her to be funny. Even though she was

funny on *Alter Ego*, people mostly remember the fighting and the crying. The first few times people laugh, her primary emotion is relief—
she's not awful!—but as the table read goes on, she starts to feel the
happy buzz of pride. She's good!

When it's over, she pauses by the display of pastries and fruit and
cookies and half sandwiches, suddenly starving. As she considers, the
lead actress catches her there. Her name is Kirsten Campos. This
Josie knows because she recognized Kirsten, not because Kirsten in-
troduced herself. Kirsten doesn't need to introduce herself, of course,
and is aware of that, but the fact she didn't enact the ritual of humble
politeness says something about her, good or bad Josie isn't yet sure.

"I'm such a fan," says Kirsten Campos. "I was *obsessed* with *Alter
Ego*."

"Oh, thank you. That's so nice."

Behind them someone says, "We're going to begin notes," which
Josie recognizes as the cue to leave even without Kirsten taking her
arm in a light grip and guiding her toward the exit. She's able to reach
back and grab a sandwich and a piece of pineapple with what she
fears is unseemly haste. Outside, the sun is stark and bright. A golf
cart whizzes by, followed by a group of background performers
decked out for the nineteen seventies. "Oh, I did an episode of that,"
one says loudly. "They were *so* behind. I was there all night."

"What show are they for?" Josie asks around a bite of pineapple.
She's really unbelievably hungry.

Kirsten gives a cursory glance over her shoulder, shrugs. "I'm so
excited to have you here," she says.

Josie nods, swallowing. "I'm excited to be here. I don't get to do
much comedy."

"It was my idea. Is it really tacky of me to tell you that?"

"Not at all. Thank you. I'm having fun!" She holds up the sandwich. "Sorry about the face stuffing. I'm starving."

"No worries," Kirsten says, but then she watches with an odd expression as Josie takes a bite. "Did you know Max Hammons shoots here?"

"Yeah, yeah, I saw his car on the way in."

"I have to admit, I always used to wonder if you two actually had a thing."

"No, no, we didn't."

"Really? Not even a little bit of a thing?"

Josie has to make a decision. Another big bite of the sandwich gives her time to weigh the options. She doesn't want to talk about Max. Or perhaps she does, but only with someone in sympathy with her—Cecelia or her therapist. Definitely not with a stranger whose face is agleam with prurient interest, Max himself somewhere nearby, close enough that she can imagine him popping into the frame with sitcom timing just as she utters some horribly embarrassing truth. But, newly revealed as the source of this job, Kirsten may be someone to keep firmly on Josie's side.

This show is in its fourth highly rated season. When it began, all the power resided with the writers, not the then unknown actors, but now that it's become a hit and made those actors stars, the power is theirs. This is the way of things. At first the actors had to say whatever lines were in the script even when those lines struck them as stupid or wrong and sent them home in impotent fury or this-show-is-killing-me creative despair; now they simply assert, "My character wouldn't say that," and the writer has to slink off in impotent fury or despair and make the change. If Kirsten likes Josie and wants to have her back, and Josie keeps getting the laughs, giving no one a reason to say no, then perhaps this could become a recurring gig. And then someone might think to cast her as a regular on a comedy. While she'd love a job on a smart single-camera, these old-school multicams have *amazing* schedules. It's only 11:45 and the whole cast is already done for the day, which blows her mind.

Making these calculations in less time than it takes to describe them, Josie relaxes into a posture of conspiratorial friendliness. "Your marriage on this show," she says to Kirsten, "does it ever feel a little like a real marriage?"

Kirsten rolls her eyes. "Totally."

"So you know how it is."

"But I mean, like, he annoys me like a real husband. You and Max, you had that whole Romeo and Juliet thing going."

Josie lets a knowing smile overtake her face. "Exactly."

Kirsten laughs, delighted and satisfied. She thinks Josie's given her something though Josie has done her best not to. Nicely played, Josie. "You'll see Max while you're here, right?"

That it doesn't seem to be a question for Kirsten makes Josie feel like it shouldn't be one for her either. "I thought I might," she says.

"Well, if you want, he usually plays basketball with his buddies every day right about now. I can show you where. A lot of people who visit me on set want to go get a look at him."

"Really?"

"Oh, yeah. I'm talking about girls who used to have *posters* of him in their bedrooms. They totally want to see him. He's Malachi! I mean, *you* know. You're Bronwyn." She sighs with rapturous melancholy. "God, I wanted to be you."

"I wanted to be me, too," Josie says, and Kirsten laughs again.

"I bet he's a really good kisser," she says. "He is, right?"

Josie shrugs. "It's been a long time." Only when she sees Kirsten's slightly wounded expression does Josie realize that her resolute good humor was flagging, that her tone was peevish. *You're Bronwyn.* "But, yeah," she says, lowering her voice, "he's a really good kisser."

"I knew it! You were acting but you weren't totally acting."

"No, not totally."

"How can you manage a real relationship," Kirsten abruptly asks, "after living a fantasy like that?"

The acuity of the question startles Josie, who dismissed this woman as a surface dweller about thirty seconds into their conversation. She pegged her as one of those actresses who never questions the existential weirdness of what they do and how they live, who announces that she's cold or hungry with a childlike belief in the importance of her needs, who takes on faith her right to specially prepared food and very expensive handbags, who tweets things like *OMG you guys are the best, I love you!* to her four million followers because it's good for her career, yes, but also because she does love them. Someone who is hyperaware of her appearance and her public image but who is otherwise without self-consciousness. Someone who has as much in common with Josie, despite their shared profession, as a pretty purring cat. Because she's caught off guard, Josie answers the question honestly. "It was hard, actually. I think in my twenties I made some mistakes because of that."

"Like what?"

"Oh, divorcing my husband, probably. I mean, I definitely divorced him. It was probably a mistake. Hard to say."

"Was he in the business?"

"No, he worked for Verizon. Very stable guy. Very sweet."

"But kind of boring?"

Josie winces. "I don't know if boring's the word."

"How'd you end up with him?"

"We met really young, when I was still on the show. At a concert, actually, which I thought was good, like a normal way to meet someone. Everyone else I knew was dating other actors. And he didn't even know who I was."

"But then he turned out to be boring."

"Well . . ."

"How long before you got divorced? I know, I'm interviewing you. I could just look all this up."

"No, it's okay. I was thirty-two."

"That's my age! And since then?"

"Since then?"

"Weren't you with Charlie Outlaw?"

Josie tenses again. "I was," she says. Then, with an effort, she returns to a playful tone: "You're thirty-two? So you were, what, ten when you had that crush on Malachi?"

"Ten, eleven, twelve, thirteen . . ." Kirsten smiles mischievously. "Thirty-two."

"Oh, I get it. So when you say your *friends* want to see him . . ."

"It might have been my idea. Now you think I'm a stalker."

"No judgments here. Have you met him?"

"Just in passing."

"Should we go see him play?"

"Definitely," Kirsten says.

On their way to the court, they pass the suburban neighborhood set, and Josie remembers how the first time she saw an exterior set like this she couldn't stop marveling that the plants in the landscaped gardens were real. *Why would they use fake plants?* someone said to her. *We're outside.* But that wasn't the point; the point was the disorienting effect of reality inside the make-believe, the way it made the whole world seem hallucinatory. Oh God, she really doesn't want to see Max. She's fighting the urge to let her pace flag. Kirsten is talking but Josie doesn't quite know about what. She knows the rhythms of conversation and can make the right sounds in the right places, and though Kirsten ought to notice that she isn't really listening, maybe she's gotten what she wanted from Josie, the promise of an introduction to Max, and so doesn't mind. Josie wishes that the fact that she expected to feel an intense confusion about seeing Max and that she observes herself feeling it did anything at all to diminish the feeling's power.

Max left *Alter Ego* in its penultimate season, and though he came back for the series finale, though the breakup scene wasn't even the last thing they shot for his final full episode, she thinks of that scene as the last time she worked with him. It remains one of her most wrenching experiences as an actor. It remains one of the most wrenching experiences of her *life*, more vivid in her mind's eye than all but a few things that have happened to her when she was only Josie. There's the memory of filming the scene and then the memory of watching it later: One comes with a sorrowful ache, the other with pride because she was *good* in that scene, she was really damn good. As they ran lines in the makeup trailer the morning of the shoot, the reality of Max's impending departure from her life slowly crept up on her, and the thought of it began to seem as unbearable to her as it did to her character. By the time they were filming, the necessary tears were easy to access. The difficulty was in saving them for the end of the scene. The camera, despite being right in her face, wasn't there. The crew wasn't there. He was there. She looked at him—his slightly crooked nose, the muscle in his jaw that flexed at least once every sad scene, his trying-not-to-cry expression, so familiar to her now, his body, too, as familiar as if she really were his lover. She knew where he was ticklish! She could recognize him by his smell. She cried so hard at the thought of losing him that when they were done shooting and he hugged her, she couldn't let go. She buried her face in his chest, and he clung to her right back. The crew members went about their business, politely looking away from the intimacy of their grief.

And it wasn't because she was actually in love with him. Beyond that emotional residue, there never was anything between them off camera, no "what if" conversation, not even a drunken kiss. What can be hard to explain, even to yourself, is how the actual doesn't matter. The subconscious leads its own rebellious life.

As soon as the basketball game comes into view, Josie identifies Max just from the way he moves before she's close enough to make out any other details. He looks to her as limber and quick and high jumping as he did twenty years ago. He isn't, of course, but that's how she first sees him. What she doesn't know is that he spotted her, too, and started playing harder, much harder. His team was down by four, but he drives for a layup, steals a long inbound pass, and hits a three-pointer for the win. He hopes she saw that; actually, he knows she did. He could feel her eyes following the arc of the ball along with his.

This has been a shitty year for Max, kicking off with the end of his marriage—and, yes, he cheated on his wife, but she was no saint either—and ever since, he's been stuck in a malaise, a bored depression, a depressed boredom. He went skydiving a couple weeks ago just to wake himself up, and it worked, but only while he was falling. Seeing Josie is a welcome jolt—that bright flame of hair. His heart is a hard, rapid beating in his chest. It's a good feeling.

He doesn't wave. He doesn't break away from the ritual of good gaming and shoulder slapping. He grabs his towel and his water bottle, takes a swig, scrubs at his hair. He walks over to Josie wiping his mouth with the back of his wrist, enjoying the pretense of being casual. A couple feet away he stops and says, "Hey, Red." He doesn't ask what she's doing there, just takes her in. She looks good. She's obviously gotten older—lines around her mouth, angular where she used to be soft—but she still looks great, sexy as ever. He was so jazzed when he read the script where he first got to take off her clothes. There was a fight scene, the two of them back-to-back against a bunch of monsters, that turned into post-victory sex. She was awesome shooting those fights, never wanted the stunt double, did as much as they'd let her, and pushed for more. To watch her move like that and then obey a desire to grab her and kiss her had taken no acting ability at all. She has two very sensitive spots in the hollows of her collarbone. If he brushed her there with his lips or even his breath, she'd sigh, her body yielding into his in a way that was so incredibly sexy, or she'd giggle and ruin the take. He rolled the dice on that one a bunch of times.

"Hey," Josie says, with girlish softness, a breathy come-on of a greeting, which is an accident, and which she feels Kirsten noticing. "Max," she offers as crisp follow-up, "do you know Kirsten Campos?"

One of the other men on the court, a character actor with comically large eyes and a long skinny neck, watches Max with a combination of admiration and resentment. Max is, in his opinion, a little bit of a dick, but one of those guys who manages to be a dick and make you like him anyway. You feel even more annoyed because you like him anyway.

Ah, Max Hammons. Who are you really? Your fans would love to know. Or at least they think they would. What they really want is confirmation that you're who they think you are, you're who they want you to be. If people love your character and you yourself are less strong, less noble, less clever, less funny, less passionate, less brave—if you yourself are an actor with an ex-wife and a mortgage, not a badass spy—they'd just as soon you keep that to yourself. Max would never make a mistake like Charlie's interview. Max never fails to behave in public with the impervious dapper charm of a leading man. His appeal is on a different order than Charlie's. He doesn't melt your heart; he makes you eager for his approval. Picture him in black and white, leaning in to light a woman's cigarette and then sitting back in his chair to regard her with an air of private amusement. He's fine with letting you believe he's a man of action and mystery, master of the art of seduction and other heroic acts. He doesn't care if you know the real Max Hammons. Maybe the man with the mean right hook and the knowing smile—maybe that *is* the real him.

Standing at the edge of the court with the two actresses, his sweat-drenched T-shirt clinging gloriously to his torso, Max directs his attention to Kirsten. So much so that the big-eyed character actor, observing from a distance while he disconsolately bounces the basketball, imagines it's Kirsten that Max wants to fuck. But Max, with subtle cues (a quick glance, an ostensibly accidental arm bump), conveys to Josie that his interest is in her. He's charming Kirsten, sure, with his twinkly laconicism and admiring appraisal. But he and Josie have a secret. Such is the magic of Max that this is somehow better than if he were paying her overt attention. When abruptly he shifts eye contact to Josie, she feels it like a kiss. "You'll be here all week?"

She nods.

"I'll come see you," he says.

Two.

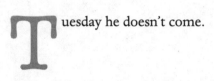uesday he doesn't come.

Three.

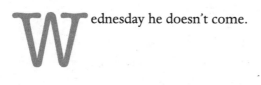W ednesday he doesn't come.

Four.

It's Thursday morning, time for camera blocking, and Josie feels ridiculous. What energy she's expended waiting for Max to show! On set today, she's walked through an unreal living room, an unreal bedroom, and an unreal restaurant wondering if she might resume an unreal relationship. All of it—rooms and relationship—carefully constructed for maximum verisimilitude. Now she sits with Kirsten at a real table in the fake restaurant awaiting an adjustment to the lights. Kirsten is on her phone, tweeting—"Sorry," she says to Josie, rolling her eyes. "They make me do this."

No one makes Josie tweet, for which she supposes she should be grateful.

"You know what I did last night?" Kirsten says, still looking at her phone. The phone chimes, Kirsten reads something and laughs, then her thumbs begin to fly again. Maybe she was talking to the phone. Though the leads normally leave the camera blocking to their stand-ins, Kirsten's here to keep Josie company, as she's told her more than once. This is nice, Josie supposes, as otherwise she'd feel like a big loser alone among the stand-ins, but also it makes her further indebted to Kirsten, and she wonders how she's going to have to pay.

Josie catches herself staring at Kirsten's screen and turns to watch two stand-ins talking at another table. What is it like for your primary value to be your resemblance to someone else? She's been around them often enough but still finds stand-ins and stunt doubles disconcertingly uncanny. Always especially unnerving was the sight of her stuntwoman dressed in an outfit identical to hers, wearing a wig that looked just like her hair.

Josie doesn't remember this, but when she was a child, her mother used to tape her daytime soap while she was at work and then curl up in bed with Josie and watch episode after episode on the weekend. When Josie was six, the show replaced an actor but kept the character, calling a new face by the old name, and when Josie saw everyone pretending like nothing had changed, she peppered her mother with angry, insistent questions, and no matter how she answered them, the whole thing seemed world-shakingly upsetting, perhaps the more so because her mother acted as if it were normal. Her mother had to stop watching the show in Josie's presence, saving her carefully labeled videotapes for nights after her daughter was in bed, because Josie started having nightmares in which a different woman claimed to be her mother and no one would believe that she wasn't. On *Alter Ego*, Josie did as many of her own stunts and fight scenes as she was allowed. People took this as a sign of her toughness, her teeth-gritted commitment to the role, and sure, those things were in the mix. But mostly she just didn't like being replaced.

Kirsten puts her phone down and looks expectantly at Josie. "It's really dorky," she says.

"What is?"

"I watched an episode of *Alter Ego* last night." Kirsten wears a look of mischievous entreaty, like a child who's done something naughty but is pretty sure she can sell it as cute.

"You did? Which one?"

"Episode seventeen."

"Which one is that?"

"The one where you and Max have your first big love scene. Oh my God, when he kisses you!" Kirsten closes her eyes and shakes her head, smiling an inward rapturous smile. "That's what I thought love would be like."

"Yeah," Josie says. "Me, too." She notices that PA, Mason, standing off to the side. It's his quality of sudden alertness that drew her eye. Ah, yes, he wants to hear what she'll say about Max. Everybody thinks they have the right. Because she did kiss him and she did touch him, but it wasn't *real* so any discussion of his lips and tongue and abdominal muscles is just a little light titillation, no harm, no foul. If Max were her actual ex-boyfriend, people wouldn't feel like his make-out strategies were in the public domain.

Unbelievable as it seems, she was a virgin when she shot that scene. If you asked her about her first time, that, not the real thing, is what her memory would summon. The real thing was nothing special. See why she doesn't want to talk about this? Does anyone want to hear how vulnerable and confused she felt? No, they just want her to say that it was sexy, that it was fun. People think they're asking for the truth, but what they want to hear is a different kind of fiction.

"Max was always very courteous about love scenes," Josie says. "Always checking with me, making sure I was okay."

"That's nice. Wish they were all like that."

Josie nods, and they sit a moment in silence. She wonders what Kirsten is recalling. Josie thinks of the time an actor slipped his hand beneath her top and pinched her nipple hard during a scene that was supposed to involve only kissing. But she doesn't ask. "I make jokes," Josie says.

"What?"

"Between takes, in love scenes. I make jokes."

Kirsten nods. "I do that sometimes. If it's awkward."

"Except with Max. I never did that with him. We were very earnest, the two of us." She glances at Mason, wondering if he's satisfied by this eavesdropping. What would he rather hear? How sometimes Max would brush his lips over the hollow above her collarbone and she'd shiver with the pleasure of it? Telling herself it was Bronwyn's pleasure, not her own.

"Those scenes were *intense*," Kirsten says. "Maybe you needed to stay in the moment."

"Right," Josie says. And suddenly she wants to say more: Isn't it still your tongue in his mouth, Kirsten? Isn't it still your breast in his hand? When we say it's purely professional, aren't we lying? When I kissed Charlie, the very first time I kissed Charlie, I was Beatrice and he was Benedick. Wasn't it still our first kiss?

Don't say that, Josie. Not to Kirsten. Not in hearing distance of Mason the PA, who might tweet it or snap a surreptitious photo and post it with a caption on Instagram. Josie Lamar's still in love with Charlie Outlaw. Josie Lamar says love scenes with Max Hammons were real. Has Josie Lamar gained weight? Oh, the possibilities for humiliation are multitudinous. That's why you don't say what you think, and when you think of something else, you don't say that either.

"Where is he, anyway?" Kirsten says.

"Who?"

"Max!" Kirsten's expression adds *Duh*.

Josie shrugs, as if to let the gesture govern the emotion, which, as she knows, it sometimes can. "I don't know."

"He said he'd come by, didn't he? I'm sure he said that."

"Yeah, he did, but you know. Maybe shooting's run long."

Kirsten toys with her phone. "I hear that show is a pretty tight ship," she says musingly. "They're usually out on time. In the beginning, I think it was a disaster—constantly going long. But now Max insists they stay on schedule. That's what I hear. Maybe it's even in his contract. So I think he could . . ." With a glance back at Josie,

Kirsten checks herself, signaling Josie that her face must reveal hurt or disappointment, which she does her best to erase. Kirsten says, "Well, I bet he'll come to the taping."

"Maybe," Josie says.

But she has a sinking certainty that he won't, that she needs to let go of the possibility that something will happen with Max. It's either that or feel like a fool. The trouble is that, letting go, she loses the bulwark between her and her grief over Charlie. For hours after she gets home, she tries and fails to occupy herself—with a book, with television, with housecleaning, with a call to her mother, who doesn't pick up. Then she stops resisting and calls Charlie. She's tired of silence, hers and his. She's tired of her own lack of agency. Be at the center of the wheel, not clinging to the rim—she read that somewhere, and it seems a good philosophy, because on the rim you're up and down, round and round, and someone else is doing the spinning. But what is at the center of her wheel? The work, always the work. Acting, she is at the center. What if she doesn't have the work? Because sometimes they give it to her and sometimes they don't and that she can't control. She doesn't know what she can control. Right now it feels like nothing. She waits for an audition. She waits for a job. She waits for Max to show. What does she have that's hers?

The call goes straight to voice mail, and she hears Charlie speak. At the sound of his voice, she feels the pressure of tears. She swallows. She's always liked his voice. It's a flexible voice, sometimes higher and gentler, sometimes deep, a bass rumble in your breastbone. He can sing, too. Not many people know that. But he has a lovely singing voice. "Hi, Charlie," she says into the silence. "It's me. I just wanted . . ." She's a good actress and she's managed to sound casual, natural, but abruptly her uncertainty catches up and she hesitates and ruins the whole performance. What is it she wants? She wants to be reminded what love is like.

Don't say that, Josie.

"I just wanted to see how you are," she says. "I hope you're okay."

He isn't okay, of course. Josie pictures him in a bar; or visiting Spain, where he's always wanted to go; or playing video games with his two best friends. But where he actually is, it has not yet occurred to Josie to imagine.

"Anyway, you can call me if you want." She swallows again. "I miss you." Then she hangs up, tosses the phone aside. She didn't mean to say *I miss you*. Or did she? What is the opposite of *despite yourself*? For yourself? With yourself? If she misses him, why shouldn't she tell him so? If she loves him, why shouldn't she take him back? If the answer is pride or self-respect, she's not feeling much in the way of either. She'll see how she feels when he calls back.

The rest of the evening, she carries the phone around the house, waiting. She checks Charlie's Twitter feed, his Instagram, but he's gone dark since demands for his head began to multiply in comments sections. She's surprised he's lasted this long. Charlie can't stand for people to be mad at him. She expected some sort of public mea culpa by now, something both earnest and humorously self-deprecating. That he's stayed quiet suggests an impressive amount of self-control. But it makes her uneasy, too. If he isn't doing what he would normally do, then two explanations are obvious: Either something from the outside has compelled his behavior, which surely would be nothing more sinister than a publicist's advice; or he's changed. She wanted him to change, but Charlie as he was is the Charlie who loved her. Her sleep is restless, and every time she wakes, she checks to see if she missed a call, an e-mail, a text. The Charlie she knows would not let *I miss you* pass in silence. The Charlie she knows would have responded by now. Has he changed so quickly? She is bereft, crying in her bed alone at 3:40 in the morning. Where has that Charlie gone?

Five.

Only once she's given up on Max does Max appear. He's learned from his characters the power of the last-minute rescue, or perhaps he always knew it. Josie doesn't even notice that he's there, standing in the video village, joking with a writer he knows. She's too preoccupied with what's happening on the stage. Tonight, Friday, is the taping in front of an audience, and after some initial nerves—Josie's not used to live performance, not having done a play since high school—she's having a great time. It's really fun being funny. What a thrill: the immediate response of laughter. What an affirming sound.

The sitcom is about a young couple and their friends. After a good long run of will-they-won't-they, the couple got married in last year's finale, so this season the writers are stepping up the workplace plot lines. All this Josie knows from binge watching on Hulu after she got the job. In her episode, she plays a colleague of the husband's, a mysterious woman, who, the husband becomes convinced, is leading a double life: She's a spy or maybe, he'd like to believe, even a superhero, which is, of course, why they cast Josie. He makes a bet with a friend about what she's up to and starts following her, and his wife, finding his explanations implausible, starts following *him*. They arrive at a scene in which the wife has followed her husband as he followed Josie to a restaurant. After some shenanigans, when the husband is distracted, the wife sits down at Josie's table just as she's about to order. They stare at each other, and then the wife blurts, "Are you sleeping with my husband?"

Josie says, "That depends. Who's your husband?"

The girl playing the waitress has one line. It's her job to hand the wife a menu and say, "I'll just give you a minute." This is her first TV job. She has one line. She wants to put into it everything she is, everything she's learned to this point, every sacrifice it took to get her here. Josie feels a pang of sympathy when the girl oversells the line and then a pang tinged with irritation the second and third times she does it. The fourth time it's all irritation. This many takes, Kirsten whispers, is very bad on a sitcom. "Losing the audience," she says, with a knowing head tilt in their direction. Josie can hear the laughter diminishing, hardening, every time they redo the scene. On the fourth take, the writers were called to the stage to laugh. Now the stand-up whose job it is to warm the audience up before the taping and keep them warm between takes does his mightiest to redirect their restlessness. He starts a contest, singing the opening bars of a TV theme song and asking people to name the show. *WKRP in Cincinnati*, Josie thinks. Charlie's from Cincinnati. Charlie, Charlie, Charlie—*shut up!* Someone shouts out the answer, and the younger audience members continue looking mystified. The writers confer near their cluster of director's chairs. The cause of the trouble stands a few feet from Josie, wearing that stricken I-fucked-up look, that shrinking posture, that dread and self-loathing and ruination and doom. Josie wishes she could pull the girl aside and tell her to calm the fuck down. But kindly. She wouldn't actually say *fuck*.

Though she can sympathize with the other actress, Josie's never been in her precise position, having gotten her first part when she was fifteen. She's been working steadily for twenty-six years. She's never had any other kind of job. The actress—her name is Emily Evans—is twenty-eight. At this very moment, if she wasn't pretending to be a waitress she'd be waiting tables for real, and lately there are a lot of days when she finds it tough to believe in herself. She knows she's got to calm down, to be easy in the moment, to say the line how her character would, which is brisk yet amusingly knowing. But *is* that how her character would say it? Who is this nameless waitress? Maybe she's a normal person stumbling through an awkward moment. Maybe she's a bit of an earnest dim bulb. Maybe she's compulsively sincere. Her agent told her that if they liked her they might cast her again because they have scenes in the restaurant all the time, and now she's fucked it up; she had one line and she fucked it up. She looks at Josie Lamar and is alarmed to find the other woman watching her, but then Josie gives her a tiny little smile, not a pitying smile but an encouraging one. *These things happen*, she imagines Josie saying. She imagines this very thing has happened to Josie and that Josie survived it. The important thing is to survive. She smiles back, trying to be brave.

On the next take, to everyone's relief, she nails the line. "Because of you," she says to Josie after the taping, nearly in tears. "Thank you so much."

"That was all you," Josie says. "It just took you a little while to get there."

"No, it was you. You smiled at me, and I thought about how brave you are and how inspiring you are and I thought, *I can do this.*"

Josie's usually uneasy when people assign her traits that properly belong to one of her characters—that properly belong to Bronwyn Kyle. But right now she's feeling too good for that concern. She just says thank you and for good measure hugs the girl. She's riding the buzz of a successful performance. Kirsten said they should have her back, and then the showrunner echoed the sentiment. For once, she's willing to let someone call her brave and inspiring without feeling compelled to demur.

When she finally does see Max standing at the craft services table pulling a stick of gum from a preopened pack, his presence seems inevitable. Of course he came. Of course. And as soon as he spots her and starts up that slow-building smile, the one that says he can read her mind, she forgives him for not showing up sooner. It seems silly, even, that she thought there was anything to forgive. He puts his arms around her. "Still got that killer timing, Red," he says.

It's nine thirty, and though she ate dinner at four, she's hungry again. Max remembers that she enjoys a nighttime breakfast. During *Alter Ego*, with all its night shoots, they ate a lot of two a.m. pancakes. He doesn't take her to Holtman's, the place they used to go back then, but to a newer one not far from the lot that he swears is better. They sit facing each other in a booth. Josie orders chocolate chip pancakes and a side of bacon. She's gained four pounds since that Oreo shake, but right now she doesn't care. The four pounds don't even cross her mind. She feels giddy, drunk, though she hasn't had a drop of alcohol. She dips her bacon in maple syrup, licks her sticky fingers, offers Max a bite of pancake from her fork, which he accepts, grinning as he chews.

"Not bad, right?" Max says.

"I don't know," she says. "I might still have to give the edge to Holtman's."

"You still go there?"

She shakes her head. "Not in years. But in my memory those pancakes are perfect."

"Not down with the night breakfast anymore? Or you just have a new place."

"No more late shoots. And you need a companion for night breakfast. Nobody should night breakfast alone."

"The Night Breakfast. Is that a children's book?"

"It should be."

"*In the Night Kitchen*. That's what I'm thinking of. 'I'm in the milk and the milk's in me.'" Josie looks at him, puzzled. Max can quote this book because he has young children to whom he's read it, but that isn't the conversation he wants to have, so he doesn't explain. Instead, he says, "I thought we should talk about what we're going to talk about on the reunion panel." He's good at avoidance. He's good at cutting the wheel hard.

"You want to rehearse?"

"I just want to be sure I don't tell any stories you don't want me to."

She smiles. "Or maybe the reverse."

"Are you implying I *ever* embarrassed myself?"

"Like when you tripped over a cable and went through a wall?"

"Oh God." He laughs. "Yeah, don't tell that one."

"What about when you thought you had to walk in slow motion for the slow-motion scene?"

"Ah, I see, we're not holding back, are we? Well, I can tell some stories, too."

"Better than mine? I don't think so."

"What about our first kiss?"

"No, sorry. You're still the most embarrassing."

"You bit me!"

"Nope. What else you got? Come on. Impress me."

He points at her. "That was good."

"What was good?"

"That was from the show, right?"

"No," she says. "Was it?"

"It was definitely from the show. *Come on. Impress me.* I thought you were doing it on purpose."

"Oh my God," she says. "I don't even know. That is really sad. Are you sure?"

"I don't know what episode, but you definitely said it," he says. "Even I know that, and I'm no expert on the show. You know how fans are like, 'In episode seventeen, what did Malachi mean when he said blah blah blah?—I never have a clue. I don't even know which one was episode seventeen. Just tell me who the monster was."

"Is that what you say to them?"

"I say, 'Which one was episode seventeen?'"

"*I* know which one that was."

"You do?"

She nods slowly, points her syrupy fork at him. "But you don't deserve to know."

"Why not?"

"Because not knowing is like forgetting our anniversary."

"What . . . ohhh. *That* one!" He grins with delight. "Wow, how could I forget?"

"I'd like to think you just forgot the number of the episode."

Max looks over her shoulder, squints as if gazing into the past. "I do seem to recall at least one or two of the major plot points."

This is real, isn't it? Both of them remembering. Their feigned desire that wasn't feigned. Because her character felt it, she did, too, and Max the same. Looking at him, she knows it without a doubt. She isn't thinking about what a good actor he is, she's thinking about what a good actor *she* is, so good she might fool herself. Is she feeling what she feels now or what she felt then, what she made herself feel in order to play those scenes? Does it matter? In all her life, has she ever been happier than when she was Bronwyn in his arms? She loved him so much, missed him so badly. What is the difference between dreaming and being awake? She is overwhelmed, at this moment, by the adrenaline rush of his presence, the push-pull of shyness and urgency. He's divorced; Charlie's gone. Why can't it be real?

"You know what story I really don't want you to tell?" she says.

"What?"

"I bet you know. Or maybe you don't remember. It might be best if you don't remember."

"Oh, *wait*." He sits back in the booth looking enormously pleased with himself. "*Of course* I remember. How could I forget one of the greatest moments of my life?"

It was during a love scene; she made a low sound of pleasure, and the director told her to keep it PG. She got teased about it after, though not by Max. Across from him, she feels herself blushing, like she must have done at the time. What are you going to do, Josie, now that you've strode confidently up to this precipice? Are you going to jump? "Listen—" she says. And that's when the girl walks up. It doesn't matter what the girl looks like. She could be anyone.

"I'm sorry," she says, though she's not sorry, not sorry at all. She's giddy. The adrenaline it took to get herself to their table jitters through her system, making her shift from foot to foot, her hands vibrating, her eyes practically pinwheels. How did Josie not notice her noticing them? She's usually so attuned to that kind of thing. Yet here she sat, focused only on Max, like someone who didn't need to pay attention. But back to the girl: "I'm sorry," she says. "You're Max Hammons."

He smiles his dazzling smile. "That's right," he says. "That's who I am."

"Holy shit," the girl whispers. Josie bets she doesn't even know she said it. "I love you."

Max touches her very lightly on her trembling arm. "Thank you," he says, his hand still there. "But listen." He lowers his voice. "I need to pay attention to her right now." He indicates Josie with his eyebrows, as though he and the girl were in subtle conspiracy, Josie oblivious. "I wouldn't want her mad at me." The dazzling smile again.

"Oh, of course," the girl stammers. She glances at Josie, her face registering recognition. "Oh, it's *you*," she says. "I didn't realize . . . You're dating Charlie Outlaw."

Josie gives her a quick, firm smile. "Hi."

The girl nods vigorously, backing away, her cheeks bright. "Thank you," she says. And then she retreats to wherever she came from. Max doesn't watch her go, his eyes on Josie as if no interruption had occurred. From somewhere behind Josie comes a burst of excited laughter.

Josie sighs. Dammit. "I'm not—" she says at the same time Max says, "Are you—" They both stop. "No," Josie says.

"You're not?"

"No, I'm not dating him. I was. I'm not now. You don't know about the interview?"

"What interview?"

"Never mind. The point is we broke up."

"I'm sorry," Max says. "If I should be."

Josie's eyes find his. She shakes her head. "You know why you shouldn't be?" she says, with sudden ferocity. "Because he couldn't do *that*." She jerks her head in the direction the girl went.

"Ah," Max says, drawing out the vowel as if he understands exactly what she means.

"He could never just be like, 'Now's not good.' He couldn't ever send them away."

He thought they deserved his time more than I did, Josie thinks, and the anger and grief she feels as she thinks this tells her not to say it aloud. Angry and sad are not what she wants to be. But Charlie didn't even call her back! If Josie knew how much Charlie loves her—if she *believed*—she'd know with equal certainty that something's gone wrong. But she doesn't believe, so all she has is an itchy little bad feeling, small enough to ignore. She wants to rewind to right before the girl walked up and reintroduced the idea of Charlie. And then erase her and rerecord.

For the rest of the conversation, she tries, but she can't get back there. Max keeps them in the past, to help her out maybe. Sensing what she needs from him to find the right emotion, the way the best actors do. But now talking about their fights and their love scenes feels searching, effortful, backward, evoking their characters' past to play a scene in their own lives. Her buzz ebbs away until she feels only how tired she is, how soul-sappingly tired. No one's going home with anyone tonight.

Still, there's a possibility between them, the convention just a week away. Out on the street, Max hugs her and steps back, his hand still cupping her shoulder. "I'll see you soon?"

She nods. He leans in to kiss her on the mouth. A light, close-mouthed kiss. A kiss like a question, like a reminder, like encourage-ment.

Josie and Max know to be discreet—public kissing, public any-thing—but it's hard to be careful all the time. Be careful, Josie! They kiss, and a camera flashes in the dark.

IV.

We may be asked, "How is it possible that an actor can experience the
life of a murderer if he has never
killed anyone?" Our reply is that it
is not necessary to commit murder
in order to experience the feeling of
a murderer. We are already being
trained in the technique of murder
when we are seized, very often for
trivial reasons, with the impulse to
drown our neighbor in a glass of
water.

— I. SUDAKOV, "The Creative Process"

One.

Charlie doesn't know how many days have passed. He has no means of keeping track. Perhaps three, perhaps three times three. All the days are the same. Already he has learned that he should ration his sleep for nighttime because the nights are far harder to endure. But of course, the human mind being a contrary animal, the days are when sleep comes without effort. It comes like a magic carpet through the window to take him away. He doesn't dream of being kidnapped, not yet. He dreams that his mother has a message for him, that she keeps saying he'll find it in the drawer, but he doesn't know what drawer she means. He dreams that it's his cue but he can't find the stage door. He dreams that Josie calls him but hangs up before he reaches the phone. He remembers little of this when he wakes, just a bright then fading image: his mother's face, Josie's face, replaced by the midnight walls.

When he's awake during the day and especially at night, he tries to summon memory like dreams. He closes his eyes because the small space inside his head is better than the small space outside it. He looks for a memory he wants to live in, and when he finds one, he plays it in his head until he wears it translucent, until he can see through it to the unimaginable present, and then he searches for another one, quick, quick, before he's overwhelmed by fear.

Right now, in what the slight lessening of darkness tells him is very early morning, he goes in his mind to Josie's house, Josie's bed, early in their relationship. The first time he stayed all weekend, not planning to, just going back there with her after dinner Friday night and finding himself still there Sunday morning. She opened a spare toothbrush for him. Both of them naked, her leg warm against his, and they're talking about learning to act, how he took so many classes and she never took one.

"You've never taken a single class?"

"Nope." She laughs. "You're so astonished. I guess that's a compliment?"

"Yes, it's a compliment. I trained for *years*, and you just do it."

"I've read a little, here and there, but I don't find a lot of it helpful."

"What have you read?"

"Let's see. Something by Uta Hagen—"

"Oh, one of my professors was obsessed with her."

"Really? I thought that whole transference thing was silly."

"No triggers for you, huh? No inner objects?"

"Remind me what those are?"

"They're . . . a visual cue for an emotion. Something that was there when you felt something. Like, if I wanted to remember how I feel right now to play a scene, I might picture that lamp."

"Why wouldn't you picture me?"

"It's supposed to be an object. Also, it's supposed to be linked with a specific memory, not your whole experience of a person."

"What *are* you feeling right now?"

He grins at her.

She grins back.

"Your thigh," he says.

"I knew you were going to say that. Try again."

"All right, I'm feeling . . . contented."

"Contented?" She pulls a wry face.

"No?"

"It lacks drama."

"I'm feeling passionate?"

"Now you've gone too far the other way."

"Happy." He wants to say *love*, but neither of them has said it yet, and so there is also *fear*.

"Happy's good. Did you ever try transference?"

"Oh sure. It was required. I was doing the speech from *Richard II* when Richard comes home to the news that he'll lose his kingdom."

"Of comfort no man speak," she says.

"Yup. So there's grief, of course."

"There's a shift from joy to terror."

"Yes! Exactly. So I remembered my girlfriend freshman year. One day I left class early because I was sick, came back to the dorm. I was actually thinking about calling her, maybe she'd bring me a milkshake, when I heard her voice through the walls. She was promising the guy next door that she'd break up with me soon."

"You're kidding."

"She was sleeping with the guy next door! She kept saying, 'It's just so awkward.' Then instead of confronting her, I waited, all pathetic, for her to break up with me, and after she did, she was dating the other guy so for months I kept running into her in the hall. That's what I used."

"What was the object?"

"The milkshake. I went out and got myself one."

"A milkshake for grief. I still think it's silly. Tell me something else you learned."

"Um, psychological gesture. That's Michael Chekhov. How you do something leads to why. Move with caution and you'll feel caution."

"Okay, that makes more sense to me."

"You were supposed to imagine your character's body, then put it on like clothes."

"Now that I don't do. I mean, I move like the character, of course, but the clothes part sounds weird."

"Well, you step into the character. You become them, and you don't need your own memories, your own emotions, because you have theirs. You're possessed, or you possess them. It's a little bit more mystical, this approach."

She leans over and kisses him with such tenderness that he's confused. "Why'd I deserve that?"

"I just suddenly felt sad at the thought of little freshman Charlie lying in his bed, listening to his girlfriend debate how to dump him."

He kisses her back, surprised by the strength of his grateful response.

"And then it's also sad," she says, flopping onto her back, "to think of you making yourself feel that again for acting class. That seems torturous."

"Yes," he says. "But it also lets you believe the bad shit that happens to you is useful."

"Sure," she says doubtfully.

"You know what I miss about that time? How sincere we were. How seriously we took it all. Standing in a circle, throwing balls at each other to practice radiating."

"Radiating?"

"Yeah, like sending each other energy. You were supposed to be able to catch the ball without looking. Do you want me to teach you other stuff I know? Stage combat?"

"Please. You don't think I've got that down?"

"Hand to hand, sure, but what about swords?"

"Are you kidding? I can swordfight."

"Oh that's right, I've seen that. Okay, I know." He jumps up. "Come on, get out of bed."

"I already know how to act. I'm naked."

"Come on, trust me."

She sighs, but she gets up.

"Okay, now walk behind me and try to walk like I do."

She says nothing, so he glances over his shoulder at her. "Watch me and do what I do."

She shakes her head at him in playful reproof. "I got it. They're not hard instructions. Go."

They walk around the house for several minutes until Charlie can tell—how? who knows?—that energy has passed between them, that they're moving in unison. He stops and she bumps against him. He turns and puts his arms around her.

"I liked that," she says. "First I was studying you, and then I was imitating you, and then I was just being you. I became you."

"Right? And how do you feel?"

She gives him a smile with wonder in it. "I love you," she says.

Then what did you feel, Charlie?

Joy.

Two.

He must have drifted at last from memory into sleep because he's startled and confused when the door opens. He's not where his mind told him he was. Thomas and Adan unchain one ankle and two wrists so he can eat his meager breakfast as usual, and after Thomas takes the empty plate away, Adan announces that he's earned the right to remain at this less confining level of confinement. "You're happy, Ben" is how he says it.

Charlie supposes he's been good. "Thank you," he says, to keep being so. He's relieved every time one of them calls him Ben. His own experience of this island suggests his captors may experience spotty internet connections. Funny to think that he found the crappy signal frustrating a short time ago, however long ago that was. Funny that what he feels right now is gratitude. He is grateful that the internet doesn't work properly. He is grateful that only one of his legs is chained. "Thank you," he says again.

Adan seems pleased. He lingers, basking a moment in his pleasure. "You walk now," he says. He makes a circle in the air with his pointed finger to indicate the perimeter of the room. "Much better."

"Much better," Charlie agrees.

"I asked," Adan says. "For you."

"Thank you."

"No problem now," Adan says. "No . . ." He puts his hand on his chest and breathes fast and hard.

"Asthma," Charlie says.

Adan smiles the smile of a successful problem solver. "No asthma!"

Charlie nods. He's not sure he can produce a fourth thank-you. He fears that if he tries he might shout or weep. Yes, it is better to wear one chain than four, but it is not nearly as good as not wearing any. There's something terrifying about Adan's cheerful conviction that he has given Charlie a wonderful thing. He's hanging about like a starstruck fan, like whatever he wants from Charlie is something he deserves to have. Charlie is well practiced in the art of polite self-extrication, but how does he perform that here? How, for God's sake, does he make this guy go away? "You're my friend," he manages, trying to sound like Ben Phillips, who might actually believe that.

Adan's smile freezes, then dissolves. "Yes," he says, with a solemn unease. Charlie imagines the boy feels guilty, though whether that guilt is about doing too much for Charlie or too little, he couldn't say. Either way, Adan wants to leave now, which is the result Charlie wanted and the one he gets.

He waits until Adan is gone to move. When they take Charlie to the bathroom, one of them hauls him to his feet. For a moment it feels as if he's forgotten how to stand on his own. He gets on one knee, like a man proposing, makes it the rest of the way from there. He's standing. Now what?

This is a stage. This is an acting exercise. Who, given his circumstances, does he need to be? To answer, he first has to consider his aims: (1) survival; (2) escape. The trouble is that the person he needs to be to survive is perhaps not the person he needs to be to escape.

For survival, Ben Phillips was an apt choice. On the show, he was a man confined to a small space who was at the mercy of a volatile and powerful person. Ben survived via his own tenderheartedness, so when Alan Reed's character wounded him, he responded to the hurt that made that person want to wound. Ben survives in the grip of power that attacks only when it sees a threat. But there are people who don't need their cruelty to contain an element of effort, people who see weakness and want to stamp it out. Ben Phillips would never survive them.

Alan Reed was himself volatile and powerful. He'd make up lines, and if the writer dared correct him, he'd say, "Well, now it's written by Alan Reed." When the second lead wanted to direct, and after he proved the earnestness of this desire by shadowing the directors of multiple episodes, the showrunners gave him the opportunity. To Alan Reed, this was usurpation. On the first day of shooting he showed up three hours late.

But Alan loved Charlie. Charlie survived like Ben survived, by being no threat to him. To this day, Alan addresses him as *kid*, and Josie is convinced that Alan doesn't actually know his name. But he survived when survival was paramount.

Who should he be if what's paramount is escape?

He paces the perimeter of the room. Then again more slowly. This time he checks all the cinder blocks, looking for a wobble, a crack. He imagines working the knife between them until he could loosen one enough to push it out. But he'd have to do it all at once, loosen the block, because as soon as someone came in, his efforts would be obvious, white powdery lines in the dark blue paint. He hates this paint. He hates this color. He imagines going through the world destroying everything this color: a dress, a house, the sky at night. And what if he did get one block loose? It's not like he could fit through it. He could shout. He could put his face in the hole and shout, but all he can see behind the house is a small scrubby yard and a fence and then a few yards past the fence some laundry hanging on a line.

He leans against the wall, puts his hands on his face. Daniel Craig wore a midnight blue tux in *Skyfall*. He remembers thinking it looked cool, wondering if he should get one for an event he was attending. What was that event? The Young Hollywood Awards, maybe. In the end, he didn't wear a midnight blue tux, and if he had, he'd go back in time right now and rip it off himself and burn it.

James Bond. That's who he should be. "Ha," he says out loud into his hands. For several minutes, he indulges again in the fantasy that his empty-hand fight training could get him out of here. He could take them all at once, them and all their guns. How satisfying that is to imagine, the deft unstoppable punches he'd throw. But when his imagination gives ground to reality, he wants, once again and forever, to weep.

All right. He has some agency now. He's on his feet. So what can he do? He has the knife but no idea what to do with it. What does he have that he knows how to use? What is he good at? He's good at people. He needs to figure out these people. Who does he need on his side for survival? Is there anyone who might be on his side for escape? Adan is the obvious possibility, but Charlie's instinct is that he won't go against Denise. Thomas is even more clearly Denise's lackey. Thomas takes pleasure in his domination over Charlie. Thomas will not hesitate to inflict pain, though Charlie suspects he'll only do so under orders. Thomas is a man who believes in hierarchy and is glad not to be at its bottom. And Darius—well, Charlie isn't sure about Darius. Darius has an air of dignified grievance, and Charlie isn't sure if he, Charlie, is the cause of the grievance or if it's something else. From what Charlie can gather, Darius is in charge, which means that he might provide necessary protection from Denise, but he has no motive for wanting Charlie to escape. Charlie's instinct tells him that, like Adan, Darius feels sorry for him. With Denise, he must neither provoke nor show weakness. With Denise, he must try not to exist.

What about the other woman, the woman who wears the housekeeper's uniform? He's wondered about her, glimpsing her from time to time through a doorway when they escort him from room to bathroom and back. Always in that uniform, with the little tree embroidered on the shirt pocket. The rest of them wear shorts and assorted T-shirts—like crew members, he thinks grimly—and so she doesn't seem to be one of them. Someone's girlfriend, he's thought, someone's sister, someone's wife. He's imagined that she might be trapped in this as he is. If this were a movie, she would be the one to sneak into his room in the middle of the night and let him go.

This woman is the one to try, should he ever get the chance. And if he does get the chance, how could he win her sympathy? Who might she want him to be?

He doesn't know. He will be anyone for her. But he doesn't know who to be.

Maybe he could use the knife to get the chain off his foot. He tugs at it experimentally, but it gives no indication of weakness. He crouches to examine first the manacle around his ankle then the padlock that holds the chain to the stake in the ground. Could he pick a lock with the knife? Only if it's as easy as it looks, which few things are. He's never even done that on TV. Could he saw through a link of the chain? He examines one, turning it over, feeling every bump and divot with his fingers, as though this will tell him something. What does he know of metal or its fragilities? And if he did get loose? The door is locked. There are armed people on the other side.

He could wait in a corner with the chain, and when the door opened, he could wrap it around the person's neck. He thinks *the person* because he's reluctant to think *Adan*. He could just knock this person out maybe. And then get his gun.

That will never work, says a voice in his head. *This is not a movie. You are not Princess Leia in the gold bikini. Are you crazy? You can't do it. There's nothing you can do.*

He sits on the floor now with his legs sprawled out in front of him, slumped forward, his hands loosely gripping the chain. He is an empty body waiting to be possessed. Move with despair and that is what you will feel. He might as well still be splayed on the ground and chained. He pictures himself that way, his long limbs stretched, not with freedom or joy or the making of snow angels but by chains; and the hands on the other side of those chains are sometimes fists, sometimes limp, rolling one way and then another, the head tilted back to the floor or sometimes rolled with the chin toward the shoulder; both hands and head moving, when they do, purely for the relief of a change in position no matter how small. He imagines he sees this body from above. Now he must put it on like clothes.

No. Imagine another body.

This one tall, too, though not as tall. Slender, with a long neck and shoulders slightly rounded in, head cocked very slightly away from the person who's talking. It's Josie he's describing. *But me she looks right at*, he thinks. He's never articulated this before, but it's true. Josie goes through the world at a defensive angle—not when she's acting, of course, but the rest of the time. With him, she's different. She turns her whole self toward him. She radiates.

And how would his body look running toward her? How would he look if he could catch her in his arms?

"I love you," Josie says. He can see himself holding her. He can feel the weight of her. He can feel her heat.

We become what we imagine, said Aristotle. Please let that be true. A kind of madness, he said.

He's going to get the knife. He's going to get it now before he changes his mind. He gets to his feet. He bangs on the door. "Adan!"

Three.

Awake in the middle of the night, Charlie feels the weight of the knife in his pocket. While there was still light enough to see, he worked the knife against the chain, producing tiny flakes of silver, so small it seems to him a million of them will have to fall before he's free. His heart caromed while he sawed, afraid that every sound he heard, and some he imagined, was someone coming to catch him. Every few minutes he scattered the flakes into the corners, burying them under gathered dust and dirt. Even now, in the quiet dark, he's afraid of the door bursting open, of Denise frisking him, of her pleasure when she finds the knife. He needs a memory. He must resist using up the first time Josie told him she loved him. He needs to ration that one, keep it for emergencies. He needs something else, another time he was happy.

I love you, he thinks, and remembers the first time he heard it from a stranger. It was toward the end of the first season of *Chef Alan*. He still lived in West Hollywood. He was in a convenience store as only the West Coast could conceive it—one that sold organic vegan sandwiches and coffee made with four-stage-reverse-osmosis-filtered water. The place sells a breakfast sandwich he still craves sometimes—probably not healthy at all, but vegan, so he can tell himself it is. On that occasion, he was waiting for his order when he sensed someone's gaze. He turned to look—he hadn't yet learned to resist that urge, still has trouble resisting it, such a primal impulse, to look at the person who's looking at you—and there was a woman gaping at him. She looked young, late teens or very early twenties. She wore glasses. On her face was such open awestruck admiration that he thought she had to be from out of town. "I love you," she blurted.

"Oh." He felt a rush of embarrassed pleasure and reddened in response. "Thank you."

It's a funny thing, how people will say I love you to a stranger more readily than to a person they actually know. What kind of love is it that can be offered up so freely? Who is it they love? Their love exists at the intersection of real and not real, like the performance that made them feel it.

"I really do love you," she said. Her name was Katelyn and she was from Sacramento, visiting LA for the weekend with her parents. She had the very particular kind of fangirl crush on Charlie that comes from being the only one of her acquaintance insisting on his awesomeness. Most of her friends said Who? at first and now rolled their eyes when she mentioned his name. Most of them didn't even watch his show. It was only on the internet that she could find like-minded worshippers bonding over their sense that, between his relative obscurity and their special ability to recognize his greatness, he belonged to them. And what a miracle that here he was in front of her! In this place she'd ducked into to grab a quick bite while her father refilled the medication he'd forgotten at the pharmacy next door! It was truly a fucking miracle! "I really love you," she said again. It was vital to her that he believe it.

Charlie ducked his head, abashed, and murmured another thank-you. In the twenty or thirty seconds of silence that followed, during which she went on adoring him with her eyes, he realized that they might stand here together in this small enclosed space for the next ten minutes, or even longer as those artisanal vegan breakfast sandwiches take a long time to produce. Now what? Where do you go next in an interaction that starts with a declaration of love? She was his fan. He knew what it was to be a fan. Now here was his glimpse of what it is to have fans. It is to be apart. To be told you're somewhat more than human and simultaneously desire and dread to disprove it. How can you love me when you don't even know me? And yet I can see in your face that you do.

She had a cell phone in her hand, he noticed, and yet she wasn't asking to take a picture with him. She was too dumbstruck, maybe. Later, she might kick herself for not asking. If he suggested it, was that kindness or arrogance? Famous people complained about the picture taking—Alan Reed certainly complained, especially when it meant flashbulbs in a restaurant as he forked his dessert to his mouth—but Charlie had not yet been given an opportunity to complain. Surely Charlie didn't have to preemptively disdain someone's desire to capture his image, to fail to suggest it out of worry that it might seem presumptuous.

The next moment would become the best part of Katelyn's story, the highlight of both her in-person anecdotes and her social media posts. "And then he asked, he actually *asked*, if I wanted to take a picture with him! Isn't that so nice? He said if he'd met an actor he liked when he was my age he would've wanted a picture."

The guy behind the cash register wielded the phone. You can still find the resulting photograph online if you're willing to click through Google images for a while. Charlie with his arm around Katelyn's shoulders, both of them grinning with a giddy, slightly unhinged happiness, behind them an array of organic power bars. Charlie found the photo himself once, in a fond nostalgic condition, wondering what had become of the girl he thought of as his first real fan.

When he saw his expression in the photo, he cringed: his open pleasure in her adoration, his needy delight. He cringed at his own vulnerability and then felt a yearning protectiveness toward his younger self. So happy. So certain in that moment that what he had was enough.

He would trade every *I love you* he's ever gotten from a stranger to hear it from Josie just one more time.

Four.

A day, or two, or three later, Charlie is absorbed in his steady, methodical sawing, the barely perceptible dent he's made in one link of the chain, when he's startled by the sound of the lock. He barely has time to conceal the knife and brush the shavings from his clothes before the door opens. Cleary he's grown too accustomed to the risk he's taking, stopped listening so hard. He's sitting on the floor by the window, and trying to hide his panic, his careening heartbeat, he pretends to be staring out through the crack in the boards. He doesn't turn as the door opens. He knows what he'll see. Sometimes it's worse to see the open door, the passageway behind it. But he doesn't hear Adan's usual, "Hello, Ben!" so after a moment, he turns, and the other woman is hesitating in the doorway, still, as always, in her uniform. His dullness vanishes. He feels a prickly alertness, a numbed limb awakening. "Where's Adan?"

She shakes her head. Maybe she doesn't speak English. She's holding a tray. It takes him a moment to understand that on the tray is his lunch because Adan just brings a plate or a bowl and hands it to him, then pulls a fork or a spoon from his pocket and hands him that, too. She takes a step toward him. He puts his hand on the windowsill and hauls himself to his feet, and she stops a few feet away. She has the watchful frozen quality of a frightened animal. Is she afraid of him? The idea is startling. He supposes it makes sense. She's a small woman, short and slight. He's a tall, broad-shouldered man, chained like something dangerous. He holds both arms out toward her, moving slowly, a gesture meant to show he won't hurt her, an offer to take the tray. She steps just close enough for him to grasp it. On the tray, a deep white bowl filled with rice and topped with a large piece of fish, five lychees stacked in a small green saucer, a napkin folded in a neat triangle to display a fork, a tall plastic tumbler of water with a single floating ice cube. And—most remarkable of all—a piece of chocolate-covered chocolate cake sealed in a bright red wrapper covered with bright yellow words. "Thank you," he says, and is struck by the sincerity in his own voice.

Her eyes flick to his. She nods. She has greenish eyes, slightly asymmetrical; a dramatic nose; a small mouth that grows smaller when she's thinking—or perhaps *withdrawing* is the better word. Slight as she is, she seems somehow to shrink still further when you look at her too long. Her hair is a contradiction: piled high on the back of her head, an explosion of dark brown curls.

"What's your name?" he asks.

"Mystery," she says.

"What am I supposed to call you then?"

She frowns. "Mystery."

"You want me to call you Mystery."

"Yes," she says. "Because it is my name."

"It's your actual name? The name your parents gave you?"

"Why not?"

"Because . . ." he says, but then he just shrugs, too demoralized for explanations. He's named Outlaw, after all, so why not Mystery? The name seems more appropriate for her than Outlaw does for him. It would be handy if people's names actually told you who they were, as in a Dickens novel. He'd like that confirmation that his impressions of these people, on whom he's helplessly dependent for survival, are correct. Denise he'd call Murderous.

The woman's body language indicates she's about to leave. "Wait," he says, and she pauses. He wants time to study her. Look at that lunch she brought. No one else would feed him like that. He feels a faint ember of hope at the thought that maybe he's right about her—she's the reluctant one, the one who might be won over. "It's a pretty name." He lifts the tray a little. "Thank you so much for this."

She nods again. "Do you need anything else?"

His mouth drops open. "I . . ." He needs so many things that he's lost track of what they are. "Something to read? Could you bring me something to read?"

She considers. "In English?"

"Yes."

"Magazines," she says decisively.

"You could bring me magazines?"

"Yes."

"That would be wonderful. You have no idea . . . I've been losing my mind without anything to do."

She frowns. Should he not have said that? But, no, it's a frown of sympathy. He thinks. She backs out of the room, locks the door behind her.

In the kitchen, Darius hears the sound of the door shutting. He's been in a fog of confusion and misery all day. He watched without comment as Mystery arranged the tray with care, assuming she was acting out of the habit of service. He knows Denise would have reacted with scorn, snatched the bowl from the tray, taken the cake for herself, or tossed it to one of the boys as if she were giving a treat to a dog.

Mystery works as a housekeeper at the hotel resort. This is where he met her when he came to do some landscaping, and they struck up an odd, silence-filled friendship. He is a landscaper, not a gardener, no matter what other people think. More than keeping plants alive and well trimmed, he's known for his ability to arrange a flower bed for maximum aesthetic pleasure. This is why the resort hired him, asked him to redo the beds out front, though they paid him only gardener's wages. Darius's original idea was to make trouble at the hotel—small persistent trouble that would drive away vacationers, a dead rat on the front walk, a leaky pipe, a dog turd floating in the pool. Darius recruited Mystery first out of a notion that he wanted an inside woman. But then his thoughts turned from sabotage to kidnapping, and he's not yet been quite sure what to do with her. Mystery doesn't seem especially devoted to either the cause or the actions he's taken in support of it. Nor does she seem to object to cause or actions. Her reasons for participating are obscure to him; perhaps she has nothing better to do.

They are alone in the house today because Darius sent Denise and the boys to deliver a letter to the police describing the hostages—the ones at the other house and Ben Phillips, his prize American—and making his demands. He has no idea if this is the right thing to do. All he knows is that he has to do something. When he planned this, the hostages were theoretical. But now that they are real, he's reminded at every moment how manifold are the difficulties of caring for them. The food that must be cooked, the rashes and sniffles that must be tended, the trouble and expense. And sometimes he feels a painful rush of sympathy for them, a sympathy that makes him angry because it makes him weak, and every time he feels weak, he looks up to find Denise watching. He doesn't know if he wants to set them all free—kidnapped and kidnappers—or murder them all. He doesn't know how much longer he can bear to be around Denise.

Back in his room, Charlie eats every bite of his lunch. His pleasure is so overwhelming that he forgets to make sure he's hidden the silver flakes of the chain. He's focused instead on the cake. He could save the cake for later, giving himself something to look forward to, but where would he put it? Inside his pocket it would get squashed. The only place in this room to keep something is on the shelf, and if he puts it there, he risks someone spotting the bright red wrapper. Adan might let him keep it, but Thomas and Denise certainly would not. Normally he avoids processed foods. In his old life, he wouldn't have eaten the cake, not when he still had the luxury of choosing what was healthy, choosing what was *worth the calories*. The cake has the slightly chemical taste of packaged desserts, but he doesn't care. He's willing to believe it's delicious. It's sweet and it leaves chocolaty bits smushed against his teeth that he works off with his tongue. It reminds him of pleasure. When he's done, he arranges the dirty dishes and the trash as neatly as he can on the tray, the lychee skins inside the bowl, the napkin on top in a neat little ball. The wrapper, licked clean, he slips into his pocket to save, for the bright red color and the memory of kindness.

Then he puts the tray in the center of the room and positions himself back by the window, cross-legged on the floor. He wants her to have to come inside the room for the tray because he hopes to get her to talk to him some more. He wants to be sure he doesn't look threatening. If pressed, he'd have to admit he doesn't have a plan exactly, but nevertheless he has the *feeling* of having a plan—he has an intention. He wants her to be on his side. What he will do if he succeeds in winning her over, he doesn't know. Her sympathy will be like the knife: something he can use if he can figure out how. Having things he doesn't know what to do with is better than having nothing.

When she comes back, he's ready. "You are so kind" is the first thing he says. "That's the best meal I've had since I came here." She ducks her head, blushes a little, an invigorating, exhilarating sight. He presses on. "You don't know how much I'll appreciate those magazines."

"I can get many magazines," she says.

"Really? Which ones?"

"*People, Us Weekly, Hello!*"

Just last month Charlie was in *Us Weekly*, filling his car with gas, one hand lifted in a wave. He saw the photographer and waved. This was the kind of thing that drove Josie crazy. "But if I acknowledge they're there, I have more control," he insisted. *No,* she said. *No, you don't.* "US Weekly," he repeats. "Do you read it?"

She shrugs. "I read English only some."

"You don't look at the photos?"

She shrugs again. "I clean them up."

"You clean them up? You work at a hotel? That's why you wear the uniform?"

"Housekeeper," she says. "At the big hotel."

He nods. "Is it a good job?"

She cocks her head. "Yes. But they do not think so." She jerks her head back toward the hall. "They hate the hotel."

"Oh. Are they activists?"

"I don't know that word."

"Are they . . . political? No one has told me why I'm here." He lets sorrow creep into his voice. "It's hard not having any idea why things are happening to you."

"That is how we all live," she says.

Is that reproof in her voice? He redirects. "Is one of them your boyfriend?"

She shakes her head.

"Your brother? Your cousin?"

No and no.

"Do you believe in . . . what they believe in?"

"Sometimes yes," she says. "Sometimes no."

"Why do you work with them then?"

She purses her lips. "I choose to."

Disheartened, Charlie sags back against the wall and asks nothing else. She waits a beat, then steps forward to get the tray. At that moment, Charlie's eye falls on the dusting of silver shavings on the floor, and he looks up quickly to see that she sees them, too. He watches her eyes flick up to his own face, her expression wary. He holds himself very still. He thinks, *I wonder where those came from*, and he believes that he doesn't know and hopes that this lack of knowledge is on his face. *Oh shit oh shit oh shit.* She proceeds to the door without a word but pauses there, looking back.

"I will bring you magazines," she says.

When the lock clicks, Charlie moves to the door as quietly as he can and presses his ear to it. He hears no raised voices, no rapid feet. What does this mean? That she didn't notice after all? That she didn't draw any conclusions? Or that she really is some kind of double agent and she wants him to escape? He waits for something terrible to happen. A desperate longing grows inside him for a clock. Has he waited five minutes or ten? Ten or fifteen? Has he waited all night? Have six months gone by? Too demoralized even to stand, he crawls over to the shavings and scatters them into the corners of the room to mingle with dust and mouse droppings. He'll have to put the knife back in the toilet tank. He can't risk having it now. But he doesn't want to draw attention to himself by asking for the bathroom just yet, so he'll wait; he'll wait as long as he can bear it, and then he'll knock on the door and request his escort, and in the bathroom he'll drop the knife back into the tank and watch it sink to the bottom.

Five.

For the next two days, nothing happens, a nothingness that weighs on Charlie even as it offers him relief. For Darius, the nothingness is unbearable. He dispatched a letter, made demands. Where is his response? His negotiator? There is not a single person in that house who doesn't feel like a caged animal. This is a crucial fact novice kidnappers fail to consider, that they themselves will be held captive until the demands are met, the ransom paid.

During that time, Charlie sees Mystery only once, when she comes to retrieve his bowl and gives him, as promised, a magazine. It's a copy of *People* with a Real Housewife on the cover. "Thank you," he says. "Thank you, thank you, oh my God." He is fervent in part because he takes this as a sign that she didn't notice the shavings, or that if she did she didn't know their meaning, or that if she did know their meaning she kept it to herself. He clutches the magazine to his chest and closes his eyes as she leaves the room, feeling again his own terrifying vulnerability. He could weep and weep over this magazine. He could kiss the Real Housewife on the mouth. He reads the magazine all the way through from the first word to the last, lingering even over the ads. Finished, he starts again.

While Charlie, poor Charlie, is in raptures, the happiest he's been since the moment the cars pulled into the clearing and the people with the guns got out, Adan is in the bathroom trying without success to flush the toilet. He makes a sound of resigned irritation and lifts the heavy clanking lid from the tank. Adan is an upbeat person, an optimist, but even he is growing cranky, mostly in response to everyone else's mood. He himself does not mind the situation. He likes taking care of Ben. He likes being part of a group. He likes that he is necessary. He sets the lid down and peers inside the tank, and right away he notices a foreign object in the tank, wavery through the water. He frowns, plunges his hand into the cold water, closes it around the knife. He holds it dripping above the tank and stares and stares. He wants to believe one of the others put it here, or that it's been here all along, but he knows that's not the case because he's had to fix the problem in the toilet before, and the knife definitely was not there, and no one else in the house had a reason to hide it. Unbelievable as it seems to him, this knife is Ben's.

Why does the world do this to us, good in the left hand, bad in the right? Why couldn't Charlie have had a little more time? He doesn't know the conversation that's taking place in the kitchen, his fate being decided, as Adan hands Darius the knife. Adan's face shows dismay and betrayal to a degree that surprises Darius, who thinks that if he were held captive and he had a knife, he, too, would try to conceal it. "Well," Darius says. "It's good that you found this."

"How could he do that?" Adan shakes his head. "I treat him well. Don't I treat him well?"

"Of course you do," Darius says, and then can't resist adding, "Don't you think you would do the same in his position?"

Adan doesn't seem able to hear this question, still shaking his head. "I treat him well."

Darius considers his options. His instinct is to throw the knife away, or perhaps keep it, say nothing, go on as before. Yes, why do anything else? He can have Adan pat the guest down again. Perhaps also Adan should check the room for signs that the guest used the knife somehow. Perhaps he should go back into his chains. He turns the knife over in his hands, admiring it. It looks expensive, with all its little gadgets. That is when Denise comes in. Darius stiffens, represses the urge to hide the knife. Why should he hide it from Denise? He's the one in charge.

She leans against the counter next to him, crosses her arms. She waits, her eyes pointedly on the knife in his hands.

"Yes?" Darius asks, and then hates himself for letting her compel him.

"We should teach him a lesson. He wants that knife, give it to him."

How did she know? Does she stand about eavesdropping in the hall? Creeping silently, imagining herself a guerrilla or a spy? "What good is he to us if our lesson kills him?"

Denise scoffs. "I didn't say kill him. I said cut him."

Darius shakes his head. "No." He shakes his head again. He pushes on the little blade, feels its resistance, lets it stay open. Then he strides to Charlie's room, bangs open the door. Charlie is where he often is, sitting by the crack in the window reading his magazine. When the door bangs open, he jerks up his head. Darius walks up to him with the knife open and Charlie braces. But Darius stops in the center of the room. He holds the knife out toward Charlie as one might hold out toward a child an item the child had broken. "No," he says firmly. He brings his other hand forward and closes the knife. Now he holds it in both hands. He shakes his cupped hands at Charlie. "No," he insists. Then he turns and goes.

In the doorway, Denise moves aside to let Darius out of the room. She doesn't look at him as he passes her; she moves only enough so that he's forced to brush past her to escape. She keeps her gaze on Charlie. Charlie looks back at her. She doesn't need to speak to convey her message: Things would've gone much worse for Charlie if she were the one in charge. Her eyes move to the magazine, and then with alarming swiftness she comes close and snatches it from his hands.

Charlie cuts off his protest, fights the upwelling of anger and grief. Wouldn't Denise love an excuse to hit him. Wouldn't Denise love to see him cry.

"This is mine now," she says with a satisfied smile.

Just like that, once again, Charlie has lost everything. The knife. The magazine. Mystery. Has he lost Mystery? Did she tell them about the knife or did someone find it? Who knows? For God's sake, her name is Mystery.

Hours go by before he sees anyone. He runs through his cache of favorite Josie memories: first meeting; first I love you; the time they saw a sea turtle while snorkeling in Hawaii and the rest of the day she'd suddenly beam at him and say, *We saw a sea turtle*; the time he cried while watching her shoot a sad scene even though he'd rehearsed this very scene with her six thousand times. She was just so good, he forgot he knew all the lines. He risks using up these memories, but they are the only things that keep him from collapsing into panic.

When someone finally comes, it's Adan. But Adan doesn't say, "Hi, Ben!" Adan doesn't smile. Charlie hadn't even considered this— he's also lost Adan. Adan thrusts his food at him without eye contact. He comes back later to take Charlie to the bathroom and refuses to let him in there alone. He stands behind Charlie waiting while Charlie urinates. Is this the greatest humiliation yet? Charlie has lost track.

Back in the room, Adan once again fixing every one of his limbs to a chain, Charlie says, "Adan, talk to me," but Adan shakes his head, won't even look at him, and what the hell was Charlie planning to do? Explain, as though his desire for escape needs justification? Apologize? Adan leaves him alone in the dark, trembling with rage at them, at himself. He was about to fucking apologize. He could kill them all.

Six.

When the noise starts, he's asleep, and his mind incorporates it into his dream: The shouting is an angry audience, the slamming door part of a set. But then the door to his room bangs open, and Adan is there, and then Adan is fumbling at his chains, and Charlie, nauseous from his abrupt reentry, says, "What? What? What?" and can't think of anything else to ask, which doesn't matter because Adan isn't answering. Adan is breathing hard, wrenching at the chains like he can break them, and he's set his gun on the ground, so Charlie might be able to grab it if he knew whether he should grab it. Should he grab it? On TV this would be an obvious choice, so it's puzzling to Charlie how it doesn't seem to be one. What would he do once he had it? Would he shoot Adan? Would he shoot them all? Could he do that before they shot him? He knows he couldn't but believes he could. He's done it before. Adan has one leg loose now and is at work on the other, fumbling the keys, muttering under his breath. Outside the noise grows louder. They all seem to be shouting. The other leg is loose, and Charlie still hasn't decided, but it's too late, because Adan picks the gun back up and starts slamming the butt against the boards on the window until he's smashed one and then another. He wrenches them away, and then he breaks the glass, too, and knocks the shards out of the window frame with the gun. "Out, out!" he says to Charlie.

"What's happening?" Charlie asks.

"They are coming," Adan says. "Go, go, go."

This is a moment that Charlie will revisit over and over. Because when Adan says *they*, he thinks he means the other kidnappers. He believes that Adan has realized the absurdity of his resentment over Charlie's desire to escape, feels such compunction that he's going to help him. With a dreamer's obedience to events, Charlie climbs out the window, then waits for Adan to tell him where to go. They are in a scrubby little yard, all brown grass and desiccated weeds, not the right yard for people who live in paradise, and at the back there's a dilapidated doghouse, and behind it a fence. "Over," Adan says, and then demonstrates, using the doghouse as a stepladder. Charlie imitates him. As he jumps down—now they're in an alley, a fence on each side, above them a cat sleeping in a window—he hears the gunfire. "Why are they shooting?" he asks Adan.

But Adan only looks incredulous and begins to run. Charlie runs after him. They sprint down the alley, dodging trash and low scrubby bushes, and then they are out into a street and still running. "Where are we going?"

"We have a meeting spot," Adan says. "In case, in case."

"Who's we? In case of what?"

"We," Adan says. "We, we." He makes a frantic circle in the air with one hand, and somehow from this Charlie understands what he means.

"Wait," Charlie says. "You mean the others?"

"Yes, yes," Adan says. "We have a place to meet. Emergency place."

"I thought we were running from them."

Adan frowns in confusion. "Not from them. From the police."

"From the police," Charlie says. "We've been running from the police."

"Yes, they will shoot us."

"They won't shoot me."

"They will, Ben. They will shoot us all."

Charlie takes a step back. "They won't shoot me."

Adan's expression shifts from urgent persuasion to wariness. "You come with me, Ben."

"They won't shoot me," Charlie says.

Adan raises his gun. "They will shoot you."

"They won't," Charlie says, and he turns to run. Even as he runs, he's bracing for impact because he doesn't know, does he, whether a bullet is already coming. He gambles this way, running back in the direction of the house. He's following his instinct, an instinct that says this is his best chance, but also, and perhaps more important, he's angry. He's as angry as though Adan were a longtime friend who deliberately played a wounding trick, a fan who turned nasty, a reporter who made him look a fool. In running, he's saying, *Fuck you, Adan*, and he's saying, *Fuck you, Ben Phillips, you pathetic, agreeable pussy, thinking you're kind when what you really are is weak, and I should have grabbed the gun, I should have grabbed the gun and shot them all. I am Charlie Outlaw, and I know how to do this. I know how to run when bullets are flying and not get hit, I never get hit, I'm the hero, and if I get hit, I'll survive. I'll survive, Josie. I'm coming. I'll survive. I'll survive.*

Only later will Charlie learn the context for the things that are happening to him right now. The police found the other house. All the hostages kept there have been released, all but one of the kidnappers captured, the last one killed. The kidnappers, being neither hardened nor particularly afraid of Darius, gave up the location of the house that contained Charlie.

And now he's free. He's free and running, his legs already burning, his lungs burning, too, but at the moment, this is beneath Char-

Leah Stewart

lie's notice. He hears sirens. He hears gunfire. He slows and looks around, suddenly not sure where to go. Around him, houses, plants, cars. Darius rounds a corner into his vision and runs right at him, and Charlie's watching him approach with a furious terror on his face so he doesn't see where the shots come from, but he does see Darius drop to the ground. All instinct, no thought, Charlie turns and runs, not toward anything, just away. Behind him he hears shouting, he hears more gunshots, and then from up ahead, he hears, "Ben! Ben! Ben!" and after a moment, he remembers that's supposed to be his name. He swerves toward the sound and finds himself in another alley, or maybe the same alley, and when he sees Adan, his chest explodes in fragments of a terrible, desperate relief. "Behind me!" Adan says. Charlie ducks behind him, and Adan leans around the corner to fire wildly at whoever is firing at them. Then he says, "Come on, Ben, run!" and though, as they pelt down the alley and then down a street and another street and on and on, Adan is ahead of him, not looking back, Charlie has forgotten about escape. Charlie follows Adan. Charlie runs.

V.

The reality you create on the stage by threading a needle and sewing, or cleaning your glasses and putting them on, is not created so that the audience will believe in you; it is created so that you will believe in yourself.

—STELLA ADLER, *The Technique of Acting*

One.

Josie is sequestered, like each of the other *Alter Ego* cast members who have recently arrived for the convention, in her own personal black Escalade with driver and bodyguard. At one point, on the way from the airport to the hotel, her bodyguard actually jumps out of the car and starts directing traffic. *You have no jurisdiction here,* Josie wants to shout, as she did during a procedural guest spot, playing a cop antagonistic to the heroes. Her bodyguard, Cyrus, is a retired policeman, an utterly humorless individual with an exhausting alertness, scanning the world. He keeps calling her "ma'am," though she'd guess he's at least ten years her senior. She's persuaded he's confused about her identity, thinks she's a visiting dignitary under threat of assassination, queen of England or president of the world. She's never played a politician. She auditioned for the role of a senator once, but she didn't get the part.

"Have you done a lot of this kind of work?" she inquires politely. They're sitting at a stoplight, her bodyguard's head literally swiveling in threat assessment. It seems rude to pull out her book or her phone, though she would dearly love to. How much farther can it possibly be to the hotel?

"Yes, ma'am," Cyrus says. He clamps his mouth shut, as though he fears she might tempt him to gossip.

Don't worry, guy. She's not asking for an inside scoop. "I wondered what kinds of incidents occur," she says. "When you have to intervene."

He keeps on sweeping for bombs. "You just don't know, ma'am."

"You don't have to worry so much with me. I'm not that famous."

He looks at her.

"I mean, yeah, people used to mob me sometimes. But not now."

"Ma'am," he says sternly.

What is he scolding her for? Distracting him? Diminishing the threat? Diminishing herself? She's just trying to be realistic here. No one is going to come leaping out at this car from the side of the road. How would anyone even know who was in here? "I'm just not sure what you're expecting."

"I don't know what I'm expecting either, ma'am," he says. "But they pay me to be ready for it."

Ah. Josie surrenders. After they filmed the second season of *Alter Ego*, Josie and her boyfriend went to New York City. They'd just started airing the show; Josie and her boyfriend watched the third episode in a relatively inexpensive hotel room in the Financial District. This was before Twitter, before website comments. She had no idea that the cult had reached saturation level. They were in the Met when someone noticed her, and then there was a mob. She remembers how that felt—the press of bodies, the shrinking air, the heat, the panicked desire to escape. All that love looked a lot like fury. She would've appreciated this guy's presence then. But now. She doesn't need him now! This is a ridiculous pretense.

True, there's been a sudden resurgence of internet interest in her, thanks to Charlie's interview and that photo of her kissing Max, which was up within hours of it happening. But that's not the kind of publicity that leads to being mobbed, not the kind she was hoping this convention would bring her. Maybe she was wrong not to bite the bullet on a publicist's fee. A publicist would have had ideas for working that interest to her advantage.

She wishes she didn't have thoughts like that.

As punishment, she returns, as she has many times since that night and that photo, to the well-worn track of Max-related worries. You can no doubt imagine some of the many questions and concerns and possibilities looping through her mind. Perhaps you can also imagine—if you've posted something on Facebook that pissed off your friend, if you've written an e-mail critical of your boss that got forwarded to your boss, if you've coyly mentioned a crush on Twitter and everyone knew exactly who you meant—how it complicates your personal life when it goes public. If Josie kisses Max and no one records it—it was such a small kiss!—then it's easier for them both to pretend it didn't happen, if that seems necessary. But now everyone knows it happened—and, oh, their insistent questions, so certain they have a right to know—and that means Josie has to answer to it for them and for herself. She can't pretend it didn't happen, and neither can Max. Max and Josie saw the picture, too.

Is the picture why Charlie hasn't called her back?

Since, her only contact with Max has been via text. She texted *Oops* and he texted back *Fuck 'em.* Ambiguous with a large potential for awkward. What Josie returns from her reverie certain of is that she needs to head that awkwardness off. She pulls out her phone, texts Max and Cecelia. *I hate my bodyguard.*

Too bad! the return text from Cecelia reads. *Mine is funny!*

Mine just scolded me.

From Max: *Mine is the type to sneak you in the back door of a club.*

Josie texts, *How do you know?*

Because he offered to sneak me in the back door of a club. A beat, and then Max adds, *Drink at the hotel bar?*

Yup from Cecelia.

I don't think my bodyguard will like that.

Don't tell him! Cecelia says.

Tell him I'll protect you, says Max.

Hey, I'm the Chosen One. I'll protect myself.

No way Cyrus would believe that this was possible. In the lobby of the hotel, he proceeds with an air that, whatever else it's supposed to do, certainly has the effect of drawing attention to her. Before she even makes it to the registration desk, a man approaches to ask for a picture, already fumbling for his phone. "No pictures!" Cyrus barks, stepping toward the man with his hand in the Heisman position.

"No, it's okay," Josie says. She feels a teenage level of humiliation. Now the whole lobby is looking. "I'll take a picture." She smiles at the man, and her agitation must have put extra dazzle in the smile because he looks stupefied. She takes a selfie with him. The trouble with selfies is that they force you to lean in very close to the fan, much closer than you have to when someone else holds the camera. This guy leans in so close his cheek brushes lightly against hers. He puts his arm around her, snugly enough to press her breast against his side. Josie catches the look of rigid alarm on Cyrus's face. The camera flashes, and she steps away from the guy quickly before Cyrus can move in. And also because she wants to. After that, there are ten more pictures before Cyrus decides to overrule her, announcing that Ms. Lamar needs to get to her room. He wields an enviable authority. The fans scatter as soon as he says the word.

On the journey from the desk to the elevator, Josie keeps her head down. Cyrus's force field holds. An empty elevator opens its doors and Cyrus hustles them both in, hits the button for Josie's floor, holds out his hand for her key card, zaps it in the slot, hands it back. The elevator doors close on someone's hopeful face and the sound of *wai—*, but Cyrus is unmoved. He says, "Ma'am, do you still want to allow pictures?"

Rebelling against Cyrus might not be in Josie's best interest, but oh how she wants to. "I'll let you know," she says.

When the elevator arrives, Cyrus steps out first, holding up his hand to stop Josie. He looks both ways down the hall before he does the come-on gesture to wave her out. She's played this scene before, wearing a prop bulletproof vest, carrying a prop gun, conscious of holding it with the proper grip. At the corner, he performs the same maneuver, holding her back until a group of twentysomething guys rumbles past. Then he actually says, "All clear."

She is relieved by the sight of the door to her room. She slides the key card into the lock, turns to him with a smile, and says, "Well, thank you," but when she presses the door handle, nothing happens. She tries the key card again, sees that the two little lights flash red, and groans. Cyrus holds out his hand for the card, tries it himself with the same result. *See?* she wants to say.

He's annoyed with the disobedient card. He clicks his tongue. "We'd better go back to the desk," he says.

"I'm fine. You can call it a night."

"I'll go with you."

"You don't have to."

"I do, ma'am."

All the way down and back up, they repeat the routine. This time they have companions in the elevator and Cyrus stands in front of her, which, sure, means no one bothers her, but also means she's pressed into the corner of an elevator behind a very large man. When she tries the new key card, she can feel herself clenching her jaw. This time the lights flash green! Thank God.

"You're all right for tonight?" he asks. He has her itinerary, knows all that's on it tonight are optional parties she doesn't plan to attend. She agrees that she's not going anywhere. "Your breakfast meeting is in the hotel restaurant at 8:15," he says. "So I'll see you at 8:10."

"In the lobby?"

"I'll come up here."

"All right," she says, weary of conflict, even, or especially, the passive-aggressive kind. She says good night and thank you, and is glad to shut the door on his face. "He'll come up here," she mutters, crossing with purpose toward the bed. "Of course he'll come up here." She turns and falls backward, snow-angel style. She lets out a long breath, closes her eyes. Cyrus took a lot out of her. Though she's been really tired in general lately. She's getting old. She should probably go to bed right now, magic the lie she told Cyrus into truth. Imagine if Cyrus catches her in the bar with Max and Cecelia. What trouble she'll be in! She can picture the stern disappointment on his face, an image that actually increases her desire to go. This reunion is tricking her into feeling twenty years younger, complete with the urge to rebel against her own well-being. But, of course, Cyrus won't be in the bar. He'll be asleep, lying fully clothed atop the made bed, with his arms crossed over his chest like a vampire.

She should be grateful to Cyrus, probably, for being so sure of his role and hers. She had no idea what to do down there in the lobby. She didn't know who to be with those fans. She's out of practice. Her self-assurance is a rusty instrument, damaged by storage. But there's such falsity in this pretense that she's special! She wanted to explain that to the little crowd of fans instead of agreeably, dutifully posing for selfies and signing her name. They see a certain Josie Lamar— Josie Lamar as an all-but-transparent container for Bronwyn Kyle— and they project that image so ferociously onto Josie's actual, inadequate body that Josie herself can see it there, a ghost, an aura, an outline, a costume that she could put on. And if she tells herself it's okay to do that, to be that for them, to accept their admiration with beneficent kindness as if she deserves it, because she'd be doing it for the fans who, after all, want that, who in no way wish to see her brought down to size? Well, then she is not telling herself the whole truth.

She thinks of how Charlie would have handled Cyrus and the scene downstairs, how he would have projected an easy goodwill, made jokes, slung his arm around his selfie partner, or suggested silly poses, and she feels a sudden sharp yearning for him or maybe to be different herself, because maybe his way is, after all, better than hers. She remembers her vehemence, her anger, as she insisted the opposite, and is sorry, so sorry that tears prick her eyes. What *is* her way? She doesn't quite know anymore, hasn't in a long time, not since the first time she realized her longing to go unrecognized had been fulfilled and—this was the terrifying, more important realization—that she didn't actually enjoy its fulfillment. And when attention returns? To receive it as her due is delusional. To lap at it eagerly is pathetic. To angrily dismiss it is unkind. So she has landed on uneasy acceptance, but she can't claim to like it there.

From the first, she loved Charlie's willingness to say what he thinks, to admit what he feels. She loved that it didn't occur to him not to. She loved his kindness, his genuine interest in other people, his desire to engage. His honesty, which brought out a corresponding honesty in her. She felt fully herself with Charlie, a whole person, not a collage. When she was with him, she stopped witnessing her own performance, stopped running everything she wanted to say through a complicated system of filters. She wasn't pretending not to care what anyone else thought. She really didn't care. She didn't care! For a brief, exhilarating time, if people looked at her, she didn't care, and if they didn't, she didn't care, and if she got an audition that was great and if all she had to do that day was go to the farmer's market with Charlie, that was also great. Over and over she experienced her own freedom with the force of revelation. This was peace. This was, at last, transcendence. She'd passed through a gate, shedding her insecurities and her disappointments and her petty, nagging jealousies, and she believed this state of calm acceptance was a permanent condition. But then he got famous. Then they went to a party thrown by one of his castmates, a party where she knew almost no one, and so very many people came between her and him that it took him two hours to notice that she'd left. "I'm so sorry; I'm so sorry," he said later, but still he didn't understand, still he seemed bewildered by how long she cried.

Her phone chimes, announcing a text from Cecelia. *We're downstairs. Where are you?*

When she opens the door, she half expects to find Cyrus standing outside it, legs spread, hands clasped gently in front of him. But he's gone. She finds herself imitating him, looking left down the hallway, then right, making sure. All clear. Though she gets some shy glances in the elevator, only one person stops her on her way across the lobby to the bar, a woman, older than Josie, who requests a hug, and when Josie grants it, gives her a little squeeze, which Josie receives as comfort, feeling an inordinate gratitude that returns that prickly feeling to her eyes. Why is she so weepy? Is it Charlie? She resolves again not to think about him. She resolves to shake off her melancholy without much hope that she'll succeed, but when she spots Cecelia and Max at a round booth in a dark corner of the bar—her friends, her compatriots—the mood lifts like a flock of birds. They wave her into the booth with a conspiratorial air. She makes a split-second decision and slips in beside Cecelia rather than Max. Cecelia leans against her, welcoming, as Max reaches across the table to lightly touch her hand.

"We got you a vodka tonic," Max says, pushing it toward her. "Cecelia says it's what you drink now."

"Cecelia is right."

"Very simple," Max says. "Very classy. Remember when you only drank White Russians?"

Josie makes a face. "I was young. I wanted everything to be sweet."

"I liked tequila shots," Cecelia says. "I thought it made me seem like a badass."

"It did," Josie says.

"I was afraid of you," Max says.

"I was afraid of *you*," Cecelia says. "At first, anyway."

"Why's that?"

"You don't know?"

Max shakes his head.

Cecelia looks at Josie with a playful display of shock. "How could he not know?"

Max spreads his arms out. "What's scary about me?"

"Ah," Cecelia says. "I won't feed your ego by telling you."

Max turns a help-me-out expression on Josie.

"She's talking about your face," Josie says.

"My face?"

Cecelia says, "Your terrifyingly handsome face." She takes a sip of her own vodka tonic. "It made us want to giggle. We were afraid we would giggle when you came around."

Max looks at Josie, who nods. "It's true," she says. "That's why you were scary. Fear of giggling."

"I'm debating how to take this," Max says. "Sure, it could be a compliment. But what does it mean that you're not giggling now? Should I conclude that I'm less handsome?"

"Oh, don't conclude that," says Cecelia. "We're just used to you now."

"You have no urge to giggle?" Max says with sorrow.

"I just want us to stop saying *giggle*," Josie says.

"That doesn't answer my question."

Josie takes a sip of her drink, makes a face at its sharp, strong taste, and puts it down. This is quite an opportunity for flirtation Cecelia has given her, with Cecelia herself there to provide cover. Does she want to take it? Maybe. She gives Max a sidelong smile. "I plead the Fifth."

"We may come back to this discussion," Max says.

"May we? Let's talk about Cecelia now."

"Yes, let's talk about me," Cecelia says. "Do you like my outfit? I don't think I like my outfit."

"She looks hot," Max says.

"You look hot," Josie agrees.

"I don't know about this stylist," Cecelia says. "I don't think I like anything she picked out."

"You're just nervous," Max says.

"That's true. Don't talk about it, though. I mean my being nervous. You can talk about *it*."

"What's *it*?" Josie asks.

Cecelia grins. "I'm up for a part in a movie."

"That's great!"

"She's going to leave us, though, any minute now," Max says. "To have a drink with the director."

"Oh, that's less great," Josie says. "What's the part?"

"It's an indie film. Based on a novel. It's the lead. And she's not a maid or a single mom or a noble social worker or whatever. It's the sort of part I never normally get. She's a middle-class woman with a family and a job, seems totally normal, but her secret is that she's a kleptomaniac. She's only ever stolen little things, but then she impulsively steals some jewelry that gets her involved in this whole elaborate crime thing—it's good, it's really good. It's a great script. The guy who's directing it, he wrote it, too."

"Do you know him?" Josie asks.

Cecelia nods. "He directed an episode of *Kidnapped* last year. He turned out to be a huge *Alter Ego* fan. So we had this conversation about how I liked Vivi best evil, because I got a break from being so reliable and good. That's why he thought of me for this." She sighs. "He's thirty-two. He's ten years younger than I am. He's never directed a movie. I've been acting for twenty years. I've been working in this business since he was a *child*. And I'm so nervous about meeting with him that I'm freaking out over my clothes like a high school girl."

"You look great," Josie says. "And you'll be great."

Cecelia rests her head briefly on Josie's shoulder. "I just want the part so badly. I forgot how much it sucks to want something this badly."

Josie's eyes go involuntarily to Max, and he looks back at her just as she looks away. She has turned her gaze quickly to Cecelia, who, of course—of course!—took note of this wordless exchange. Cecelia picks up her glass and hides her smile behind it. Cecelia is nervous but not quite as nervous as she's making it seem. The director has all but told her she has the part. She's playing up her nerves because of the double bind of friendship with another actor: She doesn't want to risk offending Josie by failing to keep her apprised, but neither does she want to risk making her feel bad at a time when getting work is a struggle. Also, Cecelia knows Josie's tying herself into knots about Charlie and Max and the photo, and whatever may or may not happen, so she's providing distraction. Then, having eased them into this evening, she'll leave them alone to do with it what they will. She's not so sure Max is the best option for Josie—that, in her opinion, is very obviously Charlie, with whom Josie was the happiest that Cecelia has ever seen her. And the one time Cecelia gambled on turning an on-screen relationship real, it was a spectacular disaster, leaving her firm in her opinion that that's never a good idea. But she wants Josie to get something she wants, even if that something is a man a little too confident of his own impenetrable charm.

Cecelia lifts her glass. "To *Alter Ego*," she says. "Because it gave me you two." They clink, and she adds, "It was a first love, wasn't it? Working together. I've never had anything quite like that again."

Max shakes his head. "Me neither. I mean we all get along on my show, but it's mostly professional politeness, more like a job, not like . . ."

"Summer camp?" Cecelia suggests.

"We're not so bonded," Max agrees.

"We're not so young," Josie says.

"Or so unencumbered," says Cecelia, who is married to a poet who stays home with their two girls. "We gave everything to that show. We were ardent."

"Good word," Max says.

Cecelia grins. "I know. Jamal likes that word. He likes to talk about words that people don't say anymore, that he wants to bring back."

"Like what else?" Josie asks. *Ardent* is a good word for Charlie, and just like that, she has already broken her resolution not to think about Charlie. What word will make her not think about Charlie?

"Now I'm drawing a blank," Cecelia says. "Hang on, I'll text him."

"What's it like being married to a poet?" Max asks.

"What's it like?" Cecelia repeats, eyes on her phone. She finishes her text, puts the phone down, and looks up at Max. "What do you mean?"

"I don't know. Is everything profound?"

Cecelia laughs. "Yes," she says. Her phone chimes and she picks it up. "Vexed," she says.

"What's that mean?" Max asks, and Josie says, "Frustrated."

"Annoyed," Cecelia says.

"Nettled," Josie says, and Max says, "I feel like you two are trying to tell me something."

Cecelia's phone chimes again. "Countenance," she says. "Now he'll be at this all night. That's what it's like to be married to a poet."

"How is Jamal?" Josie asks.

"He's good. I told you he won that second-book contest, right?" To Max, she adds, "That's how you get published when you're a poet. You win a contest."

Max says, "That's also how you get a part."

"True." Cecelia smiles at her screen. "Very true. Must be why we understand each other." She starts typing again, still wearing her inward smile.

Here it comes again, Josie. That longing you cannot conquer and cannot bear. Right now, at this very minute, Charlie is being herded into the rain forest by people with guns. If you knew that, what would you do? What lengths would you go to to get what you want?

"I miss the fight scenes," Josie says. "I miss kicking ass."

"I miss watching you kick ass," Max says. "You were so good at it."

"You were, too."

"We were good at it together."

Max leans into the table, eyes on Josie as though Cecelia weren't there, and whispers, "I don't know what *countenance* means either."

"I think it means you agreed to something," Josie says. "Or it means your face. Your 'fair countenance,'" she quotes from somewhere, and Max gives her that slow, knowing grin.

"My handsome face," he says.

"All right, you two," Cecelia says, and for a startled moment Josie thinks she's scolding them for flirting, but, no, she got a text from the director and she's leaving to go meet him at another bar. Josie's nervous about being left alone with Max, but she also wants to be left alone with Max. So it's with a complicated mixture of emotion that, as they're saying good-bye to Cecelia, she spots the *Alter Ego* show-

---

---

runner and two of their other castmates headed their way. They squeeze into the booth, so that Josie is pressed closer to Max, and as she talks to Bill, the showrunner, who sits on her other side, and Max talks to the other actors, she is hyperaware of Max's thigh lightly touching hers, his arm brushing against her arm. At one point, when their arms are touching, she notices Bill noticing, his expression speculative. Though he makes no comment, he looks at her with that assessing air, which provokes her to say, in a voice pitched below the noise of the bar, "Nothing's going on."

Eyebrows up, he murmurs back, "The whole freaking world saw that picture."

"That was just a friendly good-bye."

He cocks his head, adding skepticism to skepticism.

"I swear. It's only become a thing because some asshole took that picture. I promise, Bill. You know there's never been anything. We just have chemistry."

"All right, I believe you. Because I know when you're lying."

"No, you don't. I'm an actor."

"So you're lying?"

"No, I'm not lying. I'm just saying you wouldn't know if I was. But I'm not."

He concedes with a shrug. "Your life is weird."

"You just now noticed?"

"You know a question's inevitable, right?"

"During the panel?"

"Yeah. Someone will most definitely ask."

"Okay. I'll come up with a good answer."

Bill jerks his beer at Max. "Better get him on board with it, too." He sees Josie hesitate and says, "I have to tell you, if you don't want to talk about it there's something to talk about."

"Fine, fine," Josie says. "I'm tired of observant people."

"You're one of us. Don't hate on your own tribe." He smiles. "If you do get together, I want all the credit."

"If we do get together, I will write you an ode."

He laughs. "An ode?"

"An ode. An ardent ode."

"Ardent," Bill repeats. "That's a good word."

"You can have it," Josie says. "I give it to you."

Bill puts his hand affectionately on her shoulder. "I miss you," he says. "My star."

By the time she is alone with Max, when everyone else has wisely stumbled off to bed, he is very drunk. She knows this because of the smile he turns her way as soon as Bill is gone—it's supposed to be sexy and inviting but slides tipsily toward goofy. "Hi," he says. She herself is not drunk at all. She nursed that vodka tonic a long time before switching to water because she doesn't sleep well when she drinks and hair and makeup will be at her door at 6:15. And also because there was a part of her that wanted to erase all doubts with alcohol and tumble into bed with Max, but another part of her, the part that's in charge, thought it might be smarter to hang on to her doubts for now.

"Hi," she says.

"So," he says.

"Yes?"

"Everybody thinks we've got something going."

She nods. "Bill asked me."

"I thought that was what was happening. You weren't that subtle with the whispering. Daniel and August asked me, too. Everybody wants to know. Enquiring minds."

"Bill thinks they'll ask us tomorrow on the panel."

"Who, the moderator?"

"No, the audience. Do you think the moderator would? We could ask her not to."

"That's probably not a good idea."

"You're right. That makes too much of it. We need a plan, though."

"Sure, okay. A plan." He smiles again. "You know the audience will love it."

"I know, but what are we going to say?"

He shrugs. "What do you think they want to hear?"

"That we're really Bronwyn and Malachi and we're secretly married and I have superpowers. And we have tiny superpowered babies."

"Flying babies."

"Flying? What show were you on? I couldn't fly; you couldn't fly. Ass-kicking babies."

"Ninja babies."

"So the plan is we'll tell them we have magical ninja babies."

He laughs. "You have a better one?"

She considers. "Okay, someone will definitely ask us if we're dating, or something like that. How about I say, 'Sadly, no.'"

"You'll probably get an *aww*. And then I'll say, 'I know, it's a shame.'"

"That'll work. We can keep it going in that vein."

"Someone might ask if the kiss was real."

"We can say, 'Well, you know, we touched lips. If that's what you mean by real.'"

"That's good."

"Well, I'm good."

"You are good. You're really kind of amazing."

Josie scoffs.

"I'm serious. You're just . . . amazing. You're brave. You're strong. You're inspiring."

"Brave and inspiring. That's what that girl said. It makes me feel like I have a serious illness."

"What girl?"

"The waitress on *You & Me*. I can't think of her name."

"The one who needed all the takes?"

"That one."

"Don't try to distract me."

"Would I do that?"

"You've never been able to take a compliment."

"Really? Never?" Though she knows this is true. Charlie used to tell her to close her eyes when he wanted to be earnest, to say that she was smart and funny and the best actress he knew.

"You probably don't remember—once I wanted to tell you how much I liked the way you'd said a line, and you all but punched me in the face every time I tried."

"Were we doing a fight scene?"

He thinks. "Were we?"

"Because that would explain it."

He performs exaggerated frustration, clenching his fists. "Let me give you a compliment!"

She clenches her own fists, pounds them on the table. "No!"

"Why not?!"

Why not? Why not? A good actor strives to make the self a malleable instrument. The danger, when you succeed in making the self a malleable instrument, is that you're not the only one who can play it. You want to trust flattery, you see, but you can't. The fact that you want to trust it so badly is the reason that you can't. If you believe what people tell you about yourself, you're instantly gullible, instantly vulnerable. You become whatever they say you are. There's nothing, good or bad, you won't believe.

"I surrender," Josie says. "You can give me a compliment."

"You can't look away or make a joke."

"Oh God. Okay. I'll have to close my eyes." And she is sorry she said that because that routine was only for Charlie, and now she's used it in this scene and made it a little less real, a little less hers.

She closes her eyes anyway, to disappear. Max touches her gently, runs his fingers down her jawline, like he used to do on the show, like she's done herself before in a performance but doesn't think people do very often in real life, or at least not the people who've been in love with her. We accept that as love, on TV and in the movies, as we accept the flavor of certain candies as watermelon or grape. That's not what Charlie used to do. What Charlie would do was put his mouth very close to her ear so that his breath tickled her skin, and she'd smile like a person on the verge of laughing, and then he'd say, "Don't laugh, don't laugh," with laughter in his voice, and she'd struggle not to, and then he might kiss her and say, "Keep your eyes closed," and then he'd say whatever it was he wanted to say and have her listen, have her believe he meant.

But Max runs his fingers down her jaw. "You're amazing, you really are. I've always been a little in love with you, Bronwyn."

It takes her a second to hear it. Then she opens her eyes, sees the forthright desire on his face. No sheepishness, no wincing, no joke. He doesn't realize.

He called her by her character's name.

She musters a teasing, skeptical smile.

He called her by her character's name!

"I'm serious," he says. "I've always been a little in love with you. Don't look at me like that! Do I need to make you close your eyes again?"

"You've always been a little in love with *her*."

He frowns. "With who?"

"With Bronwyn."

"With you, Josie. Don't you think I know the difference?"

No, you clearly don't, Max, not at this moment, and it is striking Josie now that maybe you never have. It's true that Josie was flirting with you because she wanted—in some dark corner of her psyche that it distresses her to acknowledge—to be with someone who didn't know the difference, to feel again, if briefly, that there was no difference. But there is a difference, there is. She could pretend otherwise, but do you want to be with her if she's acting? If you do, she doesn't want to be with you.

She was never acting with Charlie. Not even when she was Beatrice and he was Benedick.

She lifts her hand. She runs her fingers down his jawline, doing it slowly, on her face an expression of tender regret. Good actors make acting look easy, so people pay them the compliment of thinking that it is. "It's late. I'm going to bed."

"Can I come?"

She laughs, though she, Josie Lamar, would rather cry. He is not Charlie, and she wants Charlie. She was deluding herself to think she could recast the role. "I have to sleep. Early morning."

"Tomorrow then," he says.

She wants Charlie, and what good does it do to be so sure of that now? She's afraid even to text him again. She has to perform herself tomorrow—she has to be the Josie Lamar who is funny and friendly and confident—and if she endures another cycle of hope and disappointment, she will fall apart. "Tomorrow," she agrees.

Two.

It would be an injustice to Josie to assume she is always as uncertain as she has been of late. It's an injustice Josie herself has been guilty of committing, constructing her self-image out of her weaker moments. We all shape-shift, of course. But not all of us know we're doing it. Not all of us do it on purpose. Not all of us embrace our ability to transform as our essential quality. When you know you can be different people, sometimes it's hard to figure out which one you are.

To understand Josie—to understand an actor—first understand what it's like to audition. Know that to seek love and approval is to court their opposites. Auditions hold out the promise of joyous achievement for which you must risk the far more likely possibility of rejection, disappointment, humiliation, despair. Still, far worse than auditioning is not getting an audition at all. You want those auditions so badly. When you get one, your agent tells you that you have an appointment, maybe several days in advance, maybe the night before. You get a script and are told to prepare certain scenes. You and your competition all arrive around the same time in an office in an office building. There's a sign-in sheet on a clipboard by the front door. Past that you see a desk and a guy texting behind it, indifferent to you or doing a good job of pretending to be. Don't ask him for his stapler because you forgot to staple your headshot to your résumé. He'll be annoyed and won't hide it. This is why he keeps a dish of highlighters, pencils, and staplers beside the sign-up sheet for the newer actors who failed to highlight their lines before they came in, who failed to do their stapling. If you use these supplies, that will mark you as unprofessional or a novice, and either you'll be flustered already by your own obvious inadequacy or you're so annoyingly oblivious that you're probably not any good. Maybe you'll get the part anyway, for being handsome or beautiful. If you are neither handsome nor beautiful nor good, then what are you doing there? You sign in. You'll be read in the order you appear on the list. The sides—the pages you're to read—are there, too, and if you know what you're doing, you check the sides to see if the scenes have changed since you were given the script.

Then you find a chair and wait. The room is full of people who look like you. If you're a middle-aged white woman, like Josie, the room is full of middle-aged white women. The auditioning room is the great equalizer. Some of them used to be famous. They're doing the thing that people do when they used to be famous, making themselves unnecessarily visible, either by trying too hard to be seen or by trying too hard not to be seen. The ones in the former category might, for instance, find it necessary to have a loud phone conversation with their agents. The ones in the latter category might be tucked into corners, turned away and inward in their chairs, like they're in danger of being accosted for their autographs. You can tell their money situation by their shoes. They project whatever quality worked for them when they were hot, when they were in hit shows. If it would be very easy for you to be just like them, and if you very much don't want to be, you spend your time in the waiting room thinking less about the part and more about how to walk the line, so

narrow it's invisible, between caring too much and making an obvious pretense that you don't care at all.

Then they call you in to read, and from the moment you enter
the room, they are alert to everything about you—your body, your
walk, your hair, your face, your nervous laugh, how awkward you
are when the assistant clips the mic on, how you got prickly when
they cheerfully asked you for gossip about the other actors on your
old hit show. Sometimes they know you won't get the part as soon as
you walk in the door and nevertheless must enact the charade. This
necessitates an immunity to your hope, to everyone's hope. Without
detachment, their jobs would be unbearable. They say, "Great!" They
tell you you made interesting choices. (You know they say those
things all day and most of the time they're lying. But they mean it
sometimes! Do they mean it when they say it to you?) When the audition is over, you start to walk out still wearing the mic clipped to
your shirt, and the assistant stops you, and you say, "I'm taking it
with me," and the assistant laughs politely, though he's had this exact
exchange ten thousand times. The door closes behind you, and on
the other side, in that soundproof room where you just wept or
shouted or seduced, they praise you or they take you apart. Later,
your headshot will either be pinned to the board where they display
the casts of their shows or filed in a cabinet under your gender, race,
and age.

An actor might believe she can play any part if given the chance,
that any and all transformations are possible. A casting director
doesn't believe that. A casting director is looking for the particular set
of traits a particular actor can embody, for what each actor brings to
a role. Does it even matter how well you perform when you say the
lines? It's easy to think it doesn't, especially when the report you get
later is that you were too old or too tall or didn't have quite the right
look. What is *quite the right look*? You have no idea. Could you have
achieved it if you'd worn different clothes, done something else with

your hair? When you're rejected—and you are almost always rejected—the thing that's being rejected is not your work but *you*. Do you see how easy it would be to let that destroy you? When Josie was cast as Bronwyn Kyle, she brought herself to that audition, and she turned out to be exactly what they wanted. After the show ended, she kept doing that, and it worked at first, and then it worked less often, and then it stopped working much at all. Over and over she wasn't what they wanted. So the question shifted from *What can I bring to this?* to *What do they want?* Whatever it was she thought they wanted, she tried to be it. She second-guessed her instincts. She pretzeled herself. She was driven by the whip of desperation, and casting people can read desperation. Desperation is not what they're looking for.

Why did she get the part of Bronwyn Kyle? Josie plays three conditions crucial to that character especially well—uncertainty, intensity, determination. She is excellent at the kind of close-up in which the gaze firms, the jaw tightens. The moments when self-doubt and indecision give way to resolve are Josie's forte. (She is also particularly good at longing and the struggle to repress it. She is good at the tug-of-war between emotion and control.) In high school, along with all the other seniors, Josie took a standardized test designed to measure aptitude for the military. After that, she got calls from a recruiter for the Marines. More than once, when asked by an interviewer how she knew she could play a hero, she said, smiling, "Well, I could have been a Marine." Later, during increasingly difficult times, that thought could be employed to give her confidence, and then, like so many other things that had once given her confidence, it grew to seem a placebo that she had mistaken for a cure. Dumbo's feather, which never actually made him fly.

She used to believe she could be a hero, and that is why they let her be one, but now a long time has passed in which they've told her she can't be much of anything, and she can't find her way back to her original belief. How we love the idea of the person who can't be broken, but that is a national fantasy. Find the right circumstances and there is no one impervious to diminishment. Just ask Charlie. And even if Josie could become impervious, how could she then be a good actor? Read all the acting books. Impervious is the opposite of what they tell you to be. Lee Strasberg: "For a human being, too much sensitivity is very difficult to live with. For an actor, there is no such thing as too much sensitivity." And, yes, Josie, like all actors, is a human being, but Lee Strasberg knew that as a fact of secondary importance. Sensitive: highly attuned to nuance. Sensitive: easily wounded. What a shame that what is fine is also fragile. Yes, Josie, it hurts to be too sensitive, but for you there is *no such thing*. Impervious, you still wouldn't get what you wanted, unless what you wanted was to stop wanting at all.

In the audition room, over and over, an actor is made or broken. That's bad enough. Imagine if they already know who you are and don't want you. Imagine if you can't even get in the room. Before she got the part on *Kidnapped*, and then the part on *You & Me*, both of which came to her because of *Alter Ego*, Josie had not had an audition in eight months. Over the phone, her mother has been suggesting alternate careers. Josie has seventy-five credits listed on IMDb, and her mother thinks she should go into real estate. "I just don't want you to run out of money," her mother said, and Josie reassured her that she won't and said what she always says when she wants her mother to drop this subject, which is to talk vaguely about syndication and streaming and DVDs, but the truth is, if it goes on like this, she might run out of money. She's been considering getting an appearance agent—she knows her former castmates Daniel and August both have one, maybe the same one—and joining the fan convention circuit. Tampa. Albuquerque. Cincinnati. She looked at the website for the Phoenix convention, and when she saw that the actors scheduled to appear are not only known for previous roles but currently working, she wondered if she'd even make the list. But there are plenty of smaller ones that would definitely want her, or so says Daniel. "Only do the ones where they give you a guarantee," he told her last night in the hotel bar. "Because, yeah, people pay forty or fifty dollars a pop for the autograph or the photo, but I've never earned more than the guarantee."

"You like doing them?"

He shrugged. He'd read some doubt in her voice because he was stiffer now, his voice wary. "It's fun."

"It must be nice to see how many people still care about the show," she said, trying to make up for whatever judgment she'd accidentally implied.

"It's awesome," he said, relaxing again. "They bring you presents—pictures they've drawn of you, or somebody brought me a Dinky Toys tank because she'd read I collect them. And I didn't have that one, so I was psyched. Every interaction is positive. They love you."

Josie asked about Dinky Toys, which she'd never heard of, and which proved to be small die-cast vehicles made in England in the middle of the twentieth century, and then she pursued the question of how Daniel acquired this interest and learned that his grandfather was British and that Daniel's mother used to take him back to Wales to visit him. In Wales, he'd play with his grandfather's toys, saved from childhood, and when his grandfather died, he left the little trucks and double-decker buses to Daniel, and Daniel grew misty telling her all this, which was fascinating and nothing she'd ever known about him in all these many years. She felt a tender sadness at the idea of his being so touched by a gift from a stranger even though she knows she'd be equally touched by it, and maybe that's one reason why she's afraid to take this step into the convention world, open herself to so much unequivocal love, and make a lot of money for receiving it. Such a step feels irrevocable.

There's also this story, which she didn't tell Daniel, hasn't told anyone except Charlie. A few years ago, just before she met Charlie, she accepted an offer, through her manager, to go to an *Alter Ego* fan convention in London. They paid her $16,000 in cash. The actual convention part was fine, but one of her duties was to attend a cocktail party, where she posed for picture after picture, and then, as people got drunker, groping crept into those encounters, hands crept up her side toward her breasts, and though she shifted and avoided as best she could, she was still clinging resolutely to her role, which was to be available and polite, and so she didn't shout or push anyone or storm out. By the time she got back to her hotel room, she felt dirty. She felt like she'd left a little piece of herself at that party, and she wouldn't ever get it back.

Three.

This convention, of course, is on a different order, an operation of enormous scope and size. There are 100,000 ticket holders, and bodyguards and studio publicity and hair and makeup, and big stars throwing parties that smaller stars hope to attend. Josie's itinerary includes a long list of parties she could have gone to last night, had she so desired, and also "optional lounges," sponsored by corporations or magazines, where she could go to "relax and escape the rush" for the price of being photographed while she did so.

The first item on today's agenda, after 6:15 hair and makeup and 8:15 breakfast and briefing, is the roundtable discussion for the Syfy special. She needs to be on for this, so she's glad that she managed to sleep last night. In fact, she slept so deeply she missed the alarm and woke to hair and makeup knocking on her door, and while they adjusted her appearance, she drifted between realities, playing out reunion scenes with Charlie. All through breakfast, trying to ignore this alternate life, she concentrates intensely on what the others are saying, so intensely that she sometimes doesn't realize it's her turn to speak. This doesn't bode well for the roundtable.

The moderator is a magazine writer who was a big early promoter of the show. He greets Josie with admiration and delight, and then after he poses his first question ("What's it like to be all together again?"), there's a moment of silence before she realizes the whole table is looking at her. Not at Cecelia, not at Max, but at her. They're deferring to her, waiting for her to answer. Of course! When it comes to this show, she never stopped being the star.

All right. Okay. She's team captain. She knows that job. In fact, that job is a welcome relief from her thoughts. That job insists she be *here*. She speaks first when it's clear no one's sure what to say, she brings up funny anecdotes about Max and Cecelia and tosses them the ball, she draws out August, who's shy and has barely spoken. She talks about Bill's fantastic scripts, her admiration and gratitude. She sets a good example. Everyone is sweetly grateful. Everyone is charmingly sincere.

As the hour winds down, the moderator asks her, "What was it like when Max left the show?"

"Oh," Josie says. She glances at Max. "That was awful."

"We were so broken up," Max says. "We could barely get through our last scene together."

"What was your last scene?" the moderator asks.

They say together, "It was a fight." Josie goes on, "It was that fight that goes wrong, early in the episode, when Bronwyn accidentally punches Malachi."

"It was supposed to be funny," Bill interjects. "But they kept playing it like it was the saddest thing in the world."

"It wasn't *just* supposed to be funny," Josie says. "Bronwyn was so angry at him for leaving. That punch wasn't completely accidental."

Bill smiles fondly at her. "That's why I loved working with you. You really understood that character. You really understood my writing." He adds, in a self-mocking tone, "You really got me."

"So the good-bye scene wasn't the last one you filmed?" the moderator asks.

"No, but it felt like it in the moment," Max says.

Bill says, "You'd like to be able to shoot things in order so the actors could follow the natural emotional arc. Like, how much easier to let them cry and emote in their actual final scene than try to stop them in one that has a completely different tone. But, alas, there's scheduling guest stars and locations and money and stuff."

"Petty concerns," Cecelia says with a smile.

"So the good-bye scene was also hard to shoot," the moderator says.

"Yes," Max and Josie say together. Then Max says, "I really felt like I was saying good-bye to my first love. Remember, Josie was my first on-screen love. Our relationship, on-screen and off, was profoundly important to me."

The moderator looks at Josie. She shakes her head. "I'm afraid to talk about it. I'm honestly afraid I'll cry."

Max rises from his seat and rounds the table to give her a hug. *"Aw,"* everybody says. Josie swallows hard. She tells herself she is acting so that she can hug him back and not worry about giving him the wrong impression, so that she can keep this team-captain feeling of being in control. But wouldn't it be nice to let him hold her while she wept, mourning the end of the idea of him. That beautiful idea, which could have saved her from facing the real-life loss of Charlie.

"You guys were great," the moderator says, when the cameras are off and he's shaking everybody's hand. "Please make a movie."

They laugh and thank him and walk out together with the kind of mutual understanding particular to a group of people who once shared a purposeful intimacy. They have seven more interviews to do before the panel, which starts at three. Max complains of his hangover. Cecelia is giddy about her all-but-certain part and exhausted from being kept awake most of the night by her giddiness. But Josie is warmed up now, and my God, it feels so good to do something right. The interviews are brief segments of banter for the internet, and she knocks them down one after another like a batter whose every swing connects. Publicity and their bodyguards shepherd them from one hotel to another, hair and makeup in frantic action as they go. Max grows increasingly sluggish and Cecelia's answers begin to tend toward the inchoate but that's okay, because Josie is on. "Thank God for you," Cecelia says, after Josie rescues her from an incoherent, rambling answer. "I forgot how good you are at this."

Josie says, "I did, too."

At two o'clock, they're escorted through back hallways into a tiny room in the convention center, where they eat boxed lunches of turkey sandwiches and apples. The moderator, a woman named Patricia, goes over the run of show: introductions, clips of deleted scenes from the new DVD set, Q & A. Even Josie feels her exhaustion now that she's sitting down, confronting how ravenous she is, so ravenous that she eats the entire subpar sandwich. She sags into her chair, and there is Charlie, back in her head again, without distractions to keep him and his silence at bay. If things were normal, she'd call or text him during a break like this. *Go away*, she thinks, although, of course, she wants the opposite.

When, one by one, their names get called, and they hear the audience roaring to convince them they are loved—don't worry, they aren't tired anymore. Bill comes out last, lifting two bottles of champagne above his head. From beneath the table he produces plastic champagne flutes. Max pops the corks, to whooping and applause, and Cecelia fills the flutes and passes them down the line. "To *Alter Ego*," one of the other actors cries, and Max adds, "To twenty years!" and Josie adds, "To Bill!" and then Bill, of course, says, "To the cast!" and then Cecelia and Max simultaneously say, "To Josie!" and the crowd erupts in cheers. They clink glasses with whomever they can reach, wearing wide misty smiles. Then, as the crowd calms down, Josie leans into the mic and says, "Let's do this," and the cheering starts again.

The questions recycle much of what they've already talked about today—what was it like to work with each other, what were their favorite episodes—but with considerably greater specificity, as the more intense the fans, the more they want to know why you made that particular face when you said that particular line. Josie is ready and waiting for the kiss question. She's surprised it takes as long as it does. She's pleased as well as surprised, as it suggests the show really is the thing they care about.

Then a little girl, about eight or nine, wearing a shirt that bears an image of Josie's much younger face, comes to the mic. The crowd murmurs its approval of her precocious fandom. "Hi, sweetie," Josie says. "Do you have a question?"

"Yes," she says.

"What is it?"

"Are you and Max dating?"

The crowd laughs, and so does Josie. "That's not what I was expecting," she says. "Did your mother tell you to ask that?"

The child shakes her head. "You kissed," she says.

"You saw that picture?"

"No," the child says. "My dad told me. He wanted me to ask."

The audience erupts in cheers and laughter.

"Where's your dad?" Josie asks.

The girl points out a man, also wearing an *Alter Ego* shirt, grinning and blushing hard. He waves.

"Sent your kid to do your dirty work, huh?" Josie says.

He shrugs elaborately, palms up to the ceiling.

"You must really want to know."

"Yeah," he shouts. "We all want to know."

The audience shouts and claps its agreement.

"Sorry," Josie says. She shakes her head. "Nothing to know."

"Just a friendly good-bye," Max says. "Between friends." The audience groans, and he says, "I know. It's disappointing."

Cecelia says, "They're friends who used to make out a lot. It gets to be a habit."

Josie nods in a way that allows as how she's right.

The girl says, "Okay," and winds her way back toward her dad. The woman who was waiting behind her abandons whatever she'd meant to ask in favor of a follow-up. "So you and Max have never been a couple?"

"We are not now and never have been a couple. I swear." Josie looks at Max, and says, in mock dismay, "No one ever believes us."

"It's all the making out," Cecelia says. "It's confusing."

"Make out now!" someone shouts.

"Are you crazy?" Josie frowns with mock reproof in the shouter's direction. "What kind of convention do you think this is?"

"It's not a bad idea," Max says, to whoops of agreement.

"Next question," Bill says, waving away this conversation.

The woman at the mic moves as if to relinquish her spot but then darts back with animal abruptness, startling the man who was stepping up to the mic. She blurts, "Are you pregnant?" Then she jolts off to the side.

"What? No." Josie looks down. "But I am getting rid of this dress."

The audience laughs.

"Okay," Max says. "That was weird."

"Yeah, but why did she ask me that?"

"You don't look pregnant," Cecelia says.

"Thank you, Cecelia."

Cecelia nods. "I got your back."

"None of us thinks you look pregnant," Bill says. He turns to the audience. "Does anyone think she looks pregnant?"

"No!" they roar back.

"Okay, but I'd still like to know why she asked me that." She leans back, then into the mic again, deepening her voice. "Not to be too neurotic." The audience laughs. "But seriously. Where'd she go?"

"Here!" someone shouts, and Josie spots the woman and waves her back.

"Come explain yourself," Max says.

The man waiting his turn at the mic steps ostentatiously back as the woman returns. She says, with sheepish pleasure, "I just always wanted you and Max to have a baby."

Josie lets her mouth fall open. "You're kidding."

"I always thought it would be a really cute baby."

"So just a breeding program," Cecelia says. "Not a comment on your outfit."

"Okay. I'll accept that."

"Let's get this back on track," Bill says. "I think what the audience really wants to know is, Max, are you pregnant?"

Max takes a comic pause. "How'd you know?"

Bill shrugs. "You have a glow."

Cecelia points at the man who's been waiting. "You have an important question. I can tell all this banter's driving you nuts."

"No, it's funny," he says, without conviction, and the audience roars again.

"We're not funny," Max says sorrowfully.

"What's your question?" Cecelia asks.

"It's actually for you," the man says.

"Wonderful."

"I want to know, when Vivi was evil . . ." The man goes on talking, and Cecelia gives a good answer, the audience sighing its appreciation in response. Josie listens but doesn't. She makes what she hopes are properly attentive faces. She's done so well today—she's pretended there is no weirdness with Max, she's hardly thought about Charlie at all—but now she's rattled. Why is she so rattled? She takes a good long swig of her champagne, hears someone shout, "Go Josie!" and lifts her empty glass in salute. A voice in her head speaks with startling conviction. *You shouldn't have done that*, it says. *Because you're pregnant.*

Four.

When you're scheduled for a photo shoot on the *TV Guide* yacht, and then, twenty minutes later at another location, an on-camera interview with the *Insider*, and then, at yet another location, a step and repeat (or, as Josie's itinerary puts it, "intimate red carpet and roundtable interviews"), and then a party the studio is throwing for fans who won a contest for access ("mandatory to stay for two hours as the studio is paying for your room"), and then after that, if she can still stand to wear her heels, the *Entertainment Weekly* party, it's hard to figure out when and how to acquire a pregnancy test. Because she will not be alone until she's dropped back at the hotel to get ready between the step and repeat and the fan party, and she'll have only an hour then, and she couldn't go alone to a drugstore because she has no car. Should she ask her driver to take her to a drugstore? Then Cyrus will definitely come along. Maybe hotels have pregnancy tests they can send up to your room, like a toothbrush or a sewing kit.

Josie makes these calculations sitting at a stoplight in a Mercedes van with her eyes closed, feeling the gentle pressure of eye shadow being applied. The makeup girl is holding her breath as she touches

Josie up, which Josie knows because, as she leaned in with her applicator right before Josie closed her eyes, she took a breath and held it with puffed-out cheeks. This must be what she does when she's concentrating. Josie wonders if she's aware that she does that and assumes no because it's so funny-looking, and then changes her mind because this makeup girl seems pretty comfortable in her own skin, doesn't even wear makeup herself, which is interesting for someone who's devoted her life to the beautification of the human face. Of the *countenance*. Josie is a keen observer of physical quirks. They are so telling and so useful. And she's fascinated by people without self-consciousness, people who seem to be making no effort at concealment. She hopes this girl knows about her cheek puffing and doesn't give a shit. Josie sits in the middle seat, with the girl on one side and Max on the other, and she feels Max's leg against hers and knows he's deliberately letting it stay there. "It's amazing that you can do that in a car and make no mistakes," he says to the makeup girl. "You have steady hands." Josie has to marvel at Max. His leg against hers—the woman he's "a little in love with"—and still he's talking to another woman with that hey-girl tone.

"Yep," the girl says, with a crisp lack of interest, and Josie is pleased. Good for you, makeup girl. Would the makeup girl go get her a pregnancy test? Maybe. But then would she tell anyone? Maybe her lack of concealment extends to answering, "How was your day?" with "Josie Lamar gave me a hundred bucks to go buy a pregnancy test." Would that be too much or not enough? What's the going rate for that job? The girl is working on her lips now, but Josie keeps her eyes closed. It's unnerving to look at a face so close to your face.

Even if Josie could get to the drugstore before the party, this seems a dangerous time and place to make an embarrassing purchase. Fans abound, as do their cell phones. She's got red hair and is easily spotted. She doesn't have time to don a hoodie and sunglasses, and then change into her cocktail dress. She doesn't even have a hoodie with her. She'd have to buy a hoodie, then change into it, somehow get to the drugstore and back, then get ready for the party, and also anyone who saw her, with the convention going on, is likely to assume that someone wearing a hoodie and sunglasses inside is famous. Right now, concealment and announcement are pretty much the same thing.

Josie dislikes people walking behind her, the feeling of a presence at her back, the sound of approaching footsteps, and this is yet another reason to resent Cyrus, who is so close behind her as they approach the yacht that she has an urge to stop and see if he crashes into her. Except she doesn't want to fall down in her heels, and Cecelia's in front of her and they'd all go down like dominoes, and then what if she miscarried or something? Does that actually happen from falling, like in old movies or *Downton Abbey*? *You're not pregnant*, she tells herself, but herself does not believe her. The idea that she is arrived with a clarifying conviction. Her weepiness, her hunger, her tight pants—these things suddenly make sense, as they would on TV, where people never seem to realize they're pregnant even as they're copiously vomiting. Josie has always seen this obliviousness as belonging purely to narrative, divorced from reality, and yet. She's an idiot. She can't remember the last time she had a period. At least she's not vomiting.

She can't possibly be pregnant.

Well, yes, she can *possibly* be. But it's such a strange idea.

If she is, she'll need to tell Charlie. Charlie who hasn't called her back. She could text him the news. She feels a verge-of-tears hilarity. Does her iPhone contain a baby emoticon?

They will be on this yacht for only twenty-five minutes, according to their strictly executed schedule, but the idea is to look like they're at a party for the photos. Someone gives them each a gift bag: Josie's contains several lip glosses, more makeup, and a Smartwater. She doesn't really know what to do with it and is relieved when Cyrus takes it from her without a word. Maybe he wants to inspect it for bombs. The actors strike playful poses and laugh with extra vigor and answer questions about what's on their iPods. "I don't have an iPod," Josie says irritably, and then sees the questioner's taken-aback expression. Dutifully, Josie course corrects, listing her favorite songs. Except all she can think of are Charlie's favorite songs, so she just lists those.

She could put on a costume, like actors sometimes do to walk the convention floor. It would have to be a face-covering costume. Like what, Spiderman? Where would she get a Spiderman costume in time for a run to the drugstore? "Anyone you're excited to meet?" someone asks her, and she would dearly love to blurt out something bizarre and unhinged just to puncture the idea that what's happening here is anything less than absurd. Why are they all pretending to be partying on a yacht? Why is everyone taking that in stride? Why is every solution she thinks of ridiculous? Because she can't think of a solution. That's why. She names a famous actress she'd like to meet. She asks Cyrus for her Smartwater and knocks it back like it's alcohol. She wishes that Charlie were here. Maybe Charlie *is* here, wandering the convention floor in a Spiderman costume. Charlie is a lover of comic books and video games and superhero movies. She should go walk the floor, pulling off all the masks. But they won't let her walk the floor at all. Before the panel started, she asked a convention employee, a man in a headset with a clipboard, if they could walk the floor for a few minutes, and he reacted as if she'd asked to run inside a burning building. "You'd get mobbed," he said, in that tone of finality people use when they want to scare you into dropping the subject.

She looks at Cyrus standing there with his giant hand clasped around the handle of her little gift bag and imagines trying to persuade him to take her onto the floor. Maybe he'd do it if she rode on

his shoulders where no one could reach her, and then he'd methodi-
cally pull off the masks of everyone wearing them, or at least everyone wearing them who appeared to be a six-foot-two man. This is a
vivid picture in her mind. She's losing it.

She really has to know if she is or isn't.

When they get back in the van, Josie deliberately heads for the
back instead of sitting beside Max like she has been all day so she
won't have to worry about Max seeing what she's doing on her
phone. On the way to the next interview, she checks Charlie's social
media again. Still nothing.

She manages to switch on the charm for the *ET* interview—she
thinks—but the effort that takes distracts her from the formation of
a workable plan. As they walk the two blocks between one hotel and
the next—in a tight cluster with the bodyguards on the outside, parting the seas—they pass a drugstore. Josie hesitates and nearly trips
August. He puts his hand on her shoulder to steady himself, and she
apologizes and keeps walking.

All right. Enough dithering. It's time for action. Their destination
in sight, she deliberately slows her steps, knowing Cyrus will slow
his, good soldier that he is. By the time they reach the elevator, he
and she are a couple of paces behind the pack. She stops so he'll stop,
too. She looks him in the eye. "You keep a lot of secrets, right?"

He reacts just like he did when she tried to draw him out yesterday, many, many moons ago. "Yes, ma'am," he says, then clamps his
mouth shut and refuses the eye contact, signaling that she can't make
him talk. Good. Great. He's the man for the job.

"I have a request."

"Yes, ma'am."

This does not surprise him. But whatever he's expecting, it's most
definitely not what she says. "Could you go back to that drugstore
we passed and get me a pregnancy test?"

He blinks. That's it on the reaction, but still she feels a gleeful triumph at having caught him off guard. There's an upside, people! "Yes, ma'am." He clears his throat. "Any particular brand?"

"I'm not picky. But I don't have any cash. I'll have to pay you back."

"That's not a problem."

She nods, and he nods, and then she hustles—everybody's calling her—through the open elevator doors.

The press room is set up with a red carpet—a red carpet to nowhere—and then six tables with six journalists each. It's an obstacle course. The actors take photos alone and in all possible combinations with one another and answer questions into iPhones and recorders and cameras. Josie's mind tracks Cyrus's progress. He must be back to the store by now; he must have found the right aisle. She can see him as if on camera, sternly considering his options. For Cyrus, every choice is a serious one. How will he deliver the thing to her? Surely he won't just hand it to her in a see-through plastic bag. Even double bagged is no good—it would still be clear she'd sent her bodyguard to the drugstore for an embarrassing personal item, and either people would ask and tease, or they wouldn't ask, signaling their speculations were worse. What if he is too discreet, as seems more likely, waiting until everyone is safely in their hotel rooms before he brings the test to her door? She wants to take that test the instant she's alone.

Automatically she turns slightly to the side for photos, hand on her hip, tightening her stomach. And how much longer will she be able to do *that*? She catches herself putting her hand on her stomach and jerks it back to her hip where it belongs. Going table to table, she stares at the recording devices before her, ready to catch each and every one of her words and then release them again into the internet, where they will live forever, poor words, drifting ghosts, unable to die. What words does she offer to the shiny, glowing phones? She doesn't say a single thing that matters. What a lot of effort has gone into the acquisition of these unimportant words.

When it's over, she finds Cyrus waiting right outside the door. She allows herself to lag behind again. When everyone else is ahead of them, he hands her the gift bag from the yacht, heavier now. Good job, soldier.

"I got you two," he says, in a confidential murmur. "One early response and one regular, with two in the box. Three total."

He must have children, a wife who once needed pregnancy tests. He seems convinced she'll want to use all three. She thanks him. He holds out his arm for her to proceed before him. "Ma'am," he says.

Five.

Back in his room, Max showers and dons his favorite suit, which is the exact match of his character's favorite suit, and wonders what's going on with Josie. He'd been sure the vibe between them was mutual, so sure that he'd anticipated ending up in her bed last night, but something shifted at the hotel bar, and try as he might, he can't remember why. The memories from later that night are hazy with booze. Is she being standoffish today—changing seats to get away from him in the van—purely because she doesn't want to sleep with him? Max isn't used to people trying to get away from him. Because Max doesn't push. He offers. He doesn't push. If she's worried that he'll read her public flirtiness as real or if she read his that way, well, that's annoying. She should know he knows the game as well as she does. Today has been a performance. Except for the talk during the Syfy special about their last scenes together. That was real. He hugged her because he wanted to, not because the cameras were on. No matter what, there is something real between them, something that no one but the two of them will ever understand.

In the van on the way to the fan party, she sits in the front row again, but this time by the window. He sits next to her so as not to make a show of not doing so, and she gives him a wan smile and then turns her gaze to the window. Waves of energy have been coming off her, last night and today and when he saw her after that taping—all kinds of energy, performative and sexual and also authoritative, which he'd enjoyed witnessing again, because the few times he's seen her in the last several years she's had her wattage down low, and in the old days he found her unshowy confidence to be one of her most attractive qualities. But now she's giving off no energy at all. She's gone very, very still. He doesn't try to talk to her because it couldn't be any more obvious that she doesn't want to talk. He turns to Cecelia, on his other side. "How did the fans get tickets to this party? What did they have to do?"

Cecelia shrugs. "Prove they were our biggest fans?"

"What would that involve?"

"Dress up like us?"

"Get tattoos of our faces?"

From behind them, Bill says, "Recite an episode from memory."

And Daniel says, "Change their names to Bronwyn or Malachi."

"That would be an impressive commitment," Max says.

"Hey," Bill says. "Don't you question my naming."

"I'd never question you," Max says. "I say what you tell me to say."

Josie turns from the window with eyes gone flat. "It was a website contest. They just entered their e-mails."

Max nods, but Josie has already turned back to the window. He looks at Cecelia with eyebrows raised and she shrugs. The van is silent for a moment, and then August and Bill start a conversation about a movie they both just saw.

He loses her for a while at the party, which takes place around a pool on a hotel rooftop. They're there to talk to fans, and so he talks to fans. The cocktails on offer are named for the characters. He, of course, orders a Malachi, which he's pretty sure contains Campari and Grand Marnier. More than one fan comes up to him and says, "I'm drinking a Malachi," some of them shyly and some of them knowingly and some of them with nervous aggression, and if the fan is a woman, he says, "I'm flattered," and ponies up his most charming smile, and if the fan is a man, he says, "Cheers!" and clinks his glass.

About an hour into the party, he extracts himself from a particularly garrulous fan—when you're as charming as Max, this isn't hard; he just rests a hand lightly on her shoulder and says, "It's been so nice talking to you," and leaves her still vibrating to his touch. He finds Josie with two women, a mother and daughter, who are showing her their Bronwyn action figures. "I don't know if I've ever seen this one before," Josie says, holding a little self in her hands. "I don't remember this outfit."

"That's from season four," the mother says.

"You don't have them?" the daughter asks. "I mean, they don't give them to you?"

"They did. I don't know if they gave me all of them. I didn't keep them—I gave them to my mother, and I think she gave some to other relatives. I didn't really know what to do with them."

"I think I'd keep them," the mother says.

"Oh, I probably kept a couple." She hands the figure back to the daughter. "They're in a box somewhere."

Max, watching the exchange from a couple feet away, can see the mother and daughter are disappointed in Josie's lackluster display of interest. He steps in, holds out his hand. "Can I have a look at that?"

The two women simultaneously startle, then blush.

"Hi," he says, grinning. "I'm Max."

The daughter hands him the figure without a word. He holds it up to the light and examines it with care. "This one really looks like you, Josie," he says. He puts it back in the daughter's hand, lets his fingertips linger just a moment in her palm. "The first Bronwyn they made looked nothing like her. They brought it to set to show her, and we all came to see, because we were all excited. And as soon as she picked it up to look at it, the head popped off. The guy, whoever he was—from the toy company? Or the studio? I can't remember. He was embarrassed. He kept saying the final version wouldn't lose its head like that."

"That's right," Josie says. "You said to the guy, 'Don't worry, Josie's head pops off, too.'"

The mother and daughter laugh. That line was an embellishment—or at least Max doesn't remember saying it. Good. She's making an effort.

"Why don't I take a picture?" Max says. "You two, Josie, little Josie."

They're delighted, beaming at him as the daughter, who's quicker, offers up her phone. Josie moves between them, puts an arm around each, and they produce two of the action figures and each holds one. Everyone smiles except the tiny Bronwyns, who must at all times be ready to fight.

"There you go." Max returns the phone. That's right, ladies. Max Hammons touched your phone! "The real thing."

They thank him and Josie profusely, and Max sees his moment. "I want to introduce Josie to someone." He tells them it's been lovely to meet them and they're out.

He touches Josie's arm to guide her in the right direction. "Did I really say that?"

"What?"

"About your head popping off."

She shrugs. "You could have. They liked it. Where are we going?"

"There's a VIP area. To let us take breaks. But only short breaks."

"There is?"

"The publicist told us when we came in."

Josie nods as if she's already lost interest.

The VIP area is a large cabana with a small bar and lounge chairs inside. No one in there but the bartender. Max escorts Josie to the chair farthest from the entrance. She sits with an air of just doing what she's told. "What are you drinking?" he asks her.

"Water."

"Have you tried a Bronwyn?"

She shakes her head.

"Do you want one?" He smiles. "They're powerful." Though he hasn't had one yet.

"No thanks."

So he gets one for himself. It tastes like absinthe and rum. "This will knock me on my ass," he tells Josie. "Just like you."

She summons the faintest glimmer of a smile. She won't make eye contact, her gaze skittering away every time he tries. His sense of patient effort suddenly gives way and he feels offended, perhaps even grievously. Can't she see he's trying to take care of her? Then he registers that she's struggling not to cry.

One afternoon, when he was Malachi and she was Bronwyn and they were sitting on set between takes of a passionate scene, waiting for a camera adjustment, he obeyed an impulse to keep touching her. He picked up her hand. They weren't in private—though they had a privacy between them, belonging as they did to a world no one else in the room inhabited—and if they had been in private, to touch her when they weren't acting was a complicated thing. So now he'd taken her hand and needed a purpose for having done so. He turned her palm up and wrote HI in it with his finger. She looked at him quizzically so he did it again. She got it and smiled. Then he traced the word SLOW, meaning they were taking forever and he was impatient to get back into the scene, to plug back into that energy before it drained away. She nodded. He turned his hand up so she could reply. Very slowly, her finger tickling his palm, she wrote STAY. She

paused and looked at him. He nodded and she went on: WITH. ME.
Then even more slowly—his heartbeat rapid now, the cameras forgotten—she wrote MALACHI.

That's the real thing between you, Max. She was Bronwyn. You
were Malachi.

He has a pen in his pocket, ready for autographs. He takes it out,
picks up her palm, and writes WHAT'S WRONG? across it.

She closes her fist around the question. She doesn't look at him.
He thinks she's not going to answer. Then she holds out her hand for
the pen, and he gives it to her and opens his palm. She takes his hand
and writes, I'M PREGNANT. She allows him a moment to look at it,
then takes his wet cocktail napkin and scrubs the words from his
palm.

"Charlie's?" he asks.

She nods.

"You just learned this?"

"Today." She smiles ruefully. "I sent my bodyguard to buy a test.
Bet that's a first. Or, who knows, maybe not." Now she looks at him.
"It was that question in the panel. Suddenly I knew it."

"You really called it on them wanting us to have babies."

"I really did." Her eyes glisten. She presses a finger to one, then
the other.

"Does Charlie know?" *She's pregnant*, he thinks. *She's pregnant.* It
hits him that he's tired and a little bit sad.

"I can't get hold of him. He won't call me back. I don't even know
where he is."

"You'll find him."

"I don't think that he wants to be found. At least not by me."

"You'll find him."

"If I do find him, what do I say?"

"Natalia said to me, 'Guess what?' and I knew."

"You were trying?"

193

He nods.

"Were you happy?"

"Yeah, I was."

"Do you think he'll be happy?"

His first instinct is to say *Of course* or *Who wouldn't be?* He suppresses it in favor of the truth. "I don't know the guy."

She lets out a long breath. "Shit."

"Listen, call him now."

"What? Now?"

"Just get it done. It'll be better when it's done."

"Oh God. I don't know if I can."

"I'll stay right with you. We'll come up with a line and you'll say it. And just look at me. You can say it to me."

"What line?"

"Say, 'Hi, it's me.'"

"Not 'Hi, it's Josie'?"

"Do you want to be formal or intimate?"

"I don't know. What should I be?"

"Intimate," he says. "Definitely intimate."

"Okay. So I say, 'Hi, it's me.'"

"And then something to prepare him, like, 'I have some news.'"

"'Hi, it's me, I have some news.' He'll probably think I got a part."

"Or another guy."

"So, something after 'I have news'?"

"How about, 'I'm sorry not to tell you this in person'?"

"Then he'll think I'm sick. I've got cancer or an STD."

"Or another guy."

"He'll be prepped for bad news. Do I want him prepped for bad news?"

"If the pregnancy's bad news, you prepared him. If it's good news, he's extra thrilled. If it's okay news, it'll seem better because he'll be relieved."

She's nodding intently. "You're right. You're absolutely right." She snaps open her clutch and extracts her phone, presses the screen, then abruptly loses her air of authoritative certainty. She looks at Max with fear.

"Say it to me."

She lifts the phone to her ear, grips his hand tightly with her free one. She keeps her eyes on him. She says the line.

"Good," he says. "Good."

She's looking at the phone in her hands. "What do I do if he still doesn't call me back?"

He puts his arm around her. He does this instead of saying he doesn't know. This is a moment, for Max, of piercing regret. Not because he won't be sleeping with her, or not only because of that. Because it occurs to him that this is as close as he's ever come in his real-life time with Josie to the intimacy they had when they were not themselves, to the way he felt about her on the show.

VI.

What happens to a human being when he, for some reason, undergoes tragic (or heroic) experiences? We will stress only one feature of such a state of mind: he feels as if the average boundaries of his ego are broken; he feels that psychologically as well as physically he is exposed to certain forces which are much stronger, much more powerful than he himself. His tragic experience comes, takes possession of him and shakes his entire being . . . This sensation remains the same whether it is caused by an inner tragic conflict, as in the case of Hamlet's main conflicts, or whether the blow comes from outside and is brought about by destiny, as in the instance of King Lear.

—**MICHAEL CHEKHOV,** *To the Actor*

One.

The hike is a trudging misery—step, step, slip, step, step. Charlie knows the thud of a boot on rock; the squelch of a boot in mud; the slide of a boot down a damp rock; the wet clunk of a boot slipping off a rock into water; the crackle of a boot on a dead leaf; the crisping of a boot on a live leaf; the snap of a boot on a twig; the scrape of one boot brushing the other; the susurration of a boot on sand; the grinding of a boot on gravel; the woodblock skitter of a boot on a nut or a fat stick, too tough to break, shooting backward, and jerking him forward. He knows the twinge beneath his right kneecap and the aching stiffness on the inside of his left one. The blistered heel, the cramping toes, the sore ankle that turns when he steps funny on a rock. How it feels to trudge uphill watching your feet, finding purchase on roots and rocks and indentations in the mud, and look up hoping to see an end to the incline and see no end. Small insects gather near his eyes and nose and mouth, and sometimes he closes an eye as one flies too close and catches its wet soft body between his eyelids. Sometimes he picks one off his tongue. He kills mosquito after mosquito and still wakes in his hammock itching from the bites, his legs reshaped by a multiplicity of swellings.

What if he hadn't followed Adan? Would he be free? Would he be dead?

What does it matter? He followed him.

Given a map and all the time in the world, Charlie could never re-create their route. They never stay long on any well-maintained trail—though Adan told him at the beginning, "They can't look for us on the trails, Ben. Not enough police," as though Charlie would find this reassuring. Often they walk straight into the jungle, Adan and Thomas leading the way, slashing with machetes in a haphazard manner that leads Charlie to believe they haven't had much practice at this. How do they know where they're going? He asks Adan, and the younger man shrugs and points behind him at Denise. Denise gives Charlie a hard stare. "We will get there," she says. Where is there? He doesn't ask. Does she know, or is she waiting for the thunderclap of inspiration? He can't decide whether it's more frightening to believe that Denise doesn't have a plan, or that she does.

He's thirsty. He's always thirsty. But he tries not to ask for water too often. He tries to limit the number of times he gets told no. Behind the decrepit shelter that was their meeting place, under a tarp and a pile of branches, the kidnappers had stashed supplies. Everyone has a backpack with a water pouch and drinking tube except Charlie, so when Denise does allow him water, he has to bend and sip it from Adan's pack like a baby cow. There are extra packs, but she wouldn't give him one. The others carry the extras in their hands.

Off trail, they walk through plants so tall that Charlie has to raise his arms high not to be snagged by them. As his calf brushes against the plants, it connects with something that gives him a sharp stinging pain that endures and endures. At every pause, he touches it to see if he can find something to extract—a stinger, a thorn, a needle—but there is nothing. They pass boulders so large they seem alien, or the fossils of enormous beasts, a great ridged rock like the spine of a dinosaur. Atop the boulders, gardens of small plants, parasites of the larger creature. Cascading down one boulder is a plant Charlie recognizes as a succulent. His father gardens. His father grew succulents around the fish pond in their backyard, in their neat, ordered backyard, all the plants contained in beds. In this jungle are fragrant squashed fruits, sweet and rotting, large thick vines grown into braids and loops, the remains of spindly trees tangled in a pile, as if they'd died grappling. Trees whose roots swell out above the ground, fat and fantastically shaped. Pregnant trees. Trees like creatures that go still when a human passes. Mud and shit-brown streams of mud.

The terrain is uneven. Denise sets a rapid pace. Charlie sometimes makes the mistake of looking up from his feet and stumbles over a rock or a root. He's been weakened by confinement. The others are sure-footed, and more than once he thinks of the barefoot girls in bikinis who passed him early on his voluntary hike, their feet practically folding over the rocks, toes gripping. Their smiles, their braided hair, their casual athleticism and easy grace. Sometimes Denise calls a halt to stop and listen for pursuers, and in the absence of their noise, Charlie hears birds and water and once, far above, the muted roar of an airplane—*Down here!* he thinks. So many different qualities of water sound: the dripping off the cliff face behind him, the burbling over one section of rocks below, the rushing over another, almost indistinguishable from wind. The call and repeat of sweet cartoon birdsong always seems far away, the birds nearby peeping shrilly or uttering harsh guttural clacks of remonstrance or warning. Sometimes there's a crashing through the foliage, and Charlie looks to see only the plants moving in something's wake. What is the something? Once he sees a spider as big as his hand crawling up a tree. Once they hear a thunderous crack and watch a tree fall.

It's dark under the tree canopy, and he misses the sun, until those moments when the canopy gives way and the sun shoots in with eager ferocity, and then he wishes it away again. From time to time, a sudden deeper darkness comes, and then rain percussive on the leaves. At first the rain is a relief and then it becomes a misery. His clothes are always either wet or damp. He is a human swamp.

Sometime in the second day, Charlie sees the remains of a path beneath his feet and looks up just in time to see a sign that reads, in multiple languages, WARNING. TRAIL CLOSED. CONDITIONS PERILOUS. RISK OF SEVERE INJURY OR DEATH. "Severe injury or death," he says, stopping so abruptly that Adan bumps him from behind. He turns to Adan, pointing at the sign. "Severe injury or death," he says again.

Adan leans forward to read the sign, squinting in a way that makes Charlie wonder if he needs glasses. Perhaps he's doing all this to earn the money for glasses. That is his *object*. *What's my motivation?* Charlie imagines Adan asking Denise. Denise is the director, of course, though not the sort who wants to discuss motivation. The sort who tenses with exasperation—the actor is being pretentious again, the actor thinks he *matters*—and tells you to hit your mark and say the line. Adan squints for such a long time that Denise and Thomas, not realizing they've stopped, disappear around a bend. Charlie looks at his concerned, uncertain face. *We could escape now, Adan*, he thinks, but, of course, Adan has no interest in escape. Adan is the one who brought him here. "I will ask, Ben," he says, finally. And then, as if he read Charlie's mind, he nudges him gently forward with the barrel of his gun.

True to his word, when they catch up, Adan asks, or at least Charlie assumes he does, not speaking the language. Denise turns and fires a rat-a-tat-tat of words that Charlie can't understand but can readily translate. Hit your mark. Say the line. Charlie knew that would happen. Charlie knows human behavior, which is a kind of prophetic power. Why does he try to fight prophecy? Up ahead, somewhere he can't yet see, a possible death crouches in a thicket of perilous conditions. He goes on trudging toward it, because that is what helplessness is. The director doesn't care about your motivation. The reporter's loyalty is to the magazine, not to you. The pa-

parazzi take your picture whether or not you wave. The people who love you don't really know you. The person who knows you says she has to try not to love you anymore. You can't control the rapid snare drum of your heartbeat or the bass thump of your dread. Your own legs walk you forward, but even that is not in your control. Your body is not your own, has never been your own, at least not since you began to offer it up for possession. *You always have a choice.* How many characters have uttered this line, wearing the appropriate face of grim, judgmental resolution? Bullshit! Bullshit! And yet, if he's ever given this line to say, ever given the chance to say a line again, he might have to convince himself he believes it. He might not have the power to refuse.

Is it because he's afraid that it happens? Does he bring it on himself? Did he bring all of this on himself? Yes or no, here is what happens: He is working his way along a trail that hugs the cliff face 3,000 feet up, barely wider than his foot, and then slants steeply down. He has passed more warning signs doing this, the final one reading STOP. HIGH RISK OF FALLING. He has his hands on the dirt above him, his body pressed into it as much as possible. His palms and fingers are coated with reddish mud. He reaches for a branch to help him around a curve, and the branch gives way when he puts weight on it, and he slips. He slips, and he slides, scrabbling frantically. He slides forever. This is not true—he slides for a few seconds—except that it is true. He slides forever. He doesn't make a sound, but his whole body screams. Then—he doesn't know how, will never know how—his toe finds a rock and his hand finds a root, and he is not falling anymore. He is not falling anymore. He is not falling anymore.

After the scream, silence. Except Charlie's breathing, which is loud. His right hand grips the root. His left toes press down on the rock. He pats gingerly at the dirt with his left hand, finds nothing to hold on to. He can find nothing with his right foot, either, but when he presses his leg forward, his knee slides into an indentation, for which he is so grateful. He shifts some weight onto his knee. Then he looks up. He sees their three faces looking down, a halo of sunlight behind them. They look terrified, even Denise, a fact he registers with a mild, distant surprise. They are closer than he expected. He didn't fall very far—ten feet, to be precise—but to fall at all 3,000 feet above sea level with no discernible way to climb back up is to fall very far. "I told you," he says. "I told you. I told you. I told you."

He hears them consulting, but even if he spoke their language, he wouldn't be able to understand them. His mind is a whirring blankness. It spins and throws out this thought—*I told you*—and then spins and throws it out again. Beyond that, there is only his knee, his toes, his fingers, imploring dirt and rock and root to hold.

Above him, Adan is terrified. He just watched Charlie—or Ben, as he knows him—slip and slide and fall, and he could do nothing to stop it. He doesn't know if Ben screamed because he could only hear his own scream, which stopped when he saw Ben's hands catch the root. But now Ben is dangling there and he looks so scared, and he says, "I told you," which is true. Adan has enormous capacity for empathy, though this situation has required him to block off certain channels down which it might run. To do so, he's told himself a story: Ben is his guest and his friend; he treats him well and takes care of him, and when this is over, Ben will go back to his privileged American life none the worse for his time with Adan, and yet what a gift his time will have given them! Money for all the many things Adan and his family need—school uniforms and decent mattresses and dental care. It is nothing for Ben to do this for them.

But if Ben dies now, if Ben plunges all that long way screaming, this story will be hard to tell. It will not have a happy ending for any of them. Adan will be complicit in snatching a man from his life and flinging him to his death. Also, Denise will almost certainly blame him because he is the one who was walking behind Ben. He is the one who was supposed to be watching him. He is responsible.

"Ben! Ben!" he shouts over the edge. He can see only Ben's hands clinging to the root, his outstretched arms, his upturned, terrified face, all dangling over a pit of despair. He has to save him. "I will save you, Ben!" he shouts, though he has no idea how.

Charlie thinks, as Adan's face disappears, *I will die with people who don't even know my name.* But, of course, he won't die with them. He will die alone. He will be a great unsolved Hollywood mystery, at least for a little while. What happened to Charlie Outlaw? Where did Charlie Outlaw go? Maybe they'll make a TV movie. Will they think he killed himself? *Will Josie . . . Josie!* he thinks. *Josie!* "Adan, can you do it?" he calls up. "Adan!" His arms tremble, tremble, tremble.

Adan reappears. "We make a rope, Ben."

"Make a rope? Out of what?"

"Out of . . ." Adan makes a frustrated noise. "Out of sleep." From behind him, Denise says something sharp. "Hold on, Ben!" He vanishes again.

Out of sleep? Out of sleep? What Adan means is that they're attempting to fashion a rope out of the string hammocks they've been using at night. Thomas, who's good at knots, is carefully tying them together with the tip of his tongue protruding from the corner of his mouth. But Adan couldn't summon the English word for hammock, and Charlie can't make sense of what he said instead. Out of sleep? "Adan!" he calls, in a sudden intensification of his panic, because when he can't see Adan, he is alone, he's alone, he's going to die, he is alone, he can't do it, he can't hold on, he can't survive this, his arms are shaking so hard, what will it feel like to fall so far? Once he starts to fall, will he keep on thinking, like he is now, that somehow he might survive? Or will he feel death's certainty? Would it be better or worse to be certain? How much pain will he feel on impact? Will death be instantaneous? Are they lying when they say death was instantaneous? How do they know? Will he lose consciousness in the air? Will he die in the air from fear?

Is the best he can hope for that he will die in the air from fear?

A few months ago, he was hoping he'd be nominated for an Emmy. They submitted the episode where his character's father died. Charlie was really good in that episode, or at least that's what everybody said. "Adan!" he shouts again, and when he can see Adan, he asks, "Can you do it?"

Adan frowns. "I try, Ben. Hold on, Ben. Hold on." Gone again.

"I can't hold on!" he shouts after him. "I don't know if I can hold on!"

"Hold on," he hears, faintly, from above.

If he gets back to Josie, he will do anything she wants. He will swear off parties, waving at photographers, smiling in selfies with fans. He will let everyone hate him as long as she doesn't. He will not need anyone else's love. He won't care anymore.

He will never get back to Josie.

"Adan!"

"Hold on . . ."

Beneath his knee, he feels the dirt shift, as if preparing itself to give way. It's so clear in his mind—the root pulling loose, the cascade of red dirt and rocks, his body falling. He can see it as if it's already been filmed. The trembling has colonized his body. His teeth chatter. His jaw hums. His legs vibrate against the cliff, helping it toward dissolution. He can't hold on.

Fear will not help you, Charlie. Remember what it is that you can do better than almost anyone in the world. You can make yourself believe in what you know isn't real. You are the violinist and the violin. Transform yourself and you transform reality. In one of Uta Hagen's books, she describes a director and designer arguing about how to create a downpour onstage. The lead actor stopped them cold: "Pardon me, but when I enter it will rain." Charlie's long forgotten the actor's name (it was Albert Bassermann) but easily recalls the line. He wrote it on a strip of paper and tacked it above his bed, re-read it most nights before he tumbled into sleep, reciting it like a charm. *Pardon me, but when I enter it will rain.*

What he's doing right now is nothing he hasn't done before. What actor has not spent time dangling off of something? A window ledge, a bridge, a fire escape. He survived all that. Don't remember the process, Charlie—the harness and the stunt double and the air bag that caught you when you fell. Remember only how it felt to believe you were holding on to save your life and that you could hold on to save your life. Remember determination. Remember faith. He believes the root will hold, the rock will hold, the dirt will hold. Faced with danger, he will narrow his eyes and firm his jaw. He could chase a helicopter, leap after it into the air. That is how sure he is that he can hold on. Josie is up there, though he can't see her. Josie is up there, and any minute now she'll throw down a rope.

How long can his self-convincing work? It can work for a little while. Belief must be renewed. In a play, the other actors help you with this. They react to what you said as though you didn't say it last night or the twenty-seven nights before, and you find your own surprise again. Be in the moment. Concentrate on your object. You have no idea what's coming next.

A minute passes, and then another. Hours pass. Days.

At first, he thinks a projectile is flying at him, but it's the impro-vised rope, skittering down the slope, sending dirt clods and pebbles at his face. He turns his head aside, not fast enough to keep grit out of his eyes or his teeth, and sways alarmingly. The rope stops two feet above him. Are they expecting him to grab it? He could lunge for a helicopter. But there is nothing for him to push off of to make a lunge. If he tries and misses, he will fall.

"Ben!" Adan leans precariously over, the hammock rope wrapped thickly around his waist. "I'm coming down!"

"Coming down?" Charlie repeats. "How? Where?"

Adan points and Charlie turns his head—carefully, carefully—to see a platform of rock, two feet wide, about four feet to his right.

"How, how," Charlie says, but not loud enough to be heard, and anyway Adan is already climbing down, moving slowly but sure-footed from rock to rock and slowly but sure-handed from branch to bush. Charlie watches in a terrifyingly hopeful suspense. One slip and Adan will fall. The rope might catch him or it might unravel, not actually being a rope, and if Adan falls and the rope holds and dangles him there like a child on a tire swing, will Thomas and Denise be able to pull him back up? Charlie wishes he knew what kind of movie he was watching, action or true-life survival or tragedy. When you know what kind of story it is, it's possible to predict whether anyone will die. Also, he'd like to know if he's the main character or if it's one of them. He's been thinking all along, as everyone does, that he is, but the main character must have the power to affect the narrative. Adan is the one taking action. Adan is the one standing on the platform, shooting Charlie a smile of achievement and relief, then letting resolution settle over his face as he unwinds the rope from his waist. Adan is the one with a plan.

"We put this around you, Ben," he says. "Then you . . ." He makes an arc in the air from Charlie to himself.

"I jump?"

"You step. You step."

Adan comes to the very edge of his platform, holding the rope with both hands. Above him in Charlie's direction is another, larger root, and Adan tests it, tugging hard, then nods with satisfaction. He holds on to it with his right hand and leans out as far as he can to offer Charlie the rope with his left.

Charlie takes a breath. He keeps his eyes on the rope, only on the rope. He lets go with his right hand to grab it. His left arm accelerates its trembling with the added strain. He pulls the rope across his stomach, pressing it between himself and the cliff. Then he grabs the root with his right hand again, pauses for breath, lets go with his left, and pulls the rope around himself. He manages to fling the end over the length that stretches between him and Adan, so when he lets go to return his left hand, the rope stays. "Yes, Ben," Adan has been saying the whole time. "Good, Ben. Yes, Ben, yes."

Now his right hand again. He pulls the rope through the loop around his waist to make a knot. Then he does it again. Will it hold if he slips? Maybe not. Probably not. He has no idea.

"Now," Adan says. He points at a small rock halfway between them, at another root just above it. "Step . . ." He pantomimes reaching and stepping. "You step. I pull the rope. You grab my hand."

So here is what Charlie has to do. He has to let go with his right hand, reach for that root, push to the right with his left foot, reach his foot for that rock, let go with his left hand, grab the root with it, reach for Adan's hand, swing his foot to the platform. He has to trust the rope. He has to trust Adan. Teachers and fight coordinators and choreographers and directors and other actors have all told him to do this and then do that, and he has obeyed, and so he should be able to obey Adan; this is nothing he hasn't done before except it *is* something he's never done before, and after they tell you what to do, you sometimes make a mistake anyway, but you get to run it again or do another take.

He pictures himself on the platform. He tells himself it has already happened. Then it's hand, foot, hand, foot, Adan pulling the rope taut and the root giving, but he's quick to the next one and it holds.

He's on the platform.

"Okay," he says. "Okay, okay, okay." He's still holding Adan's hand. He wobbles. Adan grabs him, puts both arms around him. Adan hugs him.

"We did it, Ben," he says.

"We still have to get back up," Charlie says into his ear. He is lean-

ing on Adan, his legs trembling so hard it's all he can do not to collapse against him entirely. This is a strange intimacy, like none he's
ever experienced. He's not conscious of noting that; he's too busy
trying to persuade his mind and body that it will be better to finish
the job of climbing back up than to live forever on this platform, this
blessed little utopia.

Adan steps back from Charlie, keeping an arm around his shoulder. "Ben, you see?" He points up the slope to the trail. "You see how
I came?"

Charlie nods, gazing up. He's not sure he does see. Above him,
Thomas and Denise peer down. He can't make out their expressions,
but he sees Denise's swinging braids. Denise calls down something.
Adan replies. She and Thomas disappear again.

"I told them you are ready," Adan says. He pats Charlie gently.
"They pull, I push, you go."

The longer Charlie hesitates, the harder this will be, so he doesn't
hesitate. They pull, Adan pushes, he goes. He is a body. He is a scrabbling animal. All he wants is his life.

Once Thomas and Denise have hauled him the last few inches
onto the trail, he crawls away from the edge and leans against the
cliff. Up here, nobody hugs him. They don't even speak. He tries to
take the rope off but his hands shake so badly that he can't undo the
knot. Thomas comes over and swiftly undoes it, pushes Charlie forward, neither roughly nor gently, so he can unwind the rope from his
waist, then moves to throw the rope back down to Adan. Charlie
puts his hands on the trail on either side of him. The dirt is warm.
He doesn't want to cry in front of them. He doesn't want to cry.

Adan calls something from below, and Denise turns to Charlie.
"Help," she says.

He crawls back to where they are. He doesn't trust his legs. He
takes hold of the rope, behind Denise, and pulls as hard as he can until
Adan is on the trail. Then he crawls away again. He watches as the

three of them slap one another on the back, as Thomas unties the rope from the tree, separates the hammocks. Denise inspects the hammocks, frowning, and then she balls them up and returns them to the packs. He watches Adan approach, crouch to offer him water, which he drinks. "I saved you, Ben!" Adan says. Charlie nods. Adan beams. He watches Denise approach, Thomas at her heels. "Up," she says. She steps over his legs and walks on past, so sure of herself she doesn't even pause to confirm obedience. Once Thomas has walked on, too, Adan helps Charlie to his feet. He keeps his hand on Charlie's shoulder as they walk single file, and Charlie is grateful for that, and grateful, too, for the warm dirt of the cliff face above him, which he hugs so closely that he will stain the side of his shirt red. He watches the shifting muscles in Thomas's back, the swinging tails of Denise's braid. He watches the trail retreat from the edge of the cliff, curving back into trees and then widening until two people could walk side by side. Though they don't. There is no way to fall here. There is nowhere to fall. It hits him with force that now he won't fall. He feels like a skeleton enchanted into animation at the moment the enchantment ends.

A few more steps to a boulder and then he collapses. First, he sits on the boulder, then he slides down it until he's sitting on the ground with his back against rock. Adan hesitates next to him, looks entreatingly after Thomas and Denise, who haven't noticed that Charlie stopped. "We go, Ben," he tries, but Charlie feels no inclination to respond. He rubs the soft moss growing on the boulder, which feels to him very much like the fur of a dog. "Ben, we go," Adan pleads. Charlie closes his eyes. He turns his face to press his cheek against the moss. He hears Adan's shifting feet as he hesitates. He touches Charlie on the shoulder, but Charlie doesn't open his eyes. "Ben," he whispers.

Charlie thinks, *That's not my name.*

Adan calls after Denise and Thomas. His footsteps move away. Charlie imagines he is alone. He would like to be alone. But all three of them return, their voices rising, that pleading note still in Adan's.

Denise's voice is like knives. Charlie doesn't care. The knives fly past him. He doesn't flinch. "Get up," Denise says. Charlie doesn't even bother to shake his head. She prods him with her foot. "Get up." Listen, Denise, who do you think you're dealing with? Charlie has been dead many times. He knows how to be still. He can slow his breathing until you'd think he wasn't breathing at all. He won't even flutter an eyelid.

Now she prods him with the gun against his leg. Subtle. "Get up," she says, layering threat on threat in her tone. She moves the gun up, pushes the muzzle hard enough against his shoulder that he slips and opens his eyes. He's angry that she got him to open his eyes. "We move now," she says.

He shakes his head. Adan starts to speak, but she interrupts him with two harsh words. She steps back and aims the gun at him. "Get up now."

"No," he says.

"Now."

"I'm going to rest. If you don't like it, shoot me."

"Now."

"Shoot me." He doesn't even look at her, though if he'd been acting, he might have stared her down as he said the line. Maybe not. It would've depended on the role. Everything depends on the role. He closes his eyes again. If she is going to shoot him, he sees no reason to watch.

She doesn't shoot him. She lowers the gun, shrugs, says something to the other two that makes them laugh. Charlie hears them move away, settle down somewhere, talking and then not talking. He doesn't know what happens after that. His mind releases him into unconsciousness, and for a while he sleeps.

He wakes to Adan gently shaking his arm. "Ben. Wake up, Ben." When he sees Charlie's eyes open, he sits back, satisfied. "Good. You rested. Now we go."

Charlie looks at Adan from far away. "No."

Adan's eyes widen. "Ben, we go now." He glances back over his shoulder. "She—"

"Fuck her."

"Ben, no. No. We need to go." Adan hesitates. "I tell you something." He drops his voice to a murmur, looks Charlie earnestly in the eye. "Darius—not police. Not police, Ben."

"What do you mean?"

"Police not . . ." He pantomimes shooting.

"The police didn't shoot Darius?"

"Yes, Ben. They not shoot."

"Who shot him then?"

Adan sighs. "Denise."

"Denise shot Darius?"

Adan nods solemnly.

All the muscles in Charlie's body tighten. "Why?"

Adan hunts for the words. "If police catch Darius . . ." He mimes grabbing. "Denise think Darius . . ." Now he rotates his hand up and away from his mouth in the gesture that usually indicates singing.

"Darius would sing?"

"Yes," Adan says, with an emphatic pleasure at his understanding, and Charlie feels an absurd urge to laugh because Adan doesn't get the pun. Adan is just confused about the right word. Adan straightens out of his crouch. "Denise," he says, with a rueful headshake. He holds his hand down to Charlie.

Denise shot Darius. Charlie didn't prove, when he defied her, that Denise wouldn't go so far as to kill him. All he proved was that she didn't kill him right then. The spot where she pushed her gun muzzle into his shoulder throbs as if it's bruised.

You always have a choice. What choice does Charlie have? He takes Adan's hand, gets wobbly to his feet.

Two.

The pregnant woman in the waiting room is doing a terrible job of pretending not to watch Josie. Under the impression that she's getting away with it, because Josie appears to be absorbed in her phone, she is flat-out studying her now, her head cocked, her mouth slightly open. When she first looked up from her own phone and noticed Josie—in the row across from hers, two seats down—she quickly looked away again, then snuck one surreptitious glance after another, but Josie never glanced up, and she grew emboldened.

The woman takes in Josie's red hair—ponytailed; her face—no makeup; her sandals—silver, with a cork-bed sole. Josie wears cropped jeans and a loose-fitting blue-and-white shirt, and sometimes the woman thinks she sees a slight abdominal curve under that shirt, and sometimes she thinks that's just the shirt. The internet can't solve the mystery: She searches *Josie Lamar pregnant* and finds only gossip long past its expiration date. She has a thrilling little hope that Josie is pregnant, that they'll meet again and again here in the doctor's waiting room, that they'll turn out to have due dates only a few days apart—though Josie will have to be a lot more pregnant than she looks, because the woman is already five months along. And Josie will also be having a girl, and they'll decide to get together outside the waiting room, first for new-mom commiseration and later, when the girls are older, for playdates, and the girls will grow up best friends, and she'll say casually, "Yeah, Josie and I are meeting at the playground this morning," and her daughter will be so used to hanging out with a celebrity that she won't even think it's remarkable. She'll be one of those people who downplays her intimacy with the famous, knowing that the information makes other people get weird.

She calls up the camera on her phone, turns off the flash, holds it up, smiles like she's taking a selfie, and clicks. She checks the picture. Josie's in profile from several feet away, and her hair looks darker than it is, so you might not recognize her if you didn't know her. She wants to send the photo to her sister because her sister figured out that she liked girls when she was twelve and got a huge, huge crush on Josie. They had a poster of Josie on the wall in their shared bedroom. Damn, she wishes it was a better photo. Should she risk another one? Should she ask if Josie will take one with her? Now she'd like Josie to look up, because maybe she would smile and seem friendly, and then she'd ask her. Her sister would just go right up to her and ask, no sneaking around, no hesitation at all. Her sister would be so thrilled! She wishes she were here.

Josie knows the woman is watching her. At the moment of recognition, Josie felt the other woman's sudden still alertness and focused more intently on her phone, though she is not reading what she is supposedly reading, which is a revised script for a studio test tomorrow that she's only just learned she has. The show is a comedy about an actress who has a meltdown and goes home to take over her small-town local theater company. The first-round audition was right before the convention, and her manager told her they weren't interested in her, so Josie hasn't thought about the part since. Revisions sent today for an audition in front of twenty people tomorrow: This is not a recipe for success. She's left a message with her manager asking if she can reschedule. She doesn't have the energy for a studio test. She doesn't have the energy to stare back at the other woman in a way that will make her stop watching, so she is pretending not to notice because that is as close as she can come to privacy. She has an unpleasant fluttering sensation high in her chest, which feels like her heart has slipped its mooring, and she wonders if this is the precursor to an anxiety attack or a pregnancy thing. She's never experienced either so she doesn't know.

Her appointment was forty-five minutes ago. The sign by the receptionist's window reads: IF IT IS MORE THAN THIRTY MINUTES PAST YOUR APPOINTMENT TIME, PLEASE LET US KNOW. But if she gets up and goes to the window, the woman's eyes will track her, the woman might even take the opportunity to speak to her, and, oh God, she doesn't want to talk to an eager, fascinated stranger right after she's peed in a cup, while she waits to put her feet in stirrups and confirm that she's pregnant at the age of forty-one by an ex-boyfriend who won't call her back and hasn't been home any of the three times she's gone by. His house has a shut-up air, as if he's out of town. She still has a key and has thought of using it, hunting clues to his whereabouts, but what if he's changed the alarm code and she ends up explaining herself to the police? *Has Josie Lamar lost it?* Alter Ego *actress caught breaking into her ex's house after photos show her canoodling with former costar.* And then a link to the police report. That probably wouldn't happen. But it might. What were the chances someone would catch her kissing Max? But someone did. And Charlie has almost certainly seen that picture. He was always a little jealous of Max. Will he believe that nothing happened? Will he doubt that the baby is his? Will they end up a sordid gossip item about custody battles and paternity tests?

She doesn't want to go alone into Charlie's dark and silent house.

She doesn't want to log on to his computer—she knows his password, her name plus her birthday—and find an e-mail in which he tells his best friend, Tony, that she's stalking him and Tony advises him not to call her back. She doesn't want to learn that he's changed his password. She doesn't want to confront evidence of some new love affair, doesn't want to bear witness to his absence, his abandoned house, his lonely things. She just wants him to appear. Please, Charlie. Just appear.

He must be on vacation somewhere, because if he was away doing a movie, she'd be able to discover that online. Charlie, as she knows him, would be instagramming the hell out of travel, but his hiatus from social media continues. If she really wants to find him, she has to send an e-mail or make a phone call she dreads: to his mother or his father or one of his sisters or one of his friends or his agent or his manager or or or. She can't bear the thought. Not because there aren't some perfectly nice people on that list, but because she's his ex-girlfriend—who broke up with him, who's been photographed kissing someone else—and it is inherently strange to be his ex-girlfriend and contact someone to ask where he's gone on vacation and how she can reach him there. And what will be her excuse? And what if he's traveling with another woman? She's been waiting for confirmation from the doctor that this is a viable pregnancy. Once she knows, then she can decide whether she can stand to wait for Charlie to resurface or whether she has to find him now.

She doesn't want Charlie to have seen that picture because it will have hurt him. Even if he's stopped loving her? Yes, even then. No one wants to imagine he could be so quickly replaced. She hopes he hasn't seen it, but alas for the information age, she knows he has. He's seen it, his parents have seen it, his sisters have seen it, his friends have seen it, his costars have seen it. She's exposed him to ridicule or smug faux sympathy or genuine sympathy that will catch him off guard, render him vulnerable, someone's kind words a quick shove into emotions he'd rather not feel. Or maybe he's not wounded but bitter and angry, and she's given him the excuse he needed to hate her. And now he hates her. He hates her now. Though she's never known him bitter and angry. She's never seen him like that. One gossip site ran the photo with *Sorry, Charlie* scrawled across it. If he has any capacity for bitter and angry—and who doesn't, who doesn't— please don't let him have seen that.

Now fifty minutes have passed. She sighs hard and lifts her face toward the ceiling, and she shouldn't have done that, because the other woman spots an opening. "They're slow today," she says.

Shit. Josie looks at her. She's smiling with a sweet and nervous eagerness, one hand resting on her belly the way pregnant women do. She has a soft, plump face, presumably plumper with the pregnancy.

"They're not usually this bad," she continues.

Josie nods.

"They'll be twenty minutes late, but not, like, *forty*. Are you way past your appointment? I bet they'll call you soon. Could I take a picture with you?"

"What?" Josie says, because this last sentence came out in an incomprehensible rush.

The woman's soft face pinkens. "Could I take a picture with you? For my sister. She loves you."

"Your sister loves me," Josie repeats, as if she can't understand the words, as if it's the first time she's been told a stranger loves her, or the friend or relative of a stranger loves her, when it's the hundredth time or the millionth.

"She's a lesbian," the woman says.

"Oh," Josie says, through a stifled, startled laugh. *Well, in that case,* she thinks but doesn't say, because why tease this pink pregnant woman who hasn't the least idea that she's tormenting her and hasn't the least intention of torment? She just wants a picture for her sister.

She just wants to express her love. *Here's a photo of Josie Lamar waiting for her pelvic exam!* "Sure," Josie says.

The woman pushes herself out of her chair and her belly comes at Josie like a ball she's supposed to catch. *Soon I'll look like that,* Josie thinks but can't believe it. "Phew," the woman says. "I can't believe I'm going to keep getting bigger."

"Right," Josie says.

"You just keep growing!" the woman says. "It's crazy. When are you due?"

"Um," Josie says, and is spared expanding because the woman is positioning herself now in the chair next to Josie's. She leans in. She holds the phone up, realizes she hasn't reversed the camera's direction, laughs nervously, fixes that, holds the phone up again. Josie sees herself in its tiny screen, first just half her face, then, as the woman adjusts the angle, all of it. She'd like to shut her eyes. The woman's cheek touches her cheek, her belly touches her arm, firm and insistent, and Josie does her best to smile.

The woman relaxes back into her seat, looking at her phone with an unabashed grin. "I took a couple," she says. "This one's the best." She shows the shot to Josie, and Josie tries not to wince. Josie watches as she texts the photo to someone named Ashleigh—her sister, Josie assumes—and then seconds later the phone chimes and a green bubble filled with *OMG!!!!!!!!!!!!* appears. The woman shows the bubble to Josie with a gratified laugh. "She loves you," she says, eyes on the screen, thumbs flying, and Josie says, "I'm just going . . . ," and heads for the receptionist's desk.

The receptionist is sorry for the wait. She'll let the nurse know.

Josie turns very slowly from the desk. The woman seems involved in her texting, but then she looks up and flashes Josie an expectant smile. And Josie left her bag in the seat next to hers. Why did she do that? Because it would've seemed rude to pick it up. Why, oh why, does she have to care about these things?

She's almost at the seat when her phone starts to ring, and she snatches up her bag and extracts it with a disproportionate rush of gratitude. It's her manager. She withdraws—politely!—to an unoccupied part of the room.

"I can't reschedule," her manager tells her. "I'm sorry."

"Today's just . . . really busy, and this is so last minute."

"I know; I'm sorry. But . . ."

Josie guesses what that trailing off means. She tests her hypothesis. "I thought they didn't want to see me."

"Oh, the role's changed. They want to see a lot of different things."

"So they want to see me but they won't reschedule."

"They want to see all three of you tomorrow."

"It's such late notice with revised sides."

"I know." Her manager sighs. "One of my other clients dropped out of the test. She booked another show."

"And you talked them into replacing her with me."

"Their instinct is that you're not right for the part, but they know you're talented, Josie. They're willing to give it another shot. Otherwise they wouldn't see you."

"But I come tomorrow or not at all."

At last, a nurse appears in the doorway of the waiting room, a folder in her hand. "Josie Lamar?" she calls.

"You'd be great for this, Josie," her manager says.

"Okay."

"You'd really be great."

"Okay, sure. Sure. I'll do my best. Right now I have to go." Then her manager says a lot of things really fast, and Josie agrees and agrees while the nurse stands near the scale smiling a tight, impatient smile.

Josie has gained seven pounds. Her blood pressure is a little high.

In the examining room, the nurse tells her to take off everything below the waist and points at a paper blanket, assures her the doctor will be right in. Josie hears the *thunk* of her file dropping into the box on the door. She obeys the nurse, folds her jeans and underwear neatly together, and puts them on a chair with her bag. She sits on the edge of the table with the paper over her lap, tries to adjust it so the curve of her buttock isn't visible, imagines the woman from the waiting room suddenly appearing in the doorway, phone at the ready. Flash. Flash.

What is she thinking, saying yes to a studio test tomorrow, when they don't even want to see her?

Seven pounds!

Do other women feel quite so disheartened by a seven-pound uptick? Ridiculous question. She knows that they do. She just likes to imagine that she could let go of that concern if her appearance wasn't so important to her job. Oh, the special torture of recording a DVD commentary, attempting insights and funny anecdotes over the background drone of insecurity. Oh God, I could have done that scene so much better. Why am I making that face? Why did they use that take? Why did I let them do that to my hair? Why do I look like that? Why do I sound like that? Why is that the way I *walk*? Some people, given access to her mind in those moments, might accuse her of being a self-obsessed narcissist, but those same people, looking at photos of her with plumper cheeks or a belly roll, would write in the comments that she'd let herself go. *The very same people.* She is supposed to look perfect without seeming to care that she looks perfect; she is supposed to age gracefully while somehow not aging at all. *He's so cute and she's a hag.* You can't win, she knows that, and sometimes she resolves to stop trying. But if it was in her nature to stop trying, she wouldn't be an actress.

When she walks into that studio test tomorrow, she will not be prepared, and they will all immediately notice the seven pounds.

Where are you, Charlie?

She closes her eyes. The paper is scratchy and uncomfortable. It wouldn't do her any good to cry. Already she's been crying an unaccustomed amount. Let's blame pregnancy for that, too.

Her phone announces a Twitter notification, and grasping at distraction, she retrieves it. *Me and @josielamar at the ob's office!* And then a photo of the waiting-room woman—@katiebird—and Josie with their cheeks touching, Josie wearing a smile that to her looks strained and terrified. Josie watches as responses appear. *OMG is she pregnant?* Someone else tweets a link to the picture of her kissing Max, and then someone else tweets one of her at the convention with her hand on her stomach. *I think so!* @katiebird tweets. *She said she didn't know when she was due.*

She wonders if the woman's last name is Bird or if her parents called her Katiebird or if it's a cutesy moniker she gave herself. Bird tweets, get it? What Josie actually said was "um."

The door opens and Josie startles. The doctor comes in. She's a compact Asian woman with close-cropped hair and a brisk, reassuring manner, and Josie must look stricken because the doctor crosses quickly to her and puts a hand on her shoulder. "So you're pregnant," she says.

Josie leans over to drop her phone in her bag. All through the appointment, punctuating the doctor's matter-of-fact descriptions of terrifying tests, the thumping whoosh of the baby's heart, she can hear the phone faintly chiming.

Three.

Remember how Charlie wanted that feeling of being where no one could find him? Ha. Ha. Ha. Welcome to the edge of the world.

The edge of the world is a beach, which makes sense, because from here there is no going forward, and because every wish Charlie makes comes true in the worst possible way. So, of course, he has been spilled out from confinement into vastness, the endless, endless ocean, bigger than anything. He knows he's not afloat but still solidly on land, sand in every nook and cranny. But afloat is how he feels when he sits with his back to the forest and them—Adan, Thomas, and Denise—and keeps his gaze on the moving water, imagining where each wave came from, the daunting miles each droplet traveled. Darius is not with them because Darius is dead. Darius is dead because Denise shot him. What it looked like when Darius died is one of the things Charlie tries not to think about, keeping his gaze on the water.

They want him on the beach where they can see him from the semicircle they've set up between beach and jungle, blocking his path. He protested that he'd get sunburned, and Adan produced a beach towel from one of the packs and gave it to him with a dampened version of his usual expectation of gratitude. Even the unnaturally cheerful Adan is finding these circumstances less than ideal. Now Charlie sits all day with the beach towel draped over his head wishing he could retract his long limbs until every part of him was under its protection. He rotates whichever part of his body is in the sun, keeping a leg out until he feels the skin tighten and warm, then switching. He's managed to avoid a bad burn, which is better than the opposite. The towel is printed with a skull and crossbones and says LEGOLAND FLORIDA PIRATES' COVE. How did they acquire it? Why did they bring it? He doesn't care. He's lost all curiosity about them. He doesn't give a fuck what their perspective is. Denise won't let him move back into the shade, where they are, not even when the sun is at its most insistent. So she can see him, she says, but Charlie knows he's the ant, she's the kid with the magnifying glass.

She's the woman with the gun.

Today, all Charlie has eaten is a package of cheese crackers. Yesterday, dried mango and trail mix and a couple of granola bars. The kidnappers are almost as hungry, Adan perhaps equally so because he snuck some of his share to Charlie when Denise wasn't looking. Now they are waiting for Mystery to show up in a boat with supplies. And when will she? And what if she doesn't? Add those questions to the list of things not to think about. The water is so blue. Blue as . . . what? Blue as blue. He's losing all descriptors. If he were on a transcendental retreat, he imagines this is what he'd be doing, depriving himself on purpose, staring at the water until all that was unnecessary fell away. And left . . . what? To be stripped down to the essential self, is that a good thing or a bad?

What is the essential self? He pictures it as something very, very small.

Since his show of rebellion, Denise has been hell-bent on reasserting her power. The rest of the hike she stopped periodically, waited for him to catch up, jabbed him under the ribs with her gun as he passed. She'd say something to Adan—maybe it was different somethings, maybe the same something, but to Charlie, whatever she said sounded like "Let's kill him," and then Adan would say something back that had, to Charlie's ear, a note of pleading remonstrance, and then Denise would laugh or fire rapid speech or say absolutely nothing, which was probably the worst. After that, she'd speed past Charlie, wait a little while to play the scene again with minor variations. He walked with tension tightening and depleting his already exhausted muscles. He flinched whenever he saw her waiting for him, his body anticipating that sharp muzzle in his side. At night, she ordered Adan or Thomas to sit awake watching him while he slept. Thomas paced and muttered beside Charlie's hammock, so when he had guard duty, Charlie's sleep was shallow and full of bright, restless dreams. Even when Charlie had to dig a hole and squat over it, Denise insisted that Adan or Thomas stand guard and glance over from time to time. Still here, guys! Did you think I dug the hole to China?

But Charlie did prove something when he refused to keep walking, and her displays of dominance don't disprove it. Charlie understands now that he still has power. To use it, he just has to be willing to risk his life.

He is so hungry. What would he eat right now, given any option in the world? The breakfast sandwich from the place in West Hollywood. A sundae from Graeter's in Cincinnati, hot fudge on black raspberry chip, whipped cream. His father's Cincinnati chili, steeped for hours with cinnamon and chocolate shavings in the crockpot, which he hasn't had in years because he no longer eats beef. No— *dolsot bibimbap. Dolsot bibimbap* from the Korean place where he used to go with Josie. They went there so often that they were recognized as regulars instead of people from TV. After they broke up—after she broke up with him—he went four times in a week hoping to run into her, but she never came, and he hasn't been since because it hurts, and even to crave the *bibimbap* hurts, but *bibimbap* is what he would like to eat right now. They both prefer it with tofu instead of meat. The dish comes steaming in a black stone bowl, too hot to touch, an egg sizzling atop the rice and vegetables. The waitress stirs in the bright red pepper paste—they both like it spicy—and then Charlie picks up a slender slice of mushroom with his chopsticks and eats it, his face pleasantly warm and dewy from the steam. Josie says, "Don't burn yourself again," because Charlie has trouble waiting for the rice to cool, and the roof of his mouth has suffered many times for his impatience. "It smells so good," he says, and she laughs though nothing is funny. She laughs with pleasure: They are together; they are about to eat this food. She says, "Eat the last dumpling." There were seven *yaki mandu* and they each ate three and politely left the last one sitting there. He picks it up with his chopsticks and bites it in half, and then offers the other half to her, and she eats the dumpling and then dips her finger into what's left of the sauce and licks it. "So rude," he says. "So unladylike." She grins at him and repeats the action. He stirs his *bibimbap*, risks a bite: The rice that was at the bottom of the bowl comes to the top golden and crispy.

"You just burned yourself, didn't you?" Josie says, and Charlie says, "Worth it."

"You have no regrets?"

"I'd do it again."

"And you will."

"I love you," he says. "Do you hear me? Can you hear me? I love you."

A shadow falls over him. Charlie looks up to see that Adan is suddenly standing beside him, and at the same time, he registers that he's been dimly aware of a buzzing sound, at first mingling with the sound of the waves and then growing ever more distinct. "Ben!" Adan says, but he doesn't stay to explain whether that was fear or excitement making him exclaim. Adan runs over the sand to the edge of the world, lifting his hand to his eyes as a small boat comes into view. He turns and shouts something at Denise and Thomas, waving them forward. Charlie waits until they've passed him to get slowly to his feet. As he stands, he realizes one of his legs and a spot on his lower back have fallen asleep, so he shakes the leg, rubs the spot on his back. He starts to drop his towel, but if he does, one of them might take it, so he drapes it over his shoulders and ties it loosely at the front. He can't risk another loss.

Adan, Thomas, and Denise currently have no interest in Charlie's towel. They're paying no attention to Charlie at all, engaged as they are in helping Mystery—because it's Mystery in the boat, arriving just as they said she would. They wade out to pull her in, and once her boat is onshore, they begin to unload the supplies. An impulse to go help them surfaces. He notes and then discards this impulse, which, of course, under different circumstances he'd follow. One of the many oddities of this experience is how the ordinary impulses arise in these extraordinary circumstances, and now he remembers the moment on the platform, after his fall, when Adan hugged him, and what Charlie felt was *rescued*. Here are feelings that go with being rescued: gratitude, relief, comfort, indebtedness, admiration. How deeply, bewilderingly at odds those feelings were with the fact that he is Adan's captive, that if he weren't Adan's captive he would never have fallen at all. Everything depends on the circumstances, on the other actors in the scene. He looks behind him at the jungle, the possibility of escape. He has no food. He has no water. He has no idea of the way. He doesn't think he could run that far before somebody shot him. His leg progresses painfully from numbness to feeling. His first impulse was to hang on to his towel. His second was to go help his captors unload the boat. He reacts to the stimulus of the moment just as he's been trained. Does he even have an essential self?

Denise looks around at him, as if she's just recollected her duty. Her gaze feels like the swinging of a gun in his direction, though her gun is on the ground. Perhaps he flinches, perhaps he looks sufficiently cowed standing there in his ridiculous towel—at any rate, she doesn't feel it's necessary to keep watching him. She says something to Mystery, who produces a white bag, stained with grease, from the boat. From this bag, Denise extracts something and takes a ferocious bite of it, chewing and swallowing before she passes the bag to Thomas. Mystery has brought them the fried pies, usually stuffed with ground beef, that can be found at roadside stands all over the island. Charlie hasn't had one because he doesn't eat beef. Ha ha ha! He doesn't eat beef!

Now: contradictory impulses, offshoots of the primal one for survival. To stay here away from Denise. To go over there and ask for food. Mystery saves him from decision, coming toward him with a pie in one hand and a plastic grocery bag in the other, and he is so grateful. Gratitude again!

She comes just close enough to extend the pie to him, then takes two steps back. She watches while he eats it, her air suggesting cautious satisfaction, like someone making progress in taming a feral child. He tells himself to eat slowly, to savor, but he can't. The pie is gone in an instant. It is delicious, though he doesn't really taste it. He licks his fingers and looks at her, hoping for another. She comes closer and holds out the bag. He restrains himself from snatching it and then tries to restrain his disappointment when he sees there's no food inside. The bag is full of magazines. "Thank you," he says.

She nods. "Something to read."

"Thank you," he says again.

"You are still hungry?"

"Yes."

She glances behind her—the others are completely absorbed by food consumption—and then pulls from her pocket another of those little wrapped chocolate cakes. She puts her finger to her lips. *"Shhhh."*

He thanks her, yet again, and eats the cake fast. She takes the empty wrapper from him and stuffs it in her pocket. "You read," she says.

He could eat more—he could eat so much more—but at least the intensity of his hunger has diminished. He tries to think like this: She brought me the food, she brought me the magazines, she has an interest in me and/or an innate kindness and maybe that can be exploited. Instead of like this: If I'm good, she'll take care of me! The latter response, a natural human reaction, is also how one trains a dog. It makes things easier that both lines of thought lead to the same action. He sits down and opens one of the magazines. Mystery watches for a moment—To confirm his obedience? To take pleasure in his pleasure?—and then rejoins the others. Satiated for the first time in days, they lounge on the beach like vacationers.

Charlie starts with the cover of the magazine, which promises a profile of a movie actor he's met once or twice. This actor is a handsome guy who first became famous for a gorgeous shirtlessness in mass entertainments but lately has been tackling more complicated roles. Charlie loved the actor's performance in the movie this profile is designed to promote—the magazine is three months old— so it takes restraint not to flip directly to the story. It's satisfying to exercise that restraint, as he could not do with the food. He starts at the beginning of the issue. He reads the table of contents. He reads the copy in the ads.

By the time he reaches the profile, two-thirds of the way into the magazine, he has a pleasant conviction of having earned it. But when the reporter describes the actor as "defensive" at a personal question, his pleasure turns quickly to annoyance. His annoyance increases when the reporter elicits from the actor the details of his preparation for the role, then comments that it's tempting to roll your eyes at his pretension. The article on the whole has a tone of fond condescension that infuriates Charlie. In fact, he feels a rage substantially out of proportion to the cause. The reporter wouldn't call an Oscar-winning critical darling pretentious even if he'd described his process in the exact same words. What does this writer know about acting? Has he ever done it? Has he ever stood alone on a stage? Or tried to believe he's alone and heartbroken with a camera two inches from his face? They permit you to think yourself an artist only once they've decided to anoint you one. Otherwise you need to cut the crap and do what you're told.

He drops the magazine, picks up another, flips it open with unnecessary force, and there is Josie. He recognizes her immediately, but it takes him a beat or two to realize that. First he feels a quick painful shock and only after does he understand why. The photo is of Josie kissing Max Hammons. Their lips are touching. Her eyes are closed. His hand is on her arm. Beneath it is a column of speculation suggesting that Josie and Max are now a couple, revisiting rumors that they were a couple in the past, that perhaps they've secretly been a couple all along.

Charlie glances up at the kidnappers to make sure they're not watching him. They're not. He checked because he's crying, and he doesn't want them to see him cry. He lies back on the sand and puts the magazine over his face. Rivulets run down his temples to dampen his hair. He tries to sniff inaudibly. In his weakened state, he believes every word he just read. Yes, it's a trashy magazine. He appeared in a gossip item in this magazine himself, at a restaurant with a costar he was never even remotely dating. But sometimes that shit is true. The article makes him believe, as he hasn't believed before, that the world will go on without him. In the story of Josie's life, he doesn't get a single mention. He doesn't matter. He isn't a person. In fact, he's a commodity, and in making him one aren't the kidnappers just completing the process he himself started? He doesn't matter, not even to Josie. He is an erasure mark. He will die out here—this thought hits him with the force of revelation. He's feared it many times, but now he believes it. He will die out here. He cries with a helplessness that feels like dissolving.

Suddenly he feels the magazine rising from his face, and he lifts his head, startled, to see Mystery regarding him. "You are all right?"

"I'm fine."

"I see you shaking."

"I'm fine."

She looks at the magazine. "This upset you?"

"No," he says.

"I can see you crying."

"I have a lot of reasons to be upset."

"You were not crying before the magazine. I thought you wanted the magazine."

"I did. I do."

"Then why do you cry?"

Why does he answer her? We all have moments when we can't resist the urge to say what's true. Charlie has those moments more than most. He points at Josie, frozen there like that. With Max Hammons! Who sprang out of Charlie's nightmares to take his place. He says, "I love her, and that's not me."

"You love this lady?"

"Yes."

Mystery holds the picture close to her eyes. He waits for her to laugh or frown with skepticism or at least ask another question. But she does a surprising thing. She reaches out to wipe his wet cheek with her finger, persisting through his automatic flinch. She looks from the picture to his face two or three times. Then she returns his magazine.

Four.

Three actresses sit on a long bench against the wall in a small antechamber; on either side of them are the doors to the bathrooms. All three parked outside the gates of a studio lot, then showed a photo ID to a security guard, who gave them badges that allowed them to proceed inside. They walked to a three-story building, entered a huge lobby, crossed it to the check-in desk. The guard at the desk has a quirk: He plays the saxophone while he sits there, a jazz sound track, sometimes sprightly, sometimes mournful, that to an anxious actor running lines in his head can be pleasant uplift or jangling interruption or ironic commentary. Whatever the feelings of these three women, they each smiled at the guard as they signed in at his desk. Then they went down the hall to the antechamber and took seats, one by one, on the bench.

Eventually the woman from the business affairs office came out with three clipboards containing their three contracts, and they signed. The contract woman has hair that makes one think of a cocker spaniel, but her demeanor is decidedly unfriendly, even mean. As she waited for all three of them to sign away seven years of their lives for a part only one of them will get, she embodied all the disappointment and cruelty of their business, or at the very least the fact that none of the contracts is an offer, that the women have to say yes first, like agreeing to a marriage in advance of the proposal just in case someone decides to propose. They all signed and smiled and thanked her as if they were already on camera.

Now they wait to be summoned, one at a time, by a casting assistant. That person will escort them into the office belonging to the studio's head of casting. In there are three couches positioned in a U-shape around a coffee table, a TV on the wall completing the square. The actor testing stands in front of the TV. The couches are crowded with nine people in suits. Six more people in suits sit in chairs squeezed behind the couches and wherever else they fit.

The actresses have twelve pages of material to perform once they enter the room, material revised since the original audition, for which all three of them had considerably more time to prepare. Each of them wishes the sides hadn't been revised or at least that they'd been given more time with the revisions. They don't care if the revisions have made the script better—they care about getting the part.

Two of the women know each other. In their twenties, they took improv classes together at the Upright Citizens Brigade. They are thirty-two and thirty-three, respectively, and they have each starred on a sitcom. One was part of an ensemble on a moderately success-ful show that ran five seasons. The other was a breakout character on a critically beloved, low-rated show that ran for three. One came very close to getting SNL. The other has had a couple of small but memo-rable film roles. Each sees the other as her primary competition, as it seems odd that the third woman is here to test at all, not being a comic actor. Maybe she knows the casting director.

The third woman—Josie—does not need access to their thoughts to know what's in them. She, too, wonders what she's doing there. Her agent came down on her quote for this, and yet she'd still guess it's higher than either of theirs. She's ten years older and more expensive and not known for comedy. Why would they hire her? They didn't even really want her to come in. Josie feels trapped in the sort of story she's always hated, the kind where characters exist only to demonstrate the inexorable workings of fate. She does not want to audition today. Auditioning today seems entirely futile. And yet she is helpless not to do it.

Last night, instead of prepping for this test, Josie went for a drink with Cecelia and did not have a drink. She marks that as the first choice she's made in fear of hurting the baby. Now she wonders if the anxiety she's feeling right now is hurting the baby. She sees the approaching edge of what will take some time to hit her fully, the fact that from now on there will be a baby to consider. Even if she got this job, how could she do it with the baby coming? If she doesn't get this job or another one, any other one, how will she support the baby? When she has someone else to feed, what will her mother say then?

This audition is for a *comedy*.

"Good luck," Josie says to the first actress, who is standing now to follow the casting assistant down the hall. As she departs, Josie and the second actress exchange quick polite smiles of rueful commiseration, then go back to studying the sides. The last line puzzles Josie. The character says it to a man she's dating. "You know what? I've got some pineapple soda." Because the scene takes place in the bedroom, Josie assumes that pineapple soda is a reference to some kind of sex act, but googling did not teach her what. All she got were recipes for pineapple mint soda or strawberry pineapple soda or links to buy pineapple soda. It's news to her that pineapple soda exists. She can't bring herself to ask the other actress if she knows what the line means.

She should have asked Cecelia if she knew. But last night at the bar, it seemed in bad taste to talk about anything except what had happened to Cecelia: Her movie part went to someone else. "Jamal's getting tired of listening to me whine," Cecelia said. "He's like, uh-huh, but you've got a job, and I've got to get the kids to do their homework. And I know, I know, but no one stops him from writing whatever poem he wants to write. No one's like, hey, I know you wanted to try a villanelle about birds, but you've got to stick to free verse about politics. This part was so good. This part was *so good*."

"I'm really sorry," Josie said. She was absent of jealousy, no part of her wanting to point out how much she'd like to be where Cecelia is right now. She understood—and understands—what a blow this is, not to get the part that spoke to you, the part that felt like the vehicle for expressing the full range of your capabilities. Yes, Cecelia is in a privileged position as an actor with steady, high-paying work. But we know from Michael Chekhov that the actor's nature longs for trans-formation. Cecelia has been Agent Corbett for years.

"I was right for that part," Cecelia said. "She's younger and thin-ner. You think this time it's not going to go that way and then it goes that way. I'm just mad at myself. I shouldn't have let myself get ex-cited about it."

Cecelia said this with tears in her eyes, and Josie scooted closer on the bench to put her arm around her. "I don't know how you could've helped it," Josie said.

Could she have helped it? Can Josie stop herself from feeling what she feels right now, which is a potent and unpleasant combination of nerves and self-loathing and hope? Hope is the irreducible ingredient. You can't get rid of the hope. Actors and gamblers are in thrall to the same irresistible fact: There's always a chance you'll win.

The second actress disappears, and now Josie sits on the bench alone. "You know what? I've got some pineapple soda," Josie mur-murs. She says it lasciviously, then coyly, then with blunt aggression. Should she try impatiently? Angrily? Apologetically? It's hard to de-liver a line when you don't know what the fuck it means.

Josie's phone ticks down toward her test—she clocked the time between the first woman's departure and the second's so she'd know how long she had to wait. Five minutes before she expects the casting assistant, Josie's phone rings. Now is not a good time to answer, but when she looks at the screen, she sees a 513 area code. She doesn't recognize the number, but 513 is Cincinnati, which is where Charlie's from. Is it possible he's gone home and is calling her from an unknown number?

When she answers, a woman's voice says, "Josie. Allison Outlaw here."

Charlie's mother always announces herself to Josie, and almost everyone else, with her full name. Charlie jokes that it's a habit so ingrained she does it with her kids as well. Josie knows that's not true. To her kids, she says, "Hi, sweetie, it's Mom." Josie once expressed surprise to Charlie that a woman like Allison had taken her husband's name. "Oh. Yeah," Charlie said. "She said she couldn't resist becoming an outlaw."

"Hi, Allison." Josie has gone very still. She feels a perfect crystalline terror, a certainty that Charlie has died.

"I still have a Google alert on your name," Allison says.

The statement takes a moment to absorb. Then Josie breathes. "Oh."

"Are you pregnant?"

Allison is never one to waste time. She probably has ten free minutes between a conference call and a meeting. She probably has CALL JOSIE in this block on her calendar. Allison has always been nice to Josie, but her businesslike certitude has the effect of making her feel like a small, faintly ridiculous child. "Yes," Josie says.

"Is the baby my son's? Or this, uh . . ." —Josie can picture Allison leaning into her computer screen, squinting at whatever she finds there—" . . . Max person."

"It's Charlie's."

"Does Charlie know about it?"

"Not yet."

"All right, here's the thing. Charlie is out of the country, I don't know if you know that."

Beneath her wary numbness, Josie feels the stirrings of relief. "I haven't been able to get in touch with him."

"Well, that's why. He said he was going to turn off his phone, that he wanted to go dark. He said he was going to hike and camp and be alone in the wilderness."

"Oh, that's why. That's why."

"Yes, so that means he won't have seen this, which I think we can both be grateful for. But I don't want him to find out this way, Josie, if that's all right with you."

"Of course."

"I don't know if you know how broken up he's been, but I don't want him to go through thinking that this baby is another man's. He said that this 'going dark' was about that ridiculous kerfuffle over the article but, of course, it's also about you. He loves you, and you're right to be angry, but I'm his mother and I can't help but tell you that he's terribly sorry."

Kerfuffle, Josie thinks. She wonders if that's on Jamal's list of criminally neglected words. *He loves me*, she thinks. He hasn't been in touch because he went dark, not because he doesn't want me anymore. Is it safe to believe that Allison is right? Allison is always so sure. "You know I didn't break up with him because of Max."

"It's all right, sweetie. You don't have to tell me anything. I know I'm intruding on your personal life. I just wanted to let you know where he is because I thought you might want to get in touch with him and tell him what's going on; I'm sure you've been trying to reach him."

"I have been trying."

"Well, of course. Of course. He's on an island I've never heard of, and he's rented a place. So all I've got is an address and the number for the management company. Do you have a pen? Never mind, I'll text it to you. I don't actually know if you can get him this way or not, but it's all I've got."

As soon as the text appears on her screen, Josie calls the number. She's conscious that at any moment the casting assistant will reappear, and the ticking clock and the nervous anticipation combine to make her feel overheated and tremulous. The phone rings fourteen times and every time she endures another tiny cycle of hope and despair. Even though she knows it won't be Charlie who answers! Pull yourself together, Josie. Someone picks up at last, a man, crisp and irritable.

"I'm looking for one of your guests," Josie says, pressing her hand to her stupid heart. "I hoped you could tell me the number where he's staying."

A pause. A heavily accented "Sorry?"

Josie repeats herself. "Charlie Outlaw," she adds.

She hears the sound of a tongue clucking in sympathy or irritation. "No English," the man says. "Sorry." And then he hangs up.

"Shit," Josie says. She sees the casting assistant approaching, but he's well across the room, and she doesn't care; she calls Allison back before he can get close enough to stop her. Allison picks up immediately and says her own name, of course, and Josie offers up what just happened to her crisp certainty.

"Well, that's a setback," Allison says.

The casting assistant has reached her. He waits with a nervous, impatient smile. "What should I do?" Josie asks.

"Josie, sweetie," Allison says, in a tone that manages to be both exasperated and sympathetic at once. "You're a grown-up. You decide."

"Miss Lamar?" the casting assistant prompts. He pronounces it *LAY-mar*.

Josie gets off the phone and follows him like she's supposed to. Is that what she should do?

The casting assistant asks, "Is it *LAY-mar*? Or *La-MAR*."

"*La-MAR*."

"Lamar, Lamar, Lamar," he mutters. He's about to lead her into the room when she remembers the puzzling line.

"Wait," she says. "Can you tell me what this means?" She shows him on the page.

"Oh, that," he says. "The writer's got it wrong; it's supposed to be pineapple *juice*."

"I still don't get it."

"Pineapple juice is supposed to make a man's semen taste better." The casting assistant turns a faint pink as Josie stares at him. "It's a blow job joke."

"Oh."

"I had to explain it to the other two people, too. It's kind of embarrassing."

"At least you don't have to say it."

He laughs. "That's true. I'm grateful for that." He turns toward the door then back again. "*La-MAR*." She nods, and as they walk in, he mutters her name once more and then raises his voice to say, "Everyone, here's Josie Lamar."

Because she's a recognizable actress, the ritual demands that she pretend to be friendly, pretend to be comfortable, pretend that she's not nervous. Even though the casting assistant couldn't pronounce her name. So she waves, friendly-like, as she makes her way past the suited people to stand in front of the giant TV. "Hey, guys!" She overshoots, the greeting weirdly boisterous. Oh my God, why is she doing this?

"Good to see you, Josie," says the casting director, a woman named Alma Josie does indeed know, if only slightly. "I'll be reading with you."

"Great," Josie says in a false, bright voice, and then, though she shouldn't, she adds, "The sides have been changed. So we'll see how this goes!"

Sometimes during a studio test no one laughs. This doesn't happen to Josie, which is a blessing. Two or three people in the room are rooting for her and they laugh, looking around to see if anyone joined them. Josie doesn't notice the looking around. She hears the laughter and is encouraged by it to believe that what she's doing is not irredeemably awful. A note often given to actors in a comic scene is "speed it up." Josie herself got this note from the director during her sitcom guest spot. Now she speeds it up without thought, just wanting to get to the end of the damn thing so she can decide what to do.

Then it's time for the pineapple soda line. Josie looks at it on the page. *You know what? I've got some pineapple soda.* She hears it in her head as if she were going to sing it: *I've got some pineapple sooo-daaaa.* This would be in a musical about blow jobs. Too much silence has happened since Alma read the previous line. No matter what these people think, Josie has good comic timing and knows very well that the rhythm often makes the joke. So it's too late now, anyway. There is absolutely no point. She looks up from the page to the people. "I'm sorry, I can't say this. This is a terrible line. I wouldn't say this."

"But it's not you saying it," Alma explains. "It's the character saying it."

Oh, thanks, Alma! Thanks for explaining my job to me. "Yes, but if I were the character, I wouldn't say this. Not that it matters, because I can't imagine you have me in mind for this character anyway. I am ten years older than the other two. I'm forty-one and I've gained seven pounds and no one thinks of me as funny. I'm not who you cast to be funny."

"I think you're funny," says a dark-haired woman in a suit.

"Thank you. One person thinks I'm funny."

"Josie—" Alma says.

"Everyone else is horribly uncomfortable."

"Josie—"

"I'm sorry, Alma. I've made everyone uncomfortable. And I don't even know if I am sorry. I just said that."

There's a ripple of nervous laughter.

"Usually in this situation I'm the only one who's uncomfortable. It's actually a nice change to have company."

The scattered laughter is more confident this time. Do they think she's doing a bit? Part of her wants to disabuse them, to really irrevocably unhinge, to announce that she's pregnant and can't find the father because he's hiding from the internet and meanwhile the father's mother called to ask if Josie's been fucking the guy she saw her with on the internet. And how many of you has *that* happened to? Anyone? Anyone?

These people might already know she's pregnant. Might know before she's told Cecelia. Might know before she's told her mother. She has a chance to keep Charlie from finding out that he's going to be a father from online gossip. She has a chance to keep him from believing Max is the father, that she's replaced him with Max. But how is she supposed to reach him? What is she supposed to do?

The woman in the suit, the one who said Josie is funny, is rooting for her to get this job because she loved *Alter Ego*, and since then, Josie has been criminally underused while that jackass Max Hammons has his own show. He was only good as Malachi because Josie made him good. Josie is one of those performers who can bring up everyone around her, raise the level of the whole production, and she deserves another chance to prove that. The woman feels a helpless frustration now, because it seems like Josie is blowing this audition and she's not sure she has the guts to advocate for her with these assholes in the face of that, and she really wanted Josie to give her a case to make. God, she hates everyone in this room. What is she doing in this shitty, shitty business? She looks at the despair and confusion on Josie's face and feels the same emotions.

How does Josie do that? Why can she make you feel what she feels when someone else can't no matter how many lessons they have? We ask and ask, but do we really want to know? Hard work and good luck can bring admiration, but it's magic that inspires awe.

When Josie's expression, her energy, shifts, the woman feels something new—the excitement that comes from watching resolution dawn. Josie's forehead smooths. Her jaw firms. "You've been a great audience," Josie says. Some people laugh. Some are silent. The woman wonders what everyone else is thinking. For a reason she can't yet articulate, she thinks maybe Josie hasn't blown this after all—she was *totally right* about that line. Josie doesn't even wait for the casting director to dismiss her with a thanks. She walks out, the woman notes with admiring envy, as if what the people in this room think no longer matters.

What just happened in Josie's mind? Where is she going? The woman would love to know.

VII.

There are two basic principles involved here, which you can write down if you wish . . . *Don't do anything unless something happens to make you do it.* That's one of them. The second is: *What you do doesn't depend on you; it depends on the other fellow.*

—SANFORD MEISNER,
Sanford Meisner on Acting

Once again, everyone waits for Mystery. It seems this will be the rhythm of life on this beach, stretching into infinity: days of sameness, a combination of boredom and impatience or hope or frustration or fear, depending on which mind you peer into, and then the sudden enlivenment of a visit from Mystery. Again and again they'll enact the narrative arc of joining and parting, joyful reunion and sorrowful longing, possibility's renewal and possibility's end. Imagine a chart with a flat line that extends and extends before it spikes, like one tracking a heart that beats only every few days, or a very occasional lie.

The kidnappers don't know any more than Charlie does exactly when Mystery will arrive. She said she'd be back in a few days when she could get the boat, which belongs to her uncle. It never occurs to any of them to worry that she won't come back at all. Given how dependent they are on her now, the absence of worry says a great deal about their faith in her loyalty. On what have they based this faith? Not much, really, as none of them knows Mystery well. She was Darius's friend, and she's not a talker. But she's given them no reason to doubt her. So far everything she has said she will do she has done. Also there's an intangible factor, an impression she gives of reliability, of steadiness and duty, an impression doubtless augmented by the fact that she's always in uniform.

When she comes, she will bring food, news of the outside world, and maybe, if they're lucky, change. When she comes, Denise needs to put a plan in motion. For that, she needs a plan. Darius's scheme to use hostages to scuttle the incipient resort died along with Darius. There is only one reason to put yourself to the trouble of keeping and feeding an unwilling guest, and that's money. This truth has long been Denise's companion. When Darius recruited her to kidnap people, he gave her the impression that ransom was the goal. That's why she agreed. Then he started blathering on about demands, a bait and switch she took as a profound betrayal. Perhaps that's part of what was in her mind when she shot him.

Another way Darius betrayed her: He knew nothing about the rules of kidnapping. He didn't know whom to contact, what to request, how negotiation works. Denise had assumed Darius had a plan for all this. That is the only reason she was willing to consider him the leader. Planning, negotiating—these are not Denise's forte. The fine machinery of interaction not only makes Denise impatient, she can't even see its workings. Certain subtleties are invisible to her, the way brushstrokes on a painting are invisible to those viewers they don't interest, to those who stand too far away to see. Her understanding is of the larger mechanics. If you hit someone, it hurts. Darius was supposed to be the brains, but Darius proved useless on all counts. It was like hiring a man to build a house and discovering he hadn't brought a hammer. No, he had brought a hammer: Denise was the hammer. Darius was supposed to design the house. She'd thought Darius was smart, but in the end he'd proven impulsive, emotional, and weak.

Were Darius alive to hear Denise express these resentments, he would want it noted that he carefully planned how to acquire the hostages and where to take them after acquisition. But even he would have had to admit that he'd had a fairly large blind spot. To overcome his ambivalence about capturing people at gunpoint, he put all his energy into that part of the plan. About the justice and necessity of his demands he'd been utterly certain, and thus it never occurred to him to work out exactly what making those demands would entail. We expect our own righteousness to part the seas.

Denise wants money. She doesn't know any more than Darius did about the process of demanding and collecting ransom. She has left it to the two boys, who've seen a great many American movies, to work it out. Several times in the last three days, since Mystery came and went and Denise opened these discussions, they've reenacted a squabble about whether it's better to call the hostage's parents or e-mail them. Those movies have them concerned about government technologies tracking them down. They can't call or e-mail from this beach—there's no service—so either way Mystery will have to do it. The boys think that Mystery is dumb. Denise disagrees. Mystery is silent and watchful. But she doesn't bother to correct them. What does she care if they think Mystery is dumb? Denise concerns herself with how much money to demand. It is her sense that all Americans are rich, but this American might perhaps be less rich than most. Another thing to hold against Darius, as if she needed one more: The best he could do was a waiter. Now the best she can hope for is that he's a waiter with rich parents. She doesn't know how things work in America. Would rich parents let their son be a waiter? Though Denise wouldn't admit this, even to herself, she feels some uncertainty about getting the amount right. It seems possible that if you ask for too much they'll just say no.

Once the boys agree on a plan and she lands on a figure, the next step will be to extract contact information from the hostage. She looks at him, huddled with his stupid magazine under his stupid

towel, and feels the usual contemptuous fury. She could walk up behind him right now and hit him hard. Then we'll see how long it
takes for him to tell her what she wants to know. She makes a gun of
her hand, closes one eye, and shoots him in the back of the head.
Many times in the last few days she's thought how much simpler it
would've been to let him fall.

Charlie assumes that the many long conversations his captors
have been having are about him, about what to do with him. After all
the time those three have spent together, what else can they have left
to discuss? For his part, he's spent the three days since Mystery came
alternating between reading magazines and running escape scenarios. He knows it's been three days because he's read three magazines.
He has five and could've read them all in the two hours after Mystery
handed him the bag, but he's rationing himself to one a day because
no one has told him when she'll return or whether she'll bring him
more. He reads one all the way through, very slowly, and then starts
over, and then puts himself to the test of memorizing the articles and
reciting them under his breath: How many paragraphs can he get
through before he makes a mistake? Only once the sun has set and
risen can he start a new magazine. He has read an interview with an
actress he admires so many times that he's begun to find a wild com-
plexity of subtexts in her words. He memorized her lines and has
said them aloud with a multitude of readings. The picture of Josie
with Max he looked at ten, a hundred, a thousand times. He could
not stop looking at it. It felt like reading the comments on his big-
mistake profile and every article that repeated the things he'd said. It
felt like searching *Charlie Outlaw asshole* and watching the internet
oblige. It felt worse than that. He had to tear the page out of the
magazine, and then he had to tear it and tear it until it was pieces that
he scattered in the sea. After that, loss closing his throat, he searched
the other magazines for a picture of Josie, but that was the only one.

In one of his escape scenarios, Charlie waits until whoever is on guard duty dozes off, then sneaks away into the rain forest. In another, he steals the boat when Mystery comes, while they're all busy rummaging through the supplies. He also imagines that Mystery rescues him, that she distracts the others somehow, then sneaks him onto the boat, pushes off before they notice. He can picture the three of them splashing after them into the water, yelling at them to stop. Maybe they'll even shoot, he and Mystery ducking into the hull of the boat until they're out of range of the bullets, and then there's just the wake behind them and the wind in their hair. There are other, even less plausible variations in which he grabs a gun and forces Mystery to pilot him out of here or Adan to lead him through the trees. He's tried to flesh out these plans, but each has a difficulty he can't surmount: He doesn't know how to start the boat's engine; he doesn't know the way back; someone might shoot him. He rehearses and rehearses but can't get anything right.

One of the kidnapping shows Charlie saw with his roommate all those years ago—which he has now had ample time and leisure to remember—involved a couple held hostage in the jungles of the Philippines for nearly two years. When the army came to rescue them, the husband was killed by friendly fire. To survive all that time in his captors' hands and then be shot by a would-be rescuer! He's glad he remembered this episode because it eases his tormenting sense that he shouldn't have followed Adan, should have run back toward the shooting. It eases his torment but doesn't banish it utterly, because maybe he still could have made it, maybe he could have run another way.

He wishes he'd watched more episodes of that show, every episode, preparing for the role he has now. He wishes he could remember one where someone escaped, but he can't, not one. Still, he can't shake the idea that escape is possible, for which he blames spy movies, fantasy novels, TV, comic books—everything that persuades us that we all might possess a hero's ingenuity, that we can trick someone out of their power over us, build a rocket out of spare parts. Evade our fates. In life you don't pick the lock on your handcuffs with a straight pin, swing yourself up from the pipe where you're chained to kick your tormentor in the face. In life you live for two years in the jungle, getting skinnier and skinnier, fighting dysentery, swallowing your rage when your captors laugh at your drooping pants, dreaming of the end, dreaming of the future—no, dreaming of the *past*. Then someone finally comes to save you and kills you instead.

The man who was kidnapped in Colombia, the man who gave a fake name—he pretended illness until his captors let him go. Charlie could try that. *Live truthfully in imaginary circumstances*, Meisner exhorts and, yes, Charlie has done that, he can do that, it is the only thing he can do. *Believe me, when I enter it will rain.* If he convinces her he's sick, will Denise just shoot him? He's valuable to her only as long as she thinks she can trade him for something. She might shoot him rather than let him go. He looks back at the kidnappers, which he shouldn't have done, because he catches Denise's eye.

Of course she gets up. Of course she comes toward him. Actions have consequences. Even if his only mistake was in glancing behind him, that glance led, a to b, to this result. Charlie sees the urge toward violence that propels Denise's approach, in her face, in her bearing, in her grip on the gun. If he cowers under his towel, she will hit him. If he stands, she will hit him. If he speaks, she will hit him. There is nothing he can do that will not give her an excuse. "Why are you coming to hit me?" he asks, when she's close enough to hear.

It breaks her momentum that he speaks. She stops two feet away. "What good will it do?" he asks. "Is there something you want?"

She calls him some names in her own language for the satisfaction of insulting him in a way he won't understand and can't respond to. He is a weakling; he is worthless; she has all the power. Then, in English: "How much money can your family pay?"

"Not much. They don't have much."

She considers him for so long he begins to feel as though she sees numbers multiplying on his face. "I will ask for a million dollars."

"What? They can't pay that. They can't possibly pay that." A million dollars! If this is what she expects from the family of a waiter, what would she want if he told the truth?

"How much then?"

"I don't know! A thousand? Two thousand? You have to be reasonable."

She smiles. "I do not have to be reasonable." She taps her finger against her gun. "You have to be reasonable."

"I will be reasonable. Take me back to where I'm staying and I'll give you my credit cards. I'll tell you my PIN number. Then you can go. You can let me go."

"We did not do all this to steal a wallet."

"You'd get money."

"You would call. You would stop your cards."

"I wouldn't. I promise. I wouldn't."

Denise scoffs. "Cash," she says. "Cash only."

"The cash machine—"

"There is a limit."

"But you could get money today. Today. This would be over. You could go back to your lives."

"No," she says, with finality. "We will contact your family."

"Let me be the one to call them then. I will ask them what they can pay." If he could gain access to a phone, he could call Josie. She could hire a K & R person, a negotiator, whatever they're called. He could pay her back. They wouldn't need to worry his parents at all.

"Ha!" So great is her scornful amusement that it carries her a few steps away from him. She circles back. "You tell me what they can pay."

"I don't know. I don't know the details of their finances. If you just let me call them—"

"No calls here. The phones do not work here."

"There's no service?"

"I said the phones do not work!"

"Mystery could take me in her boat somewhere I could call."

"No. You will not call."

"Then how will they know they can believe you? How will they know I'm alive?"

She lets out a long hiss of exasperation and drops to a crouch in front of him. She presses the barrel of her gun under his chin. "Maybe you won't be alive." She jerks back to her feet, wrenching the gun with her in a way that leaves a long scrape along his jawline. She stalks out of his view. Having learned his lesson, he doesn't turn to watch her go.

He is shaking. But she did that because she knows he's right. If she's planning to get a ransom, she has to provide proof of life. The advantage he has over Denise is that she lets her temper get the best of her. She behaves rashly. Does she realize that she didn't get an answer to her question? She is so easily provoked into abandoning her mission. He thinks again of the man who pretended to be sick.

But he has completed another circle. The advantage is a disadvantage: Denise behaves rashly. That is why Darius is dead.

Still, he considers what he'd do if he followed that man's lead, what performance he'd give. Remember what he learned back when he was sawing at his chain with a pocketknife: Even the pretense of agency helps to stave off despair. Scientists could prove beyond a doubt that our brains are programmed like computers, genetics and environment predetermining every infinitesimal choice, and we would still insist on free will. He could fake flu, but that might not be convincing without a fever. Appendicitis? He could refuse to eat. He could pretend madness, stage a panic attack. Or shock. He can summon what that feels like readily enough. Could he fake a panic attack without giving himself one? He remembers telling Adan he has asthma. Maybe he could convince them he needs treatment for it. They'd have to take him to the hospital. Appendicitis would do that, too. It seems like the performance of appendicitis would be easier to maintain. He should do it in front of Mystery, whose apparent sympathy for him might work to his advantage. (What exactly *does* she feel about him? What did their last encounter mean?) Mystery could insist on taking him to the doctor, insist they put him in her boat. Adan would want that, too, would want to help him. Mystery and Adan versus Denise and Thomas on the subject of Charlie's life.

Would Denise kill him rather than take him to a doctor?

His mind rounds the track again. Again. Again. There's an acting exercise in which each person in a pair repeats the same phrase over and over. "You looked at me." "Yes, I looked at you." "You looked at me." "Yes, I looked at you." The repetition goes on until an irrepressible urge arises in one partner to say something different, so that partner does, and the dialogue changes, and the real gives life to its facsimile. Thus the participants learn the importance of reacting rather than acting, the importance of obeying instinct. Charlie is playing this game with himself, waiting for the moment when he knows without thinking what to do.

Meanwhile, he has already changed the kidnappers' pattern. Denise went from Charlie to pace circles around the two boys. They are arguing like idiots about some idiotic movie. (What's interesting about this conversation is that they identify with the hero of the movie, who rescues a bunch of hostages, rather than the people he rescues them from. But Denise doesn't take note of that because she doesn't care.) As she continues to pace, their conversation grows uncertain. They eye her as she passes them, glance at each other nervously. Abruptly she stops. "We'll have to prove to his parents that we have him."

"Yes," Adan says. "Proof of life."

"You already thought of that?"

They exchange a quick glance. "No," they say.

"He wants me to let him call them."

"Well, sometimes they do that," Adan says.

"Who does that?" Denise snaps.

"The people asking for ransom. They call the family, and then they let the hostage talk, to tell them he's okay." Adan uses the word *hostage* because it's the term Denise prefers. In his own mind, he says *guest*, like Darius did.

Denise looks at Thomas. "You agree?"

"Yes, in the movies—"

"In the *movies*," Denise says. "In the *movies*." She regards them both with contempt. "I won't let him call. He'll play some trick. We need to send a photo."

"Mystery can take it when she gets here," Adan offers.

"And then we can send it by e-mail," Thomas chimes in. "We need an e-mail address."

Denise looks at Adan. "Go get it."

"Now?"

"We need to have it when Mystery comes. You start asking now. So there's time if you fail." She says this as if she expects him to fail, and if he does, he'll be sorry. Or Charlie will be.

Panic attack, Charlie is thinking. Or not exactly a panic attack, because he can't keep that up indefinitely. Panic attack segueing into psychotic break. Refusing to speak or speaking nonsense. Unhinged laughter. Moving in a jerky, unsettling way, darting his eyes. Crying, maybe, but not peaceful tears. Wild sobbing. He imagines it would be harder to shoot someone who was crying, but he's not sure that applies to Denise. He needs to frustrate Denise just enough for her to walk away, not enough for her to fire. He thinks he has a sense of how to do that. The preparation for this scene will not be hard. Every emotion he needs is ready at hand. If he can't get there otherwise, all he needs is to remember that picture of Josie, which he's trying not to think about so as not to provoke the very emotional experience he's now imagining provoking.

"Hello, Ben," says Adan. Something about the way he's standing reminds Charlie of PAs coming to his trailer to tell him he's needed on set. He is both tentative and determined.

"Hi," Charlie says. He sweeps an arm out to the side. "Have a seat."

Adan drops to the sand, crosses his legs like a child or a yogi. Crisscross applesauce. What teacher used to say that? "Ben," Adan says. "Ben." He reaches out and pats Charlie on the shoulder. "You are okay, Ben?"

Charlie shrugs. "Sure. I could use a cup of coffee. Cream, no sugar."

Adan looks worried. "We have no coffee, Ben."

"I know. I was kidding. It was . . . never mind."

Adan nods like all is forgiven, all is understood. "Now, Ben. When Mystery comes, we take picture."

"Of me?"

"Yes, Ben. To send your family."

"Ah."

"Proof of life."

"So you can ask for money."

"Yes, Ben!" Adan seems encouraged. "We send picture and we ask. You tell me e-mail for your family, please."

Charlie shakes his head.

Adan looks at him with earnest patience. "Yes, you need to tell me. You tell me, Ben."

"I won't tell you."

"Ben, you need to tell me."

"No."

"Ben." Adan takes a deep breath, considers. "Ben, you want to go home?"

"Of course."

"You want to see your mother? Ben, you have girlfriend, Ben?"

Charlie feels tears in his eyes, clenches his jaw against them.

"Yes, Ben. You want to see them. You want to go home."

Charlie shakes his head.

"You do, Ben. I know. I want to go home. You want to go home."

"I won't tell you."

"Ben, it is not hard."

"I won't tell you."

"You must. You must."

"I won't."

"But, Ben, if you not tell me, then Denise will come to ask."

"Adan." Charlie lifts his face. He makes eye contact. His eyes fill and he doesn't try to stop them. He blinks and feels a tear run down his cheek. "Do you remember how you saved me?"

Adan nods solemnly. "I saved you, Ben."

"Denise might kill me, Adan. Like she killed Darius. Would you let her do that? After you saved me?"

Adan swallows. He glances back at Denise.

"Don't look at her; don't look at her. She'll come over here."

Adan obeys, but he doesn't look at Charlie either. Charlie leans in, trying to compel his gaze. "Can't you help me, Adan? Can't you get me away from her?"

"I can't, Ben. I can't. She . . ."

"Please, Adan."

"She is my sister, Ben."

"Your sister?" Charlie didn't know that. How did Charlie not know that?

"Yes, Ben. My older sister. I must do what she says. I am sorry."

"Well, fuck," Charlie says. "Fuck fuck fuck fuck it all. I won't tell you the e-mail. I won't tell her."

"*Shhh*, Ben," Adan says, but he's too late, because here comes Denise, certain of Adan's failure and not at all sorry to intervene. Charlie gets to his feet, putting a hand on Adan's shoulder to propel himself upward. He walks away from Denise toward the water. Ben Phillips can't take it anymore. Ben Phillips is headed for a meltdown. Charlie doesn't know what he—Ben—will say when Denise reaches him, but something will come, something will come. His *sister*! Is she Mystery's sister, too? He hears Denise shouting behind him, but he doesn't turn around. He keeps walking past the edge of the world into the water. The water laps against his ankles, then his calves, and he thinks of a shot from a movie—What movie was it?—in which a man walks steadily into the ocean until he's gone.

On the beach, Denise is in a quandary. She shouldn't be because where can Charlie go? She doesn't for a second believe he'll drown himself. She saw his face after he fell. She saw him scrabbling back up the cliff face. She knows he wants to live. All she needs to do is wait here on the beach, turn a withering gaze on him when he comes dripping back from his pointless defiance. But Denise cannot abide defiance. As Charlie has already noted, she makes bad decisions in the face of it. She carries a gun. Will she lift it and shoot him and ruin her own plans? Or will she wait? She herself doesn't know. Once more she yells for him to return and still he keeps on walking—then the pattern changes again. Out on the ocean, Mystery comes into view.

Mystery! Thank God for her.

Charlie stops. He pictures a movie in which a man—a castaway, a long-bearded castaway—watches a boat approach, the first boat he's seen in years. The imaginary man waves his arms. He yells. Does the boat come closer? Does the boat keep going? What is that boat bringing him, rescue or despair? What is in the goddamn boat? He is up to his hipbones in the ocean.

He waits for Mystery to reach him. She looks at him quizzically, killing the engine. He smiles at her like it was his intent all along to escort her in. Then he tows the boat to shore.

After that, things unfold as they did the last time Mystery arrived, except that Charlie walks up the beach away from the rest of them into the edge of the jungle. No one tries to stop him. He climbs into the string hammock he's come to think of as his. His wet pants cling to his skin. Above him a flowering tree, a pattern of leaves and branches and bright red blossoms imprinted on the sky. What is he to make of beauty right now? One worldview suggests it's there to comfort him. *Have hope* is its message. *Even on the darkest days . . . Look, a rainbow!* Or it's torture by way of ironic contrast, making a bad thing worse. Or it's indifferent. Let it be indifferent. He can't be made to feel worse. He doesn't want to have hope.

After a while—How long? Who knows? Who cares?—he hears footsteps approaching. He closes his eyes against the urge to lift his head and find out whose footsteps they are. He knows anyway, can tell by the sounds, even before fingertips brush his forehead. It's Mystery. "I have something to show you," she says.

He opens his eyes. "What?"

"You don't want the others to see."

He sits up, swaying in the hammock. "What?"

She steps back farther into the trees out of view, Charlie assumes, of the three on the beach. She's holding another bag of magazines.

"What?" he asks again, his heart starting up in defiance of his commitment to numbness. He is so weary of dread.

"I will show you."

He climbs out of the hammock. Ben Phillips is having a panic attack. Charlie breathes. He breathes.

Mystery pulls out a magazine. She opens it to a dog-eared page. Then she holds it open. He moves closer to see. She points at a photo. The photo is of a man wheeling a suitcase toward the entrance to

LAX. The man wears form-fitting jeans and a baseball cap and a jacket that fits so well you can tell it was expensive. "That is you," she says.

"No, it isn't."

She shakes her head in quick, firm dismissal. "That is you."

The caption reads: *Is Charlie Outlaw pulling a Dave Chappelle? No one's seen Charlie since this photo taken in the international terminal at LAX. The TV star has been silent on social media since he told a reporter he doesn't really like his own show. "The fans really turned on him," says a source from the set. "That really stung. He'll need some time to get over it— and so will the fans." Is that controversy all that's got Charlie on the run, or could it have something to do with the rumors about ex-girlfriend Josie Lamar? (page 5)*

What rumors? About Max? What rumors? "Can I have that?" Charlie reaches, but Mystery pulls the magazine back. He fights the urge to snatch it from her. He doesn't want the others to notice anything going on.

"Who is Dave Chappelle?" Mystery asks. She pronounces it *chapel*.

"He's a comedian who got very famous and then disappeared for a while. He went to Africa."

"Are you very famous?"

"No. I don't know. It depends who you ask."

"But that is you."

He looks at the picture again. He is about to agree—the jig is up—but what rises in him is refusal. He wants to deny that it's him, and not just because he's been claiming a different name. That guy looks nothing like he feels. That guy has every faith that he'll get where he's going. He has no idea of the shit he's about to get Charlie into. Charlie hates that guy.

"I don't understand," Mystery says. "You tell Denise you are rich. You give her money and you can go."

"I'm not rich. I'm not as rich as you probably think."

Mystery frowns in puzzlement. She shakes the picture at him. "But that is you. You give her money and you can go."

He won't tell Denise. He already decided not to tell Denise. He doesn't know the right thing to do. He doesn't know what got him here. He doesn't know what will get him out. He only knows he decided not to tell Denise. "That is not me," he says, and he sells it, he can hear that he sells it, he can see it by the way her expression morphs toward doubt.

"That *is* you."

"That is not me."

"But the lady . . ." She jabs her finger at the caption.

"What lady?"

She huffs with frustration, flips the pages of the magazine, shows him a picture of Josie striking a pose at a staged photo op. Her hand is on her stomach. "Page five," she says. "I ask the front-desk man to read the English. He say this lady is ex-girlfriend of that man. You say you love that lady." She looks at him in triumph.

"I don't know that lady," he says.

"You cry about her."

"No." He shakes his head.

"You do."

"I'm upset. I've been kidnapped."

"You say you know her."

"I don't know her."

Mystery purses her lips, considering. "She is pregnant."

"What? That's not true." He reaches for the magazine again, and again she pulls it back. A corner of a page comes away between his thumb and finger.

"Is true."

"No, it's not!"

"You don't know her. So how do you know?"

"I just know. Can I look at that, please?"

"You tell the truth and I give it to you."

"I am telling the truth. She's not pregnant."

"She is. It is in the magazine."

"She would have told me!"

"No, no," Mystery says. "The baby not yours."

"If she's pregnant, then it's my baby."

"This say she has the other man's baby."

He shakes his head spastically. "This is a tabloid!" he says. "It's full of shit! And how would you know? How could you possibly know?"

"*Shhhh*," she hisses, reaching as if to clap her hand over his mouth. She stops just short of touching him.

"Why are you saying all this? Why are you showing me this? Why didn't you just take it to Denise?" From the look on her face, he'd guess Mystery doesn't know the answer.

She shrugs. "I wanted to ask you."

"Why?"

"I wanted to know."

"You wanted to know what? If I'm famous? If you know some-body famous? If I'll take a selfie? If I'll sign that photo? The auto-graph's not for you, it's for your teenage daughter, right? You wanted to know if I was really dating Josie? If I really loved her? If she left me for Max Hammons? Max Hammons! If she—" She is staring at him—frightened? stunned? confused?—and in her hands the magazine goes slack, tilting toward him to display its picture of Josie. He stops abruptly and snatches it. He steps back too far with his prize, out of the trees into visibility, and then even farther onto the beach, putting distance between himself and Mystery. He doesn't realize his mis-take, too busy reading. Reading over and over without absorbing any of the words.

And then the magazine is gone, because Denise has snatched it from his hands. She looks at the page, then assesses Charlie. She can see he's upset but why? "You like this lady?" she asks mockingly. "You have love for her?"

Charlie stands there shaking.

Denise doesn't read English any more than Mystery does. She barks at Mystery, summoning her from the trees with rapid questions. Mystery gives a short reply. What did she say? What did she say? What did she say?

"So the lady is pregnant," Denise says. "So?" She seems genuinely curious. This is the first time she's expressed any curiosity about him. Everybody gets more interested when your picture's in a magazine.

"She's not pregnant."

Denise looks pleased by his vehemence. She leans in and enunciates. "She is."

"You don't know! You don't know anything! You don't even know what you're doing!" He snatches the magazine back.

Denise looks at him openmouthed for a moment, her hand flexing around her gun. Then she laughs. She turns to the boys and speaks rapidly and loudly, gesturing at him, and they laugh, too. She pooches out her belly like she's pregnant and pouts in his direction. More words he doesn't understand, and their laughter grows more uproarious. He is hilarious. He is ridiculous. He is a fool. He wants that baby to be his. Denise turns back to him, the smile lingering on her face, and hits him in the stomach with the butt of her gun. He doubles over, and then she grabs his hair and drives her knee up and his face down so they collide in the gruesome crunch of his nose breaking. He drops the magazine to catch his blood in his hands. Denise leans over and swipes it up, then casually pushes on his shoulder until he is on his knees. She puts her own knee hard into his back as she flips the pages. "Clothes, clothes, clothes," she says. "Pretty ladies. Pretty men. You would die for this magazine?" She plays to her audience, making more jokes. His nose throbs. Adan and Thomas laugh but Mystery doesn't. He's never heard Mystery laugh. He tries not to vomit, wiping his bloody hands on the sand. Her knee is sharp in his back.

She stops talking. He feels her go still. He closes his eyes against what's coming. Thomas says something to continue the hilarity, and she snaps a command. She takes the knee from his back and steps to the boys. He doesn't have to speak her language to know what's happening. She's showing them the picture of him. He crawls away, as far as he can get before a foot connects with his side and he goes down. He looks up at Denise and winces against the sun. "You are Charlie Outlaw," she says.

He shakes his head.

"You are rich. You are famous. You are a liar."

"That is not me."

"We do not need to e-mail your family. We will send a picture to the news and your family will see."

"No."

"I will ask for two million dollars."

"That is not me."

She kicks him again. "Lie." Again. "Lie." Again. "Lie."

He curls up on his side, gasping.

Abruptly she stops. She says conversationally, "You take a rest. Then we talk."

She broke Charlie's nose. She cracked one of his ribs. There is sand in his eyes, sand on his tongue, sand sticking to the blood coagulating on his face. He swallows grit and iron. The sun finds him like a spotlight.

Josie.

Fingers on his broken nose, and as light a touch as it is, he cries out. "No ice," says Mystery's voice. "She say take care of you. How can I take care of you?"

Josie, I am sorry.

Fingers push his hair back, carefully pulling strands from the blood. Mystery tsks. "Charlie," she whispers. "I worry for you."

He cracks open his eyes. "Take me away from here then," he whispers. He's too hurt and frightened and the sun is too bright for him to read the microexpressions that succeed one another with rapidity on her face. All he knows is that she feels, all at once, multiple things.

"You tell her what she wants. Please, please, Charlie. I worry for you."

"My name is Ben Phillips."

"You are Charlie Outlaw," she says, pleadingly.

He closes his eyes.

Time's up. Adan and Thomas appear on either side of him. They haul him up, not to his feet but his knees so he must still look up at Denise, who stands before him with arms folded. "We will clean your face before we take a photo," she says. "Or they will not recognize you, Charlie Outlaw. Pretty man."

"You can take a photo," he says. "But you can't get two million dollars."

"I can. You are rich. It will be easy. Everyone will send money to save you. You are famous."

"They won't believe you. All kinds of people take pictures of me. They take pictures everywhere I go. They put them on the internet. They make things up. They'll think you just saw me on a beach. You have to let me call my family."

"No calls."

"They won't believe you."

"They will see the photo and they will believe."

"They won't. You won't get two million dollars."

Denise is not a patient person, and what patience she had for this exercise in prolonged frustration was exhausted by the time she shot Darius. In her hand there is a pistol. She has exchanged her usual rifle for it, doubtless for the purpose to which she now puts it. She presses the muzzle to his forehead. "We will take a picture of this, Charlie Outlaw. Will they believe this? Will they believe this, Charlie Outlaw? Will they believe this? I think they will believe this." She removes the pistol, takes the safety off, replaces it at his head. "They will believe you are dead, Charlie Outlaw, when they see the photo. I will kill you now. Will they believe you are dead?"

Charlie thinks, *I should've—* The gun goes off. He doesn't finish the thought. He just dies. Then he takes a breath and discovers he didn't.

Denise did not shoot him.

Denise shot over his head.

He puts his face in his hands. Denise did not shoot him.

She drops to a crouch beside him. "Now, Charlie Outlaw," she says, "you will tell me everything I ask."

"That is not me," he says. He rocks front and back with his knees in the sand, cradling his broken nose, his fingertips pressed so hard against his eyelids that he sees spots. Is this real? Is he acting? He couldn't tell you now, will never be able to tell you. He and the character are one. "That is not me," he says, and keeps saying it. It is his only line. "That is not me. That is not me."

VIII.

In life we often act unconsciously, unaware of the causes that determine our behavior, and the aims which our actions pursue—but on the stage we must always know what we are doing and why.

I. RAPOPORT, "The Work of the Actor"

One.

There are two paths to success. You can believe that you can succeed. You can stop caring if you fail. Picture the scene in which our heroine, four bad guys at her feet, turns her gaze on the one who remains. Moments ago, he and his fellow villains mocked her, certain of her easy defeat. Now, as the camera pushes in for a close-up, her eyes say *Run*, and that is what the last bad guy does, he turns and runs. Which path did she take to that victory? Within *Run*, we can make out both *I will win* and *I do not give a shit*.

Picture Josie descending the stairs from a plane to a tarmac, striding past slow-moving disembarkers on her way into an airport. On the plane, to Josie's amused and rueful astonishment, they showed an episode of *Alter Ego*. That was a first: Never before has she seen her tiny self replicated on all those tiny screens. They showed it because of the show's anniversary, an episode in which Bronwyn almost gives up, almost walks away, so from her seat on the plane, Josie got to watch her own face morph from fear and desperation into resolution. Despite this, none of the passengers recognized Josie on the plane, and they still don't, even the ones who might if she weren't walking by them so fast. The airport is a small one, not air-conditioned, with three bars offering tropical cocktails and racks bristling with colorful brochures and a metal fence instead of walls around two sides of the baggage claim.

Josie has not told anyone, not even Cecelia, where she is, because she didn't want anyone to try to dissuade her. She knew, for instance, that if she told her agent or manager, the other voice on the line would immediately take on that careful, don't-poke-the-bear tone, which she hates and doesn't think she deserves. In the face of the assumption that actresses are hysterical narcissists, Josie has striven to behave as a reasonable, competent adult. In the last two decades, she's put a lot of effort into not seeming fragile or crazy to people determined to treat actresses as fragile and crazy, and what has been the point of her reasonableness and competency? They treat her that way anyway. Imagine all the temper tantrums she might have thrown. Imagine all the times she might have gotten what she wanted.

For Josie, the world has contracted to a singular certainty. She'd forgotten the power of that. Find Charlie. That is the beginning and the end. To a certain point, her plan is made: rental car, hotel, shower, all prelude to the real quest. Find Charlie. She'll go to the address she got from Charlie's mother. There she will succeed or fail.

Even in a strange place with spotty cell service, Josie has confidence that she'll find her destination. She always knows which way is north. Here there is only one main road, which follows the coastline through the settled parts of the island. Eighty percent of the island is wilderness, accessible only by foot, boat, or helicopter, so the road goes only three-quarters of the way around the island. Where the last piece of the circle would be is rain forest instead—rain forest, a large canyon, and mountains that start where the beaches end and press insistently into the center of the island, with fingers of the mountains reaching out even farther. On a map, civilization appears to cling to the island's edge between the encroachments of mountains and sea. It seems to Josie, driving from airport to resort through heavy traffic and little towns dense with ramshackle houses, that the mountains maintain a magisterial remove.

As she nears the resort, billboards vanish, along with roadside food stands; undrivable vans; abandoned construction with tipped-over porta potties; storefronts that combine locksmith, printing, and legal services; small wooden rectangular buildings in need of paint; and other markers of people who don't have money. This resort is for the people who do. Everything that interrupts the beauty of the landscape is gone, as if someone has swept the porch. On either side of the road are eucalyptus trees that reach for one another, forming a canopy, so for a mile or so, Josie feels as if she were in a tunnel, though a tunnel that's spangled with light. Josie doesn't know this, having read no guidebooks, but hundreds of these trees were planted more than a hundred years ago on the orders of a man who'd grown rich off the island's resources. Part of what was once his land now belongs to the resort. He was, by all accounts, a terrible man. The tree tunnel is beautiful.

The resort advertises itself as luxurious, relaxing, and secluded, all of which is accurate. It encompasses nearly two hundred acres on a small, irregularly shaped peninsula, with seven private beaches, diving, snorkeling, and sailing, multiple restaurants, tennis courts, massage cabanas, a bar offering frozen mango cocktails, a boutique selling overpriced colorful scarves. Fluffy little donkeys roam the grounds. There are no televisions or telephones in the rooms. Josie would have stayed at a moderately priced chain hotel, but there doesn't seem to be one on this island. So here she is on a quest in this place designed for the perfect vacation, feeling a momentary confusion of purpose. She stands on her balcony gazing at the blue, blue ocean as a big white boat passes by. A breeze rustles the fronds of the palm trees. In the distance, she can see the hazy gray-blue outline of the next island. Her bedspread has a pattern of sea grasses on a sand-colored background. The same fabric is on the throw pillows on the armchair and the couch. The floor is tile—the color of a darker speckled sand—and it's cool under her bare feet. She's just out of the shower, wrapped in a thick white robe, droplets of water forming at the ends of her hair and descending over the edge of the balcony, back to the sea. What if she just stayed here for the week she booked and then flew home? No confessions, no confrontations, no rejections. No risk. But that is not the choice the hero makes.

In the hall, she passes a maid with her cart, and it seems to her that the maid looks at her strangely, turns to watch as she passes. She doesn't look back to confirm the other woman's gaze. She expected to go unrecognized here, but then again, these days it's impossible to know what people have and haven't seen. Bronwyn even followed her onto the plane.

Back through the tree tunnel and Josie rejoins the main road, heading still farther away from the airport, up and around to the island's north shore. This area is less densely populated. There are no billboards, fewer turnoffs, more places to pull over and photograph the view. Josie departs the main road for one that abruptly diminishes in size, so two cars passing each other would have to drive partly on the shoulder. The houses are neat, if slightly shabby. On her right, there is a small stone church with a peaked roof ending in a modest wooden cross over an arched door and a rose window. Its quaint loveliness is striking after the chaotic modernity of the towns near the airport and the well-brushed sheen of the resort. On her left, there is an upscale market, comprised partly of the well-kept buildings of a former plantation. Josie glimpses a sparkling fountain of mosaic tile, above it a bright parrot on a perch.

She turns onto a road that climbs to higher ground. Gated driveways appear in breaks in the trees and hibiscus hedges. Whatever wonders they protect are hidden from view, but occasionally more modest houses sit exposed and ungated by the road. Once she sees a trailer, alone in the center of a huge swath of cleared land, radiating abandonment.

A long gravel driveway takes her up higher still to the cottage where Charlie is supposed to be. It's isolated on six acres, a little yellow cottage with large windows and a small patio nestled among fruit trees and tropical flowers. Josie stops at the top of the drive. Hers is the only car here. She assumes Charlie rented one and that therefore he must be gone somewhere. She gets out anyway to make sure, to have a look around. To wait? One of the compact reddish chickens that roam free on the island crosses her path, a quartet of chicks scurrying after her. Josie sees a rooster, too, and a peacock and three peahens, one of whom has her own large chick. The peacock is in full display, his magnificent feathers fanned out while he turns in a slow circle, furiously shaking the more ordinary brown feathers at his rear. These enticements seem to interest the peahens not at all. They move around him in a way that suggests they're carefully avoiding eye contact. At the sight of his vigorous, determined silliness, Josie laughs for the first time in what feels like days or weeks, and she moves up to the house with a lightened spirit. If Charlie's not here, he will be later.

Cupping her hands around her face to look through the big front window, Josie sees a big bed under a filmy canopy, a table holding an unopened champagne bottle and two unused flutes, two wicker chairs with floral cushions, a small kitchen against one wall. It looks like a honeymoon cottage, and she feels a pang of sadness at the thought of Charlie's being there alone. For Josie, solitude is not inherently a negative, but it is for Charlie. Charlie doesn't like to be alone. How has he felt sleeping on that huge bed under that romantic canopy? The shower is an outdoor one, under the roofline of the house within a wooden enclosure. Through the heart-shaped window carved in the wood, the showerer would be able to see mountains, bushes bursting with flowers of an insistent red, a faint blue line of ocean. Has Charlie been forlorn, standing under the water, looking at a heart-shaped view?

Maybe not. Maybe he hasn't been alone.

But there are no signs of any other inhabitant, no hairbrushes or women's razors or bikini tops hung from doorknobs to dry. Just Charlie's pile of paperbacks, Charlie's Reds baseball cap, Charlie's bottle of bourbon. Charlie's things. But not Charlie. It's painful how much she wants to see him, as if he were a star and she an ardent fan, as if her longing were locked in desperate battle with the deep and certain knowledge that he'll never ever be hers.

She waits an hour until the light starts to fade and the sky takes on colors. She's tired—her body tells her it's bedtime—and she doesn't know the road well enough to want to drive it in the dark. Before she goes, though, she walks the property, which includes an orchard of guava, lychee, papaya, and mango trees laid out in long neat lines. Who picks this fruit? A fair amount of it has fallen untouched to ripen and ferment on the ground, giving the orchard a fragrance of drunkenness. She peels and eats some lychees. She walks a little while accompanied by a chicken, who keeps pace with her in companionable fashion until it abruptly veers off, pursuing its chicken ends. She's getting hungry—she's no longer fighting her hunger, seven pounds be damned. She thinks of attempting a mango, but she's never been good at telling when they're ripe, and she doesn't have a knife to slice one open, and she doesn't want to greet Charlie with strands of mango stuck in her teeth. She eats some more lychees, dropping the peels as she walks as if leaving a trail.

Back at the house, she witnesses the ongoing efforts of the peacock. Persistence: sometimes admired, sometimes feared, sometimes disdained. Sometimes, as in this case, ignored. She writes Charlie a note and slides it under the door: *Hi, Charlie, I need to talk to you. I'm staying at the resort. Please call when you get this. Love, Josie.* She doesn't hesitate over the love, and no matter what happens next, it is an undeniable pleasure to say what she means, to know what she wants, to act without questioning her actions.

She eats dinner at one of the resort's open-air restaurants and then goes back to her room to slip into her deep, dream-filled pregnancy sleep. Charlie will call, or he won't, and either way she'll go out again tomorrow to find him.

Two.

The kidnappers are at a loss. Ben—*Charlie*—won't eat, won't rise from his hammock. Once, Denise flips him out of the hammock, and he just lies there on the ground until Adan helps him back in. Only Adan can get him to drink water. It is as if he has decided to die. When they speak to him, he looks at them with faraway eyes and doesn't answer. He will no longer respond to Ben. When they call him Charlie, that is the only time he speaks. He says, "That is not me."

Thomas is sullen. He thinks often of running away. He misses his neighborhood soccer game. He misses his girlfriend. Adan is sorrowful. He thinks he's a player in a tragedy, helpless to resist fate. He goes around with tears in his eyes. Denise is angry, but her anger no longer motivates her. She has passed into a permanent state of fury that she experiences as numbness. She leaves the care of Charlie entirely to Adan, spends all day pacing the edge of the ocean watching for Mystery. Mystery—whose job it was to find an e-mail address and write a ransom demand and send it. Has she done it? Has anything happened out there in the world?

There is no way to know.

Three.

A knock at the door intrudes on Josie's sleep. She didn't expect to sleep this long or this late. She'd expected—she'd hoped—to be woken by a call from Charlie. So she didn't set an alarm, forgot to hang the do-not-disturb sign. Even at the sudden sharp knock she doesn't quite wake. Her dream clings to her. She thinks she is awake, that she is in Charlie's bedroom rearranging the items on his dresser while Charlie explains that he wants her to pose for nude photos with him, and she objects, and he is inexplicably holding a clipboard. The dream thins so she can almost see real life through it, so she hears the door open and the maid's footsteps and knows they don't make sense with the clipboard and the nude photos, but she is still lying in bed, working out the truth, when the maid walks into her room.

The maid does not realize right away that someone is in the bed. Josie shoved all but one of the ten thousand pillows to one side, so the mound of them blocks the maid's view. Not until she lifts one of those pillows, intending to unmake and remake, does she see her. At that moment, Josie thinks, *Wait, that's not right*, and opens her eyes. She and Josie make eye contact, and both of them utter a sound between a gasp and a scream.

It's easy for Josie—as she and the maid stammer incoherent apologies, the maid first in her own language, then English—to attribute all the fluster and awkwardness to the unexpected encounter of maid and half-dressed hotel guest, blowsy with sleep. But the moment goes on for too long. Why isn't the maid beating a hasty retreat? Why is she still standing there, compressing that pillow against her chest, murmuring, "I am so sorry"? Is she a fan? But she shows none of the eager, animal impulse to get closer.

"Don't worry," Josie says. "I should have put the sign on the door."

The maid nods, but still she doesn't go.

"It's okay," Josie says. She's sitting up in the bed, her oversize T-shirt adjusted so the neck no longer slips off one shoulder. Now she reaches under the covers to pull the hem over her hips, in case it takes sliding out of bed to encourage this woman to leave. She debates what's worse on the scale of vulnerability: being in the bed while the woman towers over her or rising half-clothed to tower over the woman. Well, it's all in how she plays it.

She throws the covers back, swings her feet decisively to the ground with no abashed effort at concealment. She stands looking at the maid with her hands on her hips. Her chin is tucked so that her lifted eyebrows point at the door.

But the maid—who is, of course, Mystery—hesitates another moment. Her eyes go to Josie's stomach, which is—in the sunlight from the window, through the thin white fabric of the T-shirt—visibly rounded. The T-shirt is airbrushed in blue swooping letters, I ♥ OUTLAWS, above a black cowboy hat. The heart is, like all hearts, red. Charlie brought the shirt back from a trip as a joke. "Outlaw," the maid says. She says it like two words. Then she drags her gaze back up to Josie's face. Why does she look so stricken? "I am sorry," she says again, and then at last, at last, she goes.

Josie hangs the do-not-disturb sign and engages the bar lock and, with that, believes she has dismissed the encounter. But something about it nags at her, and she catches herself in a reverie, replaying the scene under the rapidly cooling shower. She has one of those feelings we call hunches or intuition—a certainty that comes after we process so much information so quickly that we don't notice we're doing it. Josie is an empath by nature and by training.

That woman knows something about Charlie.

She dresses hastily, hoping to catch her. Only a few minutes go by, not more than ten, but when Josie stands at her doorway looking one way down the hall and then the other, she sees no cart. She's visited by an oddly fond memory of Cyrus the bodyguard. All clear, Cyrus, though she would prefer it otherwise. Strange that the maid is not cleaning the next room without an occupant—Josie sees three doors without signs dangling from the knobs.

She vanished, through a portal, in a puff of smoke, by teleport. She ran away.

In the hallways, on the grounds, even as she eats a late breakfast in the restaurant, Josie looks for her. *What is it you think she knows?* she asks herself. *What could that woman possibly know?* She challenges her own conviction but can't diminish it. She is sure, and that sureness creates a thrumming, insistent dread. She finds another maid, exiting a room, and describes to her the woman she saw. "That is Mystery," the maid says.

"She doesn't sound familiar?"

The maid looks puzzled, so Josie rephrases.

"You don't know her?"

"Yes, I know her. Mystery."

"She's a mystery?"

The maid frowns. "Yes. Her name. Mystery."

Josie would laugh if it wasn't for the dread. "Have you seen her today?"

No, the other woman has not seen her.

"Who might have seen her? Who can I ask about her?"

Now the other woman looks worried. "You need something for your room? You don't like the cleaning?"

"No, no, no, it's not that. She hasn't done anything wrong. I just wanted to talk to her about something."

The worry shifts toward puzzlement. "You want to talk to her?"

There's a why in that question. Yes, Josie, why? Why do you want to talk to the housekeeper? To seek advice about the island? There's a concierge for that. You need to think of a reason. "Okay, never mind, it's okay, thank you," Josie says.

"You need something?" the woman asks.

"No, I . . . sure, yes, sure. Could I have . . . an extra towel?"

The maid's face brightens. This is a request that makes sense to her. She gives Josie the towel and Josie thanks her again and they go their separate ways.

By the time Josie approaches the front desk, she has her reason, which should have come to her more readily, as it's the key that opens most doors, at least outside of LA. "Excuse me," she says to the man at the desk. "I have kind of a strange question." She smiles at him in conspiratorial sheepishness.

He smiles back, like a person unfazed by strange questions.

"I'm looking for one of the housekeeping staff. Mystery. I don't know her last name."

"Yes, Mystery." The clerk looks at her in expectation of more.

"She came into my room while I was there earlier today—"

"Oh!" The clerk's face changes.

"No, no, no," Josie says. "No, no, it's no problem. I'm not here to complain. I wanted to talk to her. I wanted to talk to *someone*. Let me back up. I'm an actress."

"Oh?" His eyebrows go up.

Yes, Josie thinks. *All right.* "I have a part in a movie where I play a housekeeper in a place like this."

The clerk permits himself a small smile. *Hollywood*, he thinks.

Josie barrels past the smile. "Anyway, she said that she could talk to me about what it's like, maybe I could follow her through her day. It would help so much with preparation. She just wanted to check with her boss. But I didn't find out how I could get in touch with her. Could you find her for me?"

He picks up a receiver but pauses before he pushes a button. "What happens in this movie?"

"Oh, it's a romantic comedy. I fall in love with a guest in the hotel."

"Ah. And who will play the guest?"

Josie names a famous American actor, and the man looks suitably impressed. "I will call down, Miss . . ."

"Lamar. Josie Lamar."

"Ah." He files the name away. As soon as she leaves, Josie knows he will look her up, and then if she seems sufficiently recognizable, he'll tell everyone he knows she was there. He dials the numbers, speaks to someone on the other end of the phone. He puts his hand on the mouthpiece and says to Josie, "They will go look for you."

Josie nods and smiles and thanks him, and they wait. The clerk is staring at her face openly now, as if to memorize or place it. Long minutes drag by. Josie pretends interest in a rack of brochures beside the desk. Finally he calls her back over, hanging up the phone. "They cannot find Mystery, I'm sorry to say. But the housekeeping manager says she's happy to accommodate you. Here's how you reach her." He writes a name and number on the back of a card.

"But no one knows where Mystery is?"

"No, I'm sorry." He frowns. "No one can find her."

At Charlie's cottage, it looks like nothing has changed since the day before. If he's been back, he's ignoring her note. Maybe he's angry and punishing her, but that would be unlike Charlie. Maybe he's devastated and avoiding pain, or he's over her and avoiding an uncomfortable scene. If he hasn't been back, what does that mean? No matter which window she tries, she can't get an angle that allows her to see whether the note is still there on the floor. She crouches in the driveway looking for fresh tire tracks, then feels ridiculous. What show does she think she's on? If only Agent Corbett were here.

Cecelia, Josie would say, should I go talk to the police, or is that crazy? Cecelia, after all the hours logged faking expertise, might actually know. She's interviewed real FBI agents. She knows the next step when someone is missing. But Josie has no cell service and only herself to ask. How can she persuade the police that anything is amiss? Because Charlie, who planned overnight hikes, is not home? Because a maid looked at her funny and said his name? No doubt this will sound ridiculous. But Josie's expertise, like that of all heroes, is in believing she can do impossible things.

There's no police station in the tiny town with the church and the upscale market, but a woman who sells handmade soap near the parrot stand directs her to the next town farther up the main road. This one is larger, with double-decker strip malls lining a half-mile stretch and bars already raucous with locals and vacationers. It's still light out, but some of these people are very drunk. As Josie emerges from her car in the station parking lot, she witnesses someone walk down the steps from a bar deck to vomit on the sidewalk.

Inside the station, she finds one policeman who speaks English. He listens to her with the air of someone humoring a small child. He is only thirty, more than ten years younger than Josie, but he is one of those men who treat all women like they are much younger than they are. He has heard nothing about Charlie, nothing about any incidents involving an unidentified white American man. He thinks that if Charlie has not been to his cottage since yesterday there are many reasonable explanations. People go on hikes, *long* hikes, he tells her, hikes they sleep on. He also implies Charlie might be with another woman, which is nothing Josie hasn't thought of herself. Charlie and Mystery.

"If he went hiking, where do people hike?"

"Oh, everywhere, everywhere. You would not find him." He tells her that 80 percent of the island is wilderness. He tells her there are some places you can reach only by foot, only by helicopter, only by boat. He says Charlie could be anywhere. Only he doesn't say *Charlie* he says *your boyfriend*, because that's who Josie told him Charlie is. He's forgotten Charlie's name, as proven when he stops Josie as she rises to go. "Wait," he says. "Is his name Ben Phillips?"

"No," Josie says. "Why?"

The policeman attempts to retract his eager interest. He is not a good actor. "I thought it might be."

"Why?"

"Someone said there is an American named Ben Phillips."

Josie frowns. The name sounds familiar, but she has no idea why. "I'm sure there is. I'm looking for Charlie Outlaw."

The policeman shrugs. "Charlie Outlaw I don't know."

Back at the resort, there's a new clerk at the desk, a woman, so Josie risks trying her story again. She is not yet desperate enough to call the manager and enact a further charade. This time, when the clerk calls housekeeping, the report is that Mystery left early.

"Is she sick? Where did she go?"

The clerk smiles with regret at the disappointment she must cause and says she doesn't know.

Four.

Where is Mystery? She was supposed to arrive on the beach yesterday. Twice today Denise has had Thomas inventory the supplies. He was surly the second time she asked him, but uncharacteristically she ignored it, preoccupied by Mystery's failure to appear. He was surly—still is surly—in no small part because this morning Denise decided to restrict food consumption. He's hungry, and he's sick of sand in his clothes, and every time he looks at the limp figure in the hammock he feels a nauseating disgust. The world is full of beggars and weaklings, people who do what they're told for no good reason. Why should he be one of them?

Denise worries. She is not used to worry. She would like to tear the worry out and stomp it to death. She pictures herself with a writhing snake gripped in her hand, its frantic thrashing tail.

Five.

Where is Mystery? Still not at work, and the clerk this morning is wary in the face of Josie's questions. Josie discards a half-formed notion of trying to act her way into possession of Mystery's address. Then what would she do? Just go knock on her door?

She arrived here with a plan—go to Charlie's rental house—and despite the lack of results, she's struggling to find an alternative. So she reenacts it, another rehearsal, or maybe this time the show. Already the drive has a comforting familiarity. The tree tunnel; the little church; all those hibiscus flowers, casual in their glory; the lonely trailer. "Hello," she says out loud as she passes it. For the hundredth, thousandth, millionth time, she plays out the scene in her head: This time, when she pulls up, a rental car will be in the drive, and when she knocks, Charlie will open the door. Charlie rises early even when he doesn't have to be on set, even on vacation, and he's probably been getting up with the sun, especially in that cottage with its uncovered windows. She imagines the sun all but comes in and shakes you awake. So he woke in that bed, under that canopy, and he stretched his long body until his feet pushed off the edge, and then he did a spinal twist and made a sound of either satisfaction or exasperation, depending on whether he achieved the sharp crack he wanted. Then he'd prop his head on a couple of pillows and reach for his phone. Many times she's woken to find him like that, phone in his hand, but not looking at it, looking at her. "Why are you always looking at me when I wake up?" she asks—though he isn't *always*—and he says . . .

Anyway. When she knocks, Charlie will open the door. He'll be wearing an old soft T-shirt and sweatpants. His hair will be charmingly tousled. He'll smell like sleep and fresh coffee. He'll look surprised to see her. He'll look astonished. And then she'll say . . .

Maybe she won't even get as far as the door before he opens it. He'll hear her wheels on the gravel drive, and he'll be startled and wary. He'll come out to see who the hell it is. Have people recognized him here? Will he think she's a stalker who's managed to track him down?

And then she'll say, "I'm pregnant."

She'll say, "Your mother sent me."

She'll say, "Well, Charlie Outlaw, you're a hard man to find."

I love you.

Hi.

Can we please get the writer to the set?

But there is no car in the drive. All is as it was yesterday and the day before. Even the peacock is still at it. The peahens persist in their indifference. Or maybe it's not indifference but wary watchful distance. Indifference requires either confidence or despair. If they were truly indifferent, they wouldn't avoid the peacock like that. Where they go is determined by where he is not. She, too, repeats herself, looks in the windows, checks the ground for clues.

Now what? Think of something, Josie. Something besides wishing really hard.

Mystery, policeman, long hikes, Charlie's mother, going dark, the policeman saying *You would not find him*, Mystery staring at her stomach, that photo of her with Max.

Ben Phillips.

She feels an internal jolt, a sudden cold alertness. That was the name of Charlie's character on the show he did with Alan Reed. The policeman asked if she was looking for Ben Phillips. Is Charlie going by that name? If he is, why does the policeman know it?

At home—at his house—Charlie often forgets to lock the glass door that leads into his tiered backyard, an absence of mind that Josie, who once had a stalker appear in her own backyard, finds alarming. When she stayed there, she always checked before bed or before they went out that the door was locked. Why can't he remember? Why do we make the same mistakes over and over? Before we can correct ourselves, one conviction must gain the strength to override another. Charlie, who grew up in a big suburban house, believes that if you have sufficient faith to leave the back door unlocked, that's how you know you're safe.

Here, what's unlocked is the door that leads inside from the wooden enclosure around the shower. If she'd come inside yesterday or the day before, she might have touched the bed where Charlie had slept, pressed her face to his pillow. Now, though, she's in no mood for melancholy longing. She's operating at the register of anxiety and dread. She wants reassurance. She wants evidence. It could be a coincidence. Ben Phillips is not that uncommon a name.

Here's what she learns: that Charlie is indeed without his phone, which she finds at the back of a drawer as if he hid it from himself. She tries to turn it on, but it's not even charged, and she can't find a charger. He must have brought it in case he needed it while traveling but left the charger behind so he wouldn't be able to use it after that. He planned ahead against his own temptations. This thought gives her a pang of thwarted affection, and she clutches the phone in her hand until she realizes it hurts.

On a table by the big front window she finds a guidebook with pages torn out, pages the table of contents tells her are from a section on overnight hikes. A good clue, a reassuring one, except that people die on hikes, people vanish in the wilderness, it happens all the time, or at least often enough to be possible. She can't figure out which overnight hike the torn-out pages describe, but maybe if she took the book to someone—that policeman?—he would know.

Ben Phillips is a common name.

Her dread is a tsunami, her confidence a fragile wall. She just stands there, but she's flailing, and that is when she looks out the window and sees a figure moving stealthily toward the house, keeping close to the trees. Immediately she drops into a crouch, out of sight of the window, and even through her panic there comes that sense of having done this many times before. It goes without saying that her heart is rioting, but she has the presence of mind to position herself so she can see out the window without being seen, to reach in her pocket for her phone. The signal comes and goes here, but for the moment, she's in luck. It's weak but there. She doesn't know what number to dial for the police. She has an absurd urge to call Charlie, so hard is it to believe he's out there in the world without his phone.

Out the window, the figure moves closer. Without looking away, Josie reaches behind her for the guidebook, which surely contains emergency numbers. She looks down to find the number, and when she looks up again, the figure is stepping cautiously out from the trees and she can see that's it a woman, she can see the woman's face. It's Mystery.

What the hero and the actor have in common is that they can think and think beforehand, but when the moment comes, they mustn't think at all. This is why it's called acting.

Josie drops the phone and the guidebook as she rises from her crouch, not even noticing the twinge in her knee, which she continues not to notice as she throws open the door, and shouts, "Where is he?" at Mystery, whose face flashes alarm, and who spins away into a run.

She runs into the orchard. Josie gives chase. Her object is to catch Mystery, and that is it, that is all that is necessary. She runs through the trees, pulping fallen fruit, scattering chickens into alarmed and indignant flapping. Catch her. Catch her. Catch her.

Mystery pauses at the end of a row, looking wildly around, and Josie is almost close enough to grab her, but then Mystery darts forward. Josie wills herself to greater speed and barrels into the other woman, knocking them both to the ground. Mystery is gasping, trying to wriggle away, but Josie catches her by the wrist and holds firm. She's breathing hard. She thinks she might vomit. "Where is he?" she says.

Mystery shakes her head, twisting her wrist in Josie's grasp, and Josie moves to pin her, putting her weight on Mystery's chest so they are very close, the closeness we achieve only in love or violence. Mystery looks so frightened that it penetrates Josie's consciousness that perhaps she, Josie, is the bad guy. Mystery is the maid for this property, Mystery made friends with Charlie, Mystery met him in a bar and is sleeping with him. Josie is a crazed attacker. She eases off Mystery into a sitting position but doesn't release her wrist. "What are you doing here?"

Mystery swallows. "I follow you."

It is one of the many strangenesses of Josie's life that there might be an explanation for why someone would follow her that wouldn't strike her as all that strange. Alarming, yes, but not strange. "Why?"

"You are really pregnant?"

Josie frowns. "Yes."

Tears well up in Mystery's eyes. "The baby. Is his?"

"Charlie's?"

"Yes," Mystery whispers.

Josie nods. She lets go of Mystery's wrist suddenly, dispiritingly sure she knows what's going on here. This woman is indeed sleeping with Charlie and has imagined it will become something more. Perhaps he's given her reason to imagine that. And Josie is the third-act obstacle, showing up with his baby in her belly to dramatically raise the stakes.

Mystery sits up cautiously and gingerly touches her wrist. "I will take you to him."

"Where is he?" Josie asks, feeling fairly certain she no longer wants to know.

"He is . . . on a beach. We will go in a boat."

"I don't understand. Why is he there?"

"They took him."

"They? Who are they?"

Mystery says, "Denise."

"Who's Denise? Why did she take him? Could you please just tell me what's going on?"

Mystery meets her eye. "They took him for money."

Josie goes cold. She notes with a weird detachment a buzzing sensation at the back of her skull, the way the world rushes away from her. She leans forward to put her head in her hands so she won't faint. "They kidnapped him?"

Mystery nods. "Yes," she says. "Kidnap."

Josie speaks through her hands. "But there's been no ransom demand. I talked to his mother. There's been nothing in the news."

"I was to send. But I did not."

"You were supposed to ask for ransom? Why didn't you?"

"Denise, she . . ." Mystery shakes her head. She digs in her pocket for a phone, touches its screen with trembling fingers, holds it out to Josie. On it there is a picture of Charlie—her Charlie—with his face so red and swollen that for a moment she didn't recognize him. She makes a sound of horror, zooming in on his face to see the swollen nose, the hastily cleaned-up blood, the dull and helpless terror in his eyes.

"Oh my God," Josie says. "Oh no. Oh my God. Why did they do this to him?"

Mystery's expression is sorrowful. She shakes her head again to say she doesn't know.

"We need to go to the police."

"No." Mystery snatches the phone back. "No police."

"I'll do it. I'll go to them."

Mystery gives her a hard stare. "They will not find me. They will not find him."

"I have to do something. Why are you showing me this? You want me to pay the ransom? Oh, that's why you followed me. All right. Tell me what you want." Josie tries to force the tremble from her voice, but it's the tremble that causes Mystery to soften.

"No, no," she says. She even reaches out as if to pat Josie's hand, stops short with her own hand outstretched. "I do not want this. I will take you to him."

"Why?"

"To save him."

"How can I save him? Don't these people have guns?"

"I am late to go there. I bring food. If I am late, they run out of food. Denise say if that happen maybe she just go. She go home and leave Ben there."

"Who's Ben?"

"I forget." Mystery makes a quick, irritated gesture. "Charlie call himself Ben."

"What do the police know about this?" When Mystery looks blank, Josie adds, "They asked me about Ben Phillips."

"Darius sent letter, but we not know Charlie's name."

"Who's Darius?"

"Darius is dead."

"What happened to him?"

Mystery shrugs. "Police shot him."

"Someone is already dead."

"Yes," Mystery says, as though this were obvious.

"I'm an *actress*," Josie says.

"I know. I see you in the magazine."

"You did?"

"You kiss another man. Ben—Charlie—he cry."

"He saw that picture?"

"I take him magazines. He ask for something to read. So." She shrugs again. "I did not know what he would see." What Josie feels deserves the word *anguish*. "How many people are holding him? How many are there?"

"Three." Mystery holds up her fingers. "Denise. Thomas. Adan."

"And you think maybe they left?"

"I hope." Mystery gets to her feet cautiously, as if afraid to provoke Josie into tackling her again. When Josie doesn't move, she looks satisfied, then quickly impatient. She holds out her hand, and Josie takes it, because she's forty-one, pregnant, bruised, terrified, and she needs help getting up. "I will take you to him," Mystery says, as though they've already agreed.

Josie doesn't think. She stands there while her various forces gather—superhero and cop and high-powered lawyer, everyone she's ever been. On film, the camera might spin around her, or many images of herself might succeed one another in a rapid montage. Throwing a punch. Staring a bad guy down. "All right," she says.

Six.

Thomas is gone. He slipped away in the night, when he was supposed to be on guard duty, while Denise and Adan were fast asleep. Denise can't believe he's really had the temerity to leave and take most of their food supply with him. She expresses her conviction that he wouldn't dare with force and repetition, as if force and repetition were sufficient to make her right. Adan makes murmuring sounds of agreement, trying not to give her a reason to make him the target for her anger. She paces. She goes into the jungle, and he doesn't watch what she does there, but from the sounds, he'd say she's attacking a tree. He is used to Denise being calmly and scornfully certain. It's unsettling to imagine her otherwise, so he pretends to himself that Denise still knows what she's doing.

Is it because he's afraid of Denise that he went along with this plan, continues to go along? Or because he loves her? She's been his older sister all of his life. He's never been able to tell the difference.

Maybe now Denise will decide that they, too, should leave. That is the best outcome he can envision, and if it happens, he will be forever in Thomas's debt.

He goes over to see if Ben—Charlie—is still breathing. Yes, he can make out the faintest movement in his chest. The magazines that got Charlie into trouble are in a pile under the hammock where Adan put them. He crouches to pick up the one from the top of the stack, which happens to be the one with the picture of Charlie Outlaw in it. He studies the man in that photo, who is strikingly tall and walking with confidence, and then he looks at the man in the hammock, who is bruised and thin and shabby and can make you believe, when you look at him, that he is in the process of dissolving. What is the point of being an American star if you can still end up like this? Adan shakes his head over the strangeness of it all, the fact that these two men could be the same.

IX.

SOCRATES: I wish you would frankly tell me, Ion, what I am going to ask of you: When you produce the greatest effect upon the audience in the recitation of some striking passage . . . are you in your right mind? Are you not carried out of yourself, and does not your soul in an ecstasy seem to be among the persons or the places of which you are speaking. . . .

ION: That proof strikes home to me, Socrates. For I must frankly confess that at the tale of pity my eyes are filled with tears, and when I speak of horrors, my hair stands on end and my heart throbs.

—PLATO, *Ion*

G et up!" Denise says. "Get up! Get up!" She screams in his face. Charlie hears it as if from very far away because he is dead. He doesn't feel the pain in his nose, the pain in his chest, the hunger, the fear, because the dead feel nothing. Once you're dead, what is there to fear? Even someone like Denise can't hurt you anymore. He is better at dying than anyone he knows. Josie once challenged him to prove this, and he died for her, not even closing his eyes but emptying them of life for the extra challenge, and she hated it, because he was so good that for a moment she believed him. She said, "All right, you win," and when he wouldn't stop, she punched him in the arm, and said, "Live!"

Denise and Adan engage in a long and voluble discussion, Denise's voice rising and rising while Adan's grows softer. What does Charlie care about the arguments of the living? They yell, they whisper, they attempt to persuade. It all takes so much effort. Being dead is easy. If he concentrates hard enough, he doesn't even have to breathe.

More discussion, then rustling sounds, then Adan's light touch on his arm. None of it moves him or causes him to move. Denise speaks rapidly, insistently, Adan no longer answering back. None of it has anything to do with him.

At some point, he realizes that the voices have stopped, but this could be a trick meant to reanimate him, so for a long time he goes on being dead. Eventually he can't ignore that there is a new quality to the stillness. He hears nothing but the sound of waves, some faint birdsong from the jungle. He is thinking, he is noticing, and against his will, this brings him back to life. This happens in stages. First, he opens his eyes. Above him he sees nothing but the same trees he's been seeing all along. Then slowly, slowly, he shifts his eyes to the side where normally he would see some sign of Denise or Thomas or Adan. He sees nothing. There is no hammock strung up where Adan's has always been. As he realizes that, he loses some of his caution and turns his head. Still nothing. Just the depressions they have left in the ground, a few scattered pieces of trash. Are they gone?

He sits up, swaying his hammock violently, and feels a rush of dizziness. Are they really gone? Is this a trick? Are they really gone? He closes his eyes, breathes slowly through his nose, trying to conquer the dizziness. Something fell from his lap when he sat up. Slowly he eases himself out of the hammock. His legs wobble as though they've never before supported his weight. He has thought in the past—after illness, after a long day shooting an action scene, after a three-hour workout to keep his camera-ready abs—that he was exhausted and weak. He has never felt like this. He crouches to see what fell and finds a wrapped piece of beef jerky. Adan must have left it for him. All the other supplies are gone.

He takes a couple of halting steps, leans against a tree. Minutes pass, and there is no sound. He begins to believe. They are gone. They are gone! If he wasn't so recently dead, he might be able to summon joy.

Or at least joy is what he imagined he'd feel when he so heartily wished for their absence. Now that they're gone, he realizes what he should have realized before, that without them he is alone. He is alone. He has no food. He has no water. He has no means of returning to the world. He is weak and incapable of making the hike even if he had a guide. He wanted to send away his captors and he did. Now that he is alive again, he has no one to keep him that way.

There is always a price for getting what you want.

On stumbling feet, he makes his way down the beach until there is nowhere left to go. He sits in the sand. He no longer has his towel. Perhaps they took that, too, but how could a sunburn matter now? He is glad for this time alive without them even if it will not last. He feels the sand settle beneath his weight. He watches the ocean. He watches it without internal comment, without metaphor, without meaning. He watches the waves and he hears the sounds they make. It strikes him that this is all that's meant by transcendence. The trouble with transcendence is that as soon as you name it it's over. With that thought, he remembers himself.

He turns the piece of beef jerky around and around in his hands. The last food he'll eat might be a food he doesn't eat. He wonders how long he has, how long he can eke out of the jerky and the fruit he can find in the jungle. He would like it to be a long time. He would like it to be forever. He would like to go home. He would like to tell Josie he loves her. He would like that baby to be his.

Terror and grief, he thinks. *Terror and grief.* He remembers himself attempting Shakespeare back in college, failing to summon Richard II by failing to summon what Richard felt. His kingdom was gone, he'd lost, he'd likely die. Charlie would like to go back and try the scene again. *Of comfort no man speak.* He knows how he'd say that line now. He remembers the whole speech, and he recites it here at the edge of the world. *For you have but mistook me all this while,* he says, and the tears just come, like they're supposed to, not forced, not conjured by the will, but real, real, real, all of it is real.

X.

The approach to drama and tragedy, or to comedy and vaudeville, dif-
fers only in the given circumstances
which surround the *actions* of the
person you are portraying. In the
circumstances lie the main power
and meaning of those actions. Con-
sequently, when you are called upon
to experience a tragedy do not think
about your emotions at all. Think
about what you have to *do*.

—CONSTANTIN STANISLAVSKI,

An Actor Prepares

One.

Mystery has an air of command at the wheel of the boat. Perhaps this quality is not innate to Mystery but to the steering of a boat. Anyone looks confident keeping a boat on course, cutting the ocean into crisp lines. Thoughts like this are a bulwark between Josie and her fears. Her fear for Charlie and her fear for herself and her fear for their baby and the rage and horror that return every time she remembers the image of her beloved's battered face. Yes, that is why Bronwyn was so full of wry asides. Josie knows that, having known everything about what it was to be her. People sometimes ask Josie what she thinks happened to Bronwyn after the show's conclusion, and Josie makes up a gratifying lie or asks them what they think and listens politely. The truth is that Josie can't imagine Bronwyn going on without her. The show ended, and Bronwyn went to sleep. Let's wake her now, let's put her on this boat where Josie needs her to be and tell all the people that she is doing what she was born to do, which is to save the world. Once you do that job, you define yourself by it. That is not a job you quit. Josie can go willingly into danger to rescue someone she loves. She has done it many times.

But she feels no certainty. She is beset by doubt. She remembers how momentous it seemed to pass up one drink for the baby, and what she's doing seems crazy, crazy, crazy. The only certainty she has is that she has no other plan. She believes Mystery when she says that if Josie goes to the police Charlie is as good as dead.

Look at Mystery at the wheel of the boat. She is the picture of certainty. She is so certain that the kidnappers will be gone that she has repeatedly dismissed Josie's efforts to discuss what will happen if they're not. "I waited long enough," she repeats, with weary firmness, when Josie brings it up again now.

"But—"

Mystery shifts irritably, and the boat wavers. "If they are there, I say I sent ransom, and they write back Charlie must see doctor. I say you are doctor."

"And then what?"

"You say he must go to hospital, we must take him in boat."

"You think that will work?"

Mystery shrugs. "You are actor."

She is actor! So, of course, she can be anything.

"What if it doesn't work? What if they just try to take me hostage, too?"

Mystery sighs. She says, with reluctance, "I have a gun."

Is it because she has lived so many scenes like this before that Josie is able to remain calm? "You have a gun."

"Yes, because Denise have gun." Mystery looks at Josie's face and sighs again. "They cannot keep you there, you and Charlie and also them. I bring no new supplies. They have no food. Do not worry. They must leave."

Mystery has a gun. Is this reassuring or the opposite? Josie moves away from her, to the back of the boat, and trains her gaze on the water. She thinks of something Cecelia once said to her, when one of them, she can't remember who, was struggling to recover from a particularly wrenching scene. "Actors spend their lives going to places other people avoid." Oh, Cecelia! What Josie wouldn't give to have her there right now, wearing one of her character's authoritative suits.

Bronwyn felt certainty. Once she committed to a course of action, she never looked back. Maybe that was the wrong way to play her. Or maybe it wasn't—maybe Josie just needs to allow certainty, needs to allow the blessed release of doubt. Mystery's plan seems insane and also like something that might work on TV. We breathe life into art, and then we reverse the flow.

In normal circumstances, Josie loves a boat ride. Growing up on the plains in New Mexico, she had little opportunity for water travel. In fact, she'd never been on a boat before she moved to LA. Now she's been on many. She's been on tours where you see the land from the boat—the white cliffs of Dover and the Na Pali Coast of Kauai and the lighthouses of New England—and that's fine, she enjoys that, but what she really loves is being in the middle of the ocean, surrounded by water, no land in sight. She always moves to the back of a boat, removing the human from view so she sees only the glistening expanse. She chooses the back instead of the front because she likes to watch the wake, evidence of their passing, quickly erased. Watching the water, she is able to do what she can never do in any formal attempt to meditate: observe and not think. The patterns of color made by clouds here, partial clouds there, clear sky there, gray and muted blue and brightest blue, a conversation between water and light. The jewel-like gleam of a crest under the sun, seeming for a moment carved of crystal, permanent, its loveliness heightened by the fact that its permanence is an illusion. It exists and is perfect and then vanishes—beautiful, then gone, whether anyone saw it or not.

What is on her mind right now is too much for even the ocean to overcome. But she tries. She watches the water. She at least remembers calm. Breathe, breathe, breathe, Josie. Then move to the front of the boat and look at where you're going instead of where you've been.

She rejoins Mystery at the front. Mystery smiles at her. "I wonder," she says. "What will you name your baby?"

"I don't know. How did you get your name?"

"My parents."

"It's an unusual name."

"No. Not so unusual." She doesn't elaborate. After a moment, she says, "Do you hope for boy or girl?"

"I think I would be happy with either."

"Charlie will be very happy."

"Do you have any children?"

Mystery's face closes. She doesn't answer.

Does she have a child-related tragedy in her past? Is Josie's pregnancy why she's willing to help them now? Josie looks at Mystery and sees a person she doesn't know, to whom she has committed her life, and Charlie's, and the life of their child. Does she want to know more? Does she want her backstory, her motivation, her object? Perhaps it's better to take Mystery on faith.

Mystery leans toward her to place a palm on Josie's stomach, like someone warming her hand. "Ah," she says tenderly, though there is nothing yet to feel.

Two.

They've been walking about an hour when Denise changes her mind. She doesn't bother to explain herself to Adan. Denise is not one for explanations. She just stops. She is in the lead, so Adan stops, too. Then she turns and pushes past him, back the way they came.

There is a moment when Adan considers rebellion. He doesn't want to go back. He was so relieved when she decided to leave, so thankful that Mystery hadn't appeared before the decision was made. He was nervous the whole time they debated and packed, listening for the sound of the boat, which might arrive at the last minute to keep them there. Then he was relieved again when she decided not to kill Ben/Charlie. Though things will be no better for them at home than they were before, they will unquestionably be better than slowly starving on a beach, watching a man will himself toward death. She said they would go, and he felt a new rush of love and faith. At moments like that, an optimist feels his worldview affirmed. Now, at the sight of her returning to her folly, he feels all the worse for having believed it would be otherwise.

He doesn't know what she has in mind, but it can't be good.

Either she's decided to kill Charlie instead of letting the world do the work for her, or she's decided to recommit to the ransom plan, which Adan knows—for the first time he fully admits this knowledge—is bound to end in disaster because Denise is in charge. Maybe it would've worked out with Darius, who had the strength to be reasonable. But Denise will screw it up no matter what. She will murder Charlie or she will demand so much money that the negotiations will last the length of a siege or she'll alienate Mystery so entirely that she never comes back with supplies, which is perhaps what's already happened. Adan does not have to follow her. He knows the way home. He carries more than half the remaining supplies.

Why does he follow her? He is a compliant, empathetic person, someone who wants people to like him, who hates to say no, who doesn't want Denise to fail or be furious, who doesn't want Charlie to die. It takes an enormous act of will to be other than we are, which is perhaps what we mean by fate. His moment of rebellion is so brief that Denise doesn't notice it happened.

Three.

"There," Mystery says, and points.

Josie sees a small curve of beach enclosed by trees, white sand, no figures yet visible on it. From here, it looks very pretty, a place you might be delighted to find, a picture of secluded paradise that belongs on a glossy calendar. "I don't see anyone," she says.

Mystery hands her a pair of binoculars. Through them, Josie sees trees then, with a quick downward correction, sand, then sand and sand and sand. "I don't see anyone!" she repeats, her voice full of accusation. "You think they might have taken him?"

Mystery looks worried. "He is too weak," she says. "Look back, back in the trees. They sit back. In shade."

Josie trains the binoculars on the trees at the back of the beach, but all she sees are trees. She takes a breath and concentrates on a systematic search. They are getting even closer and so are the things through the lenses. She tries to move the binoculars in steady lines down the beach. A half-remembered fact floats through her mind, something about how the eye sees, how it skips over some of the picture.

Then his face fills her vision.

Charlie's face.

On it an expression that mingles hope and fear. He is looking at the boat.

She lowers the binoculars. She can see him now without help. He is sitting in the sand cross-legged, with his chest bowed forward over his legs and his face lifted like he just this moment picked it up. "I see him! He's there, he's there, I see him!"

"And the others?"

"No, no, nothing. I think you're right. I think they're gone. I think you're right, Mystery." She turns to the other woman with an impulse to embrace her, but Mystery is driving the boat, and her eyes are narrowed, scanning the shore, and her mouth is a flat, tense line. Josie sees that Mystery has not been certain, has not been certain at all, faked enough certainty to carry them both here. Mystery is a good actress. Josie feels a rush of anger and relief and bitterness and gratitude—for faking it, for tricking her, for pretending long enough to bring her here.

She herself feels now all the certainty she couldn't conjure before. There he is. There he is, he is still alive, he is still alive, and she was right to come and get him. Any minute now she will be able to touch him. She is so impatient that she jumps out of the boat before it reaches the shore, splashing through the water, leaving Mystery to bring the boat the rest of the way in.

Charlie gets slowly to his feet as she splashes toward him, slipping in the water in her sandals. She's worried he'll fall back down, he looks so shaky, and she tries to get to him faster, before that happens. He isn't coming toward her, just standing there, and she doesn't know if that's because he's too weak to move or because he doesn't believe she's real.

He doesn't believe she's real. He sees a woman coming toward him who appears to be Josie. But that is not possible. She came from Mystery's boat. He sees Mystery behind her, pulling the boat out of the water. He is dreaming. He is hallucinating. He has lived so long in imaginary circumstances that he has gone mad. He is dead, and this is the final, merciful vision offered by his mind to his mind. Isn't it remarkable that the mind speaks to itself. Offers comfort. Offers a last beautiful thing, Josie running toward him up the beach.

"Thank you," he says, when she reaches him, speaking not to the real Josie, of course, but to his mind, so he says it with a heartfelt, melancholy calm that throws her. His tone is one of parting rather than reunion.

"What?" Her fingers and her eyes are everywhere on him, checking for damage, and also just touching him, touching him, touching him. "Are they gone?" she asks with urgency.

He nods. He catches her hands in his and he feels the bones beneath her skin and the hard metal of the ring she always wears—it belonged to her grandmother—and he sees, up close, that she doesn't look quite like his image of her, that she's fuller in the face and there's a bruise on her jawline and the circles under her eyes have never been so dark. That's when he knows she's real. He staggers with the shock of it, and she puts a steadying hand on his arm. "Sit down, sit down," she says. "You're all right. I'm here. You're all right. We're going to take you out of here."

He obeys her, sinking back to the sand, and she drops to her knees beside him. "Josie?" he says.

"Yes. Yes." She touches his cheek. "Yes, it's me. Yes."

"How did you get here?"

"Mystery brought me."

He looks past her at Mystery, standing at a respectful distance with her face averted, her eyes on the trees behind them.

"I'll explain everything later. I know it seems crazy. Let's just get you out of here."

"Okay," he says, but he can't quite stand up again, not yet. "Just a minute," he says, and then he says it again and again, though he can't get the words out for crying so hard. She is here, she is here, and all his possibilities reawaken. He can't tell the difference between pain and joy.

Four.

Denise stops, holds out her hand. "Listen," she says.

Adan obeys. He hears nothing.

"It's her," Denise says. "It's Mystery." She increases her pace and almost immediately stumbles over a root, sprawling forward, losing some of her supplies. Adan helps her up though she fights him, snarling imprecations. He sees her knee is bleeding, but she ignores his attempts to point this out. She seems furious now. He doesn't know if it's the fall or his attempts to help her—she hates to be seen at moments of vulnerability, she hates to have them at all— or if the fury is all for Mystery, who almost made her give up.

Her knee must be painful because she walks more slowly now. He can see she's trying not to limp. But she still projects her furious purpose. Which is what, exactly? To inflict something on someone. He keeps pace behind her, his dull, trudging disappointment giving way now to an agonizing dread. He had hoped Mystery would never come back. He had hoped they'd reach the beach and Charlie would be gone and Denise would turn around again. He has been Denise's prisoner, he thinks, as much as Charlie has. But, of course, there is that crucial difference. Even now he could turn around. Even now he doesn't.

Denise does not expect to find that anything has changed with Charlie. She assumes he'll still be lying in the hammock where they left him, pathetic coward that he is. So she is astonished when they emerge from the jungle to their campsite and his hammock is hanging there limp and empty. So astonished that she actually walks up and touches it to confirm this new reality. She squeezes the flimsy material of the hammock in her hand and only then, when she cannot deny its emptiness, does she step out of the shelter of the trees to look toward the beach. She does not hurry. How is she to know she has any reason to hurry? It is one of Denise's failings that she must at all times insist on her own power even—especially—to herself. She has lived so long in the belief that fear is the only motivator. She assumes Charlie heard the boat, rolled out of his hammock, crawled down the beach to beg for scraps like a dog. She assumes that Mystery would never do anything to betray her. She has already erased from her mind the defiance of Thomas's departure.

She sees the boat, she sees Mystery, Mystery sees her. Why does her mouth open wide, as if to scream? On the beach is something strange: someone else besides Charlie. A woman with bright red hair. Oh! Denise understands. She understood the moment she saw the look on Mystery's face, though it took her another moment to recognize that. Mystery has changed her allegiance, brought the redhead here to steal Denise's prize. Oh no. That is not how this will end.

When Mystery screamed, Josie looked up to see a woman, high on the beach, where none had been before, a woman who is now running toward them, her braids swinging, a gun in her hand. Josie has stood before a gun many times, has many times held one, but never until this moment has she understood what a gun is. A gun is death in someone's hand. It is no trivial thing to hold a gun or face one, and the wonder flashes through her mind that she's ever been insouciant while doing either. She cannot stop this woman, cannot stop her from taking Charlie from her right at the moment she's re-gained him. She does not have a gun, and if she did, would she use it? What is better, yes or no? *Yes, yes, yes,* we say. *Shoot! Shoot!* Josie has shouted it at the screen herself. The qualities we detest are the ones we consider most heroic. Willingness to kill. Willingness to die.

She half rises, flings herself around Charlie, against his back, be-tween him and what's coming. He tries to turn to look at her, but she presses him down with all her weight. Normally that would not be enough to hold him, but he is weakened, and she is strong right now, she is very, very strong. She closes her eyes. She opens them again when she hears the shots and realizes she didn't die.

She sees the woman on the ground, sprawled on her back. What Josie sees most clearly are the dirty soles of her boots. Now she sees a man behind her, and for a moment, she thinks the man shot her, but wouldn't he still be standing there holding the gun? She looks over her shoulder at Mystery. Mystery is the one with the gun. She keeps it raised now, pointed at the man, who pays it no mind. He drops to his knees beside the body of the woman, touches her, leans in close to her face, looks at the blood on his hand. He rocks on his knees. His mouth is open like he's making a terrible sound of pain, but if he is, Josie can't hear it over the ocean. Then there is a gun in his hand, and Josie braces herself, waiting for him to shoot her, for him to shoot Mystery, for Mystery to shoot him. But he places the barrel of the gun to his own temple. "No!" Josie shouts, but the sound is drowned out by the report of the shot and the waves.

Five.

In the boat, Josie cradles Charlie's head on her lap. He is in and out of consciousness. When he wakes, he wakes with a start, looks for her face. She says something soothing—it doesn't matter what—and he closes his eyes again. Mystery has not said a word. Not while she and Josie half helped, half carried Charlie into the boat, not when they pushed it into the water, not when they climbed in themselves, not when she started the motor and pulled away. They left the two bodies on the beach, the bodies of those two people, one of whom Mystery killed.

Josie looks at her from time to time to see if she's still crying, and every time she is, crying silently, a steady stream of tears. The crying seems to be a thing separate from her. Her face is blank, her cheeks are wet, she blinks and more tears fall.

She says nothing, still, when they reach the dock, when she ties up the boat, when she helps Josie help Charlie out. With arms around both their shoulders, Charlie makes it to where Josie parked her car. Mystery holds the passenger door open while Josie helps Charlie inside. As soon as Charlie is in, she kisses his forehead and turns to say something—she doesn't quite know what—to Mystery. Thank you, certainly, and something else, something comforting, something to say that what Mystery did was necessary. But Mystery is walking away. Josie takes a few steps after her, but Mystery does not want to be followed, does not want Josie to speak, so Josie won't. Mystery does not want to play one last scene. So Josie watches her walk away.

Josie takes Charlie to the hospital, where doctors and nurses treat his injuries and hook him to an IV for rehydration and calories. When they ask what happened to him, she says he was hiking, he got lost, he fell. They exclaim their sympathy and alarm, but Josie thinks she also sees in their manner annoyance with a tourist who did a stupid thing. "He was hiking alone?" they say. "Oh, you should never hike alone."

Once Charlie is asleep and the nurses have told her several times that she should leave and get some sleep herself, Josie goes back to her hotel. But she doesn't intend to stay there. She can't bear the thought of Charlie waking and thinking she has disappeared. She packs her things, assuming that once Charlie is released they'll go to his cottage. While she is packing, her phone rings. Her agent says, with cheerful annoyance, "We've been trying to reach you!"

"We?" She hears other voices then and understands that her manager is also on the phone, and everyone who works for them on her behalf, the whole team.

"You got the part!" they say.

"What?" For a moment, she cannot think what part they mean. They have to remind her. She sits down on the bed. "You're kidding," she says. "I totally blew that audition."

"Apparently not," her agent says. "Whatever you did, they liked it."

"They want to know if your speech about not getting the part was an act," her manager says.

"What do you mean?"

"To show them you could do the meltdown stuff."

"What meltdown stuff?"

"Didn't you read the script?"

"Yeah, I just can't, I can't . . ."

"The character has a public meltdown. That's why she goes home."

"And also," her agent chimes in, "are you pregnant?"

"What?"

"They said there was a rumor that you're pregnant."

"Oh."

"They said it's okay if you are. They said they'll write it in. Raises the stakes."

Josie laughs. "Okay," she says. "Tell them to write it in."

They don't go home for a week after Charlie's release despite increasing anxiety on the part of Josie's people in LA, who are coping with the increasing anxiety of the people who have just cast her as the lead in their show. Charlie needs to heal. He doesn't want to be photographed at LAX with bruises and scratches on his face. But neither does he want to be on the island anymore, so they take a boat to a neighboring one, smaller, far less populated, with one boutique hotel. Even there Charlie doesn't feel safe. Only Josie leaves the hotel, and only to get food. Mostly they stay in their room with all the doors locked and think of baby names. She doesn't ask questions about his time in captivity, but sometimes he tells her things.

"We can never tell anyone what happened," he says one day. "In case they look for her. Just in case."

"Okay." They are, as always, on the bed. After a moment, Josie says, "They'd love you again if they knew." She says this as fact, not argument.

Charlie is silent, and she thinks maybe he hadn't thought of this before she said it, and she wonders if she shouldn't have. She did not mean to suggest that he prostitute his trauma or that she suspected that he would. Then he says, "I know. I don't care."

He doesn't care, he doesn't care, and yet the truth is more complicated, and perhaps more to his credit, than that. If Josie asked him to, he'd willingly swear any self-abnegating vow she wanted, because his intention right now is to quit the internet, quit it forever, never give another interview, never read another review, never care what anyone but Josie thinks of him, never again run a search for his name. He thinks—here in the safety and comfort of this bed, Josie's warm body pressed against his—that he no longer wants their love. If that were true, keeping such promises would be easy. But he does want their love. Of course he does! He wants it, and can deny himself.

XI.

For every moment of real feeling on the stage there is a response, thousands of invisible currents of sympathy and interest, streaming back to us.

—CONSTANTIN STANISLAVSKI,
An Actor Prepares

Josie's day starts as it always does, as it seems like it always has, with the sound of the baby crying. She walks down the dark hallway with her hand on the wall for support, already shushing him under her breath. Through the slats of the crib, the baby's white-clad arms are visible, waving in the air. Josie grasps and lifts the solid weight of him, feels his wet face snuffle against her neck. She carries him back to their bed to nurse, Charlie warm on one side of her, the baby on the other. The baby will fall asleep again, and Josie, too, will doze a little longer before she has to force herself to slip out of bed around him and get ready for work.

An hour later, Charlie's day starts as it always does, as it seems like it always has, with the touch of the three-year-old's fingers on his face. "Daddy," she says. She thinks she's whispering, but she doesn't know how to whisper, so her voice is breathy and loud. "I'm hungry," she says, like this is a new and perplexing discovery and not one of the first thoughts she voices every day.

"Okay, honey, I'm coming," Charlie says. He touches Josie's shoulder, making sure she's awake, before going down the hall to pour cereal.

Josie showers, dresses, and brushes her teeth, checking from time to time that the baby is still asleep securely in the middle of the bed. He's on the cusp of learning to roll over, and she doesn't want him hitting the floor. When Charlie comes back to shower, Josie joins their daughter in the kitchen. While the little girl chatters, Josie eats breakfast quickly, watching the clock, and then she scoops the child into her lap and reads her a book, reaching the last page just as the nanny arrives. On cue, Charlie comes in with wet hair and the squirming baby in his arms. The baby looks as if he's considering a long crying jag, but he brightens and smiles when he sees his mother. Josie takes him, squeezes and kisses him, and then passes him to the nanny. He loves the nanny when Josie's not there, but now he'll cry until Josie leaves, which makes her hustle to get out the door.

Charlie kisses both children good-bye and walks out to the porch, where Josie's waiting for him. They're both number one on their call sheets, due on the set early almost every day. Josie's show is a critical success, and Charlie's is enjoying a ratings resurgence now that his character and his costar's are finally on the verge of consummating their romance. As well as things are going, both Charlie and Josie still worry that the work will stop. They no longer say that they're going to quit acting even on their worst days. Let's live truthfully in imaginary circumstances, but let's not pretend. There are worse things to lose than a part or a prize.

They linger on the porch for a few minutes, talking about the kids—whether the little girl ate enough breakfast, when the baby will grow out of his separation anxiety. Josie got script changes last night and is holding the new lines in the back of her mind to run through once she's in the car. Charlie's nervous about his first scene of the day because someone will point a gun at him, and he knows he'll become shaky and sweaty and have to retire afterward to his trailer. He plays such scenes very well if they're meant to be raw with emotion, but he can no longer do them any other way. He doesn't say anything about his nerves to Josie, but she knows. Normally they part with a quick, exhausted kiss, but today she hugs him hard.

"It's just make-believe," he says in her ear.

"I know," she says. Good actors that they are, they both pretend that's true.

In the car, Josie finds that she has brought Charlie's anxiety with her, so she can't focus on her new lines. She remembers the first few months after their return from the island, when Charlie attempted to reclaim ownership of his life by risking it, speeding a racecar around a track, skydiving. When he came back alive from his third time leaping out of a plane, Josie, then eight months pregnant, cried so hard and long that he promised never to do anything like that again. He said the need was finally out of his system. But she's never fully believed it.

Charlie, in his own car, counts his breaths and tries to think of nothing. Not the scene, not what it reminds him of. In through the nose, out through the mouth. One, two, three. His lot is much closer than Josie's. He's already in hair and makeup, joking with the stylist, before Josie reaches her parking spot. On the way back to his trailer, he greets everyone he sees, remembering names, asking after dogs and girlfriends and children, not thinking of the scene.

As is her own habit on set, Josie smiles at everyone she passes but doesn't speak. In the makeup chair, she closes her eyes and runs through the revised scene, fixing each word in her memory. Her character must confront her estranged mother, the climax of a long emotional arc that started in the show's first episode. She has to be both furious and vulnerable, to feel the weight of everything that's come before, to rage and cry.

Charlie paces from the video village to craft services and back again, waiting for the director to be ready. One of his castmates calls him over to watch a funny video on his phone, and Charlie laughs appreciatively. He asks the guy about the vintage motorcycle he's rebuilding and concentrates as hard as he can on the long and complicated answer. This is the actor who will, shortly, be pointing a gun at Charlie, but right now he's just a friendly guy who loves motorcycles and that's all Charlie has to think about. "About to start," the AD says in passing, and Charlie nods like he's happy to hear it.

Sitting in her director's chair, Josie waits with her earbuds in, eyes closed, letting the music summon the mood. The scene is about, she thinks, how her character can't stop wanting her mother's love even though it hurts her to keep wanting it. Loss and longing. Hope and fear. She feels the touch on her knee that signals it's time. She opens her eyes and sees Mystery.

Mystery, who rescued them.

No, of course it's not Mystery. It's the new PA. She doesn't even look very much like Mystery, just a little something in the shape of the face. Sufficient, in Josie's state of mind, to conjure her. Mystery, at the wheel of the boat, her face wet with tears. Mystery, known only by her actions, which Aristotle promised is enough.

"Thank you," Josie says to the PA, with such intensity that the girl looks discomfited. Josie rises from her chair, walks toward the camera and the lights, while Charlie, across town, does the same.

They go to work. They slip the bonds of their own lives. They channel their emotions and so become a conduit for ours. They do what the world needs them to do; they transform.

Acknowledgments

When I started this book, I knew only a little about the life of an actor. I'm enormously grateful to the many people who helped me in my research, especially Jeremy O'Keefe and Elwood Reid, who made it possible for me to visit sets, witness auditions, and talk to casts and crews. This book wouldn't exist without the crucial insights of the actors I interviewed: Jon Gries, Zoe Jarman, Matthew Lillard, Graham Patrick Martin, Kathleen Robertson, Anika Noni Rose, and the others who gave me the gifts of their time and observational skills. I can't thank them enough. My thanks also to Maria Semple for talking me through a week on the set of a multicam and giving me the basketball idea. Last but not least, thank you to k. Jenny Jones and her acting students at the University of Cincinnati for allowing me to observe their stage combat and technique classes and answering all my questions.

My research also involved a number of books and articles on both acting and kidnapping. In addition to the books on acting technique quoted throughout, I found these works invaluable: *Long March to Freedom: The True Story of a Colombian Kidnapping* by Thomas R. Hargrove; *Kidnapped: A Diary of My 373 Days in Captivity* by Leszli Kalli; *The Negotiator: My Life at the Heart of the Hostage Trade* by Ben Lopez; *A House in the Sky* by Amanda Lindhout and Sara Corbett; and "My Captivity" by Theo Padnos in *The New York Times Magazine*. I also read memoirs by actors including Alan Cumming, Tina Fey, Rob Lowe, and Amy Poehler, and watched *Hollywood Reporter* Roundtables; DVD commentaries; and a number of episodes of *Locked Up Abroad*.

I keep needing to find new ways to phrase my thanks to my editor, Sally

Acknowledgments

Kim, who always helps me find the best version of the book, and my agent, Gail Hochman, who always gives excellent advice. This is my fifth book with both of them and I couldn't be luckier.

I'm also lucky to have resources and supportive colleagues at the University of Cincinnati: Thank you to the Taft Research Center; the Office of Research AHSS Program; Jay Twomey; Chris Bachelder; Michael Griffith; and Jenn Habel. Enormous thanks, also, to the Rivendell Writers' Colony, where many of these pages were written. I'm grateful to Carmen Touissant, for being such a good host, and to Kevin Wilson and Leigh Anne Couch, for being such good company.

My daughter, Eliza O'Keefe, once said to me wisely, "When you're irritable it means your writing isn't going well." So thank you to her and her brother, Simon, for their tolerance, and for reminding me to get out and do something fun. My thanks to my husband, Matt O'Keefe, for putting every word to the test and making me a better writer—and for the last twenty-three years.